HOUSE OF BASTIION
THE HAIDREN LEGACY

1

Kristianna,
    May they captivate you, as
they've captivated me.
Madöm, for granting them room
to breathe. Tredae'Aurgnth.
                        Ky Kala

K.L. KOLARICH

ROGUE KITE
PUBLISHING

ISBN: 978-1-7354606-0-4 (eBook)
ISBN: 978-1-7354606-1-1 (Paperback)
ISBN: 978-1-7354606-2-8 (Hardcover)

Library of Congress Control Number: TXu 2-222-143

Cover Art & Design: Fiona Jayde Media
Interior Book Design: Brent Spears

Printed by Rogue Kite Publishing, in the United States of America.

First printing edition 2020.

www.TheHaidrenLegacy.com

For Amanda,
Who told me to abandon the expected and
wander into the unknown…

"*Let a single Haidren from each House preside at the arm of Thoarne throughout the generations. By inheritance or election, may these delegates of Bastiion, Boreal, Darakai, and Pilar establish a Quadren of Advisory. For the needs of the unseen are many, and the voices of the seen few; in this way, the concerns of the Ethnicam shall be heard across Orynthia.*"

—*Orynthian Accords*, Spire Age

PROLOGUE

T he shrouded figure watched her from deep within the shadows of the wood. Admired the way her bone-white hair shone in the moonlight, the slight evening breeze whispering through those tresses, waltzing with each tendril to a melody he would never hear. After all these years, even long into her maturity, Alora remained the most beautiful woman he'd ever beheld. Her face was lovely in a way that no amount of time could hope to tarnish, her movements still graceful and refined.

With a sigh, the figure huddled deeper into the folds of dark fabric encompassing him, making certain to keep his monstrous form concealed. He was the very embodiment of irony, yearning for these passing moments between assignments, even as he brewed with anxiety, knowing she'd again be forced to look upon what he'd become. Once assured not an inch of blistered flesh was visible between the weather-worn black gloves and his cloak, he resettled himself into the mist with forced patience.

The man was talking again.

Broad-shouldered and muscular, Orien Darragh boasted a frame of robust fortitude, though it was less apparent in the formal attire that such a celebratory occasion called for. As Alora listened to the words of her brother-in-law, the figure noted the way she tensed, despite Orien's good humor. She'd always excelled at hiding her inner thoughts from most, but the figure was not *most*. He was *other*. And, undeterred by his shame, he was hers.

Orien's expression turned pensive as he placed his callused hands on the rock ledge encircling the private terrace. It was a discreet spot, built into the short cliffside, abutting the tree line. It had been Alora's preferred meeting place for many years, hidden as it was from the city of Roüwen below.

"Eoine should have been here today," Orien said, overlooking their lambent city of wood and stone. "It's the most joyous day of Luscia's life—her Ascension to adulthood. Her mother should have been with us."

Ghostly light from the nearest leaves flickered across Orien's face as he gazed into Alora's eyes—her countenance so very much like his Eoine's—and seemed to imagine the wife he had lost. Nearly a decade had passed since Alora's sister disappeared into the eerie luster that set Roüwen and the lands of Boreal aglow, but the figure knew that Alora still carried a heavy burden of shame and regret. A tattered strip of bloodied linsilk, found in the undergrowth, was the only token left behind from Eoine's tragedy, one Alora believed preventable had she advised Orien differently.

The figure caught the glimmer of pain in her expression as Alora shifted away from the luminescent view. "My sister would have sent Luscia on her way with pride," Alora agreed. "Though I'm not sure how many times it would have taken Eoine to fully let go."

Orien smiled slightly, evidently lost in the memory of a woman who no longer existed. He failed to notice the strained lines forming at the corners of Alora's mouth. Silence fell between them for a moment as she contemplated her brother-in-law, clearly reluctant to interrupt his bittersweet reminiscing.

"The lumin is unsettled, Orien," Alora shared hesitantly. "I've been watching it in the wind for some time. I didn't want to alarm you—not until I was sure."

Orien snapped to attention at her mention of the lumin, threads of the *Other* invisible to his naked eye, apart from the lustrous hints in the surrounding nature. The figure felt his own otherness daily, enough to believe in the sacred light energy that threaded through every inch of the Boreali highlands. As Haidren to Boreal, Alora saw what no other could, possessing an ancestral ability to interpret the signs and warnings of what might come to pass.

"Alora, you're the most respected woman in Boreal," he sputtered. "I hear your concern, but look around you! Luscia has Ascended and will finally take her place by your side as al'Haidren, representing our people beside the throne. The High One is pleased tonight, and so am I. Aren't you?"

When Alora failed to answer, Orien's eyes narrowed in suspicion. "Do you not think she is ready?" Orien asked accusingly. "That your niece isn't suited to be your successor?"

For a brief moment, Alora pursed her lips, slighted by his suggestion, then gently rested her palm on Orien's arm. "I meant no such
thing, Clann Darragh."

The figure saw the strong shoulders of Boreal's leader soften at the
formal use of his title while Alora continued, "I have every confidence
in Luscia. Beyond her lineage and upbringing, her abilities by blood are
manifesting without her full awareness. Honestly, I am trying my best
to keep up with her training," she admitted. "But the fact remains that,
for whatever reason, the lumin is not at peace."

The Clann Darragh wasn't a foolish man, and it was clear that her
warning weighed heavily upon him. Unease tugged his features.

"Do you think it's the *Dönumn*?" Orien whispered. "The Najjani
guards haven't reported anything of significance."

Alora cast her gaze across the living fortress below, illuminated by
hazy, twinkling light. She closed her eyes and steadied herself against
the echoes of music that rocked the night to sleep after the evening
festivities. The figure groaned inwardly at the restlessness she attempted
to hide, painfully aware he would add to it once the Clann Darragh
finally took his leave.

"I don't think so. I can't tell you what is causing the disturbance,
only that it is disturbed. I've prayed to the High One for clarity, but
Aniell's answers are never straightforward. All I know for certain is that
there's a change in the wind."

"What of Luscia?" Orien posed. "She's no longer here in my sphere
of protection. How will this affect her position in Bastiion?"

"It won't concern her for now. Until the next path is made clear,
she will proceed as tradition dictates. Prioritizing her safety in light of
these revelations is my only suggestion at the present," Alora said. "It's
why I ordered her party to leave ahead of my own, to give her as much

concealment as possible. Any outside forces would assume that she and I would be traveling together, since she is my heir."

Orien's eyes widened at the possible danger. His fingers began to comb through his thick beard, the color of silvered birch. As the House of Boreal entered an ominous season of unknowns, his prized and influential daughter was commanded out of reach, away from their refuge.

Alora took his hands, each easily the size of a lycran's paw. The figure noticed how fragile her pale fingers appeared in the giant's grasp and welcomed the familiar sting as he remembered what it had been like to hold those hands once, long ago.

"The king is a good man, Orien. But you know as well as I how thoroughly the leaders of the Ethnicam have pushed me out of Korbin's confidence over the years. The throne may not be our enemy, but the other three seated on his Quadren?" Alora bit her lower lip. "Of that, I'm not convinced. Not anymore. Luscia will proceed as planned, until we know where Boreal stands within the Ethnicam."

"Then I will trust your wisdom, *Ana'Mere*," he said in the steady voice expected of Boreal's mighty Clann Darragh. Meaning *Great Mother*, it was a word chosen out of affection, not duty, for his rank did not require he use it.

With that, Orien took his leave, descending the steps that led from the lookout back into the fortress, where Roüwen's citizens continued to celebrate the Ascension of their new al'Haidren. Alora remained behind, staring out at the city that had been her home since birth. Her long, glittering skirts shuffled against the ground, and a small quirk of her lips was the only proof she'd felt the presence of the cloaked figure.

"You can come out now, if you wish," Alora said quietly. There was no need for her voice to be louder than a murmur. A trait now shared between them.

She remained stoic as he approached, apart from the tiny grin—a gift he recognized, given for his pleasure. Emerging from the brush, he adjusted the fabric further to hide his gruesome appearance.

He was almost beside her when she gracefully trapped him with those eyes, bright in the darkness as they reflected an unearthly radiance. The left was a shade of sky he could only vaguely recall after so many years sentenced to darkness; the right, grey as the iron he could never touch. A living set of truths that told the story of how far he'd fallen.

"If you insist on hiding from me during our conversations, then I must ask why we continue to have them," she said grimly to the figure. "The least you can say is hello."

"*Allöh*, my lady," he complied, receiving a cross look in return.

"How are your sores? I have the next vial of elixir. And the fever—has it returned?"

He restrained himself from madly seizing the satchel set upon the ledge. The blisters had worsened, of course, along with the aches, but it would take quite a bit more interrogation on her part to evoke any admittance of it. Especially when those vials came at the expense of a wound, now entirely healed, somewhere along her porcelain skin.

"I bring news from the towns you had me observe. Two of your traders were murdered, brutally, and a Boreali cross-caste child is missing in Port Tadeas," he said, speaking calmly and succinctly. "You'll need to stop there on your journey to Bastiion."

Alora tended to internalize the burdens of her people, so he'd found it best to deliver these reports pragmatically, to help her accept them as impersonally as he did. Despite that, she pressed a hand against her stomach, whether to keep from being sick or to comfort herself, he couldn't tell.

"We were hunted before the time of Tiergan, in the days of old," she whispered. "What if the lumin…"

"What would you have me do, my lady?" he asked hurriedly.

Alora's eyes anchored onto his. Mastering her features to resemble the cool slate they stood upon, she ordered, "Follow Luscia. Remain unseen. Protect her at all costs."

He studied the planes of her face for the thousandth time, committing them to memory. The figure then gathered up his inky cloak and retreated into the mist of the tree line. He'd taken a mere ten steps before she spoke his name into the night, as was their custom. He stilled with his back to the moonlit woman as she whispered for his ears alone; a promise that betrayed all hope, for it hinged upon the irreparable.

"There is still hope for redemption."

The figure crushed his lashless eyes shut and carried the sound of her voice into the darkness he now called home.

ONE

Luscia

Luscia stretched her neck until she felt a sharp pop of relief. Only four days on the road to Bastiion, and her bones were already weary. But as the distance ahead stretched farther than that behind, Luscia chastised herself for the silent complaint. They were still a week's journey from the lowlands of Hildur, and her neck would just have to accept it.

"Captaen!" a man's voice shouted. The greenery by the side of the road parted, revealing Declan, the brawny Najjani warrior who'd been sent to locate the next stage of their route.

Declan brought his horse up to address the handsome man riding beside Luscia. Bright, unruly copper hair fell out of the disheveled knot he'd tied at the crown of his head. Swatting it out of his eyes, Declan wiped away the beads of sweat trickling down his slightly crooked nose and paused, as if suddenly remembering protocol.

"*Ana'Sere*," he huffed in reverence, bowing his stocky frame to Luscia before turning toward Marek Bailefore, the captaen of her guard. "Captaen, the structure we recalled is just a mile south. You'll find the same broken tree marking the hidden turnoff."

"*Waedfrel*, well done," Marek answered, a hint of relief in his deep voice. "Declan, take Noxolo and scout the area for dinner. We'll reconvene at the ruin."

Luscia watched the two warriors disappear into the surrounding wood, the shock of Noxolo's off-white hair trailing in the wake of Declan's horse. Her sharpened hearing caught Noxolo attesting to the distinct flavor of possum, and a faint grunt of exasperation in response.

"This way, *Ana'Sere*," was the captaen's only directive before moving on.

It was nearing dark when they arrived at the place Marek and Declan sought. They'd ridden farther that day than expected, certainly farther than Luscia's sore limbs would have preferred. Dodging contorted branches and jutting limbs, they carefully approached a ruin comprised entirely of materials from the Lost Ages, which could have once been anything from a meetinghouse to a place of trade. With half the walls in a crumbled heap, overtaken by the elements, the remnants were beyond recognition. Arms of the nearest trees embraced the ruin, leaving the rest clothed richly in emerald moss where the jaws of nature had consumed it.

Evidence of the Lost Ages was uncommonly discovered in Orynthia. After the Forgotten Wars desolated the ancient world, the generations of survivors had only fragmented structures such as this to piece together a conclusion for what had been committed against the earth and her inhabitants. A muddied, empty conclusion about the evils of men taught still, even a thousand years later.

Instantly, Luscia understood why Marek thought it wise to make camp here. With so much of the ruin intact, the walls would block a fire from sight, as well as dull the evening's inevitable chill.

Tonight may actually provide a decent rest, she pondered optimistically.

Following Marek's lead, she dismounted the dappled mare in a graceful leap, cushioning the impact with a slight bend of the knees. Luscia wasn't a tall woman by any standard, so it was a fair distance from the saddle to the ground. She'd always resented her small stature, as men rarely took seriously a woman whose height resembled that of a large child. Blessedly, the rest of her body hardly looked like a child's. Boreali women were known for their shapely figures, and Luscia was no exception. Though, from a defensive standpoint, longer limbs would've offered a useful advantage in combat.

Still, the more cunning part of Luscia reveled in her lack of height. As a daughter of Boreal, stealth and speed were given abilities, but her smaller frame was often smoother and quicker than her average sparring partner, even among the Najjani elite.

Out of the corner of her eye, Luscia spotted Marek approaching. He stopped a few feet away, gathering back the strands of crimson hair that had escaped their leather lacing during the journey here. Luscia busied herself with unharnessing her mare, trying to ignore the appeal of Marek's chiseled cheekbones and strong jaw, each characteristic begrudgingly appreciated. Luscia wished he would keep his distance. Their close proximity suggested an unspoken familiarity between them, however inevitable it may be.

"You rode well today, *Ana'Sere*," Marek offered as she unfastened the saddle. "We'll set your quarters against the farthest wall. It's the tallest and most stable. Provides the greatest security. You must have been cold last night—do you require another set of furs?"

Luscia made an effort to soften her features, knowing they could be severe. As much as she'd like to ignore his companionship, she could not allow herself to remain petulant when addressed out of duty. Insightfully, Marek had started to use her formal title, *Great Sister,* regularly once he realized she was more receptive to it.

"*Tadöm*, Captaen," Luscia conceded, thanking him.

"*Yeh'maelim, Ana'Sere.*"

Finally making eye contact, she met a pair of cerulean lights in the darkness. His suggestion was earnest, she knew, by the way his fine brows lifted in concern.

Yet to endure each generation to the next, the peoples to the East reached outward. The eastern tribes strengthened in numbers and eventually established the Orynthian armies. As their Unitarian forces emerged, cultures of the Old-World were lost, and the New-World was born.

In the signing the Accords, the ruling powers of each House founded the Ethnicam, solidifying their allegiance under a unified Orynthian banner. From Bastiion were the Peerage of the nobility, from Pilar the Shoto Collective, from Darakai their tribal chieftains and from Boreal, her clan elders. This balance of power worked to ensure through domestic trade, service was paid in full for the benefit of all Orynthia, the central kingdom. As the Houses retained enough independence to govern their own territories, the Ethnicam provided accountability against partiality. Or so it proclaimed.

"You navigated well, I see," she acknowledged. He nodded, and an awkward silence fell between them, the air growing still. Bristling, Luscia inquired, "How do you know this place? I've seen ruins of this size only a handful of times. On my last journey to Bastiion, my aunt's guard kept us to the main roads."

"Your father—the Clann Darragh, I mean...." Marek cleared his throat. "He sent us on a scouting assignment two months ago to prepare for your journey. He thought it prudent to explore alternative routes in case we needed to avoid the main roads. Declan noticed framing underneath the overgrowth and led us to find the perfect shelter." He paused to gesture at the rotted frame. "In order to remain undetected, we haven't made our fires as large as I'd like. Tonight, we should be able to."

Marek fiddled with the bedroll he carried, clearly uncomfortable speaking so much. It was the longest monologue she'd heard him give in normal conversation. Luscia opened her mouth to reply, but was cut off when Declan and Noxolo stalked past, thoroughly engaged in an argument over venison seasoning. With a buck thrown over his shoulder, Declan trudged toward the fire another warrior had built. Noxolo dragged a sad-looking possum, yammering on about thissleweed and an old family recipe. Luscia controlled her smirk and braced for the thunderous explosion about to erupt from the bulkier Najjan.

"I'm grateful for your consideration, Captaen," Luscia finally said to Marek, despite Declan and Noxolo's brewing dispute in the background. She lowered her head a fraction, excusing herself, and turned in the opposite direction. "Oh, and *tadöm*, for the furs," she added over a shoulder, "but I'm certain Aksel will be warmth enough once he returns from terrorizing the local wildlife."

With that, Luscia headed to the farthest wall, desperate for some space.

Over the next hour, Luscia found solace in the symphony of the wild-wood. She slowly picked at her second portion of venison, savoring the flavor. He could be a real nuisance, but Noxolo was onto something with the thissleweed. An odd combination, she concluded, from an even odder family.

Her gaze followed her warriors while they moved about, going through the motions of their nightly routines. Not for the first time, she recognized why Boreal's clan elders chose each of these men to play this coveted role in her life. There was the twenty-three-year-old Marek, of course, who traversed their camp almost silently as he prepared for first watch, gliding like an extension of the mist as he searched for potential threats. His northern heritage combined with his years of training on the Isle of Viridis had honed him into a deadly warrior, and his keen mind for strategy had earned him leadership over the other four Najjan.

The musical beat of clashing metal drew her eyes to the twins as they sparred in a series of dancelike steps and arced maneuvers. The golden-haired brothers circled one another, a competitive joy radiating from both men. At twenty-one, they were the youngest members of Luscia's quintet of warriors, though still older than her own eighteen years. Outsiders often found their abstract precision to be unnerving, but the House of Boreal commended both Böwen and Creyvan Tear-lach as shining examples of its beauty and military prowess.

Beyond the crackling fire sat the eldest of the group: Declan Athdara. He had readily become Luscia's favorite among her escort. Though he tended to erupt whenever his patience tired, she felt most at peace with his otherwise quiet disposition. A superior tracker and hunter—as evidenced by the dinner he'd provided—but Luscia felt certain there were many reasons Declan had been chosen to protect her. She studied the artistic way he sharpened and polished a set of luxiron blades laid before him, admiring the way he held each with such care, like they were precious stones instead of death-bringers.

To their communal relief, Noxolo Egon snored in a corner of the ruin. It was the most reasonable he'd been that day. Translucent skin as pale as her own was concealed beneath his fine, moonlit hair, though Luscia could still see his long nose peeking through the curtain of platinum strands. It was Nox's speed that positioned him at her side—when engaged, Nox moved as fast as Luscia, despite being almost three heads taller.

Shadowmen, the people of Orynthia called them. Boreal's Najjan fought in the shadows with a chilling patience, a fearsome caste of warriors who danced with blades like the whistling tempests over the Drystan Sea. Luscia found the adopted name rather appropriate, as opposed to the slew of distasteful alternatives the realm enlisted. Even in the face of Boreal's crumbling political status within the Ethnicam, the Najjan retained their repute, and were resented for it.

It was through the Ethnicam that Orynthia maintained a careful alliance between the four Houses that ruled each corner of the realm. After the Forgotten Wars, the remnants of humanity found solace in their respective territories and cultures, struggling to survive in a land of famine and war-taint. Those who hadn't starved were either clean or unclean. Residual war-taint disfigured and drove the afflicted into grotesque madness, while mortal disease threatened the rest. Focusing inward as the land's natural resources began to dwindle, skirmishes broke out amongst the outer territories of Boreal, Pilar, and Darakai. But instead to the east, Bastiion reached outward to neighboring tribes to bolster their numbers, sacrificing their heritage to become something new and in doing so, thrived. Together, the emerging Unitarians built the strength and military might of the Orynthian forces.

It was the House of Bastiion that ultimately united the four territories, hundreds of years after the Forgotten Wars. In exchange for protection, the outer territories of Boreal, Pilar, and Darakai formed in an uneasy treaty with the prosperous Unitarians and therefore, each other. Although Boreal's history with Orynthia dated further than that of Darakai or Pilar, all owed their survival to the crown. Over a thousand years after the earth shed its taint and began to bloom, the Houses continued to pay homage to Orynthia's founding epicenter, Bastiion.

In signing the Accords, the ruling powers of each House founded the Ethnicam, solidifying their allegiance under a unified Orynthian banner. From Bastiion were the Peerage of the nobility; from Pilar, the Shoto Collective; from Darakai, the tribal chieftains; and from Boreal, the clan elders. All four owed fealty to the Royal Line of Thoarne, whose descendants sat upon the Orynthian throne. This balance of power worked to ensure that, through domestic faculty and trade, service was paid in full for the benefit of all Orynthia, the central kingdom. As the Houses retained enough independence to govern their own territories, the Ethnicam provided accountability against partiality—or so it claimed.

However, during the last century, friction had escalated within the Ethnicam when the House of Boreal suspended all trade beyond standard weaponry with the rest of the realm. Their territory was famous for its deadly luxiron blades, forged with the aid of lumin and unparalleled in battle. The Boreali guarded the secret of luxsmithing carefully, and trade of these special weapons with the rest of Orynthia had always been rare, even before Luscia's ancestors forbade their sale outside Boreal's borders. Luscia privately found the Ethnicam's resentment to be ridiculous, as Orynthia's grudge with Boreal was over the monopoly of trinkets. Corrosive and bewitching trinkets, but trinkets nonetheless. It was the Najjani warriors who were the true weapons of Boreal. It was in their blood, their very nature.

By belonging to the line of Tiergan, it was a nature that segregated Luscia even further from her five.

With some surprise, Luscia realized that she'd finished her plate of venison while studying her men so intently. She rubbed her tired eyes, then rose to her feet with a groan, making her way over to the well-made tent of Orallach hide that Creyvan had erected for her.

"Thank Aniell for privacy," she murmured as she slipped inside.

With a sigh, Luscia peeled off her layers of traveling gear, desperately wishing for a hot bath. It'd been days since her last true wash. When all that remained was the thin layer of her linsilk shift, simpler than the others she possessed, Luscia lay back against the bed of lush furs and combed her fingers through an untidy cluster of sandy knots.

As she finished fighting with the last of the tangles in her waist-length hair, a wet muzzle parted the opening of her makeshift quarters. Aksel waited until Luscia obliged him with a warm, "Well, come in, you brute."

The lycran's huge form shook the tent as he made an obnoxious attempt to lie down. The tent was good stock, but it was never intended to house a woman *and* her overgrown wolx. Regardless of his enormity and the rank stench of his latest conquest, Luscia welcomed Aksel's company as well as his warmth. She had slept safely with the animal for three years, since he was a pup. Even now that he was considered fully grown, she didn't intend to stop.

Nestling closer to Akel's thick coat, she listened to the distant tinkling of metal as Declan rewrapped his luxiron blades. Breaths later, she heard his voice rumble in the night. Gently, barely audible to most, he sang to the unseen threads of lumin in the darkness. Luscia was nearly asleep to the sound of his melody when the twins began to accompany the native Boreali hymn, forming a soothing blend of masculine tones that rose to greet the wind stirring the leaves. They sang for no one in particular, except the moon and her maker.

Taken in by the music and its simplicity, Luscia repositioned her head at the opening of the tent. She fastened a flap to the side to better appreciate the old song branded in their northern hearts. With eyes closed, she intertwined her offering with that of her warriors.

> *From the mounts of Orallach we sing,*
> *From the crest of Aksel's Keep we bring,*
> *A song of Old, a song of some.*
>
> *For those who've lost what Tiergan found,*
> *My soul turns ear to hear such sound,*
> *Of Dönum's light and Lux's stream.*
>
> *Though ash and flame and darkness came,*
> *New life and burnished day remain,*
> *Resilient against horrors sought.*
>
> *'Tis in the wind, between the trees,*
> *Whispers proof of everlasting.*
> *Though in their absence I will hold,*
> *Aniell's delight in Boreal.*

Her harmony trailed off as she felt compelled to look toward the heavens of Aurynth and its watchman, the moon. For her vow to Aniell and the children of Boreal, her life was no longer her own. Luscia knew the day would come when she'd be asked to sacrifice everything because of it.

Summoning all the bravery she could, Luscia Darragh Tiergan accepted her fate. She was, and would forever be, al'Haidren to the House of Boreal.

Luscia's eyes flashed open.

Rotating her neck in a slow, controlled motion, she locked eyes with her lycran. The eerie gleam of Aksel's irises flicked to the front of the tent, then tracked some unseen movement around the side of the cramped space.

Luscia reached for the dagger under her pillow and soundlessly pushed herself off the ground. Balancing on the ball of each foot, she inhaled deeply, but the air smelt only of moss and pine. She crept outside, listening intently all the while. The darkness was devoid of sound—even the animals had gone quiet.

"*Ana'Sere?*" Böwen advanced from his post behind the edge of the ruin. "Are you well?"

Aksel circled her legs, bare beneath her shift, sniffing the undergrowth.

"It's nothing," Lusica started to murmur, but froze when the lycran yipped at the base of the tent. Along the side, a deep gash scored the stretch of hide, ending exactly where she'd laid her head. From the laceration, a beetle writhed out between the fibers and scurried back to the earth.

"Wake the sleepers." Luscia swallowed as the hairs on her arm lifted to another calling. "We leave within the hour."

TWO

Zaethan

A familiar blade landed inches from Zaethan's left cheek and impaled the earth beneath him, still damp from the morning rain.

"As they say, 'Every gain has a loss.' Looks like the loss is yours, *Ahoté!*" Kumo Shá announced confidently as his massive weight pressed down on Zaethan's chest. The white of his smile reflected the bright afternoon sun, shining boldly against the depth of his southern skin while he boasted to the few spectators currently sprawled across the surrounding terrain.

Always putting on a show, Zaethan critiqued.

Ignoring the mix of dew and sweat bathing his spine, Zaethan studied the other man. Showmanship continued to prove his cousin's primary weakness, as much as it was his source of charisma.

"*Uni*. Yes, it does, my friend," Zaethan promised under his breath, locking eyes with the proud victor. He permitted his cousin's celebration a moment longer before slamming his forehead into Kumo's.

His cousin roared with pain and surprise. Taking advantage of Kumo's disorientation, Zaethan hooked his legs around the muscular torso that pinned him and rotated them both to the right. Before the maneuver was complete, he thrust the fingers of his dominant hand aside, stretching to find a hilt encased in worn leather. He freed the blade from the dirt and let it skim Kumo's throat, just as his left knee hit the wet earth with force.

"A loss, indeed. But let us not forget an older saying, cousin," Zaethan whispered into his second's ear, just loud enough for the present members of his pryde to hear. "'Boast in your victory, not before it,'" he quoted with a devious grin.

Zaethan's head still pound from the impact, but upon assessing the pain clouding his beta's face, he decided the drumming ache was completely worth it. He rolled and stood in one fluid motion. Flipping the blade to offer the hilt to its rightful owner, he extended a hand to the man on the ground. Kumo clasped Zaethan's forearm with a grimace and climbed to his feet, gingerly taking back his favorite knife.

From behind, Zaethan overheard Takoda Muthwali snicker smugly. Their other comrade, Jabari Ulumb, swore as he dropped three dromas into Takoda's hand, the clink of each silver coin emphasizing the mistake in doubting his alpha. Zaethan hid his amusement, lightly brushing off the blanket of dust and grime his outer tunic had collected. After binding back the woven locs that had been freed in the tussle, reforming the fall of rope-like braids between his shoulder blades, Zaethan strode to his remaining men, congregated near the horses.

A small segment of his personal militia—his pryde—had ridden to the outskirts of Bastiion to hunt in the openness between the provinces of Galina and Agoston. At least, that was the generic excuse he offered to any who questioned his absence. Bastiion had been his second home since late childhood, but it was irrefutably suffocating. Having inherited the title of al'Haidren, Zaethan Kasim was committed to serve the crown, but even after twenty-three years of partially living at court, his blood still ran Darakaian red. A blood that called to open spaces, like a hawk calls to its master.

His father—Nyack Kasim, Chief Warlord of Darakai, Commander of the Orynthian armies, and Darakai's Haidren under King Korbin Thoarne—was scheduled to return to the palace that afternoon. While his father's visits tended to inspire Zaethan's need for a hunt, a half-day's ride couldn't prevent their eventual reunion. Zaethan shook out his clenched fists as the thought itched the back of his mind.

"Are you never still, Alpha Zà? *Doru*, just stop. Take this." Zahra Hanovi, his third, tossed a canteen in his direction, shaking her shaved head. "After all that commotion, you still jostle about."

She said it in jest, for both knew Zahra was his third for good reason. Her loyalty had proven to be as reliable as her ruthlessness in combat. Even so, being a few years older than he, Zahra's maternal instinct awoke once in a while, though Zaethan rarely minded. Her spontaneous displays were even comical at times, at least when Kumo was victim to the harsher sides of her Darakaian mothering.

Zahra would be a truly terrifying mother one day, if any man was ever brave enough to suggest it.

"That is why I call him *Ahoté*," his cousin hollered, pointing his fingers against his cheeks to resemble the whiskers of bobcat.

Nepotism had nothing to do with Kumo's position at Zaethan's side, either. His cousin was bred for war. Even covered in mud, anyone could see the corded musculature hugging his bones. With a neck the width of a small tree and legs like horse haunches, the man looked like a fragment of the Andwele Mountains come to life. Truthfully, Zaethan held the upper hand in combat simply because Kumo moved first with his fists, second with his mouth, and lastly with his brain. The moment his cousin let the latter lead him, he'd evolve into an unbeatable opponent.

"When did you become so eloquent, Kumo?" Zahra snapped. "It's good to see that brain is finally trying to fill your thick skull. Eh, maybe you can give us all pet names."

Her voice always seemed to drip a preferred flavor of sarcasm when addressing his cousin. After their years of forced camaraderie, she still harbored bitterness over remaining third and never second. Despite Zahra's vicious strategies and insatiable hunger to win, Kumo's size always named him victor in formal challenges for his position.

"*Uni*, yeah, I give you plenty of names, Zahra. You just haven't heard them all yet," Kumo managed, mumbling a string of curses in Andwele. He tightened the saddle fastenings on his mount with fervor, exerting his frustration on the leatherwork instead of the svelte, aggressive woman to his side.

It was a delicate partnering of wills Zaethan worked hard to marry, but even with their squabbling, he needed them both. Ironically, their dissimilarity made him stronger. It was a fact each contender recognized, but refused to admit aloud.

"Quit your bickering," Zaethan ordered, adding a pointed, "*both* of you," when Kumo's mouth dropped incredulously.

He didn't have the energy to play the roles of both alpha and nanny today. Stepping into a stirrup, Zaethan swung his weight across the saddle, anxious to begin their trek back. He needed to meet with the crown prince before the evening was over, and he preferred to face his father in the morning, after a full night's rest.

"What's wrong?" Kumo waited, sensing Zaethan's growing disquiet.

His beta could be impulsive and unpredictable, but Kumo had grown sensitive to Zaethan's moods. Seeing the warning in his alpha's eyes, Kumo altered his tone.

"Did one of the little nasties crawl up your behind during our tussle?" he teased mischievously. "Those bites can get ugly—not so good for charming court yancies."

Zaethan shuddered. Grass-nasties were small, ugly, six-legged creatures whose bites burned like the rumored fires of the depths.

"*Uni*, I distinctly remember the time you dumped a handful down my breeches. I don't recall your being so thoughtful about the aftereffects ten years ago," he clipped back, feeling his own lips quirking.

"Eh, *kàchà kocho*," Kumo said noncommittally before he winked. "You weren't so good-looking ten years ago. But you grew into that nose eventually."

Zaethan gathered the reins and prompted Hellion to lead them out of the clearing. It was a stretch he and the stallion knew well, for the tail end of the Khan River beckoned a variety of game to her banks. The richly scenic ride along the edge of her waters, where pebbled offshoots fed neighboring flora, was his favorite trail apart from the one home to Faraji.

Hellion snorted in acceptance of the command, exuberant to move again. Zaethan had trained dozens of their revered Andwele mountain stallions, but this beast was the most feral he'd ever handled—far more wild than his twin sister, Harmonia. Breeding a set of twin Andweles was unheard of, and he'd intended to gift the male to the crown prince five years ago as Darakai's offering upon Zaethan's Ascension, following tradition. But even the most experienced riders struggled to hold dominance over Hellion—hence his naming—so Zaethan decided to give Dmitri the female, as the mare was significantly easier to manage. The prince had readily preferred Harmonia to her twin after witnessing Hellion's violent temperament firsthand.

Throughout the hours of riding, the clouds overhead rearranged to paint the evening's backdrop. Blushing skies streaked with splashes of citrine cast a warm glow over the open landscape. Zaethan pushed Hellion to run to the stallion's content, lowering his upper body to rest along Hellion's impressive frame, unifying them. He felt beads of perspiration escaping from under the horse's steely mane, a match to the sweat trickling down his own brow. It was proving a warm spring, though nothing compared to the hot, stuffy air Bastiion harbored.

He needed this. This rush, this escape. Whether natural or created by their momentum, Zaethan savored the wind beating against his skin. It would be another age before either of them could have this, and somehow, the onyx beast sensed it, too. The angry stallion, his likeness in spirit, craved the same taste of abandon.

Zaethan didn't know when they'd be able to feel such freedom again in the coming months, especially once *she* came. Ensuring the crown prince's safety against her sorcery would overrule every personal desire once the al'Haidren to Boreal crossed their city gates. When they last met, she'd been too young to wield her unnaturalness against them, but her second coming would not be the same.

Closing his eyes, Zaethan tried to forget hers.

Zaethan's pryde reached the inner Proper as *Owàa* bade his farewell and conceded to Àla'maia, his lover the moon.

Familiar scents from the market filled his chest as they rode through the streets: fine jasmine and bergamot mixed in a sickening cocktail with the stale aroma of butcher slabs. The distinct odors of old produce and imported drink mingled in the clouds of smoked pipe marrow escaping from dirtier, less frequented tents. Zaethan despised these smells, which told a story of waste and addiction, cheap trade and desperation.

This was Bastiion, the heart of Orynthia. The realm's crown city, fueled by a commerce that was equal parts luxury and rot.

Regardless of Zaethan's disgust for Unitarian custom and livelihood, the Proper was a home of sorts. Dmitri was here, and as future king, here he would remain. Over the years, the prince had grown closer to a brother than a charge, and regardless of Zaethan's wish to escape what—or rather *who*—thrived in Bastiion, he had vowed to keep his oath to never abandon his oldest friend. Two yancies—rich Unitarian noblemen—crossed the street, each towing a pair of night-callers on their arms. The young women, faces painted with immaculate artistry and bodies draped in exotic textiles, laughed sensually with their bene-factors. Their feminine chatter suggested a mutual pleasure, when the transaction couldn't have been further from the truth.

"Eh, *Jaha*! It's been a while, no?" a throaty voice called from a crooked alley to their left.

Zaethan twisted in his saddle toward a woman wrapped in layers of ruby velvet, tailored to exaggerate her figure to perfection. Her lips parted slightly as she encouraged the material to fall down a bronze shoulder.

"How 'bout you men come see me tonight?" she proposed, her tone sultry. "I'll make sure my girls show you extra love…extra *papyon*, yeah?"

"Salma. You're looking lovely, as always," Zaethan offered with an easy grin. "Unfortunately, I am otherwise engaged. Perhaps you can comfort Bastiion's lonelier souls—a pitiful yancy has more coin than my poor Darakaian pryde."

Every man in the Proper knew Salma Nabhu and, likely, most of her staff. She'd been the matron of The Veiled Lady for over a decade, and her decadent establishment was one of the most popular in the city—as were the many darker services it had to offer

"*Uni,* but none of the rich yancies look like you, *Jaha,*" Salma taunted.

The woman was old enough to be his mother, but Zaethan welcomed the sound of home. *Pretty thing*, she liked to call him. It was a useless seduction, yet hearing the broken Andwele roll off her tongue was a bittersweet memento of the mountains he'd not seen in months.

"You come see me soon, yeah?" she urged as they passed. "You bring me those eyes. Even Madam Salma gets lonely sometimes…"

With a final wink, she disappeared back inside The Veiled Lady. Music floated from the windows of the night den, though their thick garnet curtains hid Salma's patrons from the eyes of Bastiion's penniless voyeurs.

"A veiled lady indeed." Zaethan chuckled.

He'd always liked Salma; she was an exception to the norm among those of her profession. Granted, her success was far from surprising when one considered how Unitarian ancestry colored her dewy skin and vibrant, hazel eyes, haloed by the tightly coiled raven hair that came courtesy of her southern heritage. Even past her prime, she stood out in crowded Marketown.

Darakaian cross-castes scarcely made a decent life in the Proper. The product of two Houses, cross-castes were unrepresented by the Ethnicam and without a seat at the table of the Quadren. Those of any origin claimed little to their names and even less in their pockets. The lucky ones found a glimmer of normalcy in trade or shop work, while the unlucky were often sold to the highest bidder.

Salma's decision to position herself as the most infamous madam in Bastiion was a sensible gamble. Even Zaethan had to admit her brash candor was like a breath of fresh air in a land of stale aftertastes. Unitarian women of the court were haughty, tight-lipped creatures who used their beauty to ensnare men as politely as they discarded them. Meanwhile, Darakaian females exhibited the opposite extreme: fierce, beautiful warriors who boldly—and, at times, combatively—voiced their wishes. Hence Salma's universal appeal.

If her invitation had caressed his ears another night, he might have directed the men to accept—Zaethan's reputation certainly benefited from the exposure. Connections accrued in a smoky game of chance with the city vagrants often proved just as powerful as any alliance built upon a dance card, but he'd thus far avoided personally partaking in Salma's offerings, much to her dismay. The madam's selection of professional night-callers was certainly inspired, but acting on a momentary impulse was never the wisest use of her business. Many a yancy found himself owing Salma Nabhu enough coin to teach Zaethan he'd rather it be the other way around. And as Haidren, the last thing Nyack Kasim would want to learn was that his son had tainted the line by siring an heir at a popular night den.

Besides, if *The Veiled Lady* housed the only parties receptive to his attentions, then Zaethan wasn't nearly as charming as he'd been led to believe.

After an hour navigating the city, the pryde finally reached the palace grounds. Zaethan urged Hellion into a large stable connected to the exterior guard house. Dismounting, he stretched out his limbs, which had become tense during the ride through the cramped streets. Then he began the rituals required to ease Hellion into his stall. Running his hands along the stallion's stunning frame in a series of swirling motions, Zaethan soothed the animal with gentle Andwele whispers. He'd bought Hellion three stall lengths, but the beast still hated being boarded. Perhaps he should incorporate Salma's methodology and purchase a docile mare.

As he locked the stall, Kumo placed a heavy hand on his shoulder.

"Come, *Ahoté*. We need to speak," the beta directed quietly. He knew well that giving orders to an alpha had consequences.

Zaethan released a breath and brushed past. "Whatever it is, it can wait, cousin."

Ignoring the command, Kumo rushed to follow. Falling in line with Zaethan's steps, he swung a broad, muscled arm swung out to stop him.

"*Doru*, Zaeth. You're upset—what's wrong?"

Zaethan's gaze traveled up the heights of the palace and lingered on the small wing of apartments that would soon belong to *her*. Inside, where she'd do the most damage.

"Word arrived late this morning. The *ysiti*," Zaethan spat vehemently, "will arrive by week's end."

Kumo's face went slack, the blood fading from his cheeks.

"*Shtàka*," he swore. "Now? I thought the ice-witch Ascended in the summer—"

"We don't have much time. I need to go."

"You've got bigger problems at hand, *Ahoté*. The Guard just found another one. This time near the docks."

"A dead cross-caste?" Zaethan whispered. "One of ours?"

Kumo shook his wide chin. "*Ano*. Another y'siti mutt. A girl, only eleven years."

The hazy image of a lifeless child hovered in Zaethan's mind. Stepping around Kumo, he marched to the nearest entrance and paused, as the matter of the witch would have to wait. Zaethan's pryde managed the security of the Proper, so he and his beta needed to speak with the sentries right away.

Before retreating into the guard house, he glanced back toward the southern tower. To protect his friend and someday king, Zaethan would soon lock himself inside that stone cage with his father while her threat suffocated any illusion of his independence.

Every gain had a loss.

And he already hated her for this one.

THREE

Luscia

The brilliant midday sun glinted off the lethal angles of the *kuerre* Luscia held. Light bounced within the luxiron core and drenched the metal in a translucent opalescence, as if awaking it from a mortal slumber.

The sword was perfect in every way.

Luscia lovingly polished it in circular motions while her men finished their meal and allowed the horses to rest. Strategically weighted and diligently sized, the *kuerre*'s curved blade fell just below her knee when sheathed. Her father had commissioned the piece months ago as an Ascension gift for her, and Luscia couldn't imagine a more befitting tool to take with her into adulthood.

"It suits you," Declan commented. His hooded, steely eyes sparkled at her for a moment before he resumed packing the uneaten pieces of meat. "It will bring him honor for you to carry it when we reach the crown city."

Luscia agreed, smiling in quiet contentment.

She caught sight of Aksel trotting in and out of the patches of sunlight piercing the dense canopy overhead. It illuminated the lycran's pristine coat of white fur, emphasizing the streak of ecru running from between his eyes to the base of his tail. An ache of gratitude settled in Luscia's chest as she watched Aksel, who had been another gift from her father. The Clann Darragh knew his daughter well, and the tokens her guarded nature would need to move from one reality to the next.

"Hey!" sounded a frantic voice. Noxolo, sitting a few yards away, ceased digging his long fingers through a shallow satchel and frowned at the small grouping. "Who took my smoked muskrat?"

In answer to the distress contorting the Najjan's delicate features, Böwen chuckled and gave Noxolo a hard pat on the back. Creyvan, the more considerate of the two, offered him a questionable alternative from his own sack.

"This is a serious offense!" Noxolo shrieked, knocking the jerky out of Crevyan's hand. "That was fresh from home! My sister Deirdre dried that last batch right before Lady Luscia's Ascension. Jerky made to go in this belly, for this jaunt!"

Nox marched about their makeshift circle, in hopes of detecting betrayal in their faces. His grey eyes bounced between the suspects, his silvery hair whipping with his hysteric gesturing.

"*This* belly!" he carried on. "For *this* jaunt!"

"Shut it, Noxolo!" Declan shouted beside her. "Nobody cares about

your sister's muskrat…or any other piece of game on her." His square
face grimaced at his own imagination.

Luscia laughed openly for the first time that day. It was a witty, if
sadly accurate observation, she had to admit. Before that comment, she
would have listed Creyvan and his genial brother as their only source of
levity. What a relief they were not unaided. Though by the horror that
twisted Nox's thin lips into a sour knot, it registered that only Declan
earned his mention on her private list.

"Do not jest so crudely in front of the al'Haidren."

Luscia's eyes snapped up to meet Marek's across the small clearing
as the men's teasing trailed off. His admonishment was spoken to the
others, but the look he pinned on Luscia implied it was she who should
be dictating the definition of appropriate banter. An almost imperceptible narrowing of his bright eyes suggested that vulgarity was beneath
her station.

Luscia concluded that, like Noxolo, Captaen Marek Bailefore
would never make her list, either.

It was one of the many reasons she'd struggled to accept him as a
potential suitor, despite her father's urging, and another example of
the High One's unfathomable sense of humor. In Marek's shadow,
other men rarely approached to make any intention beyond friendship
known. Most Boreali women, of any age, would've been elated to be
tethered to the redheaded warrior—after all, Marek was one of the
more attractive bachelors in Roüwen. However, Luscia felt that a strong
jaw and piercing gaze couldn't compensate for his domineering tactics
and unwanted opinions.

Fortunately, Boreal's Clann Darragh hadn't assigned his protégée
and favored captaen among the Najjan as Luscia's sole escort to Bastiion.
For that, she would thank Aniell. Luscia was certain that, however

much Orien Darragh beamed at the image of them together, her safety must have overruled any ceremonial agenda. Still, she'd long reconciled that a union with the captaen was inescapable. Luscia's role as future Haidren to Boreal would require she not only make a match to preserve the line of Tiergan, but a powerful one within the boundaries of their reclusive society.

Rebelliously, Luscia wondered if enough crass joking might cause Marek to reconsider just how much nonsense he'd willingly tolerate, and perhaps seek companionship elsewhere. But, as he'd already implied with his pointed look, it *was* her responsibility to set the standard for decorum. So, instead, she settled for staring imperiously until he lowered his eyes. He would, eventually. The dogmatic captaen might be the head of her private guard, but he held no such sway over the al'Haidren herself, and in such moments, Luscia loved to remind him of it.

"It was probably just the lycran, Noxolo," Marek stated with finality.

"Don't blame poor Aksel for the grabby paws of men, Marek," Luscia interjected as she packed the polishing cloth into her traveling case and stood to sheath her *kuerre*.

As if to make her retort more believable, the menacing wolx growled from his position at her side. Even sitting, his head perched well above her waist. At nearly two hundred pounds, Aksel was massive, even for an Orallach fox-wolf hybrid. His protective instincts had only heightened since crossing Boreal's border and now showed in the way he bared his teeth at the captaen.

With pride, she clicked her tongue and chided, "Now, Aksel, we mustn't lower ourselves to the beastly standards of others."

It was petty, but she was incredibly bored. During the past fort-night of travel, the only occasion Luscia exerted effort to communicate beyond necessity was to stimulate her mind or distract it. Though there'd been no other sign of a threatening presence following them, excess boredom encouraged wary curiosity to drift into speculation about the patched gash down the side of her tent, or the dreams that still haunted her. Thus, being a perplexing product of logic and whimsy, with each trait warring against the other, she could only converse with herself for so long. If one virtue wasn't fully engaged, the other would prevail, and Luscia wasn't yet ready for whimsy to yield to cold pragmatism. Pragmatism inevitably sought answers—answers she wasn't sure she wanted to find.

Climbing into the worn leather saddle, she dipped her fingers into an inner pocket of the satchel and swiftly drank one of her aunt's prescribed tonics while the men were distracted by their departure. Her condition having been concealed by family since puberty, she aimed to prevent her next episode as long as possible. Discreetly, Luscia dabbed a drop of the liquid from her bottom lip after the others began to move.

Watching the line of Najjan plunge into the wood, she again felt the crisp, sobering premonition each step toward the House of Bastiion incited. Lifting her chin, Luscia stared ahead, determined to ignore it.

"Noxolo!" she called with renewed cheer. "Tell us more of your sister's muskrat. Our friend Marek here regularly enjoys game most tend to avoid."

"Well, Deirdre uses a variety of techniques..."

With a satisfied smirk, Luscia trotted her horse past the successfully mortified Boreali captaen.

Humidity pressed against her skin like an unwanted kiss. It must have been the hottest day of spring thus far, and Lusica had long since done away with the magnificent fox fur she'd received upon her departure from Roüwen. Her northern brethren refused to waste any aspect of a kill, viewing each as a sacrificial gift from above, and Luscia was usually more than happy to be a recipient of their resourcefulness. Furs were often worn throughout the cool, damp springs of Boreal's highlands, but the climate had progressively shifted as they descended into Orynthia's lower elevations.

Jerking his coat off each arm, Böwen seemed to share her disgust for the weather. In a huff, he shoved the Boreali jacket into a saddle bag and pulled most his chin-length hair away from where it had begun to stick to his cheeks.

"I don't understand how the Unitarians endure this soggy, sweltering pit every year," he grumbled.

"*Ana'Sere*, will it be like this the entire summer?" Creyvan asked from behind.

"*Wem*," she confirmed, "though worse, if I recall. However, my only visit was during autumn, to celebrate the prince's Ascension."

Unlike her predecessors, Orien Darragh had shielded his daughter from court life in Bastiion, relying entirely on Alora, the clan elders, and the Isle of Viridis to shape Luscia into their next al'Haidren. During her entire seclusion, there was one sole event in Bastiion that had demanded her attendance: the eighteenth birthday of Dmitri Thoarne, Crown Prince of Orynthia.

"Do you remember him much, Lady Luscia? Prince Dmitri?" Noxolo inquired, turning in his seat to glance back from the head of the party.

In truth, her recollection of the experience was vague and admittedly useless. At twelve years of age, Luscia had hardly been politically savvy or socially fluent. Faint memories painted Dmitri Thoarne as being a kind and considerate, if somewhat frail, young man. But he was no longer eighteen, just as she was no longer twelve. Luscia grinned at that. Six years could change a person exponentially.

"He was very gracious host," Luscia said, aware of her ambiguity, but it wasn't as if they'd been royal bunkmates at the time.

Clearly dissatisfied, Nox reluctantly faced forward, drooping his shoulders dramatically.

"What of the other al'Haidrens?" Böwen asked. "You must have met them during his Ascension ceremonies."

"Introductions were made, though more for formality's sake than the purpose of actual acquaintance," Luscia began, attempting to answer their curiosity as accurately as possible. Like her, they too had lived in seclusion most of their lives. "The al'Haidren to Bastiion was pleasant, though often inebriated. Or missing altogether, allegedly seeking company in noble skirts."

"Typical," Declan retorted dryly, riding up alongside Luscia as the trail began to widen.

She nodded, because it was true. While the Unitarian provinces provided the realm with various goods and reliable crops, Bastiion's nobility rarely contributed anything besides excessive legislature and needless finery. In their quest for personal fulfillment, Unitarians occupied the remainder of their time in pursuit of the next pleasure, often on a daily basis.

"What about Pilar?" Creyvan yelled excitedly from the other side. "The Pilarese Beauty is famous, but I heard she has a tongue like a Tavish horsewhip!"

"Though not as lovely as you, *Ana'Sere*, of course," Böwen rushed to counter his twin's enthusiasm.

"*Tadöm*. I'm well aware of my reflection, Böwen, but I do appreciate your reassurance." Grinning in his direction, she found Böwen blushing behind his short, golden beard, barely longer than a day's stubble.

Throughout her youth, Luscia had heard her physical beauty affirmed enough to accept the claims. Her fair eyes, one nearly the translucent hue of the *kuerre*, were prismatic like the warmed waters of the Dönumn, where the Najjan tempered their sacred luxiron. Tiergan lineage was always self-evident to any who knew to look for it in the eyes. Accented by thick, distinct brows and crisp cheekbones, hers was a fearsome beauty. Glancing down, Luscia noted how the sun high-lighted the pale tresses that framed her face like ribbons of bone, a stark contrast against her ferocious mane the color of driftwood.

Even from afar, the daughter of Orien Darragh was unmistakable.

The Najjan favored women who bore sparks of Boreal's otherness, so they celebrated a woman who appeared as hauntingly beautiful as their homeland. Yet Luscia was no longer in Boreal, and she wouldn't blame the eastern Unitarians if they didn't share that same appreciation. At best, she imagined they might classify her northern features as striking. At worst, rather unsettling.

"I can't attest to the rumors, Creyvan," she said at last. "Frankly, the al'Haidren to Pilar avoided me like war-taint."

Which was probably a blessing, Luscia added silently.

From their brief encounter, she had surmised the western al'Haidren to be a perfect reflection of Pilar; cultured and steeped in snobbery. The House of Pilar operated as Orynthia's center of learning. Devoting their lives to discovery and advancement, their shotos spent years studying and debating topics most in the realm couldn't begin to comprehend. While Bastiion's Peerage of Nobility functioned as Orynthia's political network in the foreground, Pilar's Shoto Collective supported it from behind a curtain of bribery and deceit. Backed by an economy stocked with rich mariners and continual profit from naval contracts, Pilar had become the wealthiest of the outer Houses, second only to Bastiion.

"Well, Darakai, then. Surely you remember that barbarian," Declan rumbled.

It was true—Luscia would never forget the Darakaian boy, though she'd certainly like to. She could still hear his melodic laugh at her expense, one that crinkled a pair of eyes the shade of fresh sage. She recalled thinking they were lovely one night, while admiring the way the older boy's glance caught a flare from fireworks shot across the water. Incredibly lovely, in fact. That is, until he deliberately pushed her overboard into Thoarne Bay. With Luscia's transition through puberty unfinished, her bones hadn't yet achieved their unearthly resilience. Her right arm had broken in the fall.

It had rapidly healed, of course, but that was hardly the point.

"Briefly and unflatteringly," Luscia managed. "*Ana'Mere* swears he apologized, but I doubt there was any conviction behind it. The House of Darakai doesn't apologize for what they're proud of—like inbred brutality."

The House of Boreal's opposition to the House of Darakai was expected, and had been constant for many centuries. While both territories prided themselves on strength and their capability in battle, Darakaians *reveled* in the violence it required. Orynthia's House of war craved bloodshed like a pack of rabid dogs, and their barbaric doctrine taught Darakai to misjudge Boreal's self-restraint as weakness, and their ability to heal as mystic witchery.

"If Darakai is wise, that House will muzzle their ambassador." Declan's thumb stroked the exposed hilt of his dagger. "*Ana'Mere* is more merciful than the Najjan. Unlike your aunt, we won't hesitate to strike an animal when he refuses to heel." The promise pinched fissures in his ginger brow, deepening as he stared into the distance.

A weighted emptiness resettled in her abdomen. Luscia had been trained for this honor, but the partnering burden became heavier with the surrounding air. The House of Boreal needed Luscia, their newly Ascended al'Haidren, to shift a generational bias by navigating a nest of vipers. The Quadren, consisting of one Haidren from each House, operated as the most intimate set of advisors for each Orynthian ruler. The House of Bastiion provided the fourth Haidren in order to offset an inherent bias. Though the royal descendants of Thoarne were also of Unitarian nobility, Orynthian regents could not personally represent Bastiion and still maintain an impartial posture toward the outer Houses.

Therefore, serving as both the legal and public representative on Boreal's behalf, Luscia's seat on Prince Dmitri Thoarne's Quadren offered her unmitigated influence, as well as unavoidable expectations.

Being firstborn in line behind their predecessors, ties had already formed in her absence between the other al'Haidrens and the prince himself. She had always respected her father's choice to seclude her from court life, yet found herself increasingly disagreeing with it of late as she faced the ramifications. Her upbringing had been enriched by isolation but with great consequence. Luscia would be entering the walls of Bastiion essentially blindfolded, unaware of any preexisting dynamics within Dmitri's Quadren.

Alora often alluded to hidden alliances between the active Haidrens to Pilar and Darakai, but she couldn't assume those had been adopted by their successors. All Luscia knew for certain was that the voice of Boreal had become discredited over the years, especially during Alora's seat. Not a difficult task, if the opposing Haidrens wished to achieve a mutual goal. And so, with the House of Boreal's reputation now plagued by jealousy, distrust, and wariness, the political road before her would be riddled with unending hurdles.

Yet that had not always been the case. Though the regents seated on the Orynthian throne had begun to forget their shared history, the bloodlines of Thoarne and Tiergan were as intertwined as the mossy vines encircling the nearest pines. Luscia would have to find a way to remind Orynthia's prince what had been forgotten, what remained, and what would always be.

"*Ana'Sere.*" Böwen gestured forward to a steep, rocky trailhead, where had Noxolo halted the line. "Are you ready?"

She regarded the winding trail that plummeted into the Valley of Fahime, steeling herself for the task ahead.

"By Aurynth, *Brödre.*" Luscia squinted against the sun's glare and adjusted the sheathed *kuerre.* "Nearly."

FOUR

Zaethan

limbing the stairs to the royal apartments, Zaethan gathered
his thoughts, the gravity of the coming threat magnifying with
each step he took. The lingering voice of the Khan River faded
with his memories of hunting boar and quail, replaced by the haunted
corners of Marketown.

Kumo had said it best; the emerging procession of slain children
paved the way for the y'siti's arrival like an offering of blood. Her party
was due to arrive in Bastiion within the week, and Zaethan didn't believe
in coincidences. He needed to convince Orynthia's prince of the same.

The years of merciless training and discipline hummed in agreement, though he knew Dmitri would have difficulty accepting the

witch as a threat to the crown. Despite the laughable accords holding the Ethnicam together, Zaethan would not fail his House, or his king.

He'd just rounded an ornate landing that opened to a wing of guest suites when a string of girlish giggles reached his ears. The nauseatingly familiar sound echoed off the walls, breaking his concentration.

Shtàka! Not now, Zaethan thought furiously. With difficulty, he mastered his scowl into a dashing grin, bracing himself for another tiresome exchange.

A flurry of lavender skirts rustled in his periphery. The heap of fabric belonged to a young Unitarian woman, recognizable by her tan, glossy skin and shinning auburn hair, which tonight sat pinned atop her bobbing head. Fluttering lashes drew his attention—albeit reluctantly—to her large amber eyes.

"*Oh*! Lord Zaethan, I didn't see you! How silly of me. I was just returning from dining. Such a lovely spread!" she announced in her tinkling voice. "You were missed by many, of course!"

"Ah, Flourette. I'm sure your practiced allure was too preoccupied with your usual victims to register my absence," was his best attempt at pleasantry.

He didn't have time to flatter Flourette Hastings. Nor did he care to.

"Lord Zaethan! Stop it, you are *too* charming!" she exclaimed as her palm brushed his arm flirtatiously, too obtuse to hear the barb in his bland tone.

Removing her hand, which had begun trailing patterns across his tunic, Zaethan reminded himself that insulting the Haidren to Bastiion's only daughter was not the smartest venture, even when she clearly required it. Zaethan thanked the figurative Fates that her brother, Ira, was Gregor Hasting's firstborn, as opposed to Flourette.

Otherwise, Dmitri would've had to draft strict rules regarding physical contact between his al'Haidrens.

"As much as I'd enjoy discussing all of your colorful thoughts, Flourette—for I'm sure there are many—I must be on my way," he managed, as Flourette's face lit up at some compliment only she could find. "Please give my regards to Lord Hastings."

Zaethan bounded up the stairwell in escape, only stilling floors higher at his destination. Flourette was an attractive girl, but a vapid one, and he half expected her to come skipping after to assault him with further courtier babble. The last time she'd successfully cornered him was during her own Ascension earlier that winter. She'd pulled him into an alcove and barraged him with intermittent kisses, while simultaneously recounting the latest innovations in embroidery.

It had been torture.

Zaethan briskly passed the guards on duty and made his way into Dmitri's apartments, pressing his back against the door in relief. This was one of few places he alone was permitted, and no one else—including Flourette Hastings.

"Lord Zaethan, how pleasant of you to drop by." Eugenio, Dmitri's valet of twenty years, surveyed him critically as he added, "*Unexpectedly.*"

The old crow never managed to hide his displeasure over the prince's friendship with Zaethan. Regardless of his station, evidence of it leaked into even their simplest exchanges.

"Eugenio, always such chipper reception! Tell me, have you gotten into our prince's southern *bwoloa* again?" Zaethan cheerfully provoked. "One sip too many this time, my friend?"

"I would *never* lower myself to the thievery and drunkenness of the outer Houses," Eugenio muttered with indignant pride as he gathered Zaethan's riding coat to hang, clearly horrified by the state of it.

"That's the spirit," Zaethan called over his shoulder, leaving the valet standing in Dmitri's lavish foyer, still muttering to himself.

Striding through a slightly open set of doors, a wave of heat met his face. A fire so large wasn't needed this time of year, even in the late evening, but his friend always preferred the apartment remain oppressively hot.

"Must you make a habit of tormenting my staff?" came a tired voice from behind a collection of papers. "If Eugenio spat in your growing collection of liqueurs, I wouldn't hold it against him."

Dmitri lounged on a plush emerald sofa, his untidy carob hair floating above the document he studied. He must have been waiting there a while, Zaethan surmised. An array of essays and reports cluttered the floor underneath Dmiri's costly boots, which were propped contently upon the serving table in the middle of the large receiving room.

"I don't expect you to understand the bond Eugenio and I share. It's the truest of friendships, founded on a mutual disrespect," Zaethan said airily, crossing the room to a small bar cart beside the crackling inferno. He poured himself a glass of Darakai's favored *bwoloa*, knowing well enough not to offer a second to the prince, for he'd only decline.

"You're later than expected. Trouble, or another productive hunt?" Dmitri inquired curiously, not bothering to look up.

"Business in Marketown, sentry replacements, Flourette Hastings," Zaethan listed casually, taking residence on the matching sofa.

"A reprise of your stolen moment in an alcove, I suspect?" his friend jested, still engrossed in the same document.

"Depths, no!" Zaethan shuddered at the thought. "I barely escaped her the first time—I'd rather stab myself in the spleen than endure a second round of that scourge."

At that, the parchment lowered to reveal a dubious expression distorting Dmitri's refined features. The blazing fire ignited flints of gold in his hazel eyes, giving them more life than the intermittent pallor of his olive skin. A single brow lifted in doubtful amusement.

"I'm not exaggerating—you endure that prattling menace for an hour, and we'll see how well you fare," Zaethan challenged dramatically, inciting genuine laughter from his friend.

He sat back, content to hear Dmitri laugh, for he didn't do it often enough. It was the reason Zaethan hassled Eugenio so intently—well, one of them, anyway. The sound reminded Zaethan of their many nights spent in this scorching room. In their formative years, Dmitri had insisted all his lessons be held in these very apartments, where they would sit like this, debating and unraveling the great mysteries with his Pilarese tutors. By accompanying Dmitri to nearly every lesson, Zaethan's childhood became rooted in Bastiion, breaking from the balanced upbringing expected of an al'Haidren. Yet where Zaethan's deviation had been educational, *hers* had been dangerous, secluded as she'd been in that y'siti cult they dared call a House.

The realm had only rumors to speculate what truly existed inside the House of Boreal, as few who ventured into their highlands returned to speak of it. Archaic occultists, the y'siti were their own breed—colorless, lifeless soul-eaters. Many whispered that their cadaverous appearance was the result of ritual bloodletting and sacrifice, that they drained their humanity away in hope of the moon's favor. Some suggested the y'siti carved the hearts from their offspring and traded with the Fates for something cold and savage instead. Something unnatural. The other members of the Ethnicam usually disregarded the stories, but Zaethan had witnessed their validity firsthand.

Simmering at the thought of Luscia Darragh Tiargen, and the

danger she was about to bring into the palace, he downed the golden liqueur in his glass and savored its bitter sting.

"We have to talk about your new security measures, Dmitri." At the prince's dark look, Zaethan rushed to add, "*Uni*—it's time. The witch is said to arrive soon, along with the rest of the y'siti. With that in mind, I've drafted a list of alterations to the guard rotation, a log system for private visitation, and a new training regimen for those assigned to this wing. Also, I want you to keep either Zahra or Jabari within sight of you at all times."

Heaving a sigh, the prince set the documents aside and perched forward. Clasping his hands together, he eyed Zaethan intently.

"She's not a witch, Zaeth."

Zaethan stared at him in astonishment. "In a handful of hours, another full-blooded y'siti will be walking these halls!" he exclaimed. "A y'siti raised completely outside Bastiion, fully indoctrinated in that foul Boreali sorcery! Therefore, one of my pryde *will* be with you at all times—minimum."

Zaethan glowered over the tray of food Eugenio delivered, exasperated by Dmitri's inability to see through Boreal's deceptions.

The prince's aristocratic nose crinkled as he pursed his lips. "Oh, is that all? Any other demands you'd like to make?" Dmitri asked, with practiced patience.

"*Uni*. Yes, actually. The al'Haidren is to be housed on the lower level, near the guard offices."

Dmitri's eyes widened in disbelief. "I'm not putting my newest al'Haidren in the dungeon, Zaethan."

"Our facilities are very generous," Zaethan grumbled.

"Behind bars, in the dark, with no windows?" Dmitri clarified.

"She'd burn in the daylight, anyway. It's better for her complexion."

"I've already ordered the appropriate accommodations be made to her apartments. They began earlier this afternoon," Dmitri said, dismissing Zaethan's plans.

"But her presence will be an ongoing threat just a floor below this one! *Depths*, Dmitri! How am I supposed to shield you from what you refuse to see?"

Zaethan stood, seething as he began to pace. Dmitri was his charge. For centuries, the al'Haidrens to Darakai had protected Orynthia's crown princes and, eventually, her kings. It was beyond personal consideration for a friend; it was duty. And for the first time in their personal history, Dmitri seemed to be truly questioning Zaethan's judgment.

"Boreal's Haidrens and al'Haidrens have been housed on that floor for generations, Zaeth, and none have proven to be assassins. Besides, if she was a threat to anyone's safety, it would be yours, I think."

Zaethan paused his pacing mid-step to study the other man. Dmitri smirked at a memory from their youth.

"Don't make this about me. You know that was an accident," Zaethan said defensively.

"You *accidentally* pushed her off the railing and into the bay?"

A muscle moved in Dmitri's jaw, but he retained his calm indifference. It was a talent Zaethan had envied on many occasions.

"I didn't *push* her. I…knocked her. Into the bay. Accidentally."

"Yes, so you've said. You broke her arm, you know," Dmitri countered.

"*Kàchà kocho*," Zaethan shot back. "She was fine the next day."

"You know I hate that phrase. It doesn't mean anything! Zaeth, the girl's arm was in a sling."

"She deserved it."

"She was *twelve*."

Dmitri reclined his head against the arm of the sofa and closed his eyes. He suddenly looked exhausted, apart from the triumphant grin he wore, content with the temporary win.

It didn't matter how many attempts Zaethan made to excuse what he'd done the night of Dmitri's Ascension. His friend would never understand. Zaethan had already humiliated himself enough the morning after, when he'd tried to explain. *Glowing eyes*, he'd said. The prince had merely chuckled and shook his head, convinced Zaethan's vivid story was the result of too much wine.

But he hadn't imagined or hallucinated anything, and Zaethan never touched any refreshment besides water when his father was near. It still stung that Dmitri had never considered that.

Over and over, he'd replayed those events. In the month following, Zaethan nearly lost his sanity picking that night apart. Yet, with six years to forget, it still haunted him.

Fireworks shot into the darkened sky, exploding among the stars that littered Thoarne Bay with tiny pricks of light, reflecting the tears of Àla'maia, the moon. Guests spread along the deck of the private vàssa ship, cheering hungrily for more. Bastiion's elite loved to be entertained, he'd thought, watching their lush clothing shine in the night, much like the very stars overhead.

The newly Ascended prince stood several feet away, surrounded by a cloud of ruffles and perfume. Every ambitious daughter of the nobility was eager to ensnare Dmitri Thoarne, along with his crown, now that he'd crossed into adulthood. Zaethan smirked the prince and jerked his head to the left, communicating his vote for the animated brunette who'd elbowed the contestant interrupting her.

Yes, she'd do.

He turned back to the celebratory display illuminating the docks, currently devoid of the colorful floating stalls that usually made up the Drifting Bazaar. Bastiion's young al'Haidren launched into another mono-logue about the grandness of his estate in Arune, encouraged by the bubbly intoxicant in his hand. And across the deck, the little y'siti played atop the ledge of the railing. Scanning the cluster of partygoers, he couldn't find her keeper. The Haidren to Boreal was nowhere in sight.

His obligation to protect Dmitri had won out, and so he watched her. The witchling had worn leggings beneath her formal garb, which soon proved intentional. She moved with an otherworldly grace atop the thin wall of lacquered wood, balancing, flipping, rotating. She played with more strength than he exhausted in standard drills. The formations eased into a kind of silent dance as she leapt from the ball of one foot to another, moving her palms in sharp patterns to cut through the gathering smoke of the fire show.

She paused to stand in place as she eased her entire weight onto one foot and raised her body to balance on a set of toes. Arms crept outward to create a foreign pose, clearly well-practiced by the required tension. Even slower, the y'siti angled her chin and let her eyes fall on his.

Then she smiled.

It was a look that encompassed pure euphoria, pride, and a challenge. It wasn't right for a child to move in such a way, or any human. Even in Darakai, the House of War, no man conquered his body so completely, so effortlessly. Unease tightened his throat and chilled his bones. He began to step in her direction to encourage her down, to stop the wrongness of it.

Then she changed.

Her body remained as still as the dead heart she surely carried. It was her eyes that shifted. One eye bluer than the Khan River; the other paler than the sky. Eyes seen only on the Haidrens to Boreal. And as he watched her, those eyes began to emit an incandescent light of their own. A gust of wind swept across the party, lifting her strange, pastel hair to join it.

The stories were true, he realized.

She really was a demon from the Depths.

Before his mind caught up with his body, he'd pushed her from the railing, watching without a trace of guilt as she fell into the black waters. Instinct had dictated it be done.

Stranger still was how her Haidren interceded on his behalf. Once the witchling was fished out of the bay and sent to her quarters to be tended, the Haidren to Boreal turned to where Zaethan's father and the rest of the king's Quadren stood gaping. After a series of questions, she'd set her mystic eyes upon him and insisted it had been an accident.

"Children just being children. Isn't that right, young Zaethan?" the white demon had suggested with ease. Her cool persistence forced him to nod.

"That's right—an accident. It looked as if she was going to fall, and I was only concerned for the al'Haidren's safety," Zaethan had confirmed aloud, more confused than ever.

Regardless of the spoken niceties between the members of the Quadren, his father still struck him that night to remind him of his shame. As well as the next.

It had been six years since her only visit to court, and even now, reflecting on the ordeal, Zaethan didn't regret his actions. If she pointed that *otherness* against Dmitri, he'd do it again.

This time with more…permanent results.

"Dmitri, recent events may change your position toward her coming." Zaethan rubbed the interior of his palm. "The *kakk* in Marketown I mentioned—"

"Whatever has occurred," the prince said, pinching the bridge of his nose, "Luscia cannot be faulted in her absence. That's the end of it, Zaeth."

Zaethan watched the flames lick the walls of fireplace, biting his tongue. He detected the order, hidden beneath the prince's casual composure. Despite their closeness, Dmitri was still his future sovereign.

"Thinking on Flourette's unending agreeableness, again?" Dmitri said, changing the subject. "I can see Gregor's face now, when you announce your forbidden love for his daughter."

"In the name of your crown, shut it," Zaethan barked, returning to the sofa.

It was a typical picture of their friendship. Sitting together, Zaethan felt too nostalgic to push the matter any further—not tonight, at least. The warmth of Dmitri's apartments always provided a shared haven from the demands of their outside worlds. A haven, it seemed, they both still needed. As Dmitri rested his eyes, Zaethan tilted his glass, absent of the golden liqueur, and gestured to the checkered board on his friend's wall.

"One round of darts and dice? Or does the prince need his beauty rest?"

Dmitri's eyes reopened with the promise of victory at their favorite game, though the darkening circles on his skin betrayed him.

"This calls for more *bwoloa*." With contrived enthusiasm, Zaethan bounded to the cart and poured two more glasses. He raised both in the air and twisted to shout through a corner archway. "Eugenio! The prince is in need of your talents. Now, come have his drink!"

FIVE

Luscia

They'd agreed to enter Bastiion after nightfall.

When Marek suggested they employ a concealed advantage in the relatively unknown environment, Luscia had readily approved. She concurred that in a city where men with pale faces, light eyes, and fair hair were not welcomed anymore, darkness would reduce the risk of an unexpected confrontation.

She'd chosen to make use of their pausing to privately redress and mentally prepare. Fastening the clasps along the front of her surcoat, Luscia tried to control her restlessness. Trembling finders brushed the line of fabric toward her collar to straighten it, pulling the material higher to hide the faded scar marring her porcelain neck. Given enough time, Boreali skin could heal from almost any wound—except for an encounter with luxiron.

She stared blankly into the dimming forest as her thumb traced the raised tissue that painted a jagged line from her left earlobe to her clavicle. Branding her skin, it served as a daily reminder of humanity's nature, etched by the very consort dagger strapped against her thigh, adjacent to its mate riding the other. She'd left Bastiion six years ago as a joyfully innocent, brave little girl. Returning now as a hardened woman, Luscia vowed to honor that little girl's memory in any way she could.

But tonight was not about the past, she resolved, standing under the moon's increasing glow. Tonight was the beginning of what was to come: the age of Dmitri Thoarne.

For this reason, Luscia had selected her attire with great intention, choosing a piece normally reserved for ceremonial combat. She'd last worn the garment during her final evaluation on the Isle of Viridis. Paired with a sleeved vest, the indigo skirt split in four places to allow a woman's full range of motion and hung low atop thin, black linsilk breeches. Trimmed in a radiant labyrinth of silver needlework, it boasted Boreal's interpretation of war. Her brethren were a people of balance, who executed every practice with disciplined elegance. A people who gave each stitch the precision of a tempered blade.

Uncovering a shard of grey kohl, she lined her eyes in a darkened intimidation the Najjan saved for ceremony, and for battle. She had one chance to make a memorable entrance, and despite her racing heart, Luscia planned to enter Bastiion as a warrior. Gingerly, Luscia felt for the warm metal tickling her nose.

At the sound of rustling leaves, she spun to see Aksel padding into the small meadow, his tongue dangling lazily from a mouthful of serrated teeth and sharp canines. Trotting toward Luscia, he slowed to press heavily against her side in a passing hello. Her fingertips trailed across his back as he rounded her frame.

She dropped her other hand from its fiddling, releasing the tiny, crescent shard of luxiron piercing her septum. The *solrahs* was a concrete, indisputable declaration of her station in Boreali society. Upon her Ascension, she'd undergone the bestowing like all Boreali Haidrens, including Alora. Even though Luscia had waited eighteen years to receive it, her skin was still adjusting to such intimacy with the living metal, warm against her nose.

Luscia gathered her small handful of belongings, buckled her *kuerre* at her waist, and headed toward the tree line to join her men. When she noticed the absence of four paws, she looked back to find the lycran patiently sitting where she'd left him.

Blasted beast, Luscia cursed.

"I'm leaving with or without you," she stated, continuing forward.

She heard a mass hit the earth and turned to see Aksel's reclining outline among the tall grasses. His unblinking, glowing eyes fixated on where she stood at the edge of the clearing. With a quick yip, Aksel tilted his head and lowered it stubbornly over his outstretched legs.

"Really? You think *now* is a good time for this?"

Luscia knew what the lycran waited for. It was what they were all waiting for.

Pure Tiergan blood offered the Haidrens to Boreal an ability to experience what others could not. The higher gifts gave their Ascended Haidrens the sacred ability to hear and feel things not of this world, but of the hidden existing in and around it. That gifting manifested in various forms, but Luscia had deliberately postponed exploring them.

She'd avoided attempting her initial Sight, the first sign of true Tiergan lineage, since the evening of her eighteenth birthday.

A vacancy or disturbance in the higher gifts was unacceptable in Boreal's next spirit leader. Therefore, failing the Sight would only confirm Luscia's silent fears—an uncertainty of self which could never be spoken aloud. Luscia feared something she could not endure. Something she'd witnessed Eoine, her late mother, bear until the day she disappeared. Her magical, tormented, beautiful, and strange mother.

Luscia stifled the thought of her. Now wasn't the time to linger on such fears.

She regarded the unwavering lycran across the empty clearing. The wolx was right—she'd waited long enough, and time was running out. Submitting to the inevitable, Luscia closed her eyes and remembered Alora's instructions. She imagined reaching past the blackness and felt for what her aunt described as a feather brushing the mind.

After a few absent heartbeats, Luscia's eyes began to water. She lifted her face upright, refusing the outpouring of emotion. Keeping her eyes pressed shut, Luscia inaudibly begged, "*Bolaeva. Bolaeva,* Aniell, please let me see."

A spark, then another, tingled up her spine and traveled down her arms. As with a tether, she tried to reach out and pull. Reopening her eyes, Luscia willed herself to see beyond the veil that masked the unseen.

In a flash of light, there they were.

Faint but present, as expected so far from the source, glittering threads of lumin danced with the breeze. The light energy snaked about her body and floated toward the night sky. Fleeting traces of it awoke in the striation of the nearest tree bark, the swaying blades of grass, even Aksel's coat. Luscia's breath caught at the beauty of the living luminescence. Hesitantly, she raised her forefinger toward a branch of leaves. The iridescent veining brightened at her touch, as if greeting an old friend.

The undiluted lumin, no longer sleeping in her Tiergan blood, pulsed beneath her skin. A nearly euphoric sensation lifted her upright, intensifying throughout her body. It was an awareness unlike any other. And though her Sight was gone with the next blink, she felt a magnetism to the threads as she hadn't before.

Alora promised that once the veil was removed, it would never return. Thus, in its exodus, Luscia released all doubt, finally believing the potency of her inheritance.

"*Tadöm, Aniell. Selah'Aurynth*," she whispered in a prayer of gratitude.

Suddenly a sharp, burning pain seared through her temples. Crying out, Luscia collapsed. Aksel ran to her side and with a wet muzzle, shoved her satchel toward her fingers. Gasping, she searched frantically for one of Alora's glass vials and swallowed the prescribed tonic in a panic. Then Luscia cradled her head in her hands, pleading for the familiar pain to dissipate.

Disappointment drowned her agony. She'd taken her most recent dose just a few nights ago; it was far too soon for her to need another. Forcing herself off the ground, Luscia prayed for relief and quickly grabbed her things. She shook with remnant throbbing, but made way toward where her Najjan had assembled at the overlook, just a short walk through the trees.

Reaching their position, Luscia proceeded to one of the pack horses and stored her things inside a woven case. Head aching, she barely registered the clearing of a throat behind her at first, but when she turned around, all five men were staring at her in silence.

"*Wem?*" Luscia demanded, before noticing the collective pattern their gazes traced about her figure. Luscia may have chosen that particular surcoat for two reasons, for it fit rather well, and no one ever achieved anything by dressing like a sack of produce.

"*Ana'Sere*, you look..." Declan began, trailing off in consideration.

"Vicious!"

"And enticing!"

The pair of animated blondes nodded in unison. Marek grumbled something between Böwen and Creyvan, and their eyes doubled in size.

"I was going to say *formidable*, but I think their outburst will suffice," Declan finished with a stiff nod, then returned to his horse.

Mounting her mare in a swinging vault, Luscia caught the grimace Marek gave the others. The captaen held his stern expression a moment longer to be certain some wordless message was understood before climbing into the saddle. Whatever it entailed, Luscia didn't think Noxolo registered it, as he stalked in front of them and grinned at her with genuine regard.

Neither did Marek, by the way his brows merged in renewed aggravation with the alabaster Najjan. Tugging up the hood of his emerald cloak to hide the striking hue of his scarlet hair, Marek walked his horse beside Luscia's mare. Starlight shone on his face when he leaned closer, highlighting the bristling along his jawline.

Marek's unease was evident as he spoke in a low voice. "You dress as if we ride into battle, Luscia."

She ignored his informality and settled her gaze on the city of Bastiion, alight in the distance below. "Aren't we?" Luscia asked with conviction.

Marek studied her, as if he could sense the remnant pain within her skull. "Something's changed. *Ana'Sere*, are you all right?"

Her stomach tightened. His al'Haidren should not be so frail, so susceptible to ordinary affliction. The lumin in her blood should have risen above the episode, especially after its awakening. Luscia's brethren needed to see the al'Haidren they believed in: anointed, resilient, whole.

Luscia evaded the captaen's scrutiny and shifted to address her men. "As discussed, we will hug the shoreline along the Vasil and enter the Proper at the northwest gate. Marketown does not slumber in the night, but rather wakens, so be on your guard. The streets should be quiet along the docks, which is why your captaen and I have selected this route.

"*Brödre*, I know you are tired, but our journey has just begun. We have spent the past two weeks sleeping in the dirt for this night. We will not waste it, like the Unitarians waste their coin. We will not misuse our potential, as the Pilarese misuse their pulpits. And we will not forget our calling, like the Darakaians have forgotten their own." Inclining her head to them, Luscia added, "*Se'lah Aurynth.*"

Finishing the hallowed proverb with one voice, they professed, "*Rul'Aniell.*"

As their horses' hooves trotted through the city's streets, paved in interesting patterns of Old- and New-World stone, an anthem of mismatched notes filled the air to announce Luscia's arrival in Bastiion. Arrival to a life where whimsy could have no reign; just the remote stillness of reason and resolution. To prevail, to protect the sacred, Luscia needed to bind whimsy away, along with her longing to run back to the land of mist and myth.

It was the smell which first met Luscia when passing into the Proper. Inhaling shallowly, she tried to rationalize that an entire civilization couldn't possibly stink of rotting fish, and that by traveling along the west docks, they'd invited the stench. Choosing this route had been wise, considering the port was essentially unoccupied. Perhaps trade simply didn't occur on the west side the bay.

While the other corners of Bastiion corralled her inhabitants, the inner walls appeared less guarded than Luscia remembered. However, her prior visit had been contingent upon the judgment of Emiere, the captaen of Alora's guard. He'd brought them through the extremely fortified southern gate, which served as Bastiion's formal entrance.

Even still, she considered, *only foolish yancies would leave such a weakness in the palace's defenses, vacant ports aside.*

"Noxolo, I swear if that reek is coming from you, I'm going to shove kheflre root down your throat to finally clear you out," Declan swore through a clamped jaw.

"We're riding beside fishing vessels. Don't fault me for what we all must suffer," Nox shot over a shoulder at the ginger Najjan's implication.

"I wasn't sleeping next to a *fishing vessel* for the last two weeks!" Declan barked.

"Enough."

Though her rebuke was but a whisper, each man immediately lowered his chin and murmured an apologetic, "*Ana'Sere.*"

Luscia forced her body into a posture of poise as they approached the palace gates. The evening merriment bathed the heart of Bastiion in the gluttonous glow. Tall spires threatened to pierce the underbelly of the black sky, each crowned with a shining, domed cupola and positioned at alternating heights around the exterior of the palace, like giant torches dotting a grand temple. The hazy warmth painted the structure in a shimmering polish, showcasing a glorious medley of quartz, limestone, and byrnnzite. An organic composite of petrified ash, wood, and

Old-World metallics, byrnnzite was a testament of Orynthia's recovery after the land's immeasurable destruction.

Bastiion's most precious jewel: the palace that had sheltered the line of Thoarne for nearly five hundred years. And Luscia's new home.

Marek trotted ahead to speak with the handful of royal sentries grouped behind the western gate to the royal grounds. Luscia straightened to her full height as they silently weighed her features against his words. After a few hushed directions and a clipped argument over the colossal wolx tracing her steps, two high-ranking officials escorted their company to the guest stables. With seeming reluctance, a sentry expressed in rushed Unitarian that a row of stalls had already been prepared for the al'Haidren's party.

Upon entering, a slew of stablemen dashed from the halls and began removing their gear from the pack horses. Luscia dismounted and searched for her captaen's face in the shuffle.

"Marek, my things," was her only directive before an emerald cloak whirled to delegate the relocation of her possessions. She spoke a faint *"tadöm"* without looking his way again, knowing that Marek's northern ears would hear her thanks above the clamor.

A stable boy with stunning ocher skin guided her mare into a nearby stall. Luscia was about to relay the horse's tendency to kick strangers when she heard a loud crash from the stables across the pathway. Another team of attendants ran in the direction of the commotion, only to result in further shouting.

When Luscia asked the boy if everything was all right, his eyes widened with genuine terror as he exclaimed, "That Andwele stallion is from the Depths! He injured two hands just this week." In fluent Unitarian, she hurriedly offered her condolences and gave an emphatic warning about her own mare's temperament.

Exiting the stall, Luscia froze.

At the stable entrance, her kinsmen held a defensive formation around an imposing man outfitted in Orynthian military garb. His belted navy tunic was embellished with enough bronze to discern his station was one of great significance. But it wasn't the man's livery, his stance, or the outfit of sentries at his back that had put her Najjan on edge. It was the expression he wore.

The man turned his sour grin toward Luscia, but his feigned pleasantry didn't extend above the lower half of his face, battered and dark, like burnt cacao. The skin around his eyes tensed combatively as he addressed her guard.

"I am Commander Kasim, Haidren to Darakai. Your presence will be tolerated in Bastiion, but that tolerance does not extend to your weaponry. Because of Boreal's greed, the Peerage has decided that it is unsafe to permit your witchiron on the royal grounds. Therefore, abiding by this new legislation, it will now be confiscated."

The commander's excuse for a smile broadened at their troubled silence. Though they held their position, Luscia could feel the Najjan watching her reaction to the Darakaian's instruction in their periphery. Her men would mirror their al'Haidren in this initial test of her character, even if the commander refused to acknowledge her directly.

Not for the first time, Luscia wished her father hadn't sheltered her so thoroughly from Bastiion. For unbeknownst to her, this new legislation could be completely valid, and she was here to keep the peace between Boreal and the rest of Orynthia. So, though it chafed her to comply, Luscia reluctantly removed the sheathed *kuerre* from her side. As she set it on the ground, Luscia kept herself from glancing at the set of carved bone riding her knuckles, or from betraying any hint of the consort daggers hidden beneath her surcoat.

"I knew you'd understand," the commander said smugly. "Place the witchiron in this cart, and General Lateef will see that your contraband is locked away." He motioned to his right, where another mature Darakaian stood beside a small wagon draped in tarp.

"And to ensure the proper handling of Najjani craftsmanship, one of *my* men will accompany him," Luscia interjected, keeping her voice steady and pleasant. The commander jerked at the sound, finally turning his head in her direction. "He will bear witness as the general delivers the key to the compartment into royal hands. For as you stated, Commander, taking my property is for the safety of us all, is it not?"

Commander Kasim's eyes targeted hers. Black and unfeeling, they seemed empty before abruptly flashing with the embers of a dying fire.

"You see, men?" he scoffed mockingly. "When asked nicely, even an unbroken, feral y'siti can manage civility."

Marek and Böwen launched to restrain Declan in his fury. Noxolo tried to soothe Aksel's snarling, for even the lycran, a wild wolx, understood the realm's favored slur for the Boreali.

Y'siti. *Filthy ice-witch.* A label both unclean and debased.

The commander's grin morphed into a wicked sneer when Luscia's hand flew up in a silent command, stilling her small army.

"Or maybe they can't," he spat before marching out the open door.

Luscia waited until the commander disappeared on his path to the palace before she broke the hush.

"Welcome, my *brödre,* to the House of Bastiion."

SIX

A full year had passed since the figure stepped foot inside the Proper. During the months leading to her niece's Ascension, most of Alora's assignments had required he trek the outskirts of the realm, segregated from the heart of civilization. Prowling the heights of the crown city, the vapors from inhabitant waste and depravity reminded the figure he preferred it that way. As he advanced alongside the rooftops, he covered his sensitive nostrils with the hem of his cloak.

Being a woman of divine influence, Alora had planted her watchers throughout Bastiion's inner and outer Propers, her band of eyes growing to an impressive network within the last decade. The occupants of nearly every hovel had a price, most unwilling to pass on a reliable copper crupas or two. Information procured from the low was often of the highest value to the one who knew to ask for it. And when separated from his mistress, this private transmission of intel was vital to her operation, their correspondence only made possible with the help of a mutual friend.

Tonight's assignment was no different.

After seeing her niece safely deposited at the western gate, the figure was instructed to keep away from the palace, that shining beacon of Orynthia, and undertake the next affair. Alora had received word that a young boy had been found within Marketown's backstreet, which meant he was obliged to return to the soiled pit of a city he'd rather have forgotten.

The figure tightened his ragged gloves, noting where the leather split. He'd have to nick a pair off a merchant cart later, before retreating to his makeshift hideaway on a docked vessel in the bay. It was just another fleeting sanctuary in a world of isolation; an isolation of his own wretched making.

Abruptly, the figure knelt within the basin of the wide eavestrough, fixed to the side of the building to catch the runoff. Spreading his cloak, he mingled with the darkness, watching the dark men moving in formation farther down the street. The Darakaian prydes must have taken over the policing of the city during his stint away—an unsurprising development, given their Haidren's dangerous rise to power.

The Darakaian patrol encircled something of interest—a pile of trash, or something significantly graver, by the smell of it. The nimblest of the group, a young man with lengthy braids, suddenly sprang upright and stepped away from their circle. He bit his fist, as if to keep from retching off to the side of the alley. A larger man, a head taller than the first, broke off as well, though his attempt to not vomit was less successful.

Through the opening, the figure peered into the center of their huddle. Wedged in a pile of garbage, the profile of a pale little boy shone in the moonlight. The dusk of his fine hair indicated mixed lineage, confirming Alora's suspicions. The boy was a Boreali cross-caste.

"*Shtàka*," a member of their militia swore, rubbing his forehead. "Same markings as that girl we found. Did anyone else know there were so many y'siti mutts in the city? Depths, I'd never have realized it until they started turning up…this way."

"*Ano zà*." The southern giant wiped his mouth and pushed away from the wall. "But would you crawl out of hiding in Bastiion if you were them? Probably know they aren't wanted. *Uni*, they be tempting *Jwona*, coming to this place."

The one with the tied braids turned and bent closer to the body, stooping to his knees. "Tempting fate, indeed," the young man muttered, braids swishing as he shook his head fervently. "Why do this to a child? Even cross-caste. He's just a cub."

"This is messed-up *kakk*, Alpha Zà." The big Dakaraian crossed his meaty arms. "Makes a pattern now, yeah?"

"*Uni*, cousin. We need to have the corpse examined. Look at that."

The braided leader pointed to the boy's wrists. Sleek, precise slits could be seen, even from above. They explained the exaggerated pallor of his skin—the boy had been drained.

The figure chewed the peeling flesh off his blistered lip, caught up in troublesome consideration. Squinting, he scanned the rest of the body, his lids itching from the strain as he cataloged the series of lacerations to report to his mistress. It would be impossible to analyze the boy's remains once the Darakaians took the body into custody.

The leader carefully slipped his arms around the boy's form and lifted it out of the garbage. A tuft of mussed, chestnut hair peeked over his shoulder, where the child's neck hung to the side, utterly limp. Then, in an unusual display of tenderness, the Darakaian alpha cradled the boy's skull against his chest, tucking it tightly under his chin. Defensively, even.

The figure blinked twice. In both his lifetimes—one lived in the warmth of day, the other damned to chill of night—he'd never witnessed the prydes show an ounce of concern for the lower classes. Especially a *northern* cross-caste. Even the House of Boreal disregarded their own blended offspring. The figure leaned forward, captivated by the alpha's surprising care for the boy. As one who excelled at navigating the realm's degeneracy, fluent in her sins and secrets, he was not often surprised by her players.

"We'll regroup in the guard house. Takoda, call for one of the doctors from the catacombs," the alpha instructed. "I don't want this becoming tomorrow's gossip at court."

The warrior in question pounded his chest and set off with another Darakaian, leaving the alpha and his giant to escort the corpse from the alley.

"*Doru.* Let me bear it, *Ahoté.*" Alone, the bigger Darakaian stopped walking and shifted his tone to something more informal, implying a long acquaintance between the two. "They'll expect your beta to carry it into the guard house. Have to look impartial, yeah? You know trouble comes to those who care." Then he inclined his head toward his alpha, as if asking permission. "*Shamali, Ahoté.* If you see fit."

"*Uni.* Take him, cousin."

At the alpha's solemn nod, the larger man gently scooped the dead child from his embrace and continued down the alley.

Stalking the Darakaians, the figure crept along the gutter, keeping the duo in range. Nearing an intersection in the backstreet, he swung down onto a crooked veranda, hugging the exterior of the building while they rounded the corner.

"By the Fates, you southern street sweeper!" Glass clunked against the cobblestone as the figure arced over the railing to see a pair of fine-dressed Unitarians, lost in their cups, cutting off the Darakaians' advance. "That bottle cost more crupas than the militia makes in a month!"

"Take your drunken coin back to your country estates, gentleman," the alpha warned, sidestepping in front of his beta, partially shielding the cross-caste. "Marketown has catered to enough yancies tonight."

"Who the Depths do you think you are?" the first nobleman sputtered, spitting on the alpha's shoe. "You can't talk to the nobility like that—"

"Eh, well, what do you got there?" his companion slurred, rapping his ornate cane. "I spy a diamond in the drainpipe! Yannis, you could fetch…" the stumpy nobleman burped, "…fetch a few aurus for that thing."

"The cub's not for sale." The alpha balled his fists, shifting to further block the boy from their sight.

"Now, now, not so hasty, friend…" Yannis splayed out his palms. "Last y'siti cross-caste I sold went out of Port Niall for three aurus and then some. Splitting the gains, you could be a mighty rich southerner by the morning."

The figured squinted, only then recognizing the distinct bulge in the nobleman's hooked nose. It wasn't long ago that Alora had the figure chasing a wealthy Unitarian slaver out of Port Niall. Ire shot through him, scathing his parched throat. The number of nobles managing their own slave exchange was limited, specifically out of that port, and the figure had lost faith in coincidence. His eyes fixated on Yannis, studying him. The slaver trader, sweaty and red in the face from his earlier entertainment, licked his hand and smoothed the thin hair he had left backwards, then offered the same hand to the alpha.

"*Ano zà,*" the alpha snarled. "I said, he's not for sale!"

"Uh, Yannis…" The partnering nobleman peeked around to the Darakaian beta. "Forget the deal. I think it might be dead, anyhow."

The slaver gripped his belt heartily and grinned, revealing a golden tooth. Rocking back on his heels, he sniggered, "Well, there's another market entirely after they've expired, it'll triple—"

The alpha grabbed Yannis's lapel and punched him square in the jaw. Whirling around, he snatched the partner's cane and, with one end, smashed the slaver in the gut, pitching him across the street. The huge beta lurched back when the alpha spun again, swinging the cane, and caught the other man's fine boots as he tried to run, hooking him to the ground. The Darakaian's braids whipped through the air as he threw the cane aside and seized the silk of the man's collar, then proceeded to beat him senseless.

"*Ahoté, doru.*" The beta marched forward, adjusting the corpse in his care. "*Doru,* stop. Zaeth, he's out cold."

Shoulders sagging, the alpha backed away from the groaning slaver. "*Uni.* We need to go," he agreed, panting slightly. "Don't need this to be tomorrow's gossip, either."

A few yards off, Yannis spat blood and lurched to his feet, putting some distance between himself and the retreating Darakaians. Without regard to his unconscious partner, the slaver departed the alley before he awoke, hobbling toward the safety and raucous noise of merchant row.

The body now lost to the Darakaians, the figure leapt to the next balcony, in pursuit of this older target. Dangling off a corroded pipeline, the figure dropped another story lower. Anticipation charged through his aching limbs, greasing his joints into action.

The figure sprung from the ledge as Yannis passed under the unstable balcony. The stench of liquor wafted off the plush suit when he landed on the other man's back. Grappling over the stonework, they rammed into a cart of stale grain. The figure drove Yannis's face into the feed, earning a warbled groan from the slaver. Straddling his abdomen, he wrapped both gloves around the base of Yannis's fat neck. Calculations consumed his mind, as he counted the ships of people one man could have arranged since the figure had failed to put an end to the slaver's enterprise. An inhuman strength jolted through his fingertips as they twisted ruthlessly, suffocating his prey.

A hawk's screech shot through the darkness. She screamed again, her heralding cry shrill and commanding, disrupting the figure's senses. Gradually, the ringing faded from his ears, and he let go. Quietening his lungs, he listened closely. The slaver still wheezed against the grain, his breathing shallow and weak.

Slinking off the cart, the figure left him there, falling into the shadows and looking to the skies. The hawk's wings flapped ferociously as she crossed the moon, steering him northward toward the light. Toward the only home he'd ever truly known in Bastiion.

Alora.

SEVEN

Luscia

uscia simmered as she and the Najjan were led along a wide corridor to her apartments. Being forced to surrender her father's gift—her beautiful *kuerre*—was a grievous insult, but only in private confinement would she exhale the rage that could never fill these halls. Any heated, emotional response might invoke something worse than political friction, and Boreal had significantly more to lose than their precious metal. Still, while she'd been warned to expect disdain from other members of the Ethnicam, such blatant hostility was entirely unanticipated.

How long has Alora endured this? Luscia wondered. *And why would she downplay these shocking conditions to the elders?*

Hidden behind Declan's wide breadth, Luscia tinkered anxiously with the thin bands of polished bone gracing her knuckles. Pride in her younger brother, Phalen, blossomed at their touch. He'd presented the radials to her as a farewell gift before she left Roüwen. Phalen had inherited his imagination from their late mother, who'd made every mundane thing somehow enchanting and beautiful when they were young. His recent apprenticeship under the Najjani luxsmiths had given Phalen's overactive mind an opportunity for innovative freedom, and his affinity for the dangerously practical was borderline genius. It was almost as if her brother had expected the confiscation of their weapons and crafted the perfect device to have on hand at all times, despite Bastiion's pursuit to seize such things.

To anyone else, the tiny weapons would appear as nothing more than a pair of strange, three-fingered rings. But when engaged by an unseen catch near each thumb, a series of hidden luxiron blades opened in a fan-like design, providing the wearer with an advantage in hand-to-hand combat. They were fully collapsible when not in use, so while an onlooker might remark on Luscia's odd choice of jewelry, they would never suspect to find the deadly arcs embedded within.

Flexing her grip around the delicate loops, Luscia recalled Phalen's parting words when he'd slyly slipped them over her fingers. *I can't add weight behind your punches,* he'd said beaming, cheeks covered in soot, *but I can give them sharper teeth.*

Luscia smirked to herself. Had Phalen been their family's firstborn, he would've made an exceedingly cunning Haidren to Boreal.

Fortunately, while her perfect *kuerre* was temporarily lost, Luscia retained his radials as well as the consort daggers riding her hips beneath the surcoat. She would have to be creative with their concealment, for those weapons were too dear to be surrendered with an attitude of civility.

"*Ana'Sere*," Marek whispered, brushing her elbow, gaining her attention.

Luscia blinked at the palace attendant who'd been assigned as their midnight guide. She couldn't remember his name, or if he'd even given one. The middle-aged man appeared as troubled as she felt. Perhaps her mute reflections encouraged his nerves.

"M-my Lady al'Haidren, your q-quarters..." the squatty attendant stammered, his small, beady eyes bouncing between Luscia and her possessive lycran. Face ashen, he directed them through a set of lofty, embellished doors.

Exhausted, Luscia was overcome with gratitude at the pleasant scent of the domed living space. Though her Boreali senses ensured an advantage in most circumstances, a heightened sense of smell while navigating the city docks had not been one of them. If her estimation was correct, the apartment faced north over Thoarne Bay, and Luscia had nearly convinced herself that even her private chambers would house the tang of Bastiion's briny imports.

Instead, her nose was bombarded with traces of cinnamon, nixberry, and spiced vanilla. Stepping forward, Luscia angled her head to appreciate the details of the vast canopy above the cavernous receiving room. Candlelight flickered throughout the chamber, accentuating the subtle variations in the byrnnzite. Trimmed by a ring of granite, the New-World stone shone in a galaxy of copper, red, azure, and gold.

The palace was so very different from the village fortress Luscia had known for eighteen years. In Roüwen, her people dwelt within a refuge of aerial homes, suspended in the heights of Boreal's ancient, towering trees. A carved city fixed between the treetops, like a hidden world known only to birds and men.

"Shores of Aurynth!"

A basket of linens went tumbling to the floor, dashing Luscia's memories of home and drawing her eyes to a matronly figure. Several stray hairs escaped the woman's blonde braid, liberally streaked with grey, emphasizing her ruddy cheeks and the strained rounding of her shoulders.

Boreali. One of Alora's ladies, then, Luscia surmised. It certainly explained the presence of nixberry in the chamber.

"You must be Lady Luscia. *Meh fyreon, Ana'Sere.* We were not told you'd arrived!" She scurried about, talking in broken fragments as she checked to make sure all was in proper order.

"That's quite understandable. Please, *bolaeva,* forgive our intrusion…" Luscia warmed her tone, humbled by the older woman's frazzled state. "What is your name, so I may thank you properly?"

"Ock! Yes. *Wem.* I'm called Tallulah, and the little wisp milling about would be your resident attendant, Mila." She glanced around. "Where is that girl?"

"Well, *tadöm,* Tallulah, for all your effort. From what I see here, you've made everything look very inviting," Luscia extended.

Tallulah's mouth broke into a relieved smile, exposing two very prominent front teeth, which for some reason made Luscia like her that much more. She half curtsied before vanishing into a deeper portion of the apartment, where she called for the "little wisp" to produce herself.

With a groan, the entry door reopened to admit a team of larger attendants, bearing her personal effects. Luscia scanned the items carefully until she at last located a small wooden chest, sleeved in linsilk to shroud its unconventional locking system. Alora had stressed its importance, though to Luscia's knowledge it merely housed a rare collection of Boreali herbs and apothic materials for progressive remedies. Her aunt was Boreal's most gifted healer, and at first, Alora had insisted Luscia follow her into the apothic arts. Apprenticing with her aunt through early adolescence, Luscia was initiated into the apothic tradition of herbaceous compounds and their unlimited application. But to her aunt's vexation, young Luscia—like her brother, Phalen—displayed an early partiality for sharp objects, an attribute they'd most certainly inherited from their father. Abandoning the apothic arts, Luscia had sailed to train with the Najjan on the Isle of Viridis, leaving her tutor at odds with the mighty Clann Darragh.

Once the last articles of gear were distributed, the attendants made an eager exit. As they departed, a head of disheveled, blonde hair emerged through their stampede.

"*Ana'Sere*, the key to our luxiron has been delivered into the prince's hands," Creyvan reported in a huff. His dismay was evident, and inarguably represented their collective feeling of nakedness. Though her party still carried the standard iron blades typically traded with the other Houses, any Najjan would ache for his specialized weaponry.

Tentatively—for she was not accustomed to initiating contact with men—Luscia rested a palm on his sturdy upper arm.

"You did as I required." She caught his gaze and held it intentionally, detecting his resentment. "You did well, Creyvan. *Waedfrel, Brödre.*"

His focus drifted to the other four Najjan, who'd begun shuffling items into different corners of her generous living space. Creyvan nodded his approval after taking in the beautiful stonework and magnificent view, as if to be certain it was worthy of her. Looking back to the doors, he ran a hand through his tangled hair.

"There are two Unitarian sentries outside, one stationed on each end of the corridor. The other suites we passed did not have watch-dogs," he said, mouth tight. "I inquired about their necessity and was informed they are 'for the al'Haidren's safety.'"

Luscia considered the predicament. It was another deliberate test of wills. She sensed Marek surveying her reaction from the opposite side of the room, where he deposited a patchwork sack of mixed hides. The captaen tried to appear busy when she glanced his way.

He failed.

"Return to the hall," Luscia instructed, "and tell them that if Bastiion truly insists on protecting the al'Haidren to Boreal, then they would have given me six guards, instead of two. Tell them to think twice before insulting the Crown's guest so thoughtlessly next time."

Creyvan's forehead scrunched, confused, before melting into mischief. His boyish features lit up as he reached for the bronze handle. "If they wish to treat you like a prisoner, we'll make it inconvenient for them!"

Luscia closed the heavy door to find Marek smiling. His approval irked her as much as it pleased her, which was irksome in and of itself. Marek was an opinionated irritant, but she had to admit, his judgment was very credible.

"Lady Luscia! I found the wisp!" a jolly voice sang.

Tallulah bustled into the great room with a slim girl in tow. The dark-haired attendant exhibited a shy, though not fearful demeanor as the older woman practically dragged her to where Luscia stood beside Alora's wooden chest.

"This one's Mila. She's your resident lady's maid, provided by the court," Tallulah chattered in heavily accented Unitarian, for Mila's benefit. "Well, go on," she urged, pushing the timid girl forward. "Introduce yourself! The blessed al'Haidren ain't going to bite!"

Mila performed an awkward curtsy of sorts, tucking her chin until it met her chest. "M'lady al'Haidren."

The girl was of an age with Luscia. Her braided raven tresses shone in the light of multiple sconces along the curved walls, but that wasn't what had Luscia's breath catching in her throat as Mila rose from her curtsy. The girl's chin lifted a fraction to reveal a set of cobalt eyes on a face of Boreali porcelain—northern eyes that darted away as quickly as they met Luscia's.

Luscia had only met a handful of cross-castes in her life, but never one with such contrasting features. It was remarkable. If she stopped quivering like a cornered mouse, Mila would be stunning. While the palace employed many out of Bastiion's lower classes, Luscia was pleased to see the girl had been elevated to a decent position.

"Where is the rest of your party? S-so that we may prepare for them, my lady." Mila spoke to the floor, but the question was sincere.

"The five Najjan are my party," Luscia replied, puzzled by the inquiry.

A quick rap foretold Creyvan's return. He strutted through the foyer a lighter man, smirking with genuine delight as he recounted what had transpired with the appointed sentries down the hall.

"'—*before insulting the al'Haidren to Boreal so thoughtlessly again!*' You should have seen the blubbering yancy! And he asked, '*Six men, she demanded?*' and I said, '*Would you deem the al'Haidren less worthy than half a dozen—*'"

Creyvan suddenly broke off his enthusiastic recounting. It took hardly a moment to realize the cause. The imposing, flaxen Najjan stood slack-jawed as he took in the sight of the lovely, skittish attendant. Mila didn't notice his dumfounded expression because at his attention, she directed her own gaze toward her feet.

"Half a dozen, Creyvan? That was dutifully demanding of you," Luscia said, in hopes of mending the moment. For his sake.

The Najjan pulled his stare from the self-conscious maid. Even in the dimness of the room, Luscia saw pink stain his cheeks.

"Was there anything else?" she asked, growing weary, both mentally and physically.

"Oh—uh, *wem, Ana'Sere.* I found this chap waiting outside your chambers..." Creyvan managed, poking an arm through the cracked doorway. He reeled in a young page, his fingers gripping the boy's deep blue tunic.

"The prince sent him," Creyvan announced, making the messenger shake. It was almost as if he and Mila were partners in an involuntary dance of trembles.

"The Crown P-Prince, His Highness D-Dmitri Thoarne requests your presence, L-Lady al'Haidren." The tiny ball of his throat bobbed sporadically with his sputtering. "'No matter the hour,' he said. I am to escort you to m-meet with him, as s-soon as you are able."

Marek rounded the corner and crossed his arms. She knew her men were all absorbing the fact that Bastiion did not view Boreal's Haidrens with the respect the Najjan would like to enforce. She was also aware that after weeks of travel, lack of sleep, and now being thrust into a den of enmity, each man was ready to snap.

Apparently, the night was long from over. Luscia summoned her remaining energy. She thanked Tallulah and Mila for the last time and, after assuring them she needed nothing further, urged the two women to get some rest.

"The same goes for everyone else," she told the Najjan. "Marek, I want two of your choosing to scout the apartment for vulnerabilities. The other three should retreat to their own rooms and sleep." Marek scowled when she cut off his opposition. "*Niit*, Captaen. You are of no use to me if you are sleepwalking. Aksel and I will accompany the page to the prince's quarters momentarily." Luscia glanced at the boy. "If you'll wait for me in the hall?"

The page bowed hastily and extended a piece of fine parchment sealed with copper wax. Luscia cautiously took the message and watched him depart. Once her quarters were free of Unitarian eyes, she popped the seal and read Dmitri's brief, ominous script.

Bring it. Five vials will do.

"*Ana'Sere*, what does the prince say?"

Another identically handsome face appeared in their make-shift circle. Böwen's concern grew as Luscia's brows knit together in contemplation. She looked from the crisp note to Alora's apothic chest, brushing against her traditional, upturned boots. The viridi wood was whittled with northern engravings, which twisted around its borders and encircled a lock made of bone. She didn't know what animal it had been taken from, but it matched the key Alora had given Luscia before her departure—an obscure, skeletal thing no longer than an index finger. A key she wore now on a chain underneath her elegant surcoat.

Upon being questioned, the only information Alora would share was that the key would be safer in Luscia's hands while she traveled off the main roads, ahead of Alora's party, in a much smaller, concealed group. Yet Luscia suspected she was about to become more than just the keeper of the bone key.

"He sends his regards. Excuse me, *Brödre*," she answered her brethren. Without another word, she scooped up the medicinal chest and sought the privacy of her personal quarters.

Luscia locked the door to her bedroom and placed Alora's apothe-cary upon the bed. She inserted the key, unlocked the chest, and assessed its contents. The chest emitted a familiar scent of viridi bark before the expected aroma of roots and herbs bloomed through the room.

Luscia leaned against the mattress in confusion, cataloguing the rather ordinary collection of materials. Well, ordinary for Alora's profi-ciency, at least. She couldn't comprehend why an apothecary should be locked, unless Alora anticipated Boreali herbs being confiscated next.

Atop the myriad of glass jars and empty vials sat a small, folded scrap of parchment. Alora must have packed it last, so Luscia would find it right away. Hands that favored combat over the mysteries of Boreal's apothic arts gently unraveled her aunt's delicate folding.

Luscia,

Mix only in necessity. The crown prince will request at his need.

This is now your apothecary. Be discreet. Hide it well.

Memorize this list of ingredients and instruction.

Burn it.

Rul'Aniell,

Alora

Underneath the note, scribbled with an unusual sense of urgency, was another page, this one riddled with unfamiliar terms and compli-cated instructions. The list of essential components wasn't very long, but it consisted of the rarest and most potent extracts native to her homeland. *Ennus thorn*, meant to improve immunity or lower one's fever. *Nixberry oil,* for pain. *Eüpharsis extract,* used to treat insomnia and calm the nervous system.

Luscia read through Alora's unconventional methodology, repeating each line until it was branded in her memory. She scanned the last few ingredients and felt her stomach churn.

Blood

(Five drops from the finger. No more. No less.)

Finally, she identified the ugly stain of darkened rust that decorated the sharpest point of the skeletal key. And for the first time in her life, Luscia dared to wonder if the rumors were true.

She flexed her palms, as if to ask the pulsing, sacred element held within them: "Are we witches after all?"

EIGHT

Luscia

Convincing Marek that Aksel served as a sufficient escort for the brief walk to the apartments of Prince Dmitri Thoarne had proven a taxing endeavor. Despite the fact that the lycran was one of the north's most ruthless predators, her argumentative captaen had only conceded when she pulled rank in front of his men—a tactic that Luscia loathed resorting to. Consequently, she followed the page feeling prickly, having left behind an equally frustrated, brooding Najjan.

Her finger itched where she'd applied a quick poultice over the recent puncture. Though the wound would have healed within the hour in any case, the last thing Luscia had wanted to explain was what had transpired behind closed doors to an already watchful captaen.

Her quick mixture of gilead leaf and yarrow flower had expedited the healing, thanks to the metabolized lumin within the plants. One of the benefits of the mysterious essence was its ability to amplify the original properties of any substance.

As they strode through a maze of corridors, Luscia counted every door and each sequence of turns. This would be the most important path she'd learn, and while it was wise to remember the route for navigation's sake, her time on the Isle of Viridis had taught her that it was even wiser to record the less noteworthy: guard placements, their dominant hands, assigned weaponry. Her northern ears, further heightened by Tiergan blood, beckoned Luscia to listen beyond the voiceless doors. The rumble of two snoring peacefully came from the right. From her left, the steady, thumping gait of a heavyset man pacing in solitude.

Beside her, Aksel's nostrils flared with the bouquet of changing scents. Always her frighteningly astute shadow, the lycran matched the tempo of her footsteps as he maintained contact with her hip. Luscia had expected him to have trouble adjusting to the differing extremes—the beast had spent most of his life running through the frigid peaks of the Orallach Mountains and prowling whistling forests blanketed in thick, lambent mist. Here, the russet fur of his hackles lifted, challenging the contrast of imposing stone walls and foreign sounds of strangers in the night.

Her metaphorical hackles rose with them.

After a change in floors, three byrnnzite archways, and a hall of impressive windows—which offered an intimate view of the thriving city below—the small page stopped in front of a set of doors. The adjoining, ten-foot slabs of red oak and ashwood were overlaid in stunning, swirling metalwork. Sleek bands met at the center, where a double handle was fixed. Molded from radiantly mixed materials, together the handles formed the head of a stag—the symbol of the Royal Line of Thoarne. The byrnnzite antlers sparkled in the dwindling light of the sconces.

Appropriately, it was said that Orynthia lived in the Stag Age. Hundreds of years and countless lives had been lost for the cause of peace, finally achieved during the early reign of King Korbin Thoarne. Understandably, the Unitarians immortalized the symbol.

But only in Bastiion, Luscia mused, *would such opulence serve as a door handle.*

The page used the knocker and nervously glanced about when the clanging echo shattered the stillness. Luscia couldn't understand why the boy was so distressed. Even if she wished him harm, as he'd surely been taught, the dozen sentries positioned along the corridor should have provided him with some sense of security. Yet he still jittered in place, eager to be rid of her.

Two Darakaian guards, each stationed on either side of the entrance, received Luscia with an unmistakable intensity. The male scanned her form, seeking any potential threat, while the female's posture radiated aggression. As al'Haidren to Boreal, Luscia was insulted by their hostile reception, but did not allow her countenance to show it.

The doors parted, groaning in invitation. Instinctively, Luscia's ears perked as she crossed into the prince's foyer after the page.

"Your efficiency, young Callister, is lacking," said a droll voice. Luscia saw it belonged to an elderly valet when he shut the door behind them. "You remain as hasty as my grandmother, who is dead."

"But the Lady—"

The valet ignored him and curtly cleared his throat when one of the Darakaians wedged the door back open. "No, not you lot. Prince already kicked you out once, best not to repeat it." His hands, speckled in age spots, shooed them out. "Now, Lady al'Haidren, if you and your…dog…would follow me? His Highness has been waiting," he directed after a clipped bow.

For some reason she suspected it pained him to do so, and not because of his age.

"Eugen—"

"You are *excused*, Callister. Thank you for your unexceptional service to His Highness," the valet wheezed over a hunched shoulder.

As she trailed behind the valet, Luscia silently scolded herself for not changing her attire before this visit with Prince Dmitri. There simply hadn't been time—she'd already been delayed too long by mixing Alora's tonic. In the face of opposition, Luscia had donned the northern accents to represent her Boreali pride upon entering the Unitarian city, but a private, late-night summons from the future king had not been considered in her careful calculations. She'd been led to expect him to call on her at first light. For a gender judged predominantly on appearance before skill or intellect, a woman's first impression was a powerful asset—an asset Luscia strove to wield with intention.

Alas, strolling into the Prince of Orynthia's apartment dressed as a Boreali battle cry come to life was far from intentional.

The valet led her into a domed great room, much like her own, though significantly grander. It was warmed by a freshly tended fire against the opposite wall. Luscia had thought her canopy was magnificent, but the large fire set the prince's byrnnzite ceiling aflame.

"The Lady Luscia Tiergan, al'Haidren to Boreal, has arrived, Your Highness."

Pulling her eyes from above, Luscia found a young man attempting to rise from where he lounged on a low-backed sofa. The prince struggled momentarily, putting his weight on a beautifully made walking cane. It appeared to be crafted from the same range of materials as the stag door handles.

He managed to stand, though he still enlisted the cane to maintain balance. Luscia didn't remember Dmitri Thoarne requiring an external aid for everyday mobility. He tiredly brushed ruffled, dark hair away from his handsome, if sallow face and offered her a genuine smile. It stretched widely, transforming him into the charming young man she remembered from his Ascension six years before.

The prince took pause as he regarded the fearsome lycran and Luscia's own haggard features.

"Lady Boreal," he began formally, greeting Luscia as if his Quadren were in session. "I truly apologize for the hour. I assume you and your party are exhausted, so I offer you my thanks for coming so promptly."

He went to move forward, but after a few shaky steps, seemed to think better of it.

"Sit with me," the prince offered instead, gesturing to the plush sofa opposite his own. "Please."

Luscia complied while he again took up residence on the luxurious material.

"Are you hungry? What am I thinking, of course you must be," he said, making up his mind before she could give an answer. "Eugenio! Eugenio, we must feed the lady. Oh, and send Callister to the kitchens to fetch something for her men as well."

Luscia rested a hand in her lap and let the other soothe Aksel as he settled near her legs. Thinking she ought to stop the prince from rambling, she decided to skip the expected pleasantries and treat their meeting for what it was: a late-night urgency, after a very long journey.

"Your Highness—"

"Please, call me Dmitri. 'Your Highness' becomes insufferable after hearing it all the time. You should really reserve its use for sarcastic effect, as some of my friends choose to do," he suggested with a quirk of his lips, exposing a lone dimple in the dusky skin of his left cheek.

Returning to the receiving room, Eugenio pushed a small cart full of items, his joints popping in protest as he began to transfer the containers in front of her. Waiting for privacy, Luscia watched the valet hobble into an adjoining hall, counting five breaths before she continued.

"Prince Dmitri—"

"'Prince' is also tiresome, I find."

His rich, hazel eyes crinkled in amusement. Luscia wondered if he, too, spent a great deal of time in his own company, as she did.

"Dmitri… " she tested, continuing at his nod of assurance. "I brought your elixir, although I must admit I was taken aback by the request. I'm not nearly as practiced as my aunt in the apothic arts, and this was my first attempt at its creation."

Reaching into the folds of her surcoat, she produced five vials. The murky plum fluid streaked the interior of the glass at the jerky motion. Luscia slid them across the short table, now decorated with trays of light pastries and a pitcher of pale coral liquid. Sweet wine from the vineyards of Galina, she guessed.

Dmitri's brows furrowed in puzzlement. Hiding his strain, he leaned over to collect the dark vials.

"I'm certain they will suffice. Alora assured me that you are highly skilled and suspected you might even produce stronger batches. Honestly, I'm surprised you weren't informed of the change in responsibility. Did she at least mention the need for discretion?" he asked intently.

"*Wem!*" Luscia immediately confirmed. "Yes, of course, the utmost discretion. If the Boreali are good at anything, it is silence."

He grasped a single vial and began to remove the stopper. She wondered if he knew what lurked inside it—if the Prince of Orynthia knew of the wound she'd had to make in order to conjure the elixir. That the blood of Tiergan was necessary for whatever devices he'd commissioned Alora to make possible.

Swallowing hard, Luscia dared to wonder what brewed inside her own veins.

Her face must have communicated as much, because his fingers ceased their mission to release the stopper at her stare.

"Did Alora tell you to watch me take it?" He scowled. "She did, didn't she? Depths, she knows I hate this foul stuff."

With a sigh, he brought the elixir to his lips and drank it brashly, like it was a shot of Darakaian *bwoloa*. Wiping his mouth clean of the residue, he continued, "I didn't know the Haidren to Boreal was also training up a royal nursemaid on my behalf. Next, she'll have you singing me lullabies to ensure a full night's rest."

Dmitri shook his head in exasperation with her aunt's tactics.

"If it would increase your appreciation for Boreal, then perhaps I should," Luscia crisply retorted, registering her tone only after she'd spoken.

She instantly broke eye contact and bowed in place, awaiting his anger. A growing headache and Dmitri's insistence on familiarity weren't helping her lack of expertise in small talk. But the Orynthian prince merely rumbled with soft laughter.

"I'm glad to see you haven't lost your brazen wit in adulthood. I recall your aunt determinedly trying to instruct that out of you." Dmitri lowered his oval face, reclaiming her gaze as he grinned.

To her surprise, Luscia felt a smile tugging at her own lips. "I'm surprised you picked up on that." While Luscia was well aware of

Alora's attempts to reform her temperament, she'd not realized it was so apparent to everyone else.

"When a child consistently engages in swordplay instead of attending teatime, it's difficult *not* to notice."

"*Wem*, well, I now recognize that tea and embroidery are more acceptable pastimes in Bastiion than swordplay," she quipped.

"Acceptable, perhaps, but not nearly as useful, I'd imagine."

Dmitri swished another mouthful of the water Eugenio had delivered with the wine, clearly desperate to chase away the aftertaste of the elixir.

"I'm also happy to see your arm healed perfectly since your last visit," he commented. "It seems Alora can heal almost any affliction."

"Aniell has gifted Alora greatly. That we can easily agree upon," Luscia said, alluding to nothing more than her aunt's penchant for rare herbs as she watched Aksel's ears pivot with the crackling fire.

It was not an exaggeration. Alora Tiergan was thought to be the most successful and imaginative healer Boreal had produced in a century, which was Luscia's point of perplexity regarding Dmitri's earlier sentiments. Compared to her aunt's renowned skill and anointing, there was no conceivable way that Luscia could ever produce a stronger medicinal remedy than Alora. The list of questions awaiting her Haidren's arrival was growing by the hour.

"Luscia?"

Dmitri's voice interrupted her spinning thoughts when he abandoned traditional Quadrennal address and adopted her given name. "I want you to know that I have waited for your Ascension with undeniable anticipation. With the final member of my Quadren here at court in Bastiion, we can finally begin to care for the burdens of our people. Though I've been of age for some time, my hands are often tied by restrictive legalities. A complete Quadren holds greater influence and allows us to circumvent the limitations set by the Peerage."

"You are the sole heir to the Orynthian throne. I should think that provides you with an ample amount of influence," Luscia commented dryly. She had little pity for a Unitarian who had to play by Bastiion's unreasonable decrees when the majority of those laws were pitted against the House of Boreal.

"Normally, I'd agree with you. I am the sole heir, yes, but unfortunately one who is not considered entirely legitimate until backed by a Quadren, wherein all four al'Haidrens have reached Ascension age. It's infuriating, really," he explained, rubbing his temples as he sat back. "There is so much to be accomplished. So many injustices of worthy cause, but I have little sway in the Peerage without the Houses behind my every word and deed."

Dmitri picked up a fat, dusty book in one hand and clenched a pile of parchment in the other, tightening his lips as he peered down at them.

"I am to be king, yet I'm bound to maneuver like a politician in my own home. It's why I spend countless nights reading these, over and over again, committing them to memory. Perhaps with you here, I can finally be put to use." His lips curved at the notion, revealing that lone dimple. "Luscia, I truly mean this when I say...well, that I hope we might become friends."

"Friends?"

Luscia eyed the Crown Prince of Orynthia. In this moment, sitting alone on his couch, Thoarne's heir looked like nothing more than a solitary boy, seeking escape from his isolation.

"Leadership can be a lonely state, Lady Boreal."

Wistfulness swept his features as he turned toward the fire. Luscia detected faint traces of freckles over his elegant nose and lean cheeks.

"Thoarne's friendship with Boreal was once a powerful force," she replied, treading cautiously in light of his abrupt vulnerability.

"And may it be again," were his closing words before grabbing the cane to propel himself upright.

She followed him into the foyer, mentally rejoicing at the prospect of returning to the large bed that awaited her and the restless wolx. Aksel's tail twitched back and forth, communicating he felt the same.

"Do you know when Alora's party will be returning? I assumed you'd journey together. She will be back in time for your reception, won't she?" he asked with genuine concern.

"My reception, Highness?"

"*Dmitri*," he reminded her. "And yes, your reception. My al'Haidren to Boreal deserves a welcoming just like the others. Even Ira had a reception thrown in his honor at court, and he's native to Bastiion."

"That's entirely unnecessary," Luscia protested. "Besides, I'm not certain a lavish social engagement on my behalf would be well received."

Advancing further into the foyer, Dmitri placed a hand on Luscia's back to guide her forward. She tried not to tense under his innocent, but unexpected touch.

"Nonsense! Bastiion loves any excuse to celebrate…" He trailed off when he noticed her reaction. Then, to her surprise, Dmitri took one of her hands in his own. His grip didn't feel as weak as she'd expected—Luscia could even sense shallow calluses on his palms, as if from some form of physicality.

"You are right when you say that Boreal's prestige has been forgotten by most," Dmitri said gently, "but *I* have not forgotten. If you wish to restore it, as I do, then the House of Boreal must command the same level of respect as the others."

Luscia lowered her head in submission. Dmitri was right; her people had so separated themselves from the Ethnicam that disrespect had become permissible in their absence.

"Your words bear wisdom, *Ana'Brödre,*" she acknowledged somberly. At his quizzical expression, Luscia added, "It means *Great Brother*—a title of honor among our people."

Dmitri's genial smile returned, as did his tremulous page, who was instructed to guide Luscia back to her apartments. After her muddy, upturned boots passed into the corridor, she heard Dmitri pop his head out after them.

"Oh, and Luscia, word travels fast at court. With regard to your demanding half a dozen sentries be stationed outside your apartments tonight…"

Collapsing her shoulders, she whispered defeatedly, "*Wem,* Highness?"

"Well done."

NINE

Zaethan

"Frankly, I found it quite clever of her."

Zaethan paced up and down the length of the exquisite elm-and-aspen table lining the center of the war room. He refrained from ripping off the collection of maps scattered across the tabletop, spotlighted by sunlight streaming through the glass ceiling overhead. Maintaining his composure was less for Dmitri's sensibilities than for the fact that Orynthia's king and commander were scheduled to arrive at any moment. Otherwise papers, would have blanketed the floor.

"*Clever?* You mean to say that commandeering *four* additional sentries on a whim—" Zaethan jabbed his own chest, "—four of *my* sentries, is clever?"

Zaethan couldn't believe his friend's indifference. Less than a day at court, and that hellish y'siti was already creating problems. On one hand, he was pleased she'd demonstrated the very defiance he'd predicted she would. On the other, Zaethan was furious the witch had claimed authority over his men within the first hour of her arrival.

"To say the al'Haidren *commandeered* your men is a rather dramatic perspective, Zaeth. And I doubt it was a whim—more likely a statement of sorts," Dmitri calmly mused, hands clasped behind his back. The prince spoke while he inspected a sketched map of Hagarh, as it was the true purpose for their meeting.

He hated when Dmitri did that. Unlike most Darakaians, Zaethan's education was dually grounded in the disciplines of Faraji as well as the Unitarian scholastics. It was why their friendship began so early in life—Zaethan had joined Dmitri for most of his lessons. Yet despite the years of study at his side, Dmitri's strengths always overshadowed Zaethan's when it came to the eloquent subtleties of debate.

Kàchà kocho. He shrugged it off. Debate was for yancies.

"I'll show your y'siti a dramatic perspective," he muttered aloud, accompanied by muffled curses in Andwele and slid a different map toward Dmitri, tapping a sketch of the city. "The only statement she made was of disrespect and complete lack of cooperation with Bastiion."

"Perhaps. Or merely a statement as uncooperative as your own?"

Zaethan's head whipped around. He knew he needed to calm down—his anger would only be met with further deflection. Dmitri always refused to listen to passionate shouting, which, unfortunately, was Zaethan's natural tone of voice.

"I'm trying to fulfill my duty to you, Dmitri," he said, exasperated.

"How is that uncooperative? And then she comes here and starts giving orders to *our* sentries, as if they were her own! Sentries stationed for *your* wellbeing!"

"Do you sanction guards to bookend the corridors outside the Pilarese suites? Or the Unitarian?" Dmitri posed, making his point with infuriating ease. "One sentry, surely, out of respect for the resident's status at court, but no more. She isn't incompetent, Zaeth. In fact, I suspect she's incredibly sharp."

"Sharp like wolx teeth capped in witchiron!" Zaethan bit out. "And then you went and invited her for a midnight tea, without your guard! You should have called for me, Dmitri."

Dmitri simply sighed and rubbed his right temple. Then his gaze turned sharp, and he squinted at the scabs over Zaethan's knuckles.

"Might I ask what happened to your hand?"

"Just keeping your loyal subjects in line. Some real class acts loitering around Bastiion these days."

"I do hope they remained loyal after you were through."

"Stop distracting me," Zaethan grumbled. "My pryde's patrolling isn't the issue. The issue is that creature upstairs."

"I wish for this argument to end. My al'Haidrens are equal in my eyes, so they should be in yours as well," the weary prince stated with finality.

Zaethan opened his mouth to reply, but tempered himself as Dmitri's father burst into the war room. Behind him were a pair of solemn, southern-skinned men speaking to each other in lowered voices as they trailed their king.

"Dmitri, my boy!" the king said joyously. "Congratulations at last!"

Korbin Thoarne rounded the spherical room and headed straight for his son. Outstretched hands engulfed Dmitri's thin shoulders and shook them with gaiety.

"Your final al'Haidren's arrival…what a splendid day this is!" he exclaimed, looking proudly into the face of his only heir.

Zaethan could see occasional similarities between them, enough to prove their relation, though it was Queen Lourissa who shone through Dmitri most. Her aristocratic nose, delicate bone structure, and lighter frame contrasted with his father's substantial brow and brawny stature. But while only a few might pick out Dmitri as the son of Korbin Thoarne at first glance, none could dismiss the same beaming grin they shared. It was sad, Zaethan often thought, that though all Orynthia associated that memorable feature with their king, rarely did they comment upon it in their prince.

Clapping his son on the back, nearly pushing him off-balance, the king made his way around the table to where Zaethan held the rigid position expected of a Darakian alpha. A hefty palm landed on his left shoulder and gave it a tight squeeze.

"A splendid day, indeed!" King Korbin repeated, smiling widely. "For you, too, Zaeth. A complete Quadren!"

Zaethan had expected his exuberance. While Dmitri's denial of the y'siti threat was due to sheer optimism, Zaethan had learned throughout the years that the king's regard for Boreal was downright delusional. Like most of the nobility, Korbin Thoarne classified the Boreali as archaic mystics who, like oil and water, would just never fully blend with the rest of the realm. Zaethan, of course, maintained the same judgment as most of the Ethnicam: y'siti were vile, and their witchery was from the Depths.

Nevertheless, he summoned a pinched smile and nodded at the king's statement.

"Still keeping my son out of trouble?" He raised a bushy brow mischievously, suggesting he believed Dmitri spent more time in taverns than he did reading dusty literature.

"Trying to, sire," Zaethan replied. "Regrettably, he tends to admire the trouble."

The king rolled with laughter. Zaethan relaxed a fraction and chuckled at the prospect of Dmitri wasting an evening in a place like The Veiled Lady. Knowing his friend, Dmitri would be more likely to tutor one of Salma's night-callers than employ one for his own pleasure.

Looking away from the prince in question, Zaethan's eyes found Darakai's chief warlord.

Hints of revulsion were hidden throughout his father's demeanor as he casually peered over the sea of Orynthian maps. It was disguised in his unblinking, hard black eyes. In the tautness of his shoulders, as his stance wordlessly proclaimed dominance. In the slight snarl that pulled one nostril up into a pockmarked cheek and melted into his shaved skull, etched with the scars of his victories.

In an instant, Zaethan swallowed his amusement, adopting his previous posture, and lowered his gaze to the table. Whether it was the king's affection for Dmitri's childhood friend or Zaethan's own conduct that had triggered his father's ire, he couldn't tell. Either were certainly enough to incite his father's anger, when Zaethan's birth was itself a disappointment. As the thief who stole his mother's last breath, Zaethan had long accepted that a man like Nyack Kasim could never deign to love him.

"Shall we begin, Majesty?" Zaethan's father asked, his voice smooth like Galina wine. "As mentioned, there've been displays of rebellion along the borders of Hagarh. Here and here," he tapped a forefinger at various points near the Yakov River, "the mudmen have begun tempting the perimeter. It seems these leeches are no longer content with our agreement."

"They claim we've kept control of the Miraji Forest for too long, and that the land is rightfully theirs to take," General Lateef interjected, rolling his eyes at the absurdity of the notion.

"Hmph." King Korbin studied the areas mentioned. "The mudmen haven't troubled us in ages...what do you think provoked them after so much time? They must realize how easily Orynthia could subdue an uprising."

"Apparently they say that 'the wind told them.' That 'it was time.'" Zaethan's father's upper lip curled with disdain. "As if Orynthia would bend to the will of a marsh-wader."

"But the Gulgons carry sticks and spears. They still coat themselves and their weaponry in muck, so what could they possibly hope to gain in a standoff? We've held the bulk of Mirajii, aside from their remnants, for centuries," Dmitri wondered aloud.

A fist the shade and texture of charred bark struck the table, causing Dmitri to jump, and landed in the center of the marked wetlands.

"Because they are resisters! And resisters must be broken, or they'll continue to revolt!" Zaethan's father declared.

The king and General Lateef readily nodded their consensus with the commander's harsh words. Privately, Zaethan agreed. The Gulgons, called mudmen for obvious reason, weren't a substantial threat to the perimeter, but if the prydes didn't push back, towns like Rian and Port Khmer would pay the price. However, it was also true that the Mirajii Forest had been in Gulgon possession when Orynthia first seized it.

"I agree," the king confirmed. "As commander of my armies, I trust you'll handle this swiftly for me, Nyack. As always."

Zaethan watched a flicker of anticipation flash through his father's onyx eyes before they waned back into deadness. For a moment, he absorbed the gravity of the king's blanket trust in his father's methods. With such a simple statement, the commander of the Orynthian forces was given permission to rain the terror of Darakai down on Hagarh, if he so wished it. Knowing too well the pleasure Nyack Kasim gleaned from wielding violence, Zaethan suspected he wished it very much.

Unlike any Darakaian before him, Nyack Kasim wielded a trio of powerful titles. Being the firstborn of his generation, he held the office of Haidren to Darakai by virtue of his bloodline and birthright. But in addition to representing the Darakai's interests in Bastiion, Nyack had long reigned as Chief Warlord in the House of Darakai, the elected leader over their tribes. Last, in recent years, he had acquired the most powerful title of all: Commander of the Orynthian armies, which by royal decree enabled him to exercise nearly all the same privileges as Dmitri's father, excepting the ability to declare war.

This trinity of authority had made the Ethnicam increasingly wary of Nyack Kasim of late. Zaethan could understand why—he too was uncomfortable seeing that much power in the brutal hands of his father.

His father instructed General Lateef to brief the king and the prince on recent developments in the other port towns, as well as the expansion of Orynthia's naval fleet, currently stationed in Lempeii. Having already heard the information, Zaethan's mind returned to Hagarh. The mudmen were superstitious wanderers, as Dmitri had stated. Superstitious, but rarely a group of aggressors. By nature, their community waded seasonally throughout the wetlands in migratory patterns, keeping to themselves. It was strange that they'd shift to the offensive without being provoked. Besides, who listened to the wind?

Just swamp-speak, he told himself. *Nonsensical kakk.*

"Zaethan. Report," his father ordered across the wide table between them.

Clearing his throat, Zaethan launched into a standard report, commenting on the adjustments to the guard and changes to their training regime. After proposing an additional trading regulation to enforce within the Drifting Bazaar and Bastiion's Marketown, Zaethan took a deep breath before concluding his summary.

"Lastly, my own militia, in addition to a handful of prydes monitoring the plains, have reported a series of Boreali cross-castes said to be missing or, if recovered, found dead. Barbarically, I should add. Those discovered were either completely drained of blood, or their bodies… their bodies desecrated. Most of them have been young children."

He paused here, knowing he should stick to reporting only facts of significance. His father would perceive any emotion as weakness, and Zaethan hadn't been named Alpha Zà over the Darakaian militia prydes for his ability to empathize.

"With such a clear pattern," Zaethan continued, "I'm wondering if the al'Haidren to Boreal's Ascension has inspired civil unrest among the Unitarian provinces. Perhaps the locals are lashing out against the y'siti influence?"

General Lateef and Zaethan's father snickered contemptuously. No concern for the slain cross-caste children could be found in their eyes. Taken aback by their reaction, he looked to Dmitri, who'd gone pale as he processed the news. Yet the severity of the situation had only shaken one of the Thoarne men, as the king slowly mirrored his subordinates.

"That's ridiculous," his father dismissed. "The y'siti do this to each other. It's just who they are. It's more likely the Najjan have taken their witchiron and begun hunting down their own breakaways. Some punishment for abandoning the clans."

"Probably gathering fodder for their next moon ritual," the general spat.

"I've never known a Boreali to be so vicious…or vindictive, for that matter," Dmitri added, scratching the back of his neck.

A mask of forced deference turned to the prince as Zaethan's father tilted his head to the side. "And because you have not met every y'siti, my resources should not be wasted on the testament of a few," he said, in the manner one might speak to a child, before adding a prudent, "Your Highness."

"Father—sir, I urge you to reconsider. Kumo and Takoda have been tracking the incidents for months now," Zaethan rushed on, pointing out the connecting trails across the map of Bastiion. "The most recent victims were discovered closer together these last three weeks, *within* the Proper."

Zaethan risked raising his eyes to his father, hoping to effectively convey the importance of the deaths. He felt it in the nausea that came with the replaying pictures in his mind. The victims his pryde had unearthed—children barely into adolescence, shoved into the damp, forgotten corners of Bastiion's twisting streets. Frail little bodies forever mutilated by horrific markings that ribboned their flesh to the bone. Their mixed lineage was only recognizable by the hair—darker than that of a full-blooded y'siti, yet significantly lighter than that of a Unitarian. Each victim outside the Proper had been found ripped apart, but those within mirrored the most recent boy discovered. Zaethan had held his tiny, limp hand as the pryde tried to make sense of the meticulous slits along his wrists, neck, and ankles. The cross-caste had been bled dry.

Zaethan managed to not throw up, before Kumo pulled the color-less, broken boy from his protective arms. He'd been no older than eight, perhaps nine years at most.

These were *not* meaningless patterns. It was only a matter of time before the killer grew bored of pale flesh, already the shade of corpses, and began to crave the children of Bastiion, painted in livelier skins of gold, bronze, and copper.

"I think my son has uncovered some alarming facts," his father announced to the group of men.

Zaethan's chest rose hopefully. The edge of his mouth started to lift at the rare moment of recognition.

"But since he allowed his pryde to become so distracted during these crucial months, by what are clearly misguided priorities, I've decided they would better serve our king where reinforcement is actually needed—at the border, near Hagarh and Port Khmer."

Zaethan's stomach dropped, as did any trace of his smile.

"Zaethan, you will remain at court. In my shadow as al'Haidren to Darakai, you must. Choose fifteen to go and five to remain in Bastiion. Bring me your list by tomorrow morning," Darakai's chief warlord concluded, letting his penalty settle heavily into the silence.

Zaethan stared at his father's tunic, covered in honorary fragments of metal and bone. Medals both Unitarian and Darakaian. A formidable picture of success who'd just publicly humiliated his son. By syphoning Zaethan's personal pryde and scattering them, Nyack Kasim would send a message to the House of Darakai that his son was unfit to lead. That Zaethan did not deserve to be called Alpha Zà, chief alpha of the prydes, and that Zaethan retained the title by birth rather than might.

It was a symbolic castration.

King Korbin, his father, and General Lateef continued their conversation after an awkward moment passed, but Zaethan only heard rushing in his ears. His resentment threatened to boil over, but gradually retreated, dissipating into a somber disgrace. He noticed

Dmitri trying to word something, worry pinching his expression. With a quick jerk of his jaw, Zaethan motioned him to drop it. He would not humiliate himself further by mimicking a dog, cowering before its master.

Squaring his shoulders, Zaethan lifted his chin to follow the king's exit once their meeting adjourned. He stepped forward, but his father's voice pierced his ears, halting him.

"Stay."

Zaethan watched the others depart. King Korbin, oblivious to the conflict, walked beside General Lateef and inquired further about his new naval fleet. Dmitri hesitated, but had learned many times over that it was best to leave Zaethan to fight his own demons.

Fixing his eyes ahead, Zaethan listened to his father's stiff boots striking the masonry of the floor as they traversed the room. The loose fabric of the wrapped *gunja* pants his father wore beneath his form-fitting military tunic concealed the preserved vigor of his middle-aged physique. Standing scarcely taller than Zaethan, his leathery, corded neck came into view, the side of it riddled from past trauma and poorly healed war wounds.

Zaethan didn't flinch when the force of his father's hand collided with the right side of his face.

Nor the left.

"For questioning me."

Head upright, Zaethan refused to wipe the blood off his splitting lip. His father reached out and roughly smeared it away to assess the damage. If, for an instant, Zaethan hoped it to be an act of affection or remorse, the thought died with his commander's parting advice.

"Put camilla root on that lip and hide your weakness before the y'siti's reception. You will not shame my name again today."

Zaethan hid his pain and peered into the starless black pools looking back at him. The commander seemed to hesitate as his eyes traveled the panes of his son's face, so very much like Zaethan's mother's, rather than his own.

After a few tense breaths, his father deliberately dropped his fingers and wiped them clean against the fabric stretching over Zaethan's chest. Marking his defeat.

Nyack Kasim then turned abruptly and left his bloodied son behind.

TEN

Luscia

L uscia crumpled the parchment in her grasp after reading Alora's brief message for the third time.

The courier, panting in his haste, had delivered the sealed note to Luscia's apartments just as Mila began preparing her for Dmitri's dreaded reception. In swift script, her aunt relayed she would not be in attendance that night. Alora's arrival was still days away.

From a pair of sentences, Luscia had deduced three certainties. The first, an event more momentous than Luscia's presentation to court as the Ascended al'Haidren to Boreal had occurred in Port Tadeas. Second, this event would delay Alora's much larger party for perhaps another week. Third, and most importantly, Boreal's anticipated Ascension offering—the next Sword of Thoarne—had been delayed with her.

Meaning Luscia would not only be attending this lofty reception without her predecessor, but also walking into it empty-handed.

Mila's meticulous fingers weaved gemstones throughout her hair, reminding Luscia the situation could be worse. She would not be entering a room full of Unitarian nobility and partnering members of the Ethnicam in her worn, muddied traveling gear. Thank the High One that Alora thought of nearly everything and had arranged the transfer of Luscia's possessions weeks ago, including the wardrobe her aunt had commissioned for her new role in Bastiion.

"I'm thankful for your assistance, Mila, especially in light of this news." Luscia sighed, genuinely grateful to the girl for taking so much time to coax her tedious cloud of braids and knots, unlike the intricate styles worn by the women of the court.

"It's my pleasure, Lady Luscia!" Mila's timid voice brightened. The maid's trembles always seemed to diminish while she worked. "Your requests are so simple, compared to Lady Sayuri. I'm just happy I can perform them to your liking."

"The al'Haidren to Pilar?" Luscia clarified.

"Oh yes, I served Lady Sayuri for an entire year before your Ascension. She, well…" Mila paused. "She thought it more appropriate to gift me to you."

"Because of your lineage, you mean?" Luscia presumed. "The al'Haidren to Pilar thought it more appropriate for a Boreali cross-caste to serve the al'Haidren to Boreal?"

Mila's fingers ceased their efforts for a moment, then gently began to move again.

"Did Tallulah tell you?" she asked dejectedly.

"Your coloring suggests northern ancestry. Only Tavish or Boreali blood could give you those eyes…and you're much too sweet to be from Tavaàr," Luscia added lightly. It was true.

"Lady Luscia, I'm honored by the reassignment and—if you'll pardon my saying so—quite relieved," Mila said earnestly. "Lady Sayuri is a very particular woman, and I certainly won't miss that dark, drafty stairwell!"

"Drafty stairwell?" Luscia asked, confused. "Aren't the Pilareese suites adjacent to my own?" She'd heard the nearest domed cupola belonged to the al'Haidren in question. With a little effort, Luscia could probably throw a stone from her balcony onto the other.

"This wing—the northern wing—housed the royal apartments until the late Shield Age, forty years ago, when the entire Thoarne family was moved into the southern wing of the palace. King Aquila decided the servant stair to his private chamber was too great a risk during the wars with Razôuel and Mworra," Mila explained. "But when Lady Sayuri learned of its existence, she ordered the stairwell reopened. She preferred to see us performing our chores as little as possible. So, we moved between her apartment and the servant levels by candlelight, if one had a free hand to hold it."

Luscia sensed Mila shudder at the memory. What a selfish request, to make those who serve do so out of sight. Lucia did, however, agree with King Aquila's decision to close the stairwell in the first place. One could never rely too heavily on another for protection. On her first night here, after returning from Dmitri's summons, Luscia had hidden weapons all throughout her apartment. In the bedroom alone were six blades, and that wasn't even counting those on her person.

"If you are satisfied, my lady?" At Luscia's nod, Mila shifted to help

Luscia step into her beaded, upturned slippers. They were beautifully useless but, alas, one did not wear battered boots to dine with a king.

A soft knock rapped against her door, followed by a respectful, "It's time, *Ana'Sere*."

Luscia stood and rested a hand upon the ancient, oversized handle of her bedroom door. Out of habit, the other felt to ensure the collar of her dress rose high enough to conceal the textured scar running the landscape of her neck. Confident it was hidden under the layer of sterling linsilk, etched in a brocade of cream and copper, Luscia strode anxiously into the common room to join her Najjan.

From the moment the enormous, ornate bronze doors opened to admit Luscia and her men into Thoarne Hall, lush fields of color filled her vision.

Though darkness hung outside the soaring windows positioned around the opulent space, the hall was flooded with warm, golden light. An overabundance of shining, metallic lanterns created an inviting ambiance for the assembly of bodies, dressed in only the most exquisite silks and satins. Their laughter melted into the rhapsodic melody being played on a dais at the center of the room, like a jewel-toned meadow full of chimes in a windstorm.

"The Lady Luscia Darragh Tiergan, al'Haidren to the House of Boreal," a stout herald announced as Declan, Luscia, and her wary lycran stepped onto the polished floors of marbled ebony.

To her surprise, only the nearest grouping glanced up at their entrance, but those who did immediately whispered to neighboring guests. Hushed snickers emitted from a cluster of Unitarian women as they appraised Luscia, each of them wrapped in gauzy layers of sparkling taffeta. She ignored them. Through her periphery, she instead watched Marek, Noxolo, and the twins pass into the hall once another noble was announced and seamlessly disappear into the crowded space.

Her lips twitched with Boreali pride.

Within minutes her four Najjan were concealed in the shadows, just as they'd strategized. Declan, the burliest of the five, remained nearest Luscia while the others assessed the many foreign variables from a hidden distance.

Ahead, a ripple quaked through a throng of nobles. As they parted, a tall, middle-aged man strode excitedly toward her with open arms. She instantly recognized King Korbin Thoarne by the byrnnzite crown encircling his head, which integrated the same pointed, bulbous shape of the domed cupolas adorning the palace. Though even without the crown, Luscia would've easily identified him by his vast, renowned smile. It stretched welcomingly across a face the summery hue of agost honey.

She and Declan both lowered themselves into a bow at his approach, bowing their heads.

"Nonsense!" the King of Orynthia exclaimed at their descent. "Up, up!"

Rising, Luscia saw he was not alone. Dmitri and two others chased the king's path through the gathering guests.

"Just wonderful!" King Korbin joyfully declared as he clutched her wrists. "Luscia Darragh Tiergan, here at last! We've waited for you for some time, you know. So many years, they hid you away from us. Why, I was beginning to think Alora's niece was one of those mystery-baubles in the market…Oh, my!" He flinched when, at his prolonged contact, Aksel's ears drew back and exposed his oversized canines. "Is that really an Orallach wolx in my hall? Or should I say, a lycran? How extraordinary!"

Luscia collected herself when the king suddenly let go of her wrists to study the beast. Declan, also taken aback by the man's enthusiasm, dutifully stood to the side while they conversed. She caught Declan's tight smile. People did not usually touch Luscia so abruptly—not anymore.

"*Allöh'jomn'yeh,* Your Majesty." Luscia greeted him properly, with a blessing of peace. "I, too, have impatiently awaited my own Ascension. Boreal sends her thanks and, with it, the hope that—"

"Dmitri!" The king's thick, greying hair rustled as he tried to locate his son. His grin, seated in a trim beard more silver than not, grew even larger when he did. "Dmitri, my boy! Our guest of honor is here to celebrate with us, and she's *brought a wolx*! Isn't it splendid?" The king bellowed and forcefully clapped his son on the back, forcing Dmitri to use his cane to regain his balance.

While the ornamental walking cane was in his hand, Luscia noted the prince wasn't actually relying on it. Her thumb rubbed the underside of her healed index finger.

Curious.

"Yes, Father, we're all very pleased." An identical grin emerged as Dmitri watched his father inspect the lycran's voluminous tail. "Luscia, allow me to reintroduce your counterparts. It has been quite some time," he said with a chuckle. "Please meet Ira Hastings, the Earl of Arune and my al'Haidren to Bastiion."

Dmitri moved back and gestured to a slender yancy, a few years older than Luscia. Four years, if she recalled correctly. An impish, citrine gaze skimmed her form, taking an inventory of her assets. From her northern slippers to the curve of her hips, the small of her waist, over the shape of her torso and to the bow of her lips his eyes traveled, eventually lingering on her own.

"Oh, I assure you, *Lady Boreal*, that we are very pleased indeed," Ira Hastings crooned, as if his visual undressing hadn't said enough.

Luscia gathered from his overconfident smirk that the al'Haidren to Bastiion was not accustomed to unrequited flirtation. Unsurprising, considering the way his olive skin emphasized the copper undertones in his deep mahogany hair, cut just short of his chin. Yet as he tucked it behind one ear, Luscia interpreted the fresh constellation of reddening marks on the base of his neck to mean one thing.

It was highly probable that, like diseased migratory birds, Ira Hastings was carrying more than his own feathers.

"In fact, if you'd like to see the Unitarian countryside, I would be more than willing to give you a…private tour of the Province of Wendylle." He winked.

Luscia doubted a tour with Ira Hastings would actually involve the countryside.

"I'm sure you would, and I thank you for the kind offer. But I believe Bastiion Proper is adventure enough for now," she declined diplomatically.

Luscia was rescued from the al'Haidren's next offer when the king tore himself away from examining Aksel and stood upright.

"Excuse me, everyone. It seems some members of the Peerage have cornered my wife again. Lourissa cannot stand those old buffoons, and if I don't go now, I'll never hear the end of it," he griped. King Korbin snapped his fingers in the air and retrieved a beverage delivered by a nearby attendant. "I'll need a drink for this endeavor," he confessed, leaning into their makeshift circle. By the sweet tinge of his breath, Luscia could tell it was not his first of the evening.

Dmitri cleared his throat while his father stormed across the hall to a group of elderly men. The aging politicians huddled around a stunning woman, who looked remarkably like her son.

"Right. As I was saying…Luscia, I'd also like to introduce Zaethan Kasim," Dmitri continued, motioning to the second man. "He serves as Alpha Zà over the Darakaian prydes, as well as being the al'Haidren to Darakai and one of my dearest friends."

Unlike Ira, Zaethan Kasim did not bombard Luscia with questions. In fact, he made no attempt at social etiquette whatsoever. He kept his distance as he scrutinized her, like a hunter might a rabid animal. A hint of disgust took hold of his otherwise handsome features. Despite the softer shade of his cinnamon skin, the definition of his full mouth, and a slight depression in his chin, Kasim's entire demeanor emulated that of his father—a man who was both Darakai's Haidren and had been gifted command of the Orynthian forces decades past.

Their likeness even fostered the same tension in his upper lip, which showcased evidence of a recent altercation where it split. The scent of camilla root wafted in her direction.

Very recent indeed.

His sable braided locs had grown longer over the years, but his eyes were as arresting as she remembered. Tonight, the al'Haidren's chartreuse stare seethed with an unfamiliar wrath, which explained the tautness of his jaw and the alertness of his limbs. Luscia detected his latent aggression under the clean leather pants and the plain, formal jade jacket that hugged his chest and narrowed with his hips. Nothing she couldn't easily subdue. Much had changed in the years apart, and her bones would not break so easily again.

"The Lady Sayuri Naborū-Zou, al'Haidren to Pilar," the herald's voice resounded over the music.

"How timely," Dmitri muttered in relief, glancing between his other three al'Haidrens.

A willowy young woman, draped in frothy tiers of scarlet, entered the hall dripping every bit of the rumored elegance attributed to her. Admirers rushed to surround the al'Haidren to Pilar, who was the famed daughter of not one but two Shoto Prime. With vicious, glittering eyes locked on her prey, Sayuri Naborū-Zou sauntered past and disregarded them, the train of her bloodred gown rippling in her wake, like the trail of an insatiable predator moving from one hunting ground to the next.

Slowing for only one man, she slinked toward their grouping. A manicured hand reached out and languorously descended the length of Dmitri's arm as she greeted him alone.

"Dmitri, I do hope you can forgive my tardiness," Sayuri purred through a round set of small, painted lips. The gilded detail of her tight bodice accentuated the richness of her western skin, revealed where the fabric fell off her bare shoulders. "Being tied into a dress this unforgiving takes time, but I hope you'll agree it was worth the trouble."

"Of course, Lady Pilar, you look—wonderful." Dmitri swallowed uncomfortably. "Sayuri, if you remember from years past, finally with us is our al'Haidren to Boreal, Luscia Darragh Tiergan."

Unhurried, Sayuri broke eye contact with the Orynthian prince. "I suppose you couldn't stay in the woods forever," she remarked coolly, angling her head as she beheld Luscia's wild mane, strung with precious stones. Such a contrast to the sleek, midnight tresses descending Sayuri's back.

Sayuri's inky gaze, splintered with topaz, darted aside when the prince asked Kasim to step away with him. The al'Haidren slyly watched them through her lashes, the corners of her eyes lifted alluringly. Curious what had caused the men's whispered argument, Luscia tried to listen as they wandered off, but was thwarted by the al'Haidren to Pilar and her penchant for unwanted conversation.

"You're much prettier than the Unitarians expected," she stated bluntly. "They said you'd come robed in grisly furs with feathers sticking out of your head."

"Personally, I've always found northern women to be quite exotic," Ira noted smoothly, inching closer and brushing a hand against the small of Luscia's back.

"That may not be a wise choice, Lord Bastiion," Luscia advised, adopting the formal Quadrennal address. She'd have to work hard to discourage this one.

At her lycran's snarl, Lusica felt Ira jerk his hand away. Even Unitarian ears could hear the low snicker from her robust Najjan, paces away.

"Amazing how the Boreali can cure nearly everything but their own complexion, isn't it?" Sayuri's rouged lips curled into a smirk. "I'm curious to see what Boreal presents as an offering tonight. A chest of dead rabbits, perhaps? I do hope it's as impressive as the cart of Soairse pearls Pilar sent to my reception, though those probably weren't as soiled as whatever you and your aunt dragged here." Sayuri pretended to search the room for Alora. "Is that why she hasn't joined you? Too embarrassed to show?"

Luscia wanted to punch Sayuri Naborū-Zuo in her beautiful face. Unfortunately, breaking her fellow al'Haidren's nose would likely prove more problematic than simply refusing to respond. The vivid imagery aided Luscia's resolve, at least.

A high-pitched squeal pierced Luscia's ears from across the hall. From their limited view, a young courtier was seen throwing herself into Kasim's arms in a fit of giggles.

"My, Ira, your sister is persistent," Sayuri remarked drily.

"I'd thought you would know by now how persistent we Hastings can be." He shared a telling look with the Pilarese beauty.

Luscia was grateful when a metal clash thundered over the crowd, the sound of a giant cymbal being struck upon the center dais, silencing the room. The king's voice echoed from where he stood on a higher platform before the Throne of Thoarne. On either side of a plush, indigo seat, winding antlers of sculpted byrnnzite reached toward the vaulted heights of the room and sparkled in the torchlight. A magnificent illustration of Unitarian artistry.

"Friends and guests! My family and I invite you all to join in celebrating the Ascension of the al'Haidren to Boreal. Her presence brings us into a new age as she takes her seat and completes my son's Quadren! Please, eat to your content, drink 'til your limit, and revel in the evening's entertainment!"

The room clapped and advanced to the series of tables around the room, buried under platters of choice cuisine and flagons of wine. Declan offered Luscia his arm to escort her to Dmitri's table on the platform, positioned a row lower, in front of their predecessors.

From the end of the king's table, a slim Pilarese man surveyed Luscia as she climbed the steps. With waxy skin and thinning black hair knotted at the base of his neck, he stood out from Korbin's other guests. His plate remained empty, except for a pile of seasoned, withered beetles. The man punctured one with a sharp, decorative metal finger-piece and leisurely brought it to his cracked lips. She heard him crunch down as Declan pulled out her chair, placed between Dmitri Thoarne and Ira Hastings.

"I haven't yet told you how lovely you look, Lady Boreal." Dmitri said under his breath once she was seated. "Thank you…for coming tonight."

Anchoring onto his sympathetic eyes, Luscia tried to discount the eerie prickling along her neck. With a smile and feigned confidence, she faced forward and positioned her back to the unnerving sound of metallic clicks and crumbling insects.

ELEVEN

Zaethan

"You promised me, Zaeth." Dmitri said, mouth clenched, as he put space between Zaethan and the rest of his Quadren. "You swore you'd be civil with her!"

The prince shoved his uncooperative hair away from his face in frustration, only for it to fall right back in his eyes. Zaethan walked with him, matching his stride to the *clack* of Dmitri's cane as it rhythmically smacked the floor. They meandered through a maze of chattering yancies, the majority of whom were too lost in their own amusement to even notice the crown prince weaving among them.

"I don't understand why you're so upset. Having nothing civil to say to your y'siti guest, I prudently said nothing at all!" Zaethan challenged.

Dmitri stopped and faced him. "Which was completely *uncivil!*"

"I will not degrade myself for the comfort of a witch!" Zaethan nearly shouted, inspiring people to step back and immediately form a ring of muffled gossip. "You don't know this y'siti, Dmitri, or what she is capable of. Not like I do. Don't ask me to play nice with the viper aimed at your throat!"

Zaethan knew his friend was struggling to teach him some lesson in courtly decorum, but he felt the restraint he'd demonstrated deserved to be commended, not corrected.

It was ridiculous how the Ethnicam still came together under the guise of mutual esteem. Through perseverance and countless compromises, it'd taken centuries for the other Houses to weaken Boreal's twisted hold on the line of Thoarne. With their mysticism and superstitious practices, the Haidrens to Boreal maintained an unmistakable power over the Orynthian realm and her rulers. It wasn't until the early Stag Age, when Korbin drafted treaties with Mworra, Razôuel, and Tavaàr, that Boreal's strange supremacy finally broke.

This entire event was a mockery—as if Bastiion, Pilar, or Darakai would ever truly celebrate the renewed influence of these creatures. Nevertheless, here they were, *playacting* now that the mysterious al'Haidren to Boreal had come out of the mist for all to see.

"She's not a witch!" Dmitri hissed at him. "Do not speak that abhorrent profanity in my presence again. I mean it, Zaeth, do you understand? She is your equal, and her name is *Luscia*." Dmitri's voice rose louder as the foreign name passed over his lips. "You'd better get acquainted with it quickly, because she's not going anywhere."

Zaethan was lost for words as he considered his lifelong friend. He couldn't recall the last time Dmitri had raised his voice—with him, or *anyone*.

He scanned the breadth of the room and saw the y'siti casting a cold, emotionless gaze onto Sayuri Naborū-Zuo while the Pilarese al'Haidren conversed in her notoriously catlike manner. The y'siti did not speak in return, but stood resolute like the ice she'd surely been cut from. No longer did she resemble the spirited, dauntless child he'd caught dancing in combative positions upon the railing of a ship. Gone was her vigor and youthful exhilaration. The House of Boreal must have beaten those qualities out of her when they replaced them with the stony detachment she now exuded. Her entire countenance reminded Zaethan of some fabled bird, agelessly observing her surroundings through each cursed eye, one steel and the other cerulean.

Reluctantly, his attention returned to Dmitri when an irritating jingle of jewels drew near. Zaethan closed his eyes and systematically cracked each knuckle on either hand, as the scent of poppy perfume foretold the imminent arrival of Flourette Hastings.

"What are you doing?" Dmitri asked suspiciously.

"Bracing myself."

"For wh—"

"Lord Zaethan, there you are!" Flourette squealed as she made impact, lacing both of her arms around one of his. Her pitch must have breached another octave by the ache it left in his eardrum. "I've been looking for you *everywhere!*" Her flirtatious gaze landed on Dmitri. "Oh! Hello, Your Highness! Don't you both look dashing tonight!"

Dmitri opened his mouth to respond when she took a breath, then briskly shut it again as her babble continued.

"You look so handsome in green. This fabric feels even more marvelous than it appears." Her fingers explored the surface of Zaethan's jacket. "Isn't Lord Zaethan just the finest al'Haidren to Darakai that Bastiion has ever seen?"

"Isn't he, though?" Dmitri encouraged her, stifling a laugh.

Momentary delight took precedence over their argument, at least for one of them. Dmitri rubbed the side of his face in an effort to cover a satisfied smirk. Zaethan stared at his friend, pleading for mercy, but Dmitri was punishing him. The prince attentively listened to Flourette's gossip, pretending not to notice when Zaethan reached behind to capture her wayward fingers when they brushed his hairline.

"How fortuitous it is, Flourette, that we are burdened by your company when there are so many others eager to hear your commentary," he stated blandly, releasing her spindly fingers.

Zaethan felt a swift rap below his knee as Dmitri cautioned him to remain civil with Flourette as well.

"Well, we couldn't have it any other way, could we? How would I enjoy the evening if I left you all by yourself?" She giggled and began to twirl one of his locs around another meddlesome finger.

"We'll never know until you do, Floure—*umph.*"

The cane thwacked his leg harder, enunciating the warning.

"Lady Flourette, have you a chance to meet my final al'Haidren?" Dmitri asked. "I'm sure she'd welcome the perspective of a native courtier, especially since your father serves as both Haidren to Bastiion and Minister of the Peerage. Would you like to make her acquaintance?" he seamlessly suggested, offering Flourette his royal dimples as he eyed Zaethan shaking out his leg.

"Of course, Your Highness! She's probably lost without me, you know, after all those years trapped in the highlands." Flourette's hand fluttered up to press against her heart. "Is it true the Boreali live in the trees? Do you think she knows what a bathtub is for?" She shook her head and let out another high-pitched giggle. "I can only imagine the work I have cut out for me, but I will make you proud, Prince Dmitri!"

"I'm certain your efforts will not go unnoticed, Lady Flourette."

Zaethan saw a palace attendant climb the dais to signal the king's official welcome. He picked up a cloth-wrapped hammer and struck the hall's enormous bronze cymbal.

"Thank the Fates," he mumbled.

"Friends and guests! My family and I invite you all to join in celebrating the Ascension of the al'Haidren to Boreal. Her presence brings us into a new age as she takes her seat and completes my son's Quadren! Please, eat to your content, drink 'til your limit, and revel in the evening's entertainment!"

Dmitri's father tipped back his glass as he sank into his throne. The shining cup was refilled by the time his elbows hit the table before him.

Dmitri promptly excused them from Flourette's clutches and strolled with Zaethan toward his table across the hall. "I thought you didn't believe in the Fates," Dmitri pointed out as they scaled the steps.

"I don't. But if I did, I'd be kissing their immortal feet. You were supposed to rescue me from that barnacle, not encourage her."

"Did you not hear? I just insisted Flourette refocus her attention on the al'Haidren to Boreal. Now you and Luscia will have a common interest to discuss," he replied, vaulting over the final steps.

Someone's feeling chipper, Zaethan thought with a grimace.

Avoiding his father, who sat behind them to the left of the king, Zaethan settled into his chair. In doing so, he viewed the opposite end of Dmitri's table, where the y'siti's brawny henchman dismissed a servant waiting to assist the al'Haidren and seated her himself instead. Once assured she was content, the bearded, fiery-haired man stepped aside and stationed himself against the closest wall. Her hybrid mutt laid at the y'siti's feet, though its ears shifted alertly with the noise of the hall. Being Darakaian, and not fully enmeshed in the social delicacies of Unitarian culture, Zaethan was surprised her wild animal was permitted at such a gathering.

"All this for some foul y'siti. It's absurd." Accented Unitarian whispered in Zaethan's ear as Sayuri slithered into place at their end of the table. "And she brings that vulgar dog everyone knows is the spawn of war-taint."

He couldn't agree with her more, which was a first.

"Dmitri, darling, this is truly a lovely display." Sayuri reached past Zaethan in order to drape her hand atop Dmitri's, slowing the natural staccato of her western accent to a more beguiling cadence. "Boreal's al'Haidren must be so honored by the incredible generosity you've shown her tonight."

"She is," a husky voice interjected.

Beyond Dmitri's profile, the fair skinned y'siti sat forward. Her unnerving eyes traveled up the length of Sayuri's sun-kissed arm to read the expression on the prince's face. Angling away from Zaethan, he only saw a dimple emerge on the lively skin of Dmitri's normally hollow cheeks. The witch half smiled and nodded at some unspoken understanding before she turned to answer a question posed by Ira.

Below their platform, a parade of alluring Unitarian dancers spread around the base of the dais as music enveloped the room. Zaethan caught a knowing look from a handsome woman in the back as her performers entertained the crowd of hungry nobles. Salma Nabhu tilted her head toward one of the glistening, twirling dancers, offering a temporary solution for his mood. The girl in question was beautiful, of course. In the torchlight, the dancer's vitality rolled off her skin with her sweat, and sepia-toned hair moved around her like a sandstorm from the Wastes.

"Gregor Hastings is already intoxicated, and it isn't even the second course," Sayruri murmured beside him. A howl exploded from where the Haidren to Bastiion laughed enthusiastically with the king, unconcerned with the serene queen trapped between them. "No wonder Ira is never sober."

"Sayuri, I have to suffer through the entirety of this event as is. Don't make it worse by opening your mouth," Zaethan spat in a low voice.

Per tradition, the evening was far from over. The Houses would have prepared a variety of performances to accompany each course of the meal, Boreal being the exception. Since being driven out of the Proper over the last decade, members of the northernmost House were generally less willing to participate in court gatherings with the rest of the Ethnicam. An arrangement preferred by the majority.

"There will come a time, *Lord Darakai,* when you and I will see the need for each other." Sayuri pursed her ruby lips. Peering over his shoulder, she quietly continued, "Watch her. She is not like her aunt, Zaethan. You'd do well to consider that when you choose to distance Darakai from Pilar's hand of friendship."

Zaethan despised Sayuri, primarily for her many attempts to openly seduce Dmitri, but the sharpness of her narrowing eyes urged him to rotate in his seat. The y'siti had twisted as well, except her gaze was fixed on the table behind. Zaethan followed her line of sight to the empty seat beside Gregor Hastings. Worry flashed across her face before reassuming her expressionless state. Her strange eyes caught his, and Zaethan's mouth eased into a vicious smile. The y'siti had finally realized just how alone in their world she really was.

Breathing in, she elevated her chin and faced forward to resume a dull discussion with Dmitri and Ira over the Province of Wendylle.

His thoughts returned to Sayuri's counsel. Zaethan risked a sidelong glance at her predecessor, seated near his father. Tetsu Naborū rapped his metal nailpiece against the tabletop as Lord Felix Ambrose, an entitled yancy from Galina, spoke rapidly into his ear. Zaethan wasn't surprised. As the elected Chancellor of the Shoto Collective, Pilar's congress of scholars and statesmen, Naborū had woven a web of political partnerships over the years, each to his benefit. In addition, adopting the role of Haidren after the death of his brother meant a man like Naborū encountered few limitations and knew how to circumvent them when he did.

"But you are exactly like your uncle, *Lady Pilar*. A conniving little snake," Zaethan hissed, turning back to his plate. "And that time you speak of is not tonight."

Salma's dancers glided off the floor as the cymbal clashed again, signaling a transition into the next course. Darakai's painted drummers took their place, the masculine uproar causing the staff to jump while they exchanged the empty dishware with something colorful and over-flowing. An attendant lifted Dmitri's plate, then apologized profusely when he nearly knocked the prince's cane off the edge of the table. On and on the charade went, performance after performance, delicacy after delicacy.

When the cymbal marked their final course, the original musicians took to the dais for the remainder of the night. Zaethan pinched the bridge of his nose and eagerly awaited the first opportunity to leave.

"Luscia, I think dessert is the perfect opportunity to display your skillset. I'll inform Alora how seriously you're taking your duty to sing me lullabies," Dmitri jested with the y'siti, apparently referencing some prior conversation.

"What a grand idea, Your Highness! The court would love to hear the elusive al'Haidren to Boreal sing for us all." Sayuri stretched across Zaethan once more, tugging Dmitri's arm.

"No, no. I was just referring to—"

But before Dmitri could explain the nature of his comment, Sayuri bolted from her seat and dashed to exchange words with the king. Promise twinkled in her eyes when she sauntered back down to their table.

"Dmitri! I didn't know your al'Haidren had prepared something for me!" King Korbin shouted over the noise of the hall.

"Father, it's…it's a misunderstanding."

"Everyone!" With dazed eyes and slurred words, Dmitri's father clapped for the room's attention. "My son's al'Haidren has prepared a treat for us before she presents Boreal's Ascension offering!"

"Luscia, I'm so sorry. He's—I can explain it to them," Dmitri started to say.

"It's not your fault," Zaethan overheard her respond stoically. "It is an honor to sing for you, Your Highness."

Standing, her guard escorted her to the dais. Halfway there, the y'siti paused and returned to Dmitri.

"If you'll permit?" she asked and cautiously reached out for his cane.

"Oh! Yes—of course," he promptly responded, his regal nose crinkling quizzically as he gestured to the cane in her grasp. "Whatever you require is yours for the taking."

With his permission, she gave a short bow and continued onward.

Sayuri reclined smugly and crossed her arms expectantly. "You're welcome for this," she murmured to Zaethan.

As the al'Haidren climbed the dais with the help of her escort, the imported material of her dress shifted with her graceful movement. It was strange how the modest cut was distinctly masculine, military even, yet made her look anything but. She lifted her ghostly, heart-shaped face to whisper to her henchman. He stared at her with momentary skepticism before bowing his head and retreating to his position at the end of their table. The crisp lines of the y'siti's face shifted as she closed her unsettling eyes, situated under dense, tawny brows, and began to mouth phrases under her breath.

Zaethan's gut tightened. The witch wouldn't dare use one of her arcane spells in the open, surely? Then, striking Dmitri's cane against the stone she stood upon, a deep and haunting ballad echoed off the walls of hall as the y'siti began to sing.

> *The Earth became dark, her blood spilt anew,*
> *Betrayal so deep, burning tears ran true.*
> *She drank of the shadow, then drowned in fire,*
> *Who could rescue her from our taint and mire?*
> > *Rul'Lothadim Aniell,*
> > *rul'Lothadim, On High.*

> *In the mist it hid, between trees it dwelt,*
> *Before the Light of Him, whom Tiergan knelt.*
> *A touch breeds death, this radiance would save,*
> *His Gift to Boreal, the High One gave.*
> > *Rul'Lothadim Aniell,*
> > *rul'Lothadim, On High.*

Zaethan jerked when the Najjani guard at the foot of their table took his sheathed sword, having unbuckled it, and accompanied her rhythmic clamor. His rich baritone joined her chilling tale.

> *Those of North they sang, yet of East they sought,*
> *Unaware of the terror, which Tiergan fought.*

Bold Thoarne traveled far, a brotherhood sealed,
By might nor by force their lands slowly healed.
rul'Lothadim Aniell,
rul'Lothadim, On High.

Old hunger recalled, scarred mouths of teeth drank,
Tearing flesh from bone, their thirsty claws sank.
Monstrosity pushed and would not abide,
Brothers East and North, whose fates did collide.
rul'Lothadim Aniell,
rul'Lothadim, On High.

Fallen pierced and slain, the Dönumn became
Tiergan's tomb, Thoarne dread, stolen hope remained.
On scorned knees he pled, spirit threads rebind,
Brilliant breath sprang forth, men no longer blind.
rul'Lothadim Aniell,
rul'Lothadim, On High.

Male voices resonated throughout the Hall, though from where they originated, Zaethan couldn't tell. Rage flared inside his chest. The y'siti were concealed in their midst without his foreknowledge. Zaethan pivoted and beheld Dmitri, who sat forward, listening in wonder.

An unnatural breeze swept the room, lifting the y'siti's hair like ash fanning off a fire. The raw gems knit throughout her tresses chimed as they rustled in place. Slowly, Zaethan's hand felt for the hilt of his *kopar*.

History written, and history rings,
Even leaves know for whom life sings.

He mends every wound, joins feathers to fly,
When all men forget, still the Earth will cry,
rul'Lothadim Aniell,
Rul'Lothadim, On High.

Dmitri hopped out of his seat and led the crowd in applause. The witch bowed solemnly and descended the dais, returning to their table. Reaching into her skirts, she pulled out a curved dagger.

A gasp shuddered over the crowd as Zaethan's limbs leapt into action. He pushed off the table and shot an arm across Dmitri's torso, calling for the guards. Within moments, sentries filled the hall, eliciting shrieks from nearby noblewomen when they drew their swords, the metal screeching.

"Lateef!" Zaethan heard his father shout over the frenzy, from his place at the king's table. "Seize that witchiron at once!"

This is why she came out of hiding, Zaethan thought, panicking as General Lateef tore through the swarm of men. *She wanted an audience to her massacre.*

"This is completely inappropriate!" Dmitri sputtered. "She is a member of my Quadren!"

Ignoring the crown prince, Zaethan's father hurried down the steps of the platform. Sentries moved to surround the witch, swords pointed at her neck, shielded only by a thin layer of fabric. Despite the imminent threat, the y'siti remained calm, slowly kneeling inside the circle of men and lifting the dagger in the air for all to see.

A flutter of relief skirted through Zaethan's gut, though his arm still hovered in front of their prince. Y'siti should never be trusted, even before a sea of witnesses. His left hand, positioned inches from Dmitri's plate, crept toward the napkin on the table. Zaethan stared forward as his forefinger eased under the fabric and took hold of the prince's dirtied carving knife. Flexing his hand around the hilt, he felt the cold of the iron seep into his skin.

"My offering to you, Dmitri Korbin Thoarne, Crown Prince of Orynthia, is a single dagger," she announced in a clear, strong voice. The y'siti lowered her arm and stroked the hilt, suddenly looking wistful. "Consort daggers are never to be parted, and this pair is the last remnant of my mother that I have. Its mate remains with me, as this blade will remain with you. It is named *Benevolence*."

Dmitri leaned forward, entranced. "And the mate in your possession?"

"*Ferocity*."

For an instant, her glistening, smoke-rimmed eyes blazed a searing light, but no one else seemed to notice. Zaethan lifted the knife out from under the napkin, looking around disbelievingly. Not even his father appeared to be particularly alarmed. Then, to his shock, the commander nodded jerkily to his sentries, who slowly back away from the y'siti, allowing her to rise and move toward the prince once again.

"Dmitri, I don't think—" Zaethan began.

Yet Dmitri merely brushed him aside and stepped around the table, opening his palms to receive the y'siti's Ascension offering. Zaethan held his breath, waiting for the witch's inevitable attack.

The y'siti smiled at Dmitri, holding out the consort dagger, looking innocent as a doe. Then, without warning, she suddenly seized her head in both hands and screamed. The jeweled blade clattered against the floor as her eyes rolled back into her skull and she collapsed.

"*Niit!*" a panicked voice cried.

A blur of emerald and crimson emerged from the shadows, leaping over the tabletops. A Najjan ran toward her, dropping to his knees once he'd cleared the crowd. He skidded upon them across the smooth floor, catching the unconscious al'Haidren in his arms. Cradling her head, the shadowman panted in alarm. A swarm of nobles stood in shock, gasping as three more fully armed Najjan materialized to escort their al'Haidren's body from the hall.

"Well," Sayuri said with a pout, "that took an interesting turn."

Zaethan slammed his fists down, causing cutlery to fly from the table, then stormed out of the room. There was no telling how many pale faces had infiltrated the corners of this palace. He realized then that the House of Boreal had not sent a mere sorceress into the heart of Bastiion, but a cancer. A weapon who'd bewitch their prince before slitting his throat.

The pang in Zaethan's chest foretold that this would be the night he'd always look back upon as the moment when everything changed.

TWELVE

Luscia

A spicy, floral scent struck Luscia as an invigorating breath of rhali pollen filled her sluggish lungs.

Her eyelids cracked open. Bright, hazy light forced her to blink multiple times before her vision could clear. Pressure racked the base her skull and spread forward, like webs of pain holding her hostage. An involuntary groan escaped her parched lips. Then, with a soft *click*, the aggressive aroma was capped and whisked away from her nostrils.

"There we are," said a soothing voice.

A warm palm rested lightly against her forehead. Alora withdrew her hand and began sifting through her apothic instruments, but returned it more forcefully when Luscia tried to lift herself upright.

"Ah, ah…my Boreali niece should know impatience is never prudent. Keeping your Captaen Bailefore out of this room has alone proven cumbersome, so I'd appreciate some cooperation."

Luscia huffed and pressed her aching head into the pillow.

"*Tadöm*," Alora thanked her, combing through the boxed apothecary. "How long?"

"About forty-eight hours. You've broken your record, *lu'lycran*," Alora answered kindly, though the use of Lusica's childhood name betrayed her aunt's attempt at nonchalance. She'd not uttered it in years.

Meaning "little wolx," only Luscia's father held onto the name his wife had favored. Luscia's mother used to say their daughter was more lycran than al'Haidren, whenever she found Luscia covered in mud or out of bed, exploring in the moonlight. Alora embraced it for a season after her younger sister, Eoine, was taken from them, but her aunt's parental inclinations were much more reserved than the younger, whimsical woman who'd brought Luscia into the world.

Still, Alora became an essential figure during Luscia's formative years. True to her sober disposition, hers was a distant love—ardent, but less concerned with impractical sentimentality than with Luscia's birthright and blood-calling.

"I've been in this bed for two days?" Luscia sputtered, startled by the time lost. "I don't understand how this happened. My vials ran out the night we entered Bastiion. A minor episode occurred once I initiated the Sight," she added at Alora's inquiring look. "But even so, my last dose was taken less than a week ago."

"You waited that long to awaken your connection? Luscia…" Alora scolded, disregarding the topic at hand. "You were instructed to begin communing with the threads the night of your Ascension. I was hoping your Sight would be second nature by now. The threads discern for us. The High One speaks through the Dönumn and thus through the lumin. It's your most vital gift as Haidren to Boreal."

She'd expected the lecture, but Luscia wasn't ready to admit to the fear that she'd been vacant of the higher gifts. Or that she'd yet to commune with the threads since.

"*Meh fyreon, Ana'Mere.*"

"It is forgiven," Alora dismissed. "Now, what of this minor episode you mentioned? I wasn't aware there'd been another since your departure. Your fiery captaen only reported what transpired at your reception."

Briefly, Luscia recounted what had taken place after initiating her Sight in the wood outside the Proper. It didn't make any sense; Luscia had never fallen victim to an episode so quickly after taking her standard dosage. Her aunt began brewing the medicinal treatments around the time of puberty, when an unknown, splitting head pain first took hold of Luscia. Neither Boreal's chief healer nor her Clann Darragh were able to discern what had befallen their young al'Haidren.

"Could this be because of my Ascension? The episodes used to be further apart, but they've intensified ever since," Luscia posed.

"*Niit.* What's more likely is, as you approached adulthood and entered into it, the occurrences are being triggered by external stressors. The episode in the wood and the reception were both evenings of extreme significance. The latter incredibly so. You attended without your Haidren and were forced to participate in that ridiculous spectacle," her aunt noted resentfully. "The thought of that court handling you like another plaything…"

Alora moved toward the windows of Luscia's bedroom, where

multiple, glistening jars had been set out upon the window ledge. She picked up a stone bowl and started grinding a complex mix of herbs together.

"Do you think…" Luscia stared at cracks in the ceiling. "….maybe I'm like her? That I took after her somehow?"

"*Heh'ta*. Stop that." The grinding paused before resuming at a calculated pace. "Assumption is not becoming on you, niece."

Alora was truthful. Her mother's madness hadn't exhibited physical symptoms before…before it had suddenly worsened.

"I'll simply increase the potency of your dosage as well as the frequency. You'll soon find court life a continuous stressor."

"What elements will you add to my treatment?" Luscia propped herself up on an elbow, genuinely curious.

"Many."

Knowing Alora, the complication of its creation would likely double as well. Her aunt tended to implement herbal blends and methods most Boreali healers wouldn't think to attempt.

"*Ana'Mere*, we need to discuss the nature of this elixir I'm to produce for the prince," Luscia pressed. "He summoned for more the night I arrived and, frankly, it was dishonest to pretend I'd even known about it."

"This is not the time for that conversation, Luscia, nor is it mine to have with you."

Alora positioned her back to Luscia as she worked. Her aunt would not give further comment on the matter.

"Will you at least share the cause for your delay, then?"

Luscia knew she was pushing Alora's tolerance, but she deserved an explanation. Never had another al'Haidren been presented to court devoid of their predecessor's support. Begrudgingly, she'd sacrificed one of her mother's consort daggers because of it. Her father had gifted Eoine with the set during their courtship, and now Luscia had forever separated the two blades. Meaning, Luscia lost two of his gifts to Bastiion, coupled with the *kuerre*.

Alora ceased muddling and set down the bowl of half-ground ingredients.

"You are no longer a child, so I must resist treating you as such," she confessed, threading her slender fingers together. "I was notified of a situation in Port Tadeas shortly before your party departed Roüwen. As you know, after declining allegiance to Boreal, cross-castes are not permitted to remain within our territorial borders. Most migrate to the port towns or all the way to Bastiion Proper. It is difficult to survive without the providence of a House, and recently, some of our cross-castes have gone missing.

"I instructed Emiere to reroute us near Port Tadeas so we could investigate. With an indication of darker crimes, the only option was to go and demand answers myself. I honestly don't believe anyone would have found the boy if we hadn't gone looking on his behalf."

Alora chewed her lip before continuing.

"My guard discovered his body downstream in a hidden creek bed. He looked prepubescent, perhaps ten or eleven years old. Bore-ali-Unitarian descent. I will spare you the specifics—no one should describe that degree of desecration—but the majority of his body had been ripped apart. The markings resembled that of an animal attack, but from the pattern of victims, it's clear that isn't the case." She met Luscia's gaze, her eyes full of an unspoken, depthless sorrow. "I am sorry for my absence, Luscia. You will soon learn that, as Haidren, our lives are no longer our own. And as much as I wished to see you recognized by the court, that little boy needed his Haidren to recognize him, too."

It was difficult conversations such as these which made it impossible to stare into the twin cosmos under Alora's thin brows and not see her mother's eyes in return. They were Phalen's eyes. Luscia's eyes.

Tiergan eyes.

Luscia buried her longing for the past and seized the ire swimming in her chest. For centuries, the House of Boreal had been revered, respected for their unique service to the crown. Somehow, that respect was spun into envy, and envy twisted into suspicion—a suspicion that had led to Boreal's complete defamation.

Still, the Ethnicam had never demonstrated such violence against their people before. Not after the signing of the Accords. Luscia couldn't help but imagine the pale, withered frame of a child with walnut curls and vacant, teal eyes. One more relative to Mila, than herself.

"What was—"

"Finnian Wollack," Alora murmured before Luscia could ask the boy's name. "The threads speak differently to each of us, Luscia. I, for instance, can see… climates about a person. The lumin around you pulsed with curiosity, one could say. It may take years for you to learn how to pass in and out of the Sight continuously, but eventually you'll employ it on a daily basis."

Alora patted Luscia's hand and returned to the window to complete her concoction. Her hair shimmered in the sun, much like the sheen of Saoirse pearls, but concealed any emotion by hanging over her delicate face and cascading loosely down her shoulder.

"I need to speak with the prince. He'll want to know this is happening to our people," Luscia declared. "*Ana'Mere*, if you'll help me out of this bed, Mila can assist in dressing me and I'll be on my way."

"*Niit*. Those feet aren't going anywhere," Alora ordered, seriousness altering her tone. "It is time to *think*, Luscia. Marching down Unitarian halls like some wild, northern zealot won't bring Finnian Wollack honor. Always think before allowing your emotions to dictate the path for you. I already brought the matter to the king's attention when I gave an account of my delay. His Majesty wishes for the local military to handle it, and we are going to let them."

"But Darakai controls the military. Any investigation for Boreal under their command will result in nothing!" Luscia argued zealously.

"But until this proves true, I cannot use that argument with his Majesty," Alora countered, thwarting Luscia's rebuttal. "You will not fight me on this. Our House is not in a position to make demands. My years of collaboration with Korbin Thoarne have been cordial, but we are no longer his priority now that the others have set their hooks in him. The louder Boreal screams, the more attention we bring to the fact that the Ethnicam does not see a need for us anymore. They do not know what they cannot know, Luscia, and we won't resent them for it. Korbin hasn't felt the threat of battle in decades. He has little experience in what Boreal means to his line, or the realm."

Frustrated with their political predicament, Luscia lay in silence while Alora poured the modified treatment into a tray of cloudy vials. Accepting one of the doses from her aunt, Luscia drank the marshy fluid in a rush. A sour, bitter tang skimmed the back of her tongue and slid down her throat.

A telling screech came just before a hawk soared through the open window in a flurry of wings. Alora lifted an arm as Amaranth glided onto her master's perch. A rolled piece of parchment was fastened to one of her legs. The hawk had always been a mystery to Luscia, as she was never privy to the information the lavender bird carried to her aunt, or from whom it repeatedly came.

"*Allöh*, my dearest. You're late," she cooed, stroking Amaranth's feathers before she unraveled the parchment and scribbled a response to the message within. "*Tredae'Auryth*." She kissed the hawk's beak gently. "And quickly."

Three impatient knocks suddenly battered Luscia's bedroom door, sending Amaranth shrieking back into the skies.

"Captaen Bailefore!" Alora spun and barked through the door. "If you persist in this endeavor to try my patience, then I will soon find some unpleasant use for your lack of it!"

Luscia heard another man clear his throat behind the dense wood.

"*Ana'Mere*...I've not come on my own behalf," Marek answered nervously.

"Lady Haidren, I trust you're having a lovely day," a cheerful voice interjected. "I was wondering if I might share a portion of it?"

Luscia shot up in bed, dragging the blanket higher to cover her thin shift as Alora flew to the handle. Opening the door with poise, Alora revealed the Orynthian prince, who was carrying a thorny, flowering shrub. At Dmitri's side stood the visibly displeased captaen, although Marek's expression softened when he realized Luscia had awoken.

"Your Highness." Alora's hand braced her middle. "*Meh'fyreon*. I apologize, we mistook you for our determined Captaen Bailefore. *Boleava*, do come in."

Marek made to follow the prince, only to have Alora swiftly shut the door in his face.

"Your protective services are sufficient from the common room, Captaen Bailefore," she added, aware he would listen even from a distance.

"Lady Haidren, it's so good to see you," Dmitri said, nodding respectfully to Alora. He glanced about the room before gesturing to the chair by Luscia's bedside. "May I?"

"*Wem! Boleava*," Luscia blurted, realizing she'd spoken in her native tongue rather than his own. "Yes. Yes, please do."

"*Tadöm*." Dmitri grinned as he sat down, summoning the dimple in his right cheek with his surprising use of Boreali. "I'm learning."

His face caught the afternoon light while he scanned her quarters. Again, Luscia noticed the improved vitality of his skin. Warm, mossy eyes bounced between the furs across the foot of her bed to the jars lining the edge of her open window. The incoming breeze disturbed his hair, freeing it from where it curled around his ears.

"I hope you find your apartments satisfactory. I held them specifically for your party, since there are so few facing northward," he commented, pointing to the bay below.

"Thank you, Your Highness," Luscia said earnestly. "Our view of Thoarne Bay is quite captivating. I enjoy watching the drifting bazaar transform throughout the day. It's quite eclectic."

"Yes, I suppose there's that." He chuckled. "Mainly, I thought you'd appreciate the ability to look toward home whenever you find yourself missing it."

Angling his head, the prince smiled sympathetically. His irises looked greener in the daylight against the contrast of his darker lashes. A spark of hope sprung forth that Dmitri Thoarne might indeed become the partner Boreal needed.

"That is incredibly thoughtful, Your Highness."

"Oh! That reminds me. This is for you," he said, clumsily handing the shrub he held to Luscia. "It's called a *Noculoma-Anastasis*. They're quite rare! You see, the buds bloom only after dark during nights with little to no moonlight. I had it uprooted from the royal gardens to keep you company while you recover from your ailment."

Traces of dirt showed beneath the trimmed edges of his fingernails.

The prince must have repotted it himself. Luscia found herself unexpectedly touched at the gift.

"It's beautiful. I promise to keep Aksel from consuming it," Luscia jested, setting the plant on her night table.

Alora pulled another chair around to the opposite side of Luscia's bed and set a long, wooden box across her lap. Carved from fallen timber on the Isle of Viridis, viridi wood was prized for its deep amber striation and seldom traded with outsiders.

"Your Highness, I am deeply remorseful for my absence during Luscia's reception," Alora prefaced, placing the viridi box between them. "Unfortunately, that also meant I was delayed in bringing you what is rightfully yours."

Her small hands opened the case to reveal a brilliant luxiron sword, set in a lush bed of embroidered linsilk. The sword's core emitted the same luminosity as Luscia's confiscated *kuerre*, but didn't curve as conventional Najjani blades did. Built with an untraditional hilt, their luxsmiths had crafted the metal to resemble a dozen interlocking, golden antlers.

"The Stag Age commenced with your father, but it is our hope that under your stewardship, it will thrive," Luscia explained her design. "This is hardly as historic as I envisioned, but I'm proud to reveal Boreal's true offering—*your* Sword of Thoarne."

Dmitri's fingers brushed his lips in awe as he studied the blade's intricacy. "I can't help but feel there's a great disparity between us," Dmitri said in a melancholy voice, carefully holding the case open. "You've given me this sword when Bastiion has taken your own, though at least your mother's dagger may remain in your care. Despite the commander's rather…aggressive…objections, I managed to convince my father to consider it an exception to Gregor's newest piece of legislation."

"A kindness indeed, Your Highness," Luscia managed to say.

"Its name?"

"*Communion.* The state of things so held."

Hesitantly, his thumb ran the length of it in a reverent caress. "This is truly magnificent. Luscia, I have no words."

He didn't get an opportunity to form them, either, due to a loud crash from the common room. Multiple languages rang out in what sounded like a heated disagreement.

"Where is he? I demand you open that door!" a man shouted, emphasized by a compilation of what she presumed were Andwele obscenities.

Rising from the chair, Dmitri carefully latched the case and picked it up, along with his cane. "This has been a delightful visit, if cut short," he said with a sigh, glowering at Luscia's door. "I'll forgive you your watchdog, if you'd be so gracious as to forgive me mine."

"Of course, Your Highness," Alora assured him.

Meeting Luscia's eyes once again, Dmitri added, "Truly, the sword..." He nodded to the box in his hand. "It will be cherished."

"Just as we'd hoped," Luscia told him with a heartfelt smile.

Reluctantly opening the door to her domed common room, the prince said farewell and quietly closed it behind him.

Too exhausted to protest the Darakaian intrusion, Luscia flipped on her side and admired Dmitri's *Noculoma-Anastasis* upon her nightstand, for once content to let her guard protest it for her.

THIRTEEN

Perched over the roof slats of a grand storehouse, the figure waited for the congregation of men to scatter once they came to a consensus about what to do with the butchered body at their feet.

He'd heard a woman scream an hour earlier while trudging in the forest just outside Arune, a grand estate in the Province of Wendylle. Rushing in the direction of her cry, the figure had arrived to find a grouping of nobility huddled around a gutted corpse, near the perimeter of a Unitarian estate. Though he'd never intended to travel this far from the crown city, Alora had ordered he leave Bastiion after Amaranth relayed the rumors he'd overhead of another cross-caste victim outside the Proper, concerning a merchant caravan making progress through the provinces. Convinced her niece was safe in her care, Alora had commanded him to go.

The Pilarese hawk preened her unusual, violet-hued feathers on the other side of the rooftop. Amaranth would travel with him until he drafted his return message to Alora. Sharper than previous candidates, Amaranth had proved an integral asset in their operation many times over. Use of the war-tainted bird was the least he could offer the fair woman he'd once betrayed, though there was no degree of servitude that could ever repay her clemency for his wickedness.

Amaranth twisted in her grooming to consider him, as if she sensed the damning shift of his thoughts. Perhaps she could—she had been his sole companion over the past decade of darkness and decay.

Motionless, the figure listened while the nobles debated ways to handle what they cleared considered to be an inconvenience. Having another function to attend, the body of a dead Boreali cross-caste wouldn't keep them occupied for much longer. He was unaware that the Peerage of Nobility had planned to gather that night in the residence of their Haidren and Minister, Gregor Hastings. Below, each councilman stood in the customary robes for such an occasion.

"Where is she now, that servant girl who found it?" A greying noble glanced around at the rest of the men.

"The maid's been taken to my wife, Pias. She won't raise further alarm," Gregor answered, clearly disinclined to bring attention to the death as well. "The girl's no help, anyway. She only tripped over it on her way to fetch more wine from my storehouse."

"If you've some rabid animal roaming your lands, any injury to my livestock is your concern, Gregor," the youngest councilman sputtered, crossing his arms. "I'll have you know, I spent an entire aurus on that gelding and five dromas for the mare!"

"If there's a rabid animal on the loose, your *horses* are the least of my concern, Nathune. *I'm* the man who lost property tonight," the Haidren tersely replied, nudging the corpse's arm with the toe of his freshly buffed leather boot. "This cross-caste cost me a fortune off a trader two years ago. It's criminal how much they charge for the young ones."

Loose pebbles fell from the stone ledge when the figure tightened his grip violently at their laughter. He grimaced as the rocks clattered down the side of the storehouse. Nearly all the men jumped as Amaranth shot from her post and circled the area to distract them from his concealed presence. Her instincts grew more impressive by the day.

The Houses were notorious for their mistreatment of cross-castes, but the Unitarian high nobility had evolved into the worst offenders over the last decade. Grown fat and greedy, they'd taken their era of peace and contorted it into an era of privileged indulgence. And while some cross-castes were still considered "employed" by province manors, most had been sold as slaves for a handsome fee.

It was sickening. Even to a monster like himself.

The rarer the genetic mixing, the steeper the price. And as the House of Boreal remained the most segregated of all, a northern cross-caste would cost someone like Gregor Hastings very much, indeed.

"Just bury it, Gregor. Or burn it, I don't care. The Peerage is waiting. But the members of your still-breathing staff need to hunt down the animal by morning," the eldest of them coughed into the dirt, impatient to return to the boisterous event inside the manor. "My wife dragged her two best cross-castes with us this time, and you can't afford to replace them."

"Fine. I'll have someone fetch you a drink, Larkstead, for the trouble," Gregor conceded, patting the hunched man on the back. "Kuudhà, rally the boys and get rid of this thing. Don't leave any trace of it, either—I don't want my guests questioning the quality of Hastings wine."

A Darkaian cross-caste, standing beyond the circle of lords, nodded silently and scurried off to enlist more servants for disposal. The nobles also dispersed, abandoning the cold, lifeless body crumpled in the grass. The Haidren to Bastiion led the councilmen toward his home to rejoin their comrades, joking as if the impromptu meeting had been nothing more than a lost bet.

Gripping his weatherworn cloak, the figure vaulted from the overhang and landed swiftly in a crouch. Soundlessly, he padded forward and knelt to inspect the injuries the child had endured. He didn't have much time.

The length of the dull, muddied hair wasn't evidence of gender, but the pink and coral ribbons tied throughout certainly sufficed. By the length of her torso and limbs, the young woman hadn't yet reached Ascension age, not that it would have brought her freedom if she had. Patches of cream-colored skin were visible under the light of the moon, though her flesh was smeared with blood from innumerable lacerations. Without a doubt, she fit the recent pattern the figure had begun tracing throughout the Unitarian plains.

As the other bodies had been reported to authorities or found in areas of traffic, this was the first opportunity that offered the necessary seclusion to use his unnatural talents. Slowly, he brought his scabbed nostrils near what was left of her face and inhaled deeply.

The figure reared back from the young woman's corpse, alarmed by the disturbing evidence collected in his blackened lungs. With shaking hands, he lifted her arms where larger gashes had been made, aware that

Gregor's manservant would return any moment. Again, breathing in, the figure was struck with an even stronger bouquet of rot, charred flesh, and an intimate, unmistakable scent not even Alora could wash away.

Bloodthirst.

This had been no animal attack.

Horrified, the figure careened into the shadows in a ceaseless sprint. Propelled by a speed not his own, but gifted from his mistress, he ran through the night under the steady watch of Amaranth overhead.

Whether he ran to Alora or from the defiled corpse, the figure did not know. The only truth guiding his inhuman legs toward Bastiion Proper was one he could not comprehend, for it was impossible.

The killer smelled just like him.

FOURTEEN

Zaethan

"This better be good, Kumo, after making me wait three days for a single report," Zaethan warned his cousin in a low voice, having already woken in a foul mood that morning.

"*Owàamo* to you too, *Ahoté*," Kumo hailed as he approached. "*Owàa* met you with a vengeance today."

"My temper has nothing to do with the sun or how he greets me. It does, however, have something to do with being incapable of providing the commander with an explanation for the Haidren to Boreal's delay. Report. Now."

"*Uni*, Alpha Zà," the beta acknowledged, lowering his chin as he wisely shifted to formal Darakaian address. "Zahra assigned Jabari to the guard rotation outside both the Haidren and al'Haidren apartments, hoping he'd pick up some information, but they speak mostly witch-tongue in passing. So, I had Takoda sweet-talk that southern *yaya* in the kitchens, you know the one with the—"

"I don't give two *shtàkas* how you acquired the information, Kumo, I just want to know what it entails." Zaethan scratched the stubble along his jaw impatiently as he glowered at the brass doors ahead, which led to the Quadrennal chambers he was late entering.

"Apologies," Kumo said hurriedly. "Jabari says the Haidren's party stopped in a port town...Tadeas, I think. Looked into some disappearance. The Najjan found another corpse like we've seen here in the Proper. Neither he nor Takoda caught much more, except the boy was butchered, not drained. I don't know what the y'siti did with the body. Probably served it in a stew, yeah?" Kumo crinkled his nose. "Should we keep investigating?"

"*Ano.*" Zaethan shook his head. They'd already wasted enough time on the matter, and his father wouldn't be pleased if he kept investigating the dead cross-castes against orders.

"*Uni*, Alpha Zà." Kumo struck his right fist against his chest and retreated to relay the order to the pryde.

"Wait," Zaethan called after him, reconsidering. "Keep Takoda posted near the younger witch. Just in case."

His beta twisted mid-step and nodded once.

"*Shàlàmaiamo, Ahoté.*"

"*Shàlàmaiamo,*" Zaethan uttered the Andwele farewell, requesting the moon watch over his cousin in turn.

He waited until Kumo rounded the corner before he gripped the byrnnzite door handles and heaved them open with authority. Zaethan had quickly learned from his time at court that one rarely needed to apologize for tardiness, when one arrived unapologetically. Besides, after he'd finally gathered the missing information to bring his father, Zaethan didn't plan to make excuses for being late to the political version of a tea party.

"Zaethan, there you are! Come, come!" Dmitri exclaimed, eagerly waving him over.

"Why, *Lord Darakai*, how considerate of you to finally show up," Sayuri droned from where she lounged next to their prince at the head of the immense pentagonal table. "Your belatedness was a gift, really. It offered the two of us some time to catch up. Our Prince Dmitri has been in high demand as of late."

Sayuri's dark, vulpine eyes flashed accusingly at the impassive y'siti seated across from her. The al'Haidren to Boreal remained unruffled in her modest layers of crisp linen and linsilk. Their dissimilarity was tangible, when one compared her pallid, spectral manner against the vivid, serpentine woman who'd one day serve as a conduit for Pilar's ever-evolving agenda. By the way Sayuri eased her ruby lips into a coy smirk, her personal agenda to position herself at Dmitri's side had not changed.

Not that the House of Darakai would ever permit such a union, nor would the Ethnicam's other elite. The only reason Zaethan's House bowed before the line of Thoarne was the simple fact that a drop of ancient, Darakaian blood pulsed within Dmitri's mixed, Unitarian veins. A blood which somehow contained everything Zaethan was, and yet everything he was not.

"My duties as Alpha Zà are more pressing than your list of social obligations, *Lady Pilar*," Zaethan said with a sneer as he crossed the room and came to stand behind Ira Hastings, who'd seated himself to

Dmitri's right. "You're in Darakai's seat, Ira, or did you get lost on your way from the tavern this morning?"

"Ah, right you are." The slightly disheveled al'Haidren picked up his wine and moved to Bastiion's seat beside the y'siti. "Hello, gosling, care for a drink?"

Ira reached to refill her untouched glass, only to find it was already full.

"I'll be more inclined to converse with you, Lord Bastiion, if you refrain from using these crass monikers," she corrected him, lifting a stiff, arrogant chin. "You may address me as Lady Luscia or, if you prefer, Lady Boreal, as is your right."

"Well, I do apologize, *Lady* Gosling." Ira rakishly tipped his drink to salute her. "Boreali women have my utmost admiration, I assure you."

"And here I always considered you an elitist, Ira." Sayuri lifted a brow. "My, how your palate has changed."

Zaethan couldn't fathom why his friend insisted they convene. Restrictions were still in place around Dmitri's power, and this juvenile bickering was the only foreseeable outcome of their assembly. Already annoyed, Zaethan watched the y'siti control her breathing, slowly inhaling and exhaling, as the other two al'Haidrens exchanged words about her. She draped a pale arm over the side of her chair to methodically stroke the muzzle of her uncommonly large wolx, though to keep which of them calm, Zaethan couldn't tell.

Dmitri cleared his throat and stood, using his cane for support. "I would like to officially call this Quadren to session," he said formally. "I know it may seem a bit...silly, I suppose, us meeting like this. My Quadren is politically dormant and we are bound by countless constraints, but I've decided to proceed unorthodoxly and deviate from Orynthian tradition.

"Over the last year, I've spent a great deal of time delving into the journals of my predecessors, specifically the entries recounting the dealings of their Quadrens through each generation of Haidrens. From my grandfather, King Aquila Thoarne, to his mother, Queen Roma Thoarne, and as far back as the ledgers allow. The single commonality between them is one I find rather unfortunate." Here Dmitri paused, glancing at each of them for emphasis. "Not *one* generation has managed to fulfill the true purpose of the Quadren, which is, by the way, to work *together* for the good of the realm. While each of us are divided by House, we are united under the banner of Orynthia, and it is as Orynthians that we will lead."

"Bridging the gap between our peoples starts at this table, Highness, and I for one am devoted to the cause," Ira pledged. He winked at the y'siti and lazily ran a hand that had never known labor through his shining mahogany hair.

"We all thank you, Lord Bastiion, for your personal support," Zaethan said with enough sarcasm to satisfy even Zahra, his third, had she been present.

"I'm so pleased to hear our union has become your passion, as well," Sayuri swiftly added, letting her fingertips brush Dmitri's hand as she regarded him through her dense lashes.

Zaethan audibly laughed, earning him a deadly scowl from his friend. He couldn't believe he was obligated to sit here and listen to this *kakk*. Dmitri had always been an idealist, but this discussion was absurd. Did Dmitri think the Houses would simply come together and abandon centuries-old ambitions and rivalries? That a noble like Ira would put his liquor aside for a cause beyond his own debauchery. Or that the y'siti sorceress would cease sharpening her witchiron while they slept? The notion that the four of them could set aside generations of strife was about as likely as one day referring to Sayruri Naborū-Zuo as *Her Highness.*

"Some of you may scoff at this proposition." Dmitri's eyes targeted Zaethan. "However, I still propose that we open this Quadren privately, be it prematurely. None of you serve your House as Haidren until I serve Orynthia as king. I'm aware it will likely be years before that becomes our reality, but we have an opportunity before us. This is the first and only Quadren to ever be born into an era of peace. So many of these journals, journals like this one," he passionately urged, lifting a tattered book off the tabletop, "were scribbled inside a tent on a scorched battlefield. But that is not how we begin, and it is not how we will end.

"We are going to use this time, these years ahead, to forge our solidarity. Over time, I can find ways to impose our influence within the bureaucratic realms. The Peerage and the Ethnicam will have to allow it when they see how united we've become. And because of that, we can dedicate our youth to something that matters—to the betterment of our people."

Not since childhood had Zaethan seen his friend speak so zealously about anything. He'd noticed the papers piling up in every corner of Dmitri's great room and study, but he had just assumed it was the king's way of preparing the prince for his future responsibilities. And on a day like this, when Dmitri's color waned and his cheeks shone hollow from exhaustion, his hazel eyes were brighter than ever.

"The Hastings family has always shown friendship to the different members of the Ethnicam. In fact, my father has purchased every type of cross-caste you can imagine for our manor in Arune. Quite an exotic collection, actually," Ira stated casually, as if Unitarian supremacy was welcome at the table. "Although he lost one just the other night. Rabid coyotes, I think? Anyway, she was exquisite—"

"Ira—" Dmitri interrupted, sensing the ire emanating from the other three.

"No, truly. It's really a compliment to your kind, gosling," he said, turning to address the y'siti. "Boreali cross-castes are priced steeply for a reason."

The y'siti seized Ira's forearm forcefully, startling him. "What did you just say?"

"Begging your pardon." Ira nervously grinned. "*Lady* Gosling, that is—"

"Ira, are you saying there was another attack?" Zaethan grabbed the noble's shoulder and interrogated him from the opposite side. His pryde had reported nothing of the sort since before the witch's reception. It was unlikely Zahra or Kumo knew anything—a painful reminder that his father had cut their force in Bastiion by three-quarters.

"What do you mean by *another* attack, Lord Darakai?" The y'siti pushed away from the table and loomed over Ira. She fixed her unnerving stare upon Zaethan.

The witch did not raise her voice. She didn't need to. Zaethan felt a series of pricks along the base of his neck. He didn't lift his hand to touch it, not even when the skin seemed to boil. The sensation vanished when she finally blinked. Wordlessly, she'd seared the truth of what she was into his flesh.

You aren't human, he suddenly understood. *You're a daughter of demons.*

"I'd like to invite you all to attend a hunt," Dmitri interrupted anxiously. "Zaethan and I were planning on an outing to the Outer

Proper tomorrow with some of his men. I'd like to extend the invitation. Lady Boreal, would you grace us with your company?"

Zaethan's head swung violently toward the worried prince. "Unbelievable!"

"Lower your voice at this table," Dmitri warned through strained lips.

Zaethan seethed incredulously. That hunt was the only promise of freedom Zaethan had clung to during the last weeks. He was not about to roll over and let Dmitri ransom it for political pacification. Not for the sake of this...creature. But before he could open his mouth to protest, the witch was already accepting Dmitri's invitation.

"I'd be delighted." The y'siti's icy tone defied her smile. "My Aksel has grown anxious and could use the fresh air. It's been ages since he ran with a pack of animals."

Zaethan gripped the smooth edge of the table as he witnessed this precious escape being traded away, like a measly handful of copper crupas for Marketown's most prized jewel. There was now no polite way for him to object to Dmitri's decision, and certainly not in front of the other al'Haidrens.

"Splendid!" Dmitri said, beaming at her. "Sayuri, Ira, I hope to see you both in the morning as well. I think that's enough for today. You are all dismissed," he hurriedly concluded, grabbing his cane.

"Your Highness, a moment of your time, please?" the y'siti requested coolly.

Zaethan glared at her as he rose to his feet. Her ashy hair was worn in a mess of twists, resembling a vengeful ghost in the way she stared down Orynthia's crown prince. As he strode toward the door, Zaethan's restless palms itched to strangle her, for bit by bit, this single creature would poison everything he held dear. Tomorrow's loss was just the beginning.

"Actually, Luscia, would you give us the room? I'd like a word with my al'Haidren to Darakai."

Zaethan halted at Dmitri's words, struggling to compose himself before turning around. After a brief pause, he overheard a submissive, "Of course," before the y'siti stepped around him, leaving the two men in privacy. Zaethan took a deep breath and twisted to face Dmitri, allowing the doors to close at his back.

"What is wrong with you?" Dmitri hissed at him. "This is our *legacy*, Zaethan. *My* legacy! How dare you act like it's all some joke? Or do you believe *I'm* the joke?" he accused, his brows scrunching together. "This isn't like you, Zaeth."

"*Ano zà!* All of *that*," Zaethan yelled, thrashing his arms toward her seat at the pentagonal table, "is not *you*, Dmitri! Depths! A friend who calls himself my brother would never sacrifice my few precious hours of freedom and proposition them like a stepping stone for his own advancement!"

"Zaeth…" Dmitri's lean shoulders fell. "I just—"

"Save it for your next forum…*Your Highness*."

Whatever Dmitri tried to say in defense of himself, Zaethan never heard. He rammed the brass doors open and charged down the hall, the deafening echo masking any rebuttal to his exit.

Consumed with rage, Zaethan eventually turned a corner to the wing of Darakaian suites. In a concentrated haze, he barely registered the ominous presence of the very man who fueled his urge to escape. From the clenching of his pitted jaw to the way his thick, scarred arms crossed over his chest, Zaethan's father appeared to have been waiting outside the apartment for some time.

"*Doru*, control yourself. Your brooding embarrasses my entire House, like a weak hatchling whining for its mother," his father said scathingly, sucking his front teeth. "Rumor says the prince initiated his Quadren prematurely today. What was discussed in this little gathering?"

"I was under the impression that the dealings of a regent's Quadren were of the utmost secrecy," Zaethan tested, more out of defiance than over actual principle.

His father brought his face dangerously close. His hot breath threatened Zaethan's cheeks.

"But you were not meeting with a *regent*," the commander warned. "You sit in that seat to serve Darakai's benefit. Lest you forget, *I am Darakai*. And because you've proven ineffective at the most elementary assignments, you will do exactly as I say. Is that clear?"

"*Uni. Uni zà*," Zaethan breathed, voicing his absolute yes.

"Good," his father growled, pulling back a fraction. "Now, we can use this prematurity to our advantage. The y'siti can't be trusted, of course. Keep her segregated from the others, just as I enlisted Tetsu and Gregor in alienating her aunt years ago. The Hastings brat is a fool, so it would be better to align yourself with Tetsu's neice. Pilar's and Darakai's goals are mutual for the time being. The Pilarese girl could be an asset to us."

"I agree the witch should be watched, but I doubt Dmitri would turn to her completely. Not over the friend he was raised with—and not enough to require aid from Pilar," Zaethan reassured his father.

"Meaning *you*?" The commander snorted his contempt. "That vile abomination is still female. Unless there's an aspect of your relationship with Korbin's son that you've made a point to conceal from me, then *uni zà*, he would. You may have given the prince a prized Andwele mount, but *you* are not the one he is mounting. Or are you?"

Blood rushed to Zaethan's cheeks, warming them. "We're taking it slow," he bit out sarcastically.

Instantly, his father snatched Zaethan's collar, twisting his grip so it tightened around his windpipe. His cold, black eyes narrowed as Zaethan tried to not give him the satisfaction of wheezing. "Mind her," he said, letting go. "Y'siti are deceitful by nature, and history has proven that Thoarne men do not hesitate to taste whatever they desire."

Rather than commenting that Dmitri was not the type, Zaethan cleared his throat and prudently switched topics. "Did you come for my report?"

"Is it even worth hearing?"

"One of Gregor's Boreali cross-castes was murdered this week in Arune. It may be related to the killings in the Proper or part of the reason the Haidren to Boreal was delayed in Tadeas—" Zaethan began, eager to redeem himself.

"I am your Haidren, Chief Warlord of Darakai, and Commander of Orynthia," his father said coldly. "Did you think I would wait around for you to drag these petty scraps of gossip back to me? Your old friend Wekesa is alpha of the pryde stationed in the Valley of Fahime. He does what you cannot and keeps me sufficiently informed."

The corner of his father's mouth twitched. He was *enjoying* this turn of conversation, Zaethan realized. In claiming the position of Alpha Zà, Zaethan had thought he'd finally be free of his long-standing rivalry with Wekesa—a rivalry that had earned him enough scars in failed attempts to earn his father's approval. Yet even without greatness in his line, and no family name to support his own, Wekesa still somehow maintained his hold on Zaethan's heels.

"Then perhaps I can continue to investigate the deaths within the

Proper," Zaethan suggested, trying to keep any hint of desperation from his tone.

"Wekesa is steadily proving to be *Jwona rapiki,* a fate writer for Darakai. Your victories are disappointing, and Wekesa's have written over them. He will lead the investigation throughout the plains as well as within the Proper," his father and commander declared. He crossed his arms, rolling back his shoulders and awaited Zaethan's admission of defeat.

Zaethan lowered his head, inwardly chafing at the gesture. "*Uni zà,* Fath—Commander *Zà.*"

He held his breath until the sound of his father's boots could no longer be heard, treading into the distance. Then Zaethan spun and threw open his apartment door, causing the walls to shake. Locking himself inside, he screamed until his throat became hoarse and collapsed against the wooden entrance, burying his head between his palms.

Kwihila rapiki mu Jwona.

Victory did write over fate. And so, as his rival Wekesa, the bastard fate writer, had erased him, Zaethan vowed to erase the witch from Boreal.

FIFTEEN

Luscia

An arrow soared past Luscia's shoulder, nearly enlisting a collection of blonde hairs in its lethal pursuit.

She twisted in the saddle to see that the target was an average-sized buck grazing among the farthest trees in the distance. Assessing the trajectory of Zaethan Kasim's arrow and the angle at which it sailed, Luscia abandoned her long-awaited discourse with a certain Orynthian prince and kicked the mare into a run.

The savage whooping and howling of Kasim and his warriors died when they realized she'd dashed to greet their conquest, though she hardly cared. A Darakaian wouldn't see what she did and, likely, wouldn't be too concerned if he could. Once in the animal's vicinity,

Luscia slowed her horse, but did not wait for the mare to halt. Seamlessly, she slid from the saddle and sprinted the rest of the way on foot.

Lying on the forest floor, the buck struggled to breathe. It was as she'd anticipated. Kasim's aim had been too low to strike the skull and yet too high to plunge the heart or liver. She dropped to the earth and cradled the deer's head in her lap, soothing him with Boreali hymns. With one hand she stroked the frightened animal, while the other reached beneath her surcoat and gripped her consort dagger, Ferocity.

"*Tadöm, Ana'Brödre. Tredea'Aurynth*," she whispered tenderly in the buck's ear. Her mother's blade caressed the hairs of his neck and ended his suffering.

Warm blood oozed from his throat and soaked her outer gear. Gently, she moved the head off her thighs, careful to avoid his antlers, as the band of southern hunters rushed toward the macabre scene on horseback. Never before had Luscia seen anyone ride as the Darakaians did. Bows drawn, they stood in the saddle as their stallions galloped underneath, like a tidal wave of menacing, monochromatic towers charging in unison.

"Get away from my kill!" the al'Haidren to Darakai barked as he leapt from his stunning, if erratic, Andwele stallion. "Tell me what you did! Did you curse it? Or is bathing in its blood just another filthy y'siti custom?"

Luscia studied Kasim's bright eyes. A genuine accusation of sorcery boiled behind them. Ire settled in her belly at his routine use of the derogatory term. His lip curled into a fleeting snarl, twisting his usually appealing features. A slim yet powerfully built woman came to stand at his side, though she lingered a foot behind. By her tattooed cheek, shaved head and the whittled bone sheathing both ears, Luscia quickly recognized her as the female who'd guarded Dmitri's apartment the night she arrived in Bastiion. The confidence the woman projected suggested she was either Kasim's mate or held a high ranking within his pryde.

"I saved him from the misery of a poor shot," Luscia squarely replied as she wiped Ferocity clean with the edge of her surcoat. She pushed a few stray hairs out of her face, untroubled by the trace of crimson her fingers left along her jaw.

"This is a hunt! Your kind have no authority here. How dare you mark what is mine!" Kasim pointed to the carcass and back at Luscia.

Luscia's eyes charted the jerky motion of his hand. A series of newly healed hatch marks decorated his knuckles.

Violent, this one.

"This is a life, Lord Darakai. One given for your enjoyment," she added when he started up again, refusing to be bated by his outbursts. "Make use of it all. Don't you dare waste him."

Luscia strode back to her mare, feeling no obligation to continue the exchange. She'd come on this excursion for one purpose, and it was not to be disrespected by the al'Haidren to Darakai. She heard him shout his displeasure from where they huddled over the dead buck, but Luscia ignored his remarks. If one indulged the tantrums of a child, one encouraged them—a principle she likewise applied to Zaethan Kasim.

By the time she resettled in her saddle, Marek's scarlet head had emerged through the foliage as he led Dmitri to find the rest of the group. Aksel trotted between their mounts, the white fur of his muzzle bloodstained by a recent meal. Eager to roam freely, the restless lycran had disappeared an hour earlier. Luscia knew he'd find her once finished. She whistled for him to come near, as the presence of her northern predator wouldn't help to calm the already edgy band of Darakaians.

"*Ana'Sere*," Marek murmured through tight lips, though he was still yards away. "Did anyone touch you?"

She knew he really asked if the al'Haidren to Darakai had overstepped his bounds again. Ever since Kasim's intrusion in her common room, the Boreali captaen remained watchful for any excuse to retaliate. Even though the prince had ordered his hound out of her apartment shortly after, her men would not forget Kasim's impudence so easily. In Boreal, protocol required she be spoken to with dignity and respect. It was understandable that anything less would enrage the men who'd sworn to protect her until their final breath.

"*Niit*," Luscia answered the captaen.

When he tilted his head in question, perplexed by her earlier departure, she jerked her chin toward the deer carcass being tied onto the back of a Darakaian's horse and the wound she'd made along its neck. Turning back to Marek, she watched him close his eyes and smile. He understood. As his lips stirred, she knew the captaen offered thanks to the High One for the animal's sacrifice as well.

Unaware of their silent dialogue, Dmitri urged his horse forward until parallel with Luscia. His was a beautiful steed, she had to admit. During their travel to the southeastern border of the outer Proper, the prince had shared how his mare was twin to the headstrong stallion ridden by his oldest friend. Even beyond their dispositions, his Harmonia appeared to be the exact inverse of her sibling. Where Hellion's black hide shone beneath his cotton white mane, her grey body gleamed under a mane that spilt across her neck like ink on a page.

"Ah, Zaeth! Good aim, my friend!" Dmitri cupped his hands and called to the other al'Haidren, then turned to address Luscia. "You took off so fast, I'd hardly enough time to realize what happened! Your man Bailefore insisted we'd find you all by following your wolx here."

"To Aksel, I am pack." Luscia shrugged. "He could pick up my scent a mile away, even in a snowstorm. When he was no longer a pup, we tried to introduce him to another *lycran* pack, but to no avail. The brute kept returning home to me."

"It's amazing, is it not? If not for the diluted war-taint in his veins, this fox-wolf hybrid could not exist," Dmitri said admiringly. "How'd you come to find him in the first place? My maps suggest a fair distance between Clan Roüwen and the Orallach Mountains."

Luscia grinned at the prince's earnest attempt to study every aspect of his realm, even the most remote corners.

"When I was fifteen, my father journeyed to Clan Ciann to convene with their elders. On his journey back, he heard the cries of a lycran pup, either lost or abandoned. Winter was in the wind, and he couldn't bring himself to leave it out there alone." She chuckled, reminiscing on her father's sentimentality. "The mighty Clann Darragh carried Aksel inside his bear-pelt coat the entire trek home."

Bearing the name of Boreal's second forefather, Aksel had undoubtedly fulfilled his calling. Meaning *Champion of Peace*, he was gifted to her more out of necessity than affection. Orien Darragh had sensed that, like the frightened, traumatized pup in hand, adolescent Luscia might find peace in the lycran's companionship. That perhaps Aksel's deep, untroubled breaths could lull her to sleep and help her heal the wounds beneath those marring her neck, after the initial months of turmoil three years ago.

Most nights, Luscia still needed him.

"When you meet those who offer such unwavering loyalty, it is difficult to leave them." Dmitri sighed, his melancholy dragging Luscia's mind back to the present.

She paused. Her hand rose to lift her collar out of habit, where it shielded the ugly evidence of those memories. Quickly, she dropped it to pick up the reins instead. Luscia directed the mare to follow Kasim's men, who led them out of the wood back into the plains. Time was dwindling, and despite Alora's warning to avoid the topic, Luscia was determined to take advantage of the prince's cheery frame of mind. Soundless to most, she instructed Marek to fall back and allow them privacy.

"Your Highness—"

"Dmitri."

Luscia smiled wryly at his insistent tone. "Dmitri...you must expect I wish to discuss the shocking information uncovered yesterday morning. Boreal was already abreast of the deaths in the northern port towns, but not of the cases your al'Haidrens to Bastiion and Darakai seem so familiar with." She risked a glance in his direction and found him nodding in agreement. "I'd like to request permission for our Najjan to investigate these crimes. As the emerging pattern pertains to my House, Boreal should be involved. We deserve the opportunity to seek justice for our own cross-castes. However, they'll need full disclosure—if you'll permit them access through the Unitarian plains to seek it."

"I agree, Luscia, but my hands are tied," he said regretfully, fidgeting with the reins in his hands. "My father entrusted the matter to Commander Kasim. Even as crown prince, I hold little influence in military matters."

"With all due respect, my kinsmen are being hunted, Your Highness. Hunted within this very Proper," Luscia countered, searching his hazel eyes. "Are you unwilling to even try petitioning your father on Boreal's behalf?"

"*With all due respect,* Lady Boreal, those cross-castes are breakaways.

Per the Ethnicam's Accords, they are no longer considered citizens of the House of Boreal." The prince's voice steadied and adopted a new, authoritative tone. "I might concur with your sentiments, but the fact remains that these deaths do fall under Unitarian jurisdiction and therefore must be investigated by the military and the prydes. If time does not favor their efforts, then I may eventually have reason to contest. Unfortunately, for now, both you and I are confined by the same Accords in this matter."

"If you wait to confront the king, more will be sentenced to death by the delay," she sternly warned, though mindful with whom she spoke. "Darakaians do not care for the Boreali, Your Highness. What is a Boreali cross-caste to them?"

"A cross-caste who is not permitted to reside within your own borders. So, what is a Boreali cross-caste to *you*, Lady Boreal?" He candidly shifted in his saddle to face her, waiting for an answer.

Yet it was an answer she could not provide him.

Luscia could not allude to what was at stake. Regardless of the crown that would one day grace his head, a higher allegiance required Luscia to tread cautiously. Upon her Ascension, she, too, became oath-sworn to protect the light sheltered within Aksel's Keep. However much she wished to, Luscia could not speak to Dmitri Korbin Thoarne of the *Dönumn Lux*. Not yet.

"The Boreali way of life can be…difficult for some cross-castes to embrace, as I'm sure you've heard." She severed eye contact and gazed forward, not liking the direction their conversation had taken. "Our breakaways choose to leave because they do not wish to carry our burden or follow our creed. But this does not mean our House has broken from *them*. These deaths are a horrific, legitimate assault against

Boreali blood, and there's no amount of litigation that can diminish that fact."

"My father trusts the House of Darakai to resolve it, and I must follow suit. The cross-castes belong to Bastiion," Dmitri promptly surmised, closing their debate. "I'd appreciate your support in this, Luscia. As al'Haidren to Boreal, your example will set the tone for how your people are to respond to these attacks."

Luscia's lips parted in shock. It seemed the Prince of Orynthia was just like any other Unitarian politician, gathering allegiance with the promise of betterment, but too content to actually challenge anything. She had been foolish to buy into his flowery speeches and late-night conferences. And not only had she fallen victim to Dmitri's moving words, like a naive little girl, but Luscia had also failed Boreal in her first cause for diplomacy.

Anger simmered beneath her alabaster skin. It melded with the sweat coursing down her back, a gift from the unforgiving sun.

They rode in uneasy silence over the next hour or so, while Luscia reevaluated her argument and the conclusion Dmitri had ultimately offered in exchange. She was furious with them both—the prince for proving to be the embodiment of Bastiion, and herself for not seeing it sooner. Had Alora also suffered such constricting disappointment for the last twenty-five years?

Luscia pressed her mare to keep up with the Darakaians, who beat the trail ahead with fervor. A lagoon of tall grasses danced for miles around their party, a peaceful contradiction to the fanatical rush of riders before her.

She shared their urgency. For once they'd returned to Bastiion's inner Proper, Luscia intended to have a long overdue conversation with her captaen.

"Might I ask where we're running off to, *Ana'Sere?*" Marek questioned between strides, evidently concerned by Luscia's impatience as she advanced down the corridor.

"*Niit!*" She whipped around and shushed him. "Not here, Captaen!"

Aware she resembled the very northern zealot Alora had cautioned Luscia against becoming, she hauled the confused captaen along in search of a secluded space, sheer frustration propelling her forward. She recalled a private alcove somewhere along these halls. Luscia had attended Bastiion's trivial functions, stood poised in the face of their mockery, but the time for passivity was over. Her need could not wait.

"*Boleava, Ana'Sere.* If you would just explain your distress, then I—"

Hurriedly, Luscia turned at the next bend, but ran into a chest of maroon damask. The impeccable fabric reeked of ladies' perfume.

"Well, what a treat," came an inviting tenor. "And here I thought we wouldn't see each other today. You were in a quite a rush to find me, Crumpet—in need of a more experienced escort, are you?" Ira Hastings suggestively arched a tidy brow at her.

Shtàka, Luscia cursed silently and frowned, realizing she had begun to adopt Unitarian slang. She had also assumed she'd escaped his company when the al'Haidren to Bastiion declined to join Dmitri's hunt that morning, and she didn't have time for this nonsense.

She looked from Ira, who reclined against the stone wall, to the young courtier beside him, pouting with both hands on her remarkably slender hips.

"Ira, how rude you are!" the courtier scolded, swatting his arm.

"Forgive my manners, *Lady* Crumpet." He winked at Luscia.

"Allow me to introduce my insufferable sibling, Flourette Hastings. There—satisfied, you festering measle?"

"Hardly." Flourette rolled her rust-colored eyes and reached for Luscia's clenched fists. "Ignore Ira, he's such a twiddleton. But you and I, our acquaintance is so belated! His Highness personally asked me to take you under my wing and share how we do things here in Bastiion."

"Did he, now?" Luscia felt her nostrils flare.

"Oh, I don't mind coaching you in a few areas," the girl assured as she openly studied the hair drooping from Luscia's braids, blanching slightly when she noticed the blood in it. "Ahem. Besides, friends share many effects with each other…"

Flourette's eyes jumped to the Najjani captaen, appraising his form. A coquettish grin appeared, and she batted her lashes excessively. Suddenly enraged, Luscia wrenched her hands out of Flourette's and gripped Marek's forearm. A menacing sound rattled from the back of her throat as she stepped around the Hastings siblings, jerking the captaen with her.

Behind her, Luscia heard Flourette gasp. "Ira! Did she just *growl* at me?"

"Yes. Yes, I think she did," Ira answered approvingly.

After another series of rapid turns, Luscia spotted the alcove to the left. Detecting no further pests in the corridor, she reeled Marek into the shadows, eager to move into action.

"By Aurynth, *Ana'Sere!*"

Luscia advanced, pinning Marek against the stone. "The luxiron—where is it?"

"You saw." His lips tensed. "It was confiscated."

"Marek…" Luscia whispered, shaking her head. She propped her leg on the molding, pressing against his own. Her fingers dropped to hike back the fabric of her surcoat where it split along her thigh. "You and I both know that was not all we carried with us into Bastiion." Much like their luxsmiths, Boreali woodcrafters were just as skillful in their expertise, proven by the trunks that Bastiion's own sentry had delivered to her apartments. Namely, the secret compartments built into ever single one of them. Flashing the hilt of Ferocity, she continued, "I've learned there are training spaces on the floor above. I think it's time we christened one."

Luscia saw the muscles of his jaw flex as he peered down at her, registering their rare proximity. She heard his breathing shift to a measured tempo. With each inhale, the plaited leather across his chest brushed her breasts before retreating with the next exhale.

"*Wem.*" Marek swallowed and dropped his eyes to where they touched. "I will gather the men and meet you in thirty minutes." Swiftly, his gaze darted back to meet hers. "What calls to you?"

Luscia smiled with all her teeth.

"Bring me the wraiths."

SIXTEEN

Zaethan

*Z*aethan used a damp woven cloth to scrub the dried blood from his fingers as he walked, welcoming the abrasiveness of the rough material. It was fitting.

His beta kept pace with him on the way to his apartments. Soured proof of today's hunt clung to his outer tunic, and though Zaethan tried to listen attentively as Kumo briefed him on a recent assignment, his eagerness to wash was distracting. He'd not claimed the title of Alpha Zà by having a weak stomach, but this blood was different. Y'siti hands had defiled that buck, and now its corrupted blood coated Zaethan's flesh, taunting him.

"...Dhalili spotted Wekesa's pryde passing through the southern gate this morning," Kumo reported with a frown, as neither man was fond of Zaethan's rival. "She didn't enter the city herself—just sent word through Jabari. I told her to wait for your instructions near the waypoint."

Zaethan halted in the middle of the corridor.

"What?" He blinked, confused. "*Doru,* stop…the commander mentioned the transition of authority over our investigation just yesterday. Wekesa's outfit is supposed to be stationed days away," Zaethan said suspiciously, shaking his head. "Dhalili saw this? Were they his warriors, or did she physically see *him* at the lead?"

Zaethan eyed his beta, anticipating an unfavorable answer. Dhalili Pàdomà was his best scout, and her word was typically more than reliable. Though his father had forced him to send the larger portion of his pryde to the border of Hagarh, Zaethan Kasim was still Alpha Zà of the Darakaian militia, and a boarded alpha required a pair of roaming eyes to shield his position from aspiring *Jwona rapiki*—Fate writers—like Wekesa. Apparently, even a nameless bastard could rise in the commander's favor over his own blood.

Birdlike and light as feather, Dhalili served as his eyes and ears throughout the plains, adept at both speed and discretion. Her slight form, similar to that of an adolescent boy, allowed her to adapt like a chameleon in every setting, become an unsuspecting resource outside his father's scope.

Unfortunately, her talents would not change the truth of his current predicament.

"He is here, *Ahoté.* Dhalili recognized Wekesa's face by that ugly scar you gave him, yeah?" Kumo added wickedly.

Zaethan squeezed the cloth in his fist until it bled onto the mosaic floor. This meant his father had called Wekesa to Bastiion long before their conversation outside Zaethan's quarters, less than a day ago. Enlisting Wekesa must have been his intent from the first mention of the Boreali cross-caste attacks.

"*Shtàka*," Zaethan snarled. "Where is he now?"

"At the docks." Kumo blew out a breath and cracked his knuckles. "Close to dawn, Unitarian sentries found a body floating in the Drifting Bazaar. Same *kakk*, corpse drained. They're down there inspecting it now."

Zaethan's fist met the wall, causing more damage to his already splitting skin than to the ancient rock. Dust particles rained from the ceiling at the impact. Scowling, he wrapped the fresh wound in the woven fabric before he made it worse.

"Zahra paid off the guards outside Wekesa's guest suite to relay his comings and goings, at least," Kumo said, as more dust trickled onto the shoulder of the beta's belted tunic.

"Shh." Zaethan brought a finger to his lips.

"Was only a few crupas, the yancy blockhead." Kumo lowered his voice to whisper and brushed off a third sprinkle of fine powder. "Loyalty runs cheap these days, *uni*?"

"You're the blockhead, cousin. *Now, shut up!*"

Tilting his head back, Zaethan watched increments of dust and soot repeatedly escape creases in the limestone wall. Keeping an index finger at his lips to signal silence, he rested an open palm against the cool rock. Routine vibrations greeted his skin, like a muffled heartbeat from the opposite side.

"Kumo," he ordered, pivoting to his beta without breaking contact with the stone. "Tell Dhalili to keep watch over the gates and inform me of any more visitors. I want Zahra on top of Wekesa's operation within the city, specifically the palace. She is to report both morning and night."

"Ah, yeah…" Kumo paused, blinking at Zaethan's erratic fondling of the walls. "And I, Alpha Zà?"

"Stay near Dmitri until I relieve you."

"*Uni zà.*" The beta lowered his chin and struck his chest, then hesitantly turned to leave. "*Shàlàmaiamo.*"

Zaethan wandered along the corridor, dragging his open palm against the stones as the slight tremors grew stronger. Beating twice, a pause, then twice again, his initial image of a heartbeat suddenly became unsettling. Originally reserved for the local military, Darakai had little need for this wing ever since Dmitri's father secured treaties with neighboring kingdoms, leaving the rooms vacant. Spinning off the main walkway, he took the next left down a narrow, less frequented passage. The pulses led Zaethan through another deserted hall, or so he thought. About to change course, he noticed the outline of a man standing in the shadows, near the door of a forgotten training chamber.

Picking up his pace, Zaethan's fingers rustled over the hilt of his *kopar* as he drew closer. Distant torchlight casted an eerie, inconsistent halo around the intruder's golden mane of hair.

Y'siti.

"You there!" he yelled, gripping his sickle-sword as the vibrations became more audible. "This is a restricted area! Y'siti are *not* permitted on Darakaian floors!"

The Ethnicam allowed the Najjani shadowmen to roam in Bastiion for one purpose: protecting their Haidrens to Boreal. The Najjan blocking the old door appeared to be roughly the same age as Zaethan, which meant he must have belonged to Boreal's al'Haidren. Making it highly probable the younger witch was breaking Unitarian law on the other side.

The thought brought a sneer to Zaethan's lips.

"Open this door immediately," he commanded her man.

Up close, Zaethan watched the shadowman sigh, seeming fully at ease. His stance was immobile. Only blue-green eyes shifted to acknowledge that anyone had spoken at all.

"By refusing to open this door, a chamber under the jurisdiction of the Darakaian military, you condemn your y'siti al'Haidren to more of the Ethnicam's discipline than her actions have already earned her," Zaethan threatened.

Boreali eyes shot to his and narrowed as the shadowman considered the warning. Just when it seemed the man would not yield, he warily cracked open the door and allowed Zaethan to pass through.

He'd not stepped into one of these rooms in years. Nor was there evidence to support another body had either, before today at least. The rhythmic beating boomed louder once he was inside the octagonal space. Tattered mats and filthy equipment couldn't damper the sound when clashes of metal accompanied the ruckus.

For a moment, Zaethan couldn't speak. The criminal display before him was too rare to expel—yet. Gaping, he watched the y'siti wielding their coveted weaponry, moving as if they carried mere cutlery instead of the most magnificent blades in the realm.

Crescent wraiths.

Due to the ban on witchiron, no Orynthian of any House, including Darakai, had come across the deadly instruments in decades. To see them in action was even more unheard of. Beautifully crafted with captivating intricacy, the shining arcs cut through the air like water and proclaimed gravity a human myth. Held in each hand by a shielded center hilt, the shadowmen battled in rotating offensive maneuvers.

No man warred like the Najjan. Zaethan's jaw slackened even further when he saw who warred alongside them.

Two shadowmen faced forward, their backs to Zaethan, immersed in the duel. The witch's ginger henchman carried a strange, vented staff carved from bone that he used to strike the floor repeatedly. The second man stood much taller, whittled from the iciest winters. His snowy fall of hair swung as he clapped in approval.

And in the center, two beings circled each other hungrily.

Between rapid, blurred movements, Zaethan recognized the larger fighter as the al'Haidren's escort from their hunt. Captaen Bailefore, he'd heard Dmitri call the shadowman. The captaen's opponent, notably smaller, fought swiftly, evading his strikes. When he missed a fourth time, Zaethan saw the witch smile widely, laughing aloud at Bailefore's failed attempts.

As to how her evasion was possible, Zaethan couldn't begin to fathom—for the al'Haidren to Boreal fought blindfolded.

The rhythm of the red-haired shadowman keeping time faltered when he realized they'd acquired an audience. Bailefore's face shot to Zaethan, causing his footsteps to stumble in their graceful dance. Not perceiving the change in atmosphere, the al'Haidren sprinted off the wall and flung herself at the Boreali captaen, similar to a falcon diving after her prey. Twisting her surprisingly agile body through the air, an arced talon sliced his shoulder on her descent as he spun to the right, barely in time.

She landed in an animalistic crouch, hardly out of breath. Zaethan felt history creep down his spine. He should have killed her six years ago, when she was still a cub. This y'siti moved faster than the captaen of her own Najjani Guard. She used their sorcery to see without her eyes. It'd made her laugh with pleasure.

Zaethan's dread rapidly shifted to a feeling of triumph. Finally, he had enough evidence to take to Dmitri, to the entire Ethnicam. Boreal's seat on the Quadren would be no more. Both witches would be banished, along with their shadowmen. Zaethan would restore honor to his birthright, to the name of Kasim. He would singlehandedly dethrone the House of Boreal.

Grinning sardonically, Zaethan brought his hands together and applauded their demonstration.

The witch ripped off the black silk blindfold. Her unnerving eyes widened, but he looked away, avoiding them and noting her choice of attire. Instead of the garb expected of her station, she'd donned humble sparring gear: a collared, sleeveless jerkin tightened at the waist over men's trousers, emphasizing the curves of her figure. The y'siti's pale arms showed more muscle than he'd expected—more like his third, Zahra, than a courtier. Most of her ghostly hair was pulled into an efficient knot. His gaze stopped just above the collar of her jerkin, where a taut, withered scar crept toward her earlobe, disfiguring her smooth neck.

The Orynthians believed Boreali skin couldn't bleed. He was happy to see that was not the case.

"Oh, don't stop on my behalf," Zaethan remarked, picking at a hangnail. "It's a spectacular show. The king will appreciate it, don't you think?"

The one with locks of fire—Bailefore—pushed through the others, wraiths in hand, and shouted some *kakk* in witchtongue.

"I wouldn't suggest that, but your call. *Kàchà kocho.*" Zaethan shrugged, then folded his arms. "First count, illegal contraband on royal grounds." He released a finger to count for the y'siti. "Second, lying about said illegal contraband to royal authorities...hm, that's not so good. *Ano*." A second finger joined its neighbor, followed by a third. "Do we want to add number three, assaulting the al'Haidren to Darakai, to the list? I'd think not. Unless you'd all prefer to be sentenced to death, in which case by *Owàa*, do continue. You have my full support."

Her men began to argue in Boreali, much to his amusement. It was moment he intended to savor.

"Lord Darakai," the sorceress spoke above their disagreement, "my men and I reserve the right to privacy, which you have infringed upon once again. Is this the foundation you want to lay for our diplomatic relationship?"

"I don't *want* a relationship with the y'siti," he spat, earning a snarl from one of the shadowmen. "Nor do any of the others on Dmitri's Quadren."

Staring at Zaethan, she murmured under her breath. The shadowmen glanced between each other and back to their mistress.

"I said, leave us!" She raised her throaty voice to a shout, shocking her men.

Gradually, they laid their witchiron on the floor and departed the room one by one until only the captaen lingered near the door. Raising her brow, she mouthed something to him all but silently in witchtongue.

Her peculiar gaze didn't leave Zaethan's face while she waited for the captaen to exit. Unable to stomach it, Zaethan looked elsewhere. They were wrong, those eyes. One iris of beryl, the other a swirling, iridescent emptiness. Two sinister globes that hosted pupils like delicate pinpricks. Once they were alone in the training room, the y'siti cocked her head and allowed several seconds to pass before speaking again.

"What is it you want, Lord Darakai?" she asked calmly. She knit her hands behind her, as if they merely spoke about the weather.

"I just told you," he spat. "Is your head as empty as your chest? My greatest wish is for the Boreali to be exposed as the treacherous, abominable creatures you are."

"That is only partially true, Zaethan Kasim. Oh, you would enjoy it immensely, that much is plainly evident," she posed, stepping closer to him. "Everyone desires something very few can give. Therefore, I suggest you think carefully in this moment, and ask yourself what it is you *truly* desire."

"What do you know about desire or what I want?" Zaethan's hand flexed around the hilt of his *kopar*. "You aren't even human, you're a *thing*. A plague upon Orynthia."

"I know you are caged by superstition. It's a noose around your neck, suffocating you more every day." She peered down and smirked at something unsaid. "It's time to think, Lord Darakai. Always think before allowing emotions to dictate your path for you."

By her rigid posture, he knew the al'Haidren was not offering what women like Sayuri or Flourette used to manipulate men. Fleeting uncertainty nudged Zaethan to reconsider his plan. On one hand, he could become a hero to Darakai. His actions might result in a war with Boreal. Lives would be lost, but for a cause such as this, Darakai's sacrifice would not be in vain. It was unlikely the Ethnicam would defend Boreal's seat when for the last century, the other Houses had fought to lessen their influence. He would almost certainly be praised, and his father would finally see his value beyond the underlying hatred he held for his son.

Then, Zaethan would never be replaced by a nameless *Jwona rapiki* like Wekesa.

Zaethan shifted his weight to the other foot, along with his thoughts. Orynthia's commander honored Wekesa—he'd brought him into Bastiion against territorial protocol. If Wekesa was in the city, then there was always a chance he'd be given credit for Boreal's fall. Zaethan needed to become his own Fate writer, his own *Jwona rapiki*. For in the event that his father allowed the bastard to rechallenge Zaethan for the title of Alpha Zà, he'd need a new advantage to defeat Wekesa again.

Chance had delivered him the first victory. Only a strong upper hand could deliver him a second.

Zaethan's spinning thoughts traveled to the witchiron blades sprawled across the mats. In all of their history with the Ethnicam, a Darakaian had never carried a set of crescent wraiths. An unexpected coupling of emotions seized his gut.

Jealousy.

Exhilaration.

"The crescent wraiths. That's what I want," Zaethan declared, his decision made. "Teach me."

The y'siti contemplated his trade, taking her time. Finally, she shook her head.

"My men can teach you another blade. Either the *kuerre* or the consort daggers. Whichever you choose, in private, as long as you agree to bind yourself to mutual secrecy."

"*Ano zà.*"

"*No?*" the witch questioned. "Crescent wraiths are advanced Boreali weaponry, Lord Darakai. Luxiron is corrosive. It's unlike anything you've ever handled. You'd likely decapitate yourself and sentence me to execution for it. The former is permissible, the latter is not."

"Despite your arrogance, y'siti are not the only beings capable of prolonged stamina and flexibility. I promise you, I can handle myself."

Zaethan smirked. "The wraiths, or I join the king for a drink and share with him the sweet tale of Boreal's demise."

He watched her bite down. The tension dragged the scar up her neck.

"Fine. Declan or Marek will train you. I will ask them to be discreet."

"*Ano*," he repeated.

"This is tiresome, Lord Darakai." The witch straightened her shoulders. "Are you a child?"

"*You* will train me."

If he was going to study the enemy's blade, Zaethan needed to learn from the victor. She'd fought more fiercely and fluidly than her shadowman. Zaethan would have to become even faster to eradicate her when the moment came.

A low chuckle escaped her shapely lips. It was a shame they were so pallid and cadaverous.

"Let the record show this course is ill advised," she boasted, raising that dainty chin. "We are each beholden to keep this secret. If you utter a word of our arrangement outside this conversation, I will expose you for betraying your own kind by dabbling in, as you so tastelessly put it, *y'siti custom*."

Zaethan assessed the creature before him. Deadly. Underestimated. He wasn't sure how he'd endure training sessions in such closeness without smothering his tutor.

The struggle had better be worth it.

"Then it's settled." Zaethan grinned. "I hope your dead Boreali flesh can face the light of dawn. We start tomorrow."

SEVENTEEN

Luscia

I nquisitive, arctic eyes charted the training space as Luscia tallied the new additions to the formerly forgotten, dirty chamber. Where yesterday lay battered mats and dingy cushions, durable leather replacements rested in their place. Gone were the musky rags that had littered the multiple corners of the room. Instead, various pieces of freshly polished equipment were positioned along the walls, ready for her enlistment.

He'd been busy, this Zaethan Kasim. Luscia peered down at her lycran, her lone confidante, and heaved a sigh.

"What say you, Aksel?" she asked, depositing the wooden globe she carried onto the edge of a mat. "*Wem*, I concur. This is a wretched idea."

An energetic swish of his lush tail conveyed her wolx was in higher spirits that morning than she. Unlike her canine accomplice, it was Lusica who'd agreed to commit some degree of treason. But had she not, defiance of Orynthian legislation could have brought charges of sedition against the entire House of Boreal. After all, each member of her party had concealed additional weaponry in their arrival to the city. Conversely, committing infidelity to Boreal by allowing this adulterous handling of luxiron would implicate Luscia alone, though the disciplinary action would surely be severe.

In an unexpected moment of demarcation, she'd chosen to defy her own House—a feeble attempt to save it from her own folly.

Planting her feet hip-width apart, Luscia rolled her shoulders and initiated a series of standard stretches. A shrill yip pierced her ears. Upside down, she turned to watch the lycran's enormous body spasm theatrically. Opening his elongated muzzle, he released a pink, textured tongue from behind his serrated fangs. Luscia rolled her eyes when he started panting.

"*Niit*," she chastised, and extended her body to the opposite side, savoring the sting of her muscles as they embraced the day. "You are not dying of thirst, you manipulative ogre."

Aksel's rump thumped against the mat in a slobbery huff. Byrnnzite monoliths and unfamiliar scents were not the only elements of life in Bastiion the animal was adjusting to. Though in Aksel's defense, he'd spent the majority of his existence traversing freely, drinking from every body of water he happened upon. Luscia hated instructing Mila to limit his consumption while they resided at court, but she'd hate the inverse exponentially more.

Natural adaption, boosted by the hints of metabolized lumin that bridged the genetic rift between fox and wolf, gave the Orallach hybrid a knack for marking pack territory throughout even the iciest winters. Unfortunately, Aksel refused to accept that it was not wintertime in the highlands, and the last thing Luscia desired was for her apartments to smell like his urine during the heat of a fast-approaching Unitarian summer. Being noxiously pungent, a single accident could take months to dispel from her quarters.

Snaking into her next pose, a distant succession of steps pricked Luscia's ears. "Aksel, *heh'ta*." Recognizing the vexed tempo of the harried pace, she prepared herself for company.

"You are late, Lord Darakai," Luscia remarked as he eased the aged door open.

By his abrupt muteness, she imagined his southern features warping suspiciously at her foreknowledge. She'd never know if it was an accurate assumption, as she didn't bother to face him.

"Wicked y'siti ears," the al'Haidren cursed under his breath. "Damn you all to the Depths."

"*Nii'boleava*," Luscia rotated her stretch to reply. "I'd rather not visit this time of year."

His uncommonly jade gaze narrowed as he greeted her with an unfriendly snarl. It would be tedious to avoid riling him during their sessions. Even in her limited time at court, Luscia had already discovered that it took very little to arouse the temper of Zaethan Kasim. Keeping him in a calm state of mind would be akin to waltzing through a forest of wind chimes in silence—highly problematic, but not impossible.

"I see your witch flesh survived first light." He eyed her arms as if they were combustible. Perhaps he thought they were.

"Highly observant of you," she stated, dodging the barb. "Shall we begin, or would you prefer to spend our time admiring my flair for punctuality in your absence of it?"

His nostrils, the same hue as her morning viridi tea, flared as he constricted his fists. He flicked a glance at the wooden sphere beside her feet. Interesting, what motivated this man.

"Where are the wraiths?" Kasim surveyed the room. "We had a deal, you and I—unless you've decided to withdraw your trade? Our king takes his breakfast early and is not difficult to track down."

"Luxiron will be of no use to you today." Luscia's hand shot out to hush a second threat. "I promised to teach you how to wield the crescent wraiths, and I will. But first, we must prepare your undisciplined Darakaian body to do so."

"The House of Boreal has restricted witchiron for centuries," the opposing al'Haidren cautioned. "My *undisciplined Darakaian* patience has run its course."

"Yet I wonder, in all of those centuries, did Darakai share their prized stallions with the rest of the realm?" Luscia countered.

"Our Unitarian prince rides the twin of my own."

"*Wem*, but your House has never shared them with Boreal."

"And we thought the y'siti would never deign to ask for anything." His ample upper lip curled back to reveal a row of immaculate, well-bred teeth as the obscenity passed between them.

"The point remains," she finished, eager to begin his lesson so she might sooner conclude it. "Do not begrudge the House of Boreal for protecting what they hold sacred. Luxiron blades are far more valuable than a horse."

"Have you ever run an Andwele stallion? I doubt there could be anything more sacred." A distant ember sparked behind his verdant irises, momentarily melting his hostility.

"Then your definition of 'sacred' is rather grounded," Luscia added dryly. She bent to pick up the wooden globe and repositioned it at the center of the largest mat.

"As much as yours is vain, *Lady Boreal*," Kasim muttered, following her lead. "I assume your little ball is supposed to prepare me, then? Did you bring the henchman's stick, too?"

Impatient hands rested on his narrow hips. The other al'Haidren was dressed strangely that morning. A trim but breathable linen vest freed his arms from constraint, whereas his legs stood swathed in draped, loose fabric that tightened at the waist and ankles. Truthfully, it didn't matter what attire the man selected, however bizarre, as long as it allowed him to move.

"The *bomaerod* is not necessary for your kind," she noted, anchoring the sole of her foot on top of the globe to keep it upright.

"My kind?" Kasim's features darkened.

"*Wem.* That is what I said, were you not listening?"

It was not an untrue statement. Naturally, Darakai's fickle al'Haidren would interpret offense where it didn't exist. A Najjani *bomaerod* was not meant for his kind, or any other, as it would deliver him nothing but a migraine, an affliction Luscia was rapidly developing herself.

Kasim's ears were not attuned to the many layers of sound that drowned the senses of the Boreali. During advanced training, the children of Boreal required a tool like the *bomaerod* to focus that clamor by honing it to a limited sphere of impact. Each beating reverberation maintained a field of range. It concentrated one's attention solely on the indicators of activity immediately surrounding them. This aid was particularly essential for Tiergan ears like Luscia's, which were far more sensitive to the constant, buzzing disharmony than those of her own guard.

Not that Luscia could clarify such things to the likes of Zaethan Kasim.

"This," she established, rolling the object under her sole, "is called a *klödjen*. Stand upon it, so we may begin."

Cords of ebony, braided locs swung to the side when he titled his head and assessed the *klödjen*. The fissures of his brow doubled the longer he studied it. Approximately the width of his shoulders, the globe was encircled by a lateral pane of viridi wood, crafted just wide enough to seat a man's boot on either side. Luscia grinned as he scratched the back of his neck before shifting to crack his knuckles.

"If you'd like me to assist—"

"Don't touch me, witch," he hissed and instinctively placed his right foot on the circular panel, weighing it to the mat.

Luscia didn't stop him in his endeavor. She'd seen the routine before. His stubbornness deserved the multiple tumbles he was about to take.

Succeeding with the right, his left heel touched down on the oppo-site side, causing his arms to reach out into nothingness for balance. A proud smirk promptly replaced his scowl. He swung his head to boast in her direction, which disrupted his fragile balance atop the *klödjen*. In a clumsy dance, he plummeted to the mat, landing firmly on his backside.

"Again," Luscia ordered, banishing her desire to laugh. It was going to be a long morning, and chuckling at his misfortune would only prolong it.

He snapped into an upright position. Darakaians despised postures of submission, much less at the feet of a small Boreali woman. Standing, he brushed off his pants and tried again, repeating his initial approach. This time, Luscia watched his knees bend beneath his abdomen, causing him to land directly atop the globe. Being male, she imagined that was far from pleasant and expected it to alter his methodology once he recovered.

It did not.

Again, he collapsed, but to the side this time, crashing upon his hip bone. Then to the other, nearly bending an ankle. He landed on his palms, dislocated his shoulder, and on one attempt almost shattered an elbow. His ordinary bones were so breakable, but he refused to stop.

"*Heh'ta*, enough," she finally interrupted, weary from his failed attempts. "Crescent wraiths rely on three principles—predominantly, balance of the body and mind. The *klödjen* cannot be conquered unevenly. *This*," Luscia emphasized, pushing one side of the viridi panel to the mat, "will never work. You cannot center yourself upon a foundation of unbalance."

"Then how do you suggest one mount your stupid *klödjen*?"

Luscia stilled her mouth. Due to his lingering Darakaian accent, he pronounced the northern term more like *cloud-june*, which in Boreali loosely translated as "master's hog."

"You jump," she answered, spreading her feet apart into a leveled stance. "The whole body must leap from one balanced position to another. Your entire form must commit in order to succeed."

Bending at the knees, she pulled her shoulders back and evened her elbows. With an exhale, Luscia leapt atop each side of the wooden panel and dipped into a crouch to lower her center of gravity. Once secured, Luscia rose into stable position.

Hopping off, she returned to the edge of the mat and nodded at the *klödjen*. "Again."

Grimacing, he mumbled foreign syllables but proceeded to mirror her example. With an angry grunt, he launched himself at the globe, almost overshooting it. Rocking back on his heels, he crouched deeply and waited for the swaying *klödjen* to settle before rising.

"Good. *Waedfrel*. Now, focus on your breathing. Uncontrolled, breath alone can undo this symmetry," Lucsia instructed as she moved to a wall that hosted an assembly of weighted discs. Selecting a few, she returned to his side. "In a moment I am going to touch you, and I'd prefer we not repeat the last hour. Do hold still."

With a fleeting tap of her fingertips, Luscia nudged his forearms to open and extend outward. Choosing one of the discs, she slid the accompanying leather tie over his fist and upward, to rest upon the muscle. Observing he was right-handed, she switched to his left and did the same, yet doubled the weight on the weaker arm. She saw the veins in his forearm protrude beneath it while he adjusted to the difference in heaviness.

"Second, the wraiths demand a balance of strength," Luscia continued as she added another disc to each arm, assessing his frame could handle more. "You have two arms. Both must carry the same burden. Your right is sufficient, but your left is too weak. Without balance of strength, there is no unity. Without unity, there can be no balance in your mobility. And as I said yesterday, neither of us would benefit from your self-inflicted beheading."

The al'Haidren snorted stiffly as he stretched his neck from shoulder to shoulder. "So considerate. What a puzzle, that a heartless y'siti would care about my possible decapitation."

"Despite the bias of your first education, the Boreali are not sorcerers, nor are we heartless." Luscia shook her head, picked up a bag of chalky gripping powder, and began to scatter it over the mat around the circumference of the *klödjen*. "On the contrary, we tend to feel a great many things," she whispered to the floor.

"A bold claim from a House of creatures who hunt their own offspring."

"The murder of our cross-castes is gruesome and tragic." Luscia felt her teeth clench as she rose and positioned her face directly under his, more than a foot higher. "Had jurisdiction been extended to our Najjan, the guilty party would've already been apprehended and brought to justice. Darakai's delay is bought at the price of *our* innocents, not yours. Don't you dare pretend these deaths are of any consequence to the House of Darakai."

A flippant laugh broke free from his flattened lips.

"All I know—" Kasim grunted when his corded forearm constricted under the weight of the disc. "—is that my men never found a slaughtered child floating in the water like another stall in the bazaar until your colorless kinsmen entered my city."

A wave of vertigo washed over Luscia's senses. Alora had never mentioned a body in the bay. His tone was callous, but lacked any trace of sarcasm. The al'Haidren wasn't misleading her; he thought she'd already known.

Luscia put space between them, as if his nearness made the words truer. Methodically, she dusted the gripping powder from her palms and clutched them behind her back to bridle their shaking. Luscia needed to inform Alora straightaway, but a rush to her side might solidify Darakai's suspicion of Boreal's role in the cross-caste deaths. An absurd deduction, but substantial enough to threaten her House's insecure standing with the Ethnicam.

"The third principle," Luscia managed, "is sheer endurance. The resolve of the wielder must be greater than the discomfort of his circumstance. The chalk will reveal how many times you dismount. Your objective is to do so only once, when you can endure no longer."

"That's it? *This* is your lesson?" The al'Haidren scoffed, irritation calling a flush to his angular cheeks. "How much time do you expect me to waste standing here like this? An entire hour?"

"If you consider a mere hour the extent of your endurance, then *wem*. Yes."

At her challenge, he sucked his teeth defiantly. "What is the record?"

"Twenty-six."

"Hours?" The corners of his lips fell, teasing hers to rise. "Twenty. Six. Hours?"

"Darakaians really do have terrible hearing."

Kasim blinked at her mutely. It was the most pleasant he'd been all morning.

"If you'll excuse me, I've much to accomplish today," Luscia offered in lieu of a farewell, and started toward the old door.

"You aren't seriously going to leave me here, standing on this *kakka-shtàka* wooden ball!"

"The only assistance I could possibly provide would be to clean you once you've pissed yourself. But, since you've made it abundantly clear how you feel about my being—what was it? Ah, *wem*, a 'plague'—I trust you'll manage."

With a snap of her fingers, Aksel trotted to Luscia's side, growling at Kasim in passing. She wrenched the door open by its rusting handle, ready to be rid of him.

"The record," he suddenly called out. "Which of Boreal's men can claim it?"

"None." Hesitantly, Luscia brushed her chin over her shoulder. "I do. Good day, Lord Darakai."

Entering the solitude of the dank passageway, Luscia tore into a soundless race toward the Boreali suites, praying to the beat of her boots. Another cross-caste child, dead.

Aniell help them.

EIGHTEEN

Luscia

L uscia's fingers scrambled desperately for the vial.

Only minutes into Luscia's trek to her apartment, the episode seized her entire nervous system. Searing, exploratory needles stemmed from each temple in search of the other. Despite the paralyzing intervals of pain, she remembered tying a single tonic under her tunic, just above her mother's dagger.

The privacy of darkness held Luscia captive within the winding, abandoned corridor. She tried to shush the shrill, whimpering lycran while she fumbled with the stopper of the vial and swallowed her aunt's acrid remedy. Condensation enveloped her now-dampened skin, adding a chill to her feverous delirium. Luscia pressed her forehead against the wall as her hands cleaved the masonry. Each fissure in the stone marked a different loved one she pleaded to, begging just them to take away her agony. Panting, Luscia pressed her cheek into the rock and waited for the pressure to subside.

This is the price of my unfaithfulness, she whimpered to herself.

Luscia wasn't worthy of the High One's mercy and wouldn't dare beg Him for it. She'd broken her covenant to Boreal, to *Aniell*, by agreeing to teach Darakai's al'Haidren how to wield their sacred blades. Luscia submitted to the piercing penance willingly; the shame was hers alone to bear.

An unknown number of minutes passed before Luscia's vision sharpened and her chest expanded to its true fullness again. Beneath her touch, Aksel's ears twitched irregularly. The disorienting, buzzing fog slowly evaporated, revealing the distant voices that had caught his attention.

Silently, Luscia eased away from the wall. She and the lycran were not alone.

"No, you lied to me! I put a lot at stake for this agreement, Naborū!"

Luscia shook out the remaining cloudiness in her ears.

"I offered you an opportunity. It's no lie you needed my assistance. Would you prefer your lordly debts come to light, Felix? You've always been a gambler. Will the Province of Galina celebrate the habits of their Lord Ambrose, or condemn them?"

Preoccupied by their brisk exchange, the two men had not yet detected her presence. Unfortunately, they were about to. That turnoff ahead was the only passage in the direction of the Boreali suites.

"This was not *part of our bargain, Naborū! Fix it. Now!"*

"I cannot reverse what you've elected to become, Felix. But I warn you

not to forget with whom you're speaking. You were nothing to Galina before I extended my resources to satisfy your…appetites."

Luscia didn't wait for the conclusion of their dispute—she had no desire to hear what despicable arrangement it entailed. She released the knot caging her mane at the top of her head, raked her fingers through the tangled ends, and smoothed the wrinkles out of her sparring tunic. None could learn of Luscia's disgraceful pact with Kasim, least of all Tetsu Naborū, the notoriously shrewd Haidren to Pilar.

With a groan, Luscia rushed down the corridor at her original pace, clucking at the lycran. "Come along, Aksel, I don't have all day," Luscia called, raising her voice as she rounded the upcoming turn.

Though the passage was dimly lit, Luscia witnessed an abrupt shift in the men's countenance. Ambrose, she deduced, was younger than anticipated. His untrained yancy build, similar to that of Ira Hastings, posed her no threat. Regardless, he promptly stood as lordly as he presumed himself to be and jerked on a pair of fine gloves, as if he was ready to leave. Squinting at her approach, the hue of Ambrose's eyes was indistinguishable, though it aligned with the rich coloring of his noble Unitarian skin and even richer curls.

An odor cradled her nostrils, akin to the sickening tinge of sweet onions just as they've begun to rot. Luscia's bravado receded when she faced Ambrose's companion.

Luscia would not have believed Tetsu Naborū, to date Pilar's wealthiest Haidren and Shoto Prime, could possibly fall victim to something so ordinary as addiction, especially that of common pipe marrow. Its cloying scent explained the unsightly yellowing of his eyes, which melted into his waxen complexion. The sallow skin over his cheeks was pulled taut by the slick loop of oiled hair fastened at the nape of his neck.

"Little Lady al'Haidren," he crooned. Naborū flipped his head studiously on its side, resembling a featherless owl. "I wonder what could have possibly brought Boreal's fledging here, to *our* clutches, this morning? Tell me…" She tried not to gag when he leaned closer. "…do you and the crossbreed often play in ancient shadows?"

Luscia didn't respond, and the Haidren did not compel her to. Instead, he raised two spindly fingers and twirled the tapered hairs of his sharp beard around the claw of his pewter nailpiece.

"I wished to walk the lycran about the palace to better familiarize him with our new home," she said carefully, unnerved by his probing interest. "We were not welcome on this floor and made to leave. I quickly became lost, but I believe this direction leads to an exit. We should be on our way."

Inclining her head to both men, she took a step around the pool of Naborū's billowing white robes. With a nauseating gulp of stale pipe marrow, Luscia looked up to find his calculating, jaundiced eyes dangerously near her own. Aksel snarled at Naborū, and bile climbed the walls of her throat.

"Even the great, *venerated* Alora Tiergan came to learn her place." Reedy, chapped lips hissed her aunt's name as if it were a curse. "And so I ask you, little al'Haidren—will her niece?"

Luscia's diaphragm constricted. Logic promised the willowy, opiated man couldn't inflict any real harm. But as the ache in her skull returned, his nearness threatened logic to reassess its claim.

"She should hope so," Naborū warned, easing back barely enough to permit their passing.

With a single snap of her fingers, Luscia mutely led Aksel away from the Haidren to Pilar. Keeping an unassuming pace, she refused to look back. When the hulking double doors to her apartments finally came into view, Luscia sailed into her makeshift haven. Inside, she pitted her back against the wood and pressed her eyes shut.

"Lady Luscia, thank the High One!" a woman cried, disrupting Luscia's solace. "They've been out searching all morning for you, your men have!"

"Tallulah." Luscia sighed; another complication of her contract with the younger Kasim. "*Meh'fyreon.* I began the day walking unaccompanied. It becomes oppressive, constantly being around the others." She despised the sour tang of the half-lie. "But more pressing is my aunt—do you know where I might find her?"

"*Ana'Mere* has left the city," Tallulah answered, tears collecting along her sparse lashes. "They found an orphaned cross-caste dead in the bay, and…the Peerage denied her request to send the body to the nearest Boreali kin in Port Tadeas. The Haidren to Bastiion, him being M-Minister…he overruled the Peerage, b-but only under the condition that *Ana'Mere* escort the body herself." The maid sniffled into a handkerchief. "They ordered her to r-remove the remains and depart before noon."

Tallulah reached into the swollen pocket of her apron and retrieved a folded scrap of parchment. Offering it to her mistress, the maid's oversized teeth bit back a freckled lip as Luscia read the hurried script.

Luscia,

I trust Tallulah relayed the urgency of my departure, as you were nowhere to be found. I do hope your absence was purposeful. While I am away, do not respond brashly to these events.

Submit emotion to reason. We must trust His Majesty to seek justice for Boreal.

Ethnicam eyes watch for any misstep.

rul'Aniell,

Alora

Luscia delicately refolded the parchment, her lips pursed. It was irrational to take offense from her aunt's instruction, but she felt rebuked all the same. Discrediting the sting, Luscia gently thanked the maid and sought the canopied terrace outside her bedroom for air.

Not a moment later, a crash of oak and stone had Luscia whirling around as the captaen of her guard stampeded into the apartment. By the tremors across his forehead, he wasn't pleased.

"LUSCIA!" Marek barked as he marched into her bedroom, trapping her on the balcony. "Not one, Luscia. Not *one* Najjan knew your whereabouts. You left your entire guard behind! Here, in this yancy shrine, of all places!"

"Am I a prisoner in my own apartments, Captaen?" Two alabaster fingers shushed his lecturing. She was not his inferior, and it was a gross overstep to speak to her as such. Her spine straightened as she leveled her gaze, "There are elements of my station which require attention outside of this room."

"Your father holds me accountable for your safety! In the name of Aksel's Keep, why did you conceal yourself from us?" Marek demanded.

"Perhaps I needed space from my warden. He's insufferable."

"An al'Haidren is to be protected at all times, Luscia." Marek scratched the rust-colored stubble on his jaw in visible frustration. "You don't get to have these juvenile disappearances anymore! And certainly not here."

Luscia's face felt aflame.

"I do not answer to you, Marek Bailefore," she said, flattening her voice and staring into his strained, oceanic eyes. "Do not allow your speech to turn so informal with me. You may be my father's choice, but you were not mine. If I must submit to rank, so must you."

Marek's gaze plummeted to his wrist. Trailing his line of sight, she saw her father's beaded cuff tied snugly around it. Flooded with shame, her chest caved in.

She'd rejected his *kurtfrieri*, a token of courtship, when he'd offered it on the eve of her Ascension. Luscia stared at the beads in the lacing, rebuking herself. It was extremely unusual for a suitor to wear the *kurtfrieri*, for if accepted, it was worn by the suited. The cuff's prominent display implied that Marek still waited to be acknowledged; for Luscia to change her mind. She'd not handled their conversation graciously that night, and she was cruel to so callously remind him of it now.

"Marek, I—" Luscia moved toward the cuff, but her hand fell, unwilling to take it from him.

"*Tadöm, Ana'Sere*, for reminding me where we stand," he whispered vacantly. "*Meh'fyreon*, for forgetting. It won't happen again."

His nose twitched as the captaen quietly bowed his head, and left.

Luscia swallowed, watching him depart. Though he wouldn't admit it, she'd been justified in rejecting him that night, for there simply wasn't reason enough to accept his courtship. She had no need for a union, not until conditions require her to continue the line of Tiergan. Having just embarked into her new life, Luscia wasn't ready to lay down her blades, or her independence. And were he to be honest, neither was Marek.

A midday breeze swept her reddening cheeks, guiding her to look out over the colorful floating stalls below. Luscia slumped against a limestone column, guilt and resentment coiling her thoughts. Children were being butchered, tossed like trash into those very waters, while she was forced to become an idle figure, watching by. Were Luscia to gather her weapons and seek answers herself, her own Najjan would remain an obstacle. The men were obligated to uphold Alora's mandate for passivity, including the passivity of her niece.

Shaking her head, Luscia glared across the vast openness to the adjacent terrace, where the nearest byrnnzite cupola glimmered in the sun. *Even the servants of Sayuri Naborū-Zuo come and go more freely than I,* she brooded.

Gradually, a sly grin replaced her frown.

"Mila!" Luscia abruptly yelled through her bedroom, into the common room. "Mila, my Aksel is parched. Let him drink his fill."

Balmy air lapped the side of her face, beckoning disobedient hairs to stick to the thin blanket of sweat coating her moonlit skin. One would've imagined nightfall might lessen Bastiion's smothering humidity, but the crown city had proved more disappointing by the day in that respect.

Gripping the decorative cutouts on the palace walls, Luscia became one with the stone as she slid her body along the exterior. Despite confidence in her own nimbleness, Luscia was keenly aware of the steep drop awaiting a fall, should her footing falter. Mentally reciting Boreali poetry to keep her wits about her, she slithered to the edge of a narrow overhang. As she'd done the night prior, Luscia felt for a beam on the underside of the cupola, secured her grip, and on an exhale, hoisted her entire frame to the opposite flank.

Inching toward where the beaming met a column, Luscia pushed her upturned boots against the pillar and ran toward the ceiling of the dome, landing on the balcony in a backward crouch. It would have been perfect, a soundless dismount, if not for the jangle of luxiron blades secured about her person. Luckily silence was not the present priority, considering Sayuri Naborū-Zuo no longer occupied the apartment.

Since her earsplitting shrieks early that morning, the al'Haidren to Pilar had refused to enter her former quarters. Luscia had overheard the entire ordeal as she drank her breakfast cup of ennus and viridi tea. The al'Haidren had screamed to her staff about some fetid odor and demanded her belongings be relocated immediately. Palace staff had yet to find the source of the stench, or a remedy for it.

Luscia grinned. They wouldn't.

She'd ventured into Sayuri's apartment the previous evening with Aksel's contribution in hand, sprinkling lycran waste over every piece of upholstery. Luscia had even coated the wood moldings while Sayuri dreamt, none the wiser. Luscia didn't harbor any remorse for repurposing the al'Haidren's unique quarters—by Mila's testimony, Sayuri had abused the hidden stair to better regulate her inferiors. Under new stewardship, it could be used to save them.

Locating the main chamber, Luscia squatted low and plucked a few hairs from her scalp. Suspending them aloft, Luscia studied the pastel strands for movement. The entire suite had been boarded upon the al'Haidren's transfer, so any breach in the interior wall would emit a subtle draft, though probably imperceptible. Her superior eyes caught a slight sway of the ends and tracked the course of airflow to a massive, ornate armoire, situated in front of a floor-length tapestry.

Moving toward the piece of furniture, Luscia angled her body to shove the hunk of timber away from the wall, only to realize it was fixed in place. Circling it, she knelt to feel under the bottom lip. A cool draft caressed the back of her knuckles.

"How clever you are, Sayuri Naborū-Zuo," Luscia credited.

She had been foolish to assume the entry point would be so blatant. Because Dmitri's grandfather, King Aquila, had the passage sealed, Luscia doubted Sayuri's reopening of it was exactly sanctioned. Ingeniously, Pilar's al'Haidren had concealed her unauthorized stair in plain sight, as just another article of her overzealous decor.

Luscia opened the face of the armoire. There, a few steps inside the piece of bulky furniture, stood a humble wooden door within the stonework. Pausing, Luscia reached into the black cloak concealing her personal armory and produced a round, glossy stone.

Entering the stairwell, she brought the *lumilore* to her lips, the pebble's warmth a familiar kiss of home and history. Luscia inhaled the dank flavor of mildew and let her breath pass over the surface of the *lumilore*, awaking it to life.

A subtle, kaleidoscopic light flooded the emptiness, set off by tendrils of lumin pulsing inside the small stone. Even Tiergan eyes needed aid to see in complete darkness, and the moon could not follow her into the stairwell. Luscia stretched the *lumilore* before her feet, grateful she'd thought to bring it with her to Bastiion. When they were young, Boreali children spent days during *Ana'Innöx* searching for the strange pebbles among the rocky banks of the *Dönumn*. Phalen swore she always found the brightest stones, as his never seemed to shine quite the same.

Luscia smiled tightly, trying not to miss him.

The stair descended in a steep spiral, the quiet stuffier with each step. After what she estimated as seven stories lower, another modest door came into view. Luscia pressed her ear against the rough grain. Muffled, racing chatter and clanking pots indicated the kitchens lay on the other side; a less than preferable route.

Curious, she crept off the landing and slunk deeper, where the temperature dropped to a refreshing chill. At the final door, the whoosh of rushing water beyond met her ears. Luscia cast the *lumilore* about, spotting a soiled pot near her boot.

Gripping the corroded handle of the door, left unlocked, she pushed it open. Luscia dry-heaved at the smell, so much stronger to her nostrils than those of a Unitarian maid. A brackish brew of excrement and sludge flowed past the archway.

After all, who would lock a servant's access to a sewer? Luscia chuckled to herself.

"Pretentious yancies."

She renewed the *lumilore's* glow and studied the architecture. An adjacent ledge bordered each side of the outtake conduit. Luscia entered the slimy tunnel and skirted along to the west. Something flickered in the distance. Following the direction of the flowing muck, the offshoot bent and narrowed until the conduit ended. Brown water spilled over like a murky tongue into an external aqueduct, carrying it away from the palace main. Gulping the newly fresh air, she'd never been so grateful for the seedy odor of the west docks.

Luscia huffed victoriously. Over the edge of the sewer aqueduct sprawled the freedom of the backstreet, stories below.

She pulled her hood over her fair braids and secured a veil to hide most of her northern face. Standing atop the rim of the waterway, Luscia gazed over the trembling embers of decadence and depravity illuminating the night sky.

Unbeknownst to the monsters within, tonight the city of Bastiion would host a hungry al'Haidren to Boreal. Taking a step into nothing-ness, Luscia leapt, eager to greet them.

NINETEEN

Zaethan

Teetering atop the witch's wooden orb, Zaethan's weight bobbed to the side when she offered him another curved rod, mirroring the first in his right hand.

"No, *niit*. Lower your center if need be," the y'siti scolded, strutting to her trunk against the wall. "You breathe, you balance."

"'*You breathe, you balance,*'" he mocked in her raspy accent and bent his knees. "*Meme qondai*, I get it already."

"Then do it without being told."

Zaethan all but fell off the *klödjen*, eager to retaliate, but stabilized himself when the rim almost dipped into the faint ring of powder encircling the base. Last time, he'd gone the entire session without disrupting it. Damn him to the Depths if he couldn't do it again.

"*Waedfrel,*" she remarked as she bent into the trunk. "Get down."

"Yesterday, you kept me on this *kakka-shtàka* ball for over an hour."

"Were you to look—" The y'siti snaked a long, braided whip around her neck and closed the lid. "—you'd realize this is today, and not the day before. Would you prefer we repeat it?"

Zaethan tensed his grip on the rods and jumped off the orb, coming toward her. "One of these mornings you won't be able to run that mouth anymore."

"Because I'll finally be able to sleep in again." The leather whip wrapped around the front of her crisp tunic, where she casually held each end in either hand. "Toward the middle, arcs at the ready."

Unmoving, Zaethan cocked his head at the weapon, noticing flakes of crimson along its tail. Uneasiness stiffened his posture. The witch carried a whip, while he only had two sticks.

"*Ano zà.* Not until you tell me what that's for."

"Incentive," she answered, suppressing a grin. "Now come along and stop pouting."

Her chin lifted defiantly, passing him across the mat, as if she were his equal in height. In reality, she barely stood taller than his scout, Dhalili, who frequently and convincingly impersonated children while gathering intel. The y'siti unraveled the whip, sending its length tumbling to the ground, uncoiling around her feet. Like his, they were naked.

"Crescent wraiths require agility as well as balance. Move too slow, and their length becomes a hindrance. Moving fluid like water…" She furled the whip, cracking it on itself. "…the wraiths become a sphere of death, both offensive and defensive. One weapon, one being. If you are unable to sustain their momentum, the victim is you, instead of your intended."

Zaethan repositioned the curved rods, raising them between his gut and the witch. "You're not using that on me."

The corners of her lifeless lips flicked upward as she tenderly slid the whip through her open palm. "My own Captaen Bailefore used this same *feidierdanns* during my training, on the Isle of Viridis. These bloodstains are proof of his effectiveness." She tilted her neck, scanning him up and down. Shrugging, she sighed, "On a Darakaian, it's unlikely to be worth the time. Few can stomach it."

He knew the y'siti was baiting him. She'd become rather good at it, too. But based on the skill with which she'd wielded the wraiths alongside her captaen two weeks ago, he also knew she was telling the truth.

Flexing his shoulders, he hoisted the rods in the air and gritted his teeth.

Her unnatural eyes twinkled with excitement. "Start spinning."

Several hours later, at another one of Dmitri's useless Quadrennal meetings, Zaethan watched the y'siti crane her ghostly neck from across the historic pentagonal table.

How he wanted to strangle it.

Zaethan's toes curled while Ira blathered on. It was miraculous that Gregor's son had managed to button his own coat today. The smell of stale ale wafted off his lapel. Zaethan readjusted in his chair, trying not to wince at the sharp pain in his feet. He refused to give the y'siti any gratification by hinting at the lingering sting of the shallow cuts she'd made. Irritatingly, the gauze stuffed inside his pigskin boots only made things worse.

Weeks under her peculiar and rather vexing tutelage, she still avoided the crescent wraiths. Consequently, he imagined the y'siti's death on a regular basis. He might've moved to orchestrate it—she'd certainly driven him mad enough—were it not for the subtle enhancements her training had made to his balance and endurance. *Shtàka*, even his posture. Zaethan would never admit it aloud, but the northern methodology had even started to influence his drills with the palace guard, as well as his exercises with the pryde.

"Lady Boreal, you've stayed silent the majority of this debate. I'd love to hear your perspective on the matter," Dmitri ventured, halting Ira's passionate insistence that his estate would serve as an optimal venue for royal guests.

Faint shadows pooled beneath the y'siti's cryptic eyes, adding to her spectral appearance. He'd noticed them earlier that morning, when she'd lashed his feet as he spun in circles like a fool. By the time he ended their session in favor of the sentry drills, he'd left her standing upon a scarlet canvas of his own making.

Damn her to the Depths, Zaethan thought with a scowl, knowing it would only make him faster tomorrow.

"I'm not convinced the best use of this Quadren is to discuss lodging arrangements for the Queen of Razôuel during their official visit." Disinterested, the witch spoke to the table, but eyed Dmitri intently. "The Zôueli are no strangers to massacre. Perhaps they would enjoy the newest attractions of the Drifting Bazaar."

Zaethan's eyes narrowed at Sayuri's knowledge of the body pulled out of the bay upon Wekesa's arrival to Bastiion. But then again, what need did the valley pryde have for confidentiality. Court rumor was their ally, anything to bolster confidence in Wekesa's investigation.

"It *is* a ma-massacre." Ira hiccupped back into his seat. "The price those greedy merchants demand for the *shtàka* they tout is criminal!"

"Lady Boreal raises a real concern." Sayuri brushed her jet hair over a glistening shoulder, baring it for Dmitri as if it were a cup of sweetened cider. "We certainly can't parade the Zôueli queen along Thoarne Bay, not after it's been polluted with Boreali scum. It's an embarrassment, really," she added haughtily.

"Lady Pilar, this Quadren mourns the loss of—"

"Another exotic prize, squandered." Ira threw his courtier hands in the air, cutting off the prince. "My father has yet to replace our northern cross-caste! They were rare to begin with!"

It amazed Zaethan how the witch did not move to strike either of them. His feet stung, the pain a vivid reminder of the violence her petite frame could inflict; the confidence she masked under layers of poise and linsilk. Even he, a Darakaian alpha, was sickened by the recent crimes against the north's forgotten children. Each an innocent, lost to Bastiion's cruelty.

Had it been Darakai's cross-caste floating in the very public waters of the Bazaar, Zaethan would've painted each al'Haidren in bruises for their privileged snobbery.

"I will never understand why you trouble yourself, Ira." Unconcerned, Sayuri trailed three elegant fingers to the base of her throat. "What is your father willing to pay for another? A few silver dromas? His gold?" She slunk leisurely into her seat and peered through thick lashes at the y'siti. "How can any creature be worth an entire auras when it looks just as dead while it's still alive?"

"Lady Pilar!" Dmitri exclaimed, stunned.

A loud *thump* sent tremors across the tabletop, rattling the glassware.

At last, the y'siti stood. Her grip tested the limits of the wood table. Although she uttered not a single word, her expression spoke volumes. A flush of rage erupted over her taut cheekbones. Zaethan squinted at her. He could've imagined it, but he swore the ends of her hair lifted, floating in a nonexistent breeze.

Her Orallach beast bared his elongated canines at Sayuri. It was insulting that the same animal had slept contently while his mistress whipped Zaethan's feet just hours prior.

"Today's session is concluded." Dmitri gathered his walking cane abruptly. "All but Lady Boreal are dismissed. Please, leave us."

Zaethan stood with the others, but had no intention of leaving them alone.

"She's rabid, Ira," Sayuri declared as the al'Haidren to Bastiion opened the door for them to exit. "Absolutely *rabid!*"

Dmitri looked expectantly to Zaethan. In a wordless exchange, Zaethan's gaze bounced to the upset y'siti and back to his charge. There was danger in isolation, and the prince knew it. Nevertheless, Dmitri's eyelids fell before he tilted his chin toward the corridor, a clear reinforcement of his earlier dismissal. Bridled into obedience, Zaethan downed the remainder of his *bwoloa,* slammed the glass onto the tabletop, and left Orynthia's foolish prince to learn for himself.

Entering the lofty, sweeping hall outside the Quadrennal chambers, Zaethan kneaded the back of his neck as he turned eastward, toward his office in the guard house. Suddenly, his arm dropped rigidly to his side. Near the wall of arched windows, brightly lit by the midday sun, General Lateef nodded in conversation with a braided man. While the alpha's face wasn't in view, the wicked scar on the shaved side of his skull was enough to identify his rival. Zaethan's teeth ground against each other.

Wekesa.

Zaethan approached them, making an effort to relax his shoulders. "*Owàamo,* General."

"Ah, *owàamo,*" General Lateef muttered with a gruff nod. "Alpha Wekesa and I were waiting for your little cub party to disband. The commander asked that we relay your orders before joining him to evaluate Wekesa's pryde and their assignment in the Proper."

The general gestured at the third man, who reclined smugly against the nearest column.

Zaethan took his time assessing his rival, savoring the intimate view of the scar he'd carved into Wekesa's head during their final challenge. It had not healed well, but in an unseemly patchwork of discolored flesh. Unblinkingly, Zaethan met Wekesa's coal eyes. They were usually ravenous, each poisoned with an unquenchable anger. Never changing, even when they were cubs in child's play. But today, a spark of victory had settled in his dark irises; a spark Zaethan needed to extinguish before it grew into a wildfire.

"Zaethan," Wekesa said in place of an appropriate greeting, jutting his long chin higher.

Taking two steps forward, Zaethan squared his shoulders and brought his chest an inch away from the subordinate alpha.

"Again," Zaethan coolly suggested.

"*Owàamo,*" Wekesa bit out, though his line of sight did not waver, "Alpha Zà."

Zaethan gave him a lazy grin before pivoting back to Lateef. "What orders do you bring me, General?"

"Our commander has arranged the delivery of certain...southern indulgences…for the king's private enjoyment. Tonight's shipment requires a stand-in," the general explained. "You are to arrive at The Veiled Lady at quarter past midnight and retrieve the next shipment from Salma Nabhu. She is expecting a proxy. Order the 'Crown Special' at the tavern bar. You will be escorted to her office. Take the shipment and bring it to a Darakaian cross-caste named Druska, in the kitchens. He will see it's delivered to the king's chambers."

Zaethan swallowed the bitterness foaming in his mouth. Wekesa watched his features as they contorted, obviously anticipating Zaethan's poor reaction to the assignment. It was an *errand*. His father had sent Zaethan's greatest rival to deploy him on a smuggler run.

"*Shamàli,* General, might I volunteer one of my pryde or a less recognizable party?" He phrased the request carefully, so as not to question his superior.

"*Ano zà.*" Lateef jerked his head, leaving no room to refute. "Your father's orders were very specific. He also tasked me to relay that, had you not been late the past week of morning drills, he wouldn't have to assign you during the night. Like yourself, he says, smugglers are not known for their punctuality."

Zaethan heard a snicker from behind and shifted to see an arrogant smirk pulling Wekesa's rough skin into a series of creases. He made no attempt to hide it, for Wekesa didn't need to anymore. Their commander called him *Jwona rapiki*, and it would not be long until Wekesa attempted to write over the fate of Zaethan's victory for the title of Alpha Zà.

Without an unexpected advantage, Wekesa could take it. He could rip it away. Zaethan knew it, as did his rival. It wasn't overconfidence, it was acknowledgment. Had Wekesa not slipped in the wet earth as it had begun to rain that vicious day of their challenge, the ugly scar he now bore would've marked Zaethan as inferior. It had been intended for him until that timely downpour, and neither man was able to forget it.

"Fine," Zaethan said, then turned to address his rival. "But before I go…Wekesa, starting tonight, five of your pryde will pull double rotation in the Proper. *You* may report directly to the commander now, Wekesa," he added darkly, "but your pryde still belongs to me. Their efforts have been futile, so I will give them no relief until this killer is found. And for each new body discovered, another in your pryde will lose sleep. *Yeye qondai?*"

Wekesa's wide nostrils flared. "*Uni.*"

"Again!"

"*Uni. Zà. Alpha. Zà.*" Emphasizing each syllable, Wekesa sluggishly brought his right fist to his heart and then let it swing limply to his side.

Zaethan's gaze lingered on Wekesa before remembering the general. "*Shàlàmaiamo,* General. I will see that my father's task is carried out."

Striking his chest, he lowered his face to their superior and was just turning to leave when the doors of the Quadrennal chamber slammed into the adjacent wall. The witch released a snarl of frustration as she and the wolx stormed in the opposite direction, ripping a string of metal beads out of her own hair in the process. She looked positively feral, and Zaethan's jaw clenched at the soreness in his boots.

That y'siti better show her witchiron soon, he thought, *or I am going to cut it off her.*

Zaethan's index finger circled the rim of his glass impatiently before he kicked back the contents with a grimace. The *bwoloa* seared his gut as it made impact. It tasted terrible.

Zaethan hated cheap *bwoloa*.

"Another," he barked to the tightlipped barkeep. He slid two copper crupas to the man, who grunted in response.

It was unclear whether the fellow was unable to respond, or simply refused to add to Zaethan's illuminating conversation as he waited inside The Veiled Lady. After Zaethan ordered the "Crown Special", the barkeep disappeared for a handful of minutes only to return in utter silence. It'd been an hour since then, and patience was not a prominent quality of Kasim men.

He spun on the stool to resume his watch over the tavern and its evening rabble. Packed with thirsty yancies and tired sentries, Zaethan estimated Salma would be content with her profits tonight. A diverse array of beautiful women swathed in colorful scarves catered to the gambling tables, their laughter and flirtation enticing poor fools into deeper debt. In the darker corners, curtains disguised pockets of pleasure and pathways to the tavern's darker dealings. Salma Nabhu was a true entrepreneur who understood the value of limiting supply to a sea of demand.

Lukewarm glass touched his forearm. The barkeep nudged it across the lacquered wood and pointed to a staircase opposite them, where Salma waited at the top. With a graceful crook of her finger, she gestured for him to ascend before again disappearing behind a fall of heavy fabric.

"About time," Zaethan grumbled.

Clutching his drink, he pushed between the drunken patrons and made his way up the narrow steps. Sweeping the drape of opaque velvet to the side, he entered a dimly lit hallway. His entry was immediately halted by two meaty guards: one Unitarian, the other a Darakaian cross-caste like Salma, each taller than Kumo.

An inviting chuckle drifted toward them from a cracked door at the end of the hall. Flickering light danced over the maroon damask rugs inside the room.

"He is the one, Ràoko," Salma called to the cross-caste, who appeared to be her appointed lead. "I must speak to the *jaha*."

Permitted to pass, Zaethan offered the surly guard a toothy grin and strolled into Salma's private office. Tipping an imaginary hat, he winked at the middle-aged businesswoman.

"You certainly know how to keep a man waiting, Salma." Zaethan took a seat on the divan and raised his half-empty glass. "I was starting to wonder if all I'd get from you is this cut-rate *bwoloa*."

"And still you kept buying it." Her eyes sparkled deviously. "But eh, it is a treat to see you, *Jaha*. It's been too long since you joined your men, yeah?"

Salma rose fluidly from her satin armchair and crossed the room to an ornate, wooden desk.

"They do fine without me. Takoda won't shut up about some new *yaya* you recruited." Zaethan rolled his eyes toward the ceiling. "He'd probably drag her home to Halona if he could."

"*Uni*, if he could. The girl does well here, happy, fed, with family. He comes often, your cub warrior." She bent to pick up a shabby crate, the clinking indicating its contents. "But I was pleased to find it was you who came for this, not he."

Salma rested the crude box on the short table between them. Drawing back the pigskin duster, she revealed a set of dark red bottles. Zaethan sucked in a breath. Apparently, Orynthia's king had developed a taste for *pammu*. Mworran *pammu*.

Zaethan rubbed his chin, considering the bottles on the table which could only be obtained through some very risky black-market trade. "This is highly illegal, Salma."

"Eh, but what isn't these days?"

"It's a dangerous game, playing the hands and feet in the transaction of another."

"You should know, son of Kasim," Salma quipped, "for we are sitting here together."

She produced two goblets and commenced pouring the syrupy liquid. It reminded him of clotted gore. When Salma proceeded to fill the second, Zaethan hastily covered it.

"*Ano, ano.* None for me." He shook his head adamantly, adding a polite "*shamàli*", when she gestured to his *bwoloa* in hand. "I've already had enough for one evening."

"You amuse me, *Jaha,* still clinging to our native tongue and its leash." Salma fell back and laughed musically. Her tight coils bounced as she gracefully rested her chin upon the edge of her hand. "A proper 'please' or 'thank you' doesn't sting too much, yeah? Surely a little indulgence wouldn't hurt." The look in her eyes made it clear that *pammu* wasn't all Salma was offering.

"We all maintain our allegiances," Zaethan said, brushing off her suggestion. "Besides, how do I know this brew isn't as foul as the *shtàka* your barkeep serves, eh?"

"I test my product personally," she emphasized, taking a slow sip of the dark red liquor. "I'm surprised it doesn't suit your palate."

"As a general rule, I tend to avoid bloodlike brews when they're smuggled in from a nation of cannibals."

While the rumors were simply that, one could never be sure that fermented pam sap and withered beetles were the only contents of a bottle coming out of Mworra. Orynthia was technically at peace with the Mworrans, but all trade with Calluc, their largest mining tribe, was currently outlawed due to the longstanding conflict between Mworra and Razôuel, Orynthia's highly temperamental ally. Zaethan's father was tempting many political forces by contracting Darakaian smugglers to secure the Mworran liquor, even for the king.

"Men gravitate toward mystery." Salma wiped a drop of *pammu* from her moistened lip. "Taste is not so different."

"Mysteries are dangerous," Zaethan remarked, setting down his empty glass in order to latch the crate and grip it in both hands.

"As are the rules which require them, *Jaha*," she replied in a strange tone, then called for her lead guard.

Salma didn't glance up from her goblet when the Darakaian cross-caste appeared in the doorway. "Ràoko, show our loyal friend to the alley stair so he may exit discreetly. Goodnight, *Jaha*." She lifted her lichen eyes to meet Zaethan's and added affectionately, "May Àla*'maia* watch you tonight as fondly as I do."

"*Shàla'maiamo*, my favorite *yaya*." Zaethan smiled in parting and followed her man into the hall.

Though the crate wasn't heavy, it was certainly cumbersome to maneuver down the constricted stair, which was barely wide enough to accommodate Ràoko's hulking shoulders. Zaethan shuffled around his trunk of a torso at the base of the landing, wincing as the bottles jostled. Receiving an expected grunt to his farewell, he stepped out into the shadows of Marketown's alleyways, thinking Salma needed to reevaluate the charisma of her staff.

Turning onto an abandoned footpath, the odor of piss and garbage clouded the air. A few yards off, Zaethan made out the shape of a boot where a drunken yancy slumped on the ground, passed out. Continuing onward, he caught an indistinct movement in the darkness. It shifted near the form Zaethan had mistaken for a yancy, revealing a dirtied, lifeless, empty face.

Crouched inches from it was the slim profile of a hooded figure.

Rushing toward the crumpled body, Zaethan's stomach dropped when the fair profile twisted and stopped him with unapologetic, inhuman eyes. He caught the crate in his arms just as it began to fall.

"*You!*"

TWENTY

She moved swiftly, as if she weighed no more than the sheer, midnight linen veiling her features. A face that strongly favored her father, yet held so little of Eoine; of Alora. Luscia Darragh Tiergan embodied the shadow, as skillfully as any Najjan, and he often felt as if he was chasing a wisp.

From the heights of Marketown, the figure had trailed his mistress's niece for a fortnight. Initially, her haphazard routine had perplexed him. Each night, the young al'Haidren ran through Bastiion's streets, eventually navigating back to the palace. Only last night had he realized that she'd completed a spherical formation. By charting the imagined spokes on a wheel, night after night, Alora's niece was mapping the city Proper.

From memory.

The figure leapt from one rooftop to the next, two buildings behind her. It was difficult to keep up without drawing attention to his presence. Amaranth's lilac feathers rustled as the hawk dove ahead, recognizing their game. Below, the little al'Haidren dodged a vacant stall, jumped to an overhang, vaulted her body through the empty space, and caught a railing off a second-story ledge. Without decelerating, she surveyed the street from her new, higher vantage point.

Approaching a junction between structures, she flew around a corner and froze. Alora's niece cocked her head, listening. The figure shrank back when she peered over a shoulder into the night. When she turned forward again, seeming pacified, he crept along once more, pulling the scratchy hood tighter over his unevenly balding scalp for concealment. The material aggravated the fresh sores and tempted infection, but he couldn't risk being seen.

After another block, she halted abruptly and frantically glanced about. As she pressed a pale hand to her skull, the figure leaned forward, concerned. Reaching into her cloak, she withdrew a familiar vial—one of Alora's—and hurriedly drank the contents. Shaking her head as if something rattled inside, she took two steps, then paused again. Angling herself a second time, the figure strained to hear what had caught her attention so intently.

Rash laughter from a nearby tavern tickled his blistered ears. An elderly woman coughed in a merchant tent. A group of men squabbled in the next. Blocks away, an infant's cry pierced the common melodies of Bastiion Proper.

Without warning, the al'Haidren took off. Bounding forward, she bolted into a maze of abandoned alleyways. When she finally stopped, the figure caught himself before he careened into the open, panting wildly. A strange nostalgia awoke his lungs. It'd been ages since he'd needed to gasp for air.

He watched her hesitate before entering a soundless backstreet, as if being irresistibly drawn into its depths. Carefully, he kept pace with her from above until she came to a halt and collapsed to her knees.

"*Niit*," he heard her breathe out.

The figure's decaying insides contorted. Beside Alora's niece rested a cross-caste corpse, propped against soiled brick and mortar. Squinting, he distinguished an adolescent in a tattered velvet dress. Moving to touch the lifeless face, the al'Haidren's eyes started to glow. Their light flickered with what he presumed were unseen threads of lumin, mingling around the body. Furrows of concentration decorated her brow as she witnessed an invisible dance the figure could not see.

Entranced, he didn't notice the intruder until it was too late. Panicked, the figure searched the skies for Amaranth. He'd remain hidden unless there was no alternative.

Gradually, Alora's niece tore her attention from the corpse and stared blankly at the man. He fumbled with a crate in his hands, adjusting his grip to avoid dropping the burden he carried.

"*You!*" he said accusingly.

She offered no reply. The figure chewed on his scabbed lip. Whoever the intruder was, he'd recognized the al'Haidren's identity immediately, even under layers of masking.

"Step back!" the man shouted with authority. In one swift movement, he deposited the unsteady crate on the ground and unsheathed a Darakaian *kopar* from the weapons belt at his waist. "Back! Against that wall, y'siti, or I'll be carrying the skin of a sorceress into Thoarne Hall."

The figure suddenly realized he'd seen this man before. The night they both gave Yannis the slaver a well-earned beating.

Alora's niece ignored the alpha's derogatory slur and his threat alike. Her disregard seemed to rile him further, and the figure prepared to leap when the Darakaian alpha brought the tip of his *kopar* to her throat.

"Now, Lady Boreal."

She blinked a few times, withdrawing from the Sight. Unconcerned, she swatted the blade away with the back of her hand and untied the veil covering her mouth.

"Why don't you make yourself useful, Lord Darakai?" she said dryly. "Those rampant emotions of yours are rarely of any value."

The al'Haidren to Darakai? What business does the son of Nyack Kasim have in Marketown this time of night? the figure mused, stunned by his appearance in the alley.

He had always wondered what became of the child. The brutish result standing on the cobblestones was less than shocking, though the way Nyack's son had protected that cross-caste's body from a slaver... that compassion was very like his mother. Perhaps their son had inherited something of hers after all.

"Do you honestly think anyone would believe your innocence?" the young Kasim spat in a harsh whisper. "A lone y'siti next to a cross-caste corpse...it only proves your reputation as the twisted, heartless witch—"

Ignoring his slander, she began a verbal assessment of the body, raising her voice above the other al'Haidren's. "Look—incisions were made along the wrists, neck, and ankles. Whoever did this was educated in human anatomy. That much is evident. Here, do you see?" Alora's niece pointed to a wound on the right arm. "Each cut was cleaned thoroughly. They killed her, drained her, cleaned her, and left the body for us to find...like a rag doll."

"I said, *step back!*" Kasim's *kopar* pointed toward the wall. "This isn't a game, Witch."

"Whatever gave you the impression it was, Lord Darakai?" She bent her nose to the cut and inhaled deeply, as the figure had done with the body in Arune.

"What the Depths are you doing!" Kasim yelled, stepping back in fear.

Jerking away, she covered her mouth. The figure shifted uncomfortably. She smelled it—the depravity, the lingering *wrongness* where the corpse had been touched. Tension curled his thoughts. The girl was another victim, like the young woman in Arune, but this time, the killer had been deliberate—careful, even, as with the boy discovered in the bay.

"Wait." Suddenly less concerned with Alora's niece, the southern al'Haidren bent to look closer. "I know that dress—the style, I mean. *Uni*, yeah, that…she's one of Salma's girls."

He cupped his chin and studied the lacerations. As Kasim reached to sweep a clump of hair off the wound across the neck, her hand shot out and grabbed his arm.

"Don't touch it," Alora's niece warned, wide-eyed. "It has been defiled. Something's not right."

"Nothing about this is right," he snapped, ripping his forearm out of her grasp. "You speak of Darakai like we're the animals, but look at this! Look what the northmen do to their own children! Depths, the girl probably didn't even live to see her own Ascension. Now she never will."

"Boreal has no part in this wickedness!" Alora's niece bared her teeth. "Our blood is precious. We *never* waste it. It's Darakaians who crave bloodshed in their lust for power, not my kinsmen."

"The Boreali drained the color from your eye." Kasim shook his head violently. Evidently, he'd heard, and believed, one of the more ridiculous rumors about her people. "They blinded you from your own savagery."

"You claimed you know the girl's mistress," she said, considering the other al'Haidren. She nodded, appearing to make a decision. "You will take me to her at once."

Alora's niece rose on her heels, secured the linen veil across her face, and waited expectantly.

"Tonight, Lord Darakai."

"The only place I'm taking you is a dungeon, for whatever you've done to this poor girl," Kasim asserted, visibly unsettled by the body at his feet.

The figure bent over the roof slats, intrigued. It was extraordinary behavior—a Darakaian caring for the fate of yet another cross-caste, especially of Boreali lineage.

"Those wounds were cleaned, but the corpse is covered in refuse. Had I any part in her death, the evidence would be on my person, which it is clearly not." She stalked past Kasim in the direction he'd originally come. "We are speaking to her mistress tonight."

"*Ano.* No, we are not. This body belongs to Bastiion. These deaths fall under the pryde's investigation. And Boreali participation is not welcome," he snarled.

"Neither is your own, apparently," she shot back. "I heard this investigation was taken from your pryde. But I have a feeling you will seek out her mistress regardless, and when you do, I expect to be there."

"I found you stalking the streets of Marketown, unescorted, at the scene of the crime." Kasim's son started toward her. "I'm within my rights to take you in on that alone."

"Lord Darakai, I may not know what exactly lies in that crate, but it's obvious you've gone to great lengths to avoid trafficked areas with it in tow." She crossed her arms and stopped just short of his chin. "There are a number of goods prohibited by our allies, goods which come in bottles just like those in your care. I wonder what our prince would say about that? His beloved friend, a common criminal."

Alora didn't give her niece nearly enough credit, the figure decided. Were she to ease her strict governance, she might see the cleverness of her Luscia. It was one of the few traits the al'Haidren had inherited from her aunt; a quality Alora had not displayed so brazenly since their youth.

An ache panged through his chest at the memory.

"Then we are at an impasse." Kasim glared down his nose at her, a creature his superior in so many ways, then sighed with disgust. "*If* I take you with me, we go my way. No arguments. None."

She stared at him for a moment before giving a stiff nod. "*Wem.* Agreed."

"Good, because you aren't going to like it," he muttered under his breath with a smirk, and knelt to pick up the crate.

"I am more than capable of discretion. You've no cause for concern," she replied defiantly to his back.

"I have to sneak Boreal's self-righteous al'Haidren into a house of ill repute. That's plenty of cause for concern." He grinned into the darkness and headed deeper into the alley, calling back, "I better see you holding two wraiths at dawn."

The figure thrust his arm in the air and awaited the bite of Amaranth's talons as they clutched his sleeve. It was time his mistress learned of the rebellious pattern her niece was weaving, and the young Darakaian who held her by one very dangerous thread.

TWENTY-ONE

Luscia

L uscia fidgeted with the scarf, careful not to disturb the fine layer of cacao paste darkening her hairline and thick brows. She wrapped her hair tightly in the silky material, as Unitarian women of the lower classes often did with their own. Tucking the loose blonde strands underneath, she arranged the tail of the scarf so that it cascaded over the scar tissue carved into the left side of her neck.

"Depths, aren't you finished yet?" her escort demanded for the second time.

"Disguising me as a cross-caste scullery maid was your idea, Lord Darakai," Luscia bit out, picking up the dress she'd borrowed from Mila and eyeing it apprehensively. "*Shtàka*," she swore. "As you frequently remind me, I'm to follow your lead without complaint."

To avoid suspicion, they'd waited three nights since finding the corpse. She tried not to dwell on that evening, though the waiting provided ample opportunity to do so. The more Luscia pondered the series of bizarre events, the more unsettled she became. It wasn't the first occasion she'd felt eyes on her back during a hunt through Bastiion, but it was the first night she'd heard the whispers, and the only since. The trail of voices had hummed indecipherable secrets and teased her into that alley, departing once she entered it.

Luscia's mother had heard voices, too. They'd made Eoine laugh, and cry.

Still, the whispers weren't the most troubling incident that night. It was for Boreal's Haidrens to choose when to use their gift of Sight. But the Sight, of its own accord, had summoned Luscia to seek behind the veil and into the *Other*. While in its captivity, that *otherness* had revealed a cloud of fractured lumin about the corpse. Those threads had shuddered away from the defiled flesh and pooled around Luscia instead, like they were fleeing something dark indeed.

Fiddling with the stitching of the borrowed garment, Luscia suppressed an itch of alarm creeping down her spine. The benefit of Kasim's delay was that it had allowed Luscia time to procure the items needed for her transformation, although neither she nor Mila had accounted for their variance in size. Imitating the majority of women at court, Mila had the appetite of a sparrow, the evidence of which was painfully obvious as Luscia stepped into the slim clothing. The attendant's taut, linen dress cinched tightly at her waist, causing Luscia's breasts to practically spill out over top.

"This is why we don't starve ourselves like the yancy women, Mila," Luscia grumbled, shoving her biceps through the narrow sleeves.

"What are you going on about?"

Squatting, Luscia stashed her far more practical gear under a stray wooden pallet and stepped around the corner in the vacant alley, praying the likes of Zaethan Kasim would not notice how her bodice quite literally busted at the seams.

By the way his bright eyes flicked up and lingered where they didn't belong, he most certainly did.

"Finally." He coughed, clearing his throat, and stomped away.

Wrapping her arms around her torso, Luscia gingerly followed.

In awkward silence, Luscia trailed him through the dancing street-lights of Marketown's busy district. Even approaching midnight, it was teeming with traffic. Eventually Kasim stopped in front of an embel-lished red door fixed between shabby brickwork and heavily curtained windows, which did little to trap the revelry within.

Seizing the handle, he hesitated and muttered, "Do try to pretend you like me, otherwise we might as well turn around right now."

Luscia's eyes rolled skeptically. "And why is that?"

"Because there's only one reason an al'Haidren would bring his maid to a place like this," he said in a dark tone.

Luscia stiffened at the sudden pressure of his fingertips on the small of her back. Leading her into a haze of smoke and laughter, he didn't remove his hand. Though the rowdy banter of drunken men occupied the tavern, exotic rhythms blurred their thunder. As Kasim steered her through cracked archways to a lengthy, crowded bar, feminine giggles lilted above the noise. Lingering by each gambling table were women dressed akin to the dead cross-caste. Angling their bodies and encircling players, they fawned over the men as they wagered coin in desperate games of pride and chance—yancy, sentry, and lower classes alike.

If Boreal's Clann Darragh could see the hovel his daughter had just entered…

Luscia swallowed hard.

Beyond the farthest table, a woman emerged from behind a split tapestry with a sentry in tow. Her tawny Unitarian skin was pinked with a flush that spread across her exposed neck and shoulders. The night-caller batted her tinted lashes as she languidly skimmed a fallen sleeve higher and bid the sentry goodnight.

Luscia knew of such transactions, naturally, but had never witnessed one unfold. Suddenly, she felt altogether too exposed. An unnamed anger hardened her jaw as she stiffly took a seat on the stool beside the other al'Haidren.

"Try harder, Lady Boreal." Kasim's hot breath brushed her ear as he instructed her through his teeth. "Your pious notions are starting to show."

"I *am* trying." Luscia forced a rigid grin.

"Tell that to your face." He spun away and addressed the solemn barkeep. "The Crown Special."

The Unitarian paused in his task, shared an edgy look with Kasim, and left his post.

"You seem familiar with the service menu," Luscia commented quietly, attempting to appear at ease while she scanned the large room for its exits. Two public, two concealed. "I'm curious—how often does a Darakaian alpha buy his women?"

"As often as he likes. Darakaians don't hide their dealings. We don't slink in the shadows like cockroaches and infect a city we're not wanted in, like y'si—"

"*Shamàli, shamàli.*" An intoxicated sentry bumped into Kasim, nearly displacing him off his stool. "*Di yaya,*" he slurred. Licking his bottom lip, he jutted his chin in Luscia's direction. "*Ni yeye ràtomdai na wewe?*"

"*Uni zà,*" the al'Haidren barked, startling Luscia when he reached over and gripped her thigh possessively.

"Eh, eh…*uni*, Alpha Zà." The Darakaian sentry threw his hands up and stumbled as he eased back into the crowd.

"Remove your hand," Luscia hissed.

"Just playing the part." Kasim sneered and withdrew his palm, wiping it discreetly against his pantleg.

Luscia watched the drunkard trip over a chair as he approached another grouping. "What did he ask you?"

"If I claimed rights to you—a courtesy, of sorts." He shrugged, hopping off his stool when the barkeep reappeared and mutely pointed to a staircase along the opposite wall.

"*A courtesy!*" she sputtered, darting after Kasim as he cut between the betting tables. Luscia swatted prying fingers as she passed through the crowd of intoxicated men.

"*Uni*, a courtesy." He climbed the steps, glancing over his shoulder. "You should be pleased I said yes—some men like to share."

Luscia's fists tightened around Phalen's radials. She calmed herself with the knowledge that they were sharp enough to take out Zaethan Kasim, should his next comment justify doing so.

At the top the landing, he swept a drape aside and halted at the sight of a wall of muscle.

"Ràoko. Delightful." He glanced up to the massive cross-caste. The wordless guard stood a head taller than Kasim, who himself surpassed six feet. "With your excellent conversational skills, who could stay away?"

For a moment, Luscia thought Kasim was about to be struck in the mouth, and found herself disappointed when he wasn't.

Ràoko retreated to a makeshift office at the end of a musky hallway. Not large, it housed a snug sitting area and a single desk, where a woman sat hunched over stacks of paper and clusters of coin. Her flock of wild, lustrous curls shone in the lantern-light when she peered up at them.

"Back so soon, *Jaha*?" the woman inquired breathily, despite the constrictive corset around her middle. "To what do I owe this rare pleasure?"

Rising from the desk, her shapely hips swayed as she moved to greet Kasim. The woman gently pulled him toward her by the neck and placed a fleeting kiss along his upper jaw. Up close, delicate fissures around her eyes indicated that she was older than her figure suggested. More interesting was the distinct contrast between her Unitarian complexion and pronounced southern features. The Veiled Lady was operated by a cross-caste.

Cross-castes seldom owned much of anything, much less an enterprise of this magnitude. It was unheard of, particularly for a cross-caste who would gather and market individuals like herself for profit.

"Ah, what have you brought me? A gift?" Luscia shifted uncomfortably when the woman walked a semi-circle to appraise his guest, chuckling in her assessment. "Had I known your preference was so… unusual, I could've offered one more seasoned from my own house, *Jaha*. You don't need to raid your palace kitchens for it, yeah?"

"Not necessary, Salma," Kasim interjected at Luscia's scowl, motioning to the divan and pair of satin armchairs. "But in a way, that is why we've come."

"And who, exactly," the woman took a seat, leaning over the small table, "is 'we'?"

Out the corner of her eye, Luscia waited for his go-ahead, honoring their agreement. At his nod, she unraveled the scarf imprisoning her distinctively northern hair.

"I didn't bring you a kitchen maid," he explained. "We need to ask you about the girl, Salma. The cross-caste they found, yeah? And unfortunately, this is a conversation the al'Haidren to Boreal insisted she be present for."

The brothel matron blinked repeatedly as her full lips separated. After a moment, her playful smirk returned.

"Cacao paste…*uni*. Rather sly, Lady al'Haidren." One black brow lifted at the residue on Luscia's scarf. "And wise. You were right to disguise her, *Jaha*. She would not be well received by my guests."

"Agreed. Now—the girl, Salma. She was one of yours, *uni*?" Kasim sat forward, cupping one fist in the other. "I need to know who she was, her friends, who visited her. There've been no leads in our investigation thus far. Your tavern may provide us with the first clues."

The sultry madam reclined in her armchair, crossing her legs slowly, and glanced between them. Luscia heard her breathing grow shallow as her eyes narrowed at some internal debate.

"*Bolaeva*." Luscia's voice cracked. "Please, help us find who is behind these atrocities. For all of Boreal, I beg you, please help us."

Several minutes passed before Salma answered.

"Her name is—*was*—Wren. The girl only came to us last year. No family."

"*Little songbird*," Luscia murmured the meaning behind the northern name. "But how did she end up here, in a…" She trailed off, too embarrassed to continue.

"…a whorehouse, Lady al'Haidren?" the madam pointedly finished. She laughed without humor. "In my experience, it is never the high and mighty who protect the cross-caste or the breakaway. *Ano,* it is the underworld. Even our Unitarian king refused to grant us a voice in the Ethnicam." Salma swept a mass of curls to the side and tilted her head. "I know what you are thinking—looking down on us, our family, yeah? What you do not realize, my *lady,* is I can only provide my family with food, shelter, protection, whatever they need because I am willing to feed Bastiion's wolves—" Two fingers pointed to the tavern underfoot. "—what they hunger."

"*Meh fyreon,* I do apologize. I meant no disrespect to your... household." Luscia grimaced, unsure how to navigate the path between etiquette and conviction.

Kasim glared at her. "Just stop talking." Inching closer to the short table, either to angle toward Salma or distance himself from Luscia, he asked, "How old was Wren? What was her role here at The Veiled Lady?"

"Sixteen, perhaps? She never said, I never asked." Salma shrugged, and Luscia's stomach knotted at the confirmation of her youth. "Wren went straight into night-business—*papyon.* She wanted the money. And she gained popularity, fast. Eh, novelty always does."

"Who called on her, habitually employed her services?" Kasim pushed.

"You know yancies prefer cross-castes, something normally off-limits. Members of the Peerage made up the majority of her clientele. Oh," she added, tapping her lip, "and the other alpha—the harsh one, with the scar." The madam pouted at him. "Your friend takes advantage of our amenities, even if you won't. The girls don't like him as much as they'd like you, *Jaha.*"

Luscia's forehead wrinkled as she glanced toward Kasim, confused at his lack of patronage. He'd suggested quite the opposite.

"Can you think of anyone who'd want to harm Wren, or ever tried?"

the southern al'Haidren rushed on, nostrils flaring, clearly irritated by Salma's mention of the other alpha.

"*Ano zà*. My house indulges these men to protect our family from who they are in the outside world. My clients know such behaviors are never tolerated inside." Salma rubbed her slender wrist in her lap. "The desires we pacify are just shadows, *Jaha*. Desire is erratic, tied to so many things. Outside, men allow desire to turn ugly, violent." Her eyes flashed to Luscia. "At least, in the world of a lowly cross-caste."

Luscia met her gaze levelly. "I am well aware of the things you speak."

Salma's eyes dropped to Luscia's bare neck and the ugly tale etched into her skin. "*Uni*, I see you are."

A chasm reopened in her chest as she maintained eye contact with the matron of The Veiled Lady. Loss, pain, and anger were equalizers; emotions that crossed class or territorial boundaries on a map. Behind an unspoken yet recognizable sadness, there was strength in the other woman's eyes. It rimmed her earthy irises in a green aura of defiance.

What an odd sensation it was, for Luscia to suddenly find herself coveting something in Salma, the owner of a brothel.

"Did you see anything else, hear anything else that night?" Kasim interrupted.

"*Ano, Jaha*. As you know, I was with you."

"*Uni*." He stood and rubbed the back of his neck. "Then we should go, before questions are raised about my maid. We'll leave the way we came. Business as usual. *Shàlàmaiamo*, Salma."

"*Tadöm*, truly. Boreal thanks you for your candor," Luscia said as she covered her hair, resembling Mila once again, and followed Kasim out the office.

"Zaethan," Salma called his given name when they reached the end of the hall. "Remember *Owàa's* fate."

Luscia didn't understand her farewell, but Kasim seemed unconcerned by the madam's ominous message.

As they descended the rickety steps into the ruckus of the tavern,
Kasim went rigid. She watched his shoulders roll back to embody
his full height. After a breath, he marched to a corner gaming table
shrouded by a throng of dancing women.

"I can see why your pryde disappoints, Wekesa." Kasim glowered
at a Darkaian alpha lounging at the table, dice in one hand and empty
glassware beside the other. "Get up."

Roughly his al'Haidren's age, the alpha's arrogance was palpable in
his delay to fulfill Kasim's order. Plucking unseen lint off his navy tunic,
he rose from the chair and strutted to stand in front of Kasim. Bone
beads swung in his braids, though they only hung from one side of his
scalp. The damaged flesh of the opposite was gruesomely uneven.

"Is this why you're so obsessed with my investigation, Alpha Zà?"
He sucked his teeth and scanned Luscia's assets, on full display in Mila's
poorly sized dress. "*Ni yeye ràtomdai na wewe?*"

The alpha posed the Andwele question to his superior, but fixed his
overconfident smile on Luscia.

"*Ano,*" Kasim answered in an amused voice. He then repeated
himself, emphasizing the final syllable. "*Ano. Zà.*"

Astounded, Luscia careened toward Kasim. Her furious stare glided
like darts into his cinnamon skin. Kasim stepped aside and gestured
obligingly in her direction. Before she could object, Luscia felt a sweaty
heaviness land on her hip, urging her forward.

"Yeah, you want some real *papyo*—ahh!" The other alpha screamed
when Luscia crushed his knuckles in her hand. Thrusting her thumb
into a pressure point, she twisted his wrist mercilessly. "*Y'siti bitch!*"

"The y'siti bitch belongs to *herself*!" She bent his wrist further and threw his hand back. "And she does not want your *papyon*!"

He cradled the injured hand to his chest and swung his good fist toward her face, but its impact was thwarted by Kasim's grip on the alpha's dark, corded forearm.

"The *yaya* doesn't want you, Wekesa." He clutched Luscia's shoulder, spinning her toward the door. "Now stand down. That's an order, Alpha."

The tavern hadn't quieted much during their scene, but the nearest parties watched intently as she and Kasim exited. Returning to the streets, he released her. Luscia assumed he was too distracted to remember to wipe his hand this time.

They hugged the exterior buildings to pass behind a row of bustling market stalls. She glanced over, perturbed by his unusual silence, and saw that Zaethan Kasim was grinning from ear to ear.

"Did that display please you somehow?" she asked scathingly.

"Incredibly." He beamed, strutting contently. "My cross-caste scullery maid did what I am not permitted to do at present."

"Injure his dominant hand?"

"Publicly humiliate him."

Luscia chewed on his statement as they returned to the abandoned alleyway. Rounding the corner alone, she located her things and began to undress. Pausing, she toyed with the unraveled lacing from the lining of Mila's garment as curiosity nipped her thoughts.

"Why didn't you correct me earlier?" she wondered aloud. "When I accused you of frequenting Salma's tavern for...you know."

"You're Boreali. I'm Darakaian. Would the truth have mattered if I had?" Kasim asked from the other side of the brick.

Half undressed, Luscia slumped against the wall and struggled to formulate a response. For some puzzling reason, against all understanding, it did.

The truth mattered.

TWENTY-TWO

Luscia

The vibration of Aksel's snore lulled Lusica to sleep as her head sank further into the pillows of her lavish Unitarian bed. With a weighty sigh, she let go of the evening she'd spent at The Veiled Lady; her seductive song and ravenous banter, the skeletons her matron masked with desire. Troubled but limp from exhaustion, Luscia melted into the sea of sheets. At last, rest would come.

Rapid murmurs in the receiving room outside licked her ears. Rolling over, Luscia buried her face in a blanket.

"—claims it's important, m-madam. I'm not to return without her."

"I'll say it again. The al'Haidren is not to be disturbed at this hour. Now go, you little twit!"

Groaning, Luscia swung her feet to the ground, much to Aksel's dismay, and cracked her bedroom door. In the foyer stood Dmitri's young page. Shakily, he extended a sealed scrap of parchment to her enraged lady's maid. Tallulah ripped it from the timid boy and studied the impression in the wax. Straightening her nightcap, the older woman looked up, bewildered.

"Ock, why'd you not show me this ten minutes ago? Making me all upset when the prince's seal was in that sorry pocket of yours!"

"It's okay, Tallulah," Luscia said with a yawn, making the maid jump. "Let's have it," she added, reaching for the correspondence.

"Oh, Lady Luscia, I'd have woken you if I thought the boy was speaking truth! This foolish lad here, he—"

"*Wem*, the prince's message, Talluah. *Boleava*, please."

"Ah." She handed over the crisply folded note. "Right."

Luscia,

Another five. Please, it is urgent.

Yours,

Dmitri

Pushing the unbound hair from her face, Luscia caught the page's eye and nodded. "Allow me to prepare myself and we'll depart immediately."

Retreating to the privacy of her bedroom, she rushed to complete the tedious steps necessary to produce the requested vials. Repeating Alora's bizarre instructions in her mind, Luscia took the edge of a knife and crushed the ennus thorn, releasing its savory odor. Scraping the chalky powder into a mixing glass, she carefully poured nixberry oil into the beaker and held it over a candle until it boiled. Hastily, she stirred in eüpharsis extract, encouraging the thick, bluish serum to slide into the bubbling liquid. Luscia rested the elixir on her dresser and tugged at the long, gilded chain around her neck. Using the sharp bone key, she added the final ingredient from her index finger.

Five drops of Tiergan blood—no more, no less.

Dividing the liquid between a set of vials, Luscia quickly set them aside and ground the poultice for her finger, dabbing it onto the wound. Tucking the vials in a pocket of her dressing robe, Luscia thrust her feet into a pair of upturned boots and returned to the foyer. If Dmitri's page questioned her appearance, as it hadn't improved during the time she'd made him wait, he didn't voice it as they traversed the halls of the palace. When the page turned down an unfamiliar corridor, Luscia grabbed his arm to correct their path.

"P-please don't hurt me!" The boy shook in her grasp.

Luscia released him. "I'm not—I just..." She rubbed her temples, cursing the Unitarians for their tales of northern witchery. "Isn't His Highness's suite in the southern wing?"

"The prince asked that you meet elsewhere, m-m'Lady al'Haidren." He ducked his head and gestured to a stairwell.

"Of course." Luscia made to comfort the nervous page in some fashion, but faltered. "Thank you...Callister, isn't it?"

Callister murmured something affirmative in response and signaled for her to descend the stairs, apparently alone. As she neared the base, an exquisite set of crystal doors came into view. Though night had long fallen, torches lit a curving path through an impressively manicured garden on the other side. Luscia hadn't a chance to visit the famed gardens herself, but had heard many stories of their beauty.

Unsurprisingly, a trim Darakaian was stationed to the right of the entryway. A spray of southern coils flanked his stern expression. Luscia lifted her chin as she entered the maze of trimmed hedges and flowering towers, painfully aware of the unspoken implications of her ill-suited attire.

Handsomely wrought sconces painted amber patterns across the back of Dmitri's crushed velvet jacket and played with the edges of his dark, wavy hair. Seated on a bench, the prince perched against his gleaming cane with an intent expression, as if he contemplated the universe. Hesitating to interrupt his ponderings, Luscia stopped just short of the bench and waited.

"Breathtaking, isn't it?" Dmitri angled his face as he peered into the flickering darkness. "I often come here to think when sleep evades me. It drives my guards mad. Will you sit with me, Lady Boreal?"

Wrapping her dressing robe tighter, Luscia dutifully took a seat beside her sovereign. She felt in her pocket for his vials, the faint clinking of glass disturbing the quiet.

"Five, as requested, Your Highness."

"Dmitri." When the prince shifted to retrieve them, a noticeable tremble ran through his fingers. Without hesitation, Dmitri brought one to his mouth and swallowed, pressing his eyes shut. "*Shtàka*, that is vile," he said, coughing.

After a few measured breaths, Dmitri faced Luscia. His cheeks showed little color, which was ironic, for his Unitarian skin was shades darker than her own. Higher, a plum hue cradled his lashes. Wan lips twitched sheepishly as he regarded the four remaining doses.

"I am indebted to your promptness, Lady Boreal. I apologize for calling you from your bed." Dmitri glanced at the hem of her robe. "I know I am not your favorite person as of late," he noted, keeping his gaze fixed there. "You've been avoiding me."

"It's true I have been…cross with you." Luscia chose each word prudently. "But you are my future king. You are owed promptness."

He nodded, yet seemed displeased by her reply. Luscia didn't know what else to say. The Prince of Orynthia refused to fight for the children of Boreal as they were slaughtered in his own city, and she could no longer expect him to. Luscia wouldn't be so naïve again. Justice for her cross-caste brethren floating in the bay, massacred and strewn in the streets, demanded vigilance. And if such vigilance demanded an illicit alliance with the al'Haidren to Darakai, then so be it.

"Do you like my garden?" Dmitri waved to the manicured land-scape around them.

"It—it's lovely."

He chuckled. "But?"

"It *is* lovely, really," Luscia insisted as his brow rose. "I just prefer the way things are out there, within nature. Free, I suppose. When something grows amidst adversity, it becomes strong. Place it in a stone box, and it remains stunted. Frail, like a bird with its wings clipped."

"Fascinating." Dmitri sat forward in thought. "You exhibit such masterful self-discipline, but prefer a wild beauty to a cultivated one."

"What you are insinuating, Your Highness?" Luscia crossed her arms before quickly uncrossing them again. Best to keep defiance under the skin, where it could not be seen, at least when it came to discussions with her aunt.

"I simply appreciate the irony. Here, you can't stand to see even the most delicate of things, such as a flower, trapped in a controlled environment, yet you control yourself meticulously. What contradic-tion your entire being must hold together every day. But—" Dmitri gripped his cane to stand, extending Luscia his arm before she could protest. "—enough of that. Come, I want to show you something."

Rising, she warily took the arm of his expensive coat. His cane rapped the cobblestones as they walked the exterior of the vast gardens. Pointing out his preferences, the prince notated each uniqueness and rarity of origin. Confined as she'd been to the peninsula of Boreal, Luscia had never travelled beyond its borders, excepting Bastiion Proper. Her eyes widened at the High One's imagination. There was so much mystery to the shapes and colors he'd crafted, the artistry he'd etched across a world she'd never seen.

"Look, there's yours." Dmitri moved to a pair of modest, thorny blossoms. Their petals were a radiant pearl under the moonlight, apart from hints of yellow at the edges. "The *Noculoma-Anastasis* is always overlooked in these gardens. We don't have many, only this pair and the third in your possession."

"I'm honored." Surprised, Luscia studied the plant and asked, "What inspired you to uproot it?"

"I wished for the third to dwell beside its match, as the other pair. Like you, I suspect, it will continue to bloom even when the light seems lost. Most especially when it is lost." He ushered her onto a narrower walkway, past the *Noculoma-Anastasis*. "Almost there—this way."

Distracted by the bordering procession of shrubs, fashioned into every type of creature, Luscia felt Dmitri's hand tighten around her own on his arm when he lifted a finger to his mouth.

"Wait," he whispered, pointing ahead to the sentries posted outside a smaller, more secluded garden within the walled paradise.

Luscia could not see who occupied it at this hour, but the list of court residents with royal sentries was quite short. Beside her, Dmitri stared at the mossy gate, a tendon skipping along his jawline as his lips pursed crookedly. Cane in hand, he fiddled with something in his pocket, but ceased when the gate creaked open and a slim woman emerged.

Dmitri stood a fraction taller as his mother tucked away her hand-kerchief and lowered a lace veil to cover her glistening, tear-stained face. Without a glance toward where her son stood silently in the dark, the elegant queen lifted her head and mutely left her guard to somberly follow. As the prince watched his mother disappear behind the maze of hedges. Luscia swallowed and looked away, suddenly feeling as if she were intruding on something immensely private.

Moving more slowly now, Dmitri led her into the little garden. After locking the gate, he directed Luscia to a bench in the center of the rounded landscape. Encircling the bench were an array of toy replicas carved from stone: a horse, a chess piece, a soldier, a rabbit. Nine in total, bedded in the flowering groundcover.

With the aid of his cane, Dmitri bent a knee to the earth and produced a carved wooden bird from his pocket. Heaving a breath, he blew bits of sawdust off its tiny beak, as if it'd been carved by his own hand. As he placed it gently beside the marble rabbit, Luscia realized the bird was not alone—similar objects littered the soil, time-weathered and dressed in foliage.

These were not children's toys, she realized.

They were graves.

Coming to sit beside her, Dmitri exhaled as he began, "I brought you here because…because it is unfair of me to ask for your trust, without first offering my own." The prince kneaded one of his palms and considered the marble rabbit in the dirt. "As history tells, the line of Thoarne has ruled the last centuries during steady conflict. Reason-ably, it's difficult to produce heirs during wartime. Over those years, the line became ever narrower, most monarchs lucky to sire two healthy children. Eventually, each sired only one, generation after generation.

"My father accomplished what no other could. He secured Orynthia's peace. Yet here we sit, at the start of an age that ought to be defined by renewed vitality…among my nameless brothers and sisters, who will never see it."

Luscia's forehead furrowed as she followed his line of sight to the carved figures.

"My mother became skilled at hiding her pregnancies while I grew up. The court couldn't be allowed to see a pattern, lest the Peerage lose faith in our line. The youngest of my siblings would've turned five this summer, had he or she lived to their birth."

"Dmitri, I—" Luscia knew loss intimately, but struggled to form an adequate response to his pain. "My brother, Phalen, is everything to me—everything left of my mother. I cannot imagine the agony of losing him. But…" She paused, genuinely baffled. "I still don't understand. Why entrust me with this secret?"

"Because Accords are capricious things, Lady Boreal. Since my Ascension, I've made a practice of studying our own. Not just what was written long ago, but the things unwritten…things not written at all. Our forefathers, yours and mine, they concealed a loophole for the outer territories. You see, the Accords between Orynthia and the Houses are not tied to the realm, or even to Bastiion. They are tied to my line, to the descendants of Thoarne himself.

"My closest cousins are so far removed from the original line, chaos would ensue if they were to fight over the regency. Now self-sustained, the Houses would pull away to solidify their independence. Broken into factions, our insecure borders would lure neighboring kingdoms to action. Prudently, our allies to the east would invade Pilar before Darakai could assume it." Dmitri's disheveled hair brushed his cheeks as he shook his head. "The realm as we know it would collapse entirely."

"So, you produce an heir of your own," Luscia concluded aloud, familiar with the burden of carrying on one's lineage. "With an heir secured, those dangers are easily circumvented."

"That is the logical solution, yes. The Peerage favor *Bahira'*Rasha, heir apparent to the Queendom of Razôuel. They believe a union with the Zôueli princess would yield the strongest heir in a century. It's why we've formally invited *Bahira'*Rasha and the Zôueli queen to join us during the solstice."

Luscia searched his eyes and the foreboding sadness hidden within. "Then there is no need for distress. Your heir will follow in your footsteps, as you will after your father."

The prince looked wistful. "That is such a wonderful dream. A favorite, when sleep permits it."

"Your Highness, I'm afraid I don't follow."

Dmitri fiddled within his pocket, pulling out his elixir, and peered into the empty vial. Then, looking up, he smiled at her. Uncertain, her smile in return faltered.

"I'm dying, Luscia."

Slowly, Luscia's eyes abandoned Dmitri's and dropped to his chest. Rustling leaves, the company of evening crickets, it all faded as her gifted ears sought only the sound of his inhale and exhale. In, then out; a smooth, uninterrupted rhythm. Back and forth, like a rocking cradle, cocooning her mind as it spun. Luscia felt her head shake.

"*Niit,*" she heard herself say, having gone numb. "No, no. There are tonics. Boreal has a remedy for everything—"

"I'm dying, Luscia," he repeated. "It's all right. Luscia, *look at me.*" Dmitri reached over and squeezed her fingers. "It is—it's all right. I've known for a few years. Alora has known even longer, I assume."

"Alora…?"

"She saved me. When I was a boy, maybe six or seven, I became very ill. Dangerously so. When the court physicians failed to find a solution, Alora came. I'm told she spent days, even nights at my bedside. When I finally woke, my parents were told my ailment had been cured. To this day, they still believe it was.

"Alora concocted a multitude of therapies throughout my youth. This elixir sustains me, but the dosage increases as I grow older. I feel…I feel myself dying, a little more each day. I don't know exactly what these contain," Dmitri set the empty vial on the bench between them, "and I don't need to know. But Alora's predictions proved more than accurate—your mixture offers me more longevity, like a spike with a slow taper. However, it too is only temporary."

"*Niit*, we will keep trying," Luscia protested, a new kind of defiance rising in her chest. "There is an answer, a different substance or ratio—"

"We've accepted there is no cure. I *will* die, Luscia. Perhaps not this year, or the next, but the night approaches when I won't be able to wake up."

A single bead of moisture trailed down her cheek and splashed her knuckles. Against logic or reason, Luscia suddenly felt very alone.

"Tell me what to do," she pleaded. "Tell me what you need."

"I need time," he said gently. "I need you to continue giving me that, just long enough to produce an heir to the Orynthian throne."

"Who else knows of this? Suspects it?" Luscia cataloged the obstacles in keeping such a secret.

"After tonight, Alora and yourself. My mother can't bear the burden of knowing the truth, and my father won't hear of it." He rubbed his forehead. "The Peerage cannot be allowed to sense a weakness in the line. At best, each noble would use it to his own advantage. We need the Peerage behind the regency to protect my heir during the rest of my father's reign, and to uphold the Accords once the child takes the throne."

"What will you tell the Quadren?"

"Nothing. Ira will inherit chairmanship of the Peerage after his father. It's typical for the Haidren to Bastiion to hold the majority seat. Sayuri…well, it's better Pilar believes the facade than learn the reality. Pilar would exploit Bastiion's weakness, rather adeptly I fear."

"And Darakai?"

Dmitri diverted his gaze and straightened his shoulders.

"Zaethan will not learn of my condition. I have my reasons for that." A sudden tension pinched the prince's neck. "Reasons which are not eligible for discussion."

Luscia slid her hand across the bench to console him, then remembered her place.

"I'm sorry, Dmitri, for what it's worth. I am so very sorry."

"*Tadöm*," he whispered in her native tongue.

They sat in the quietness of the garden together, each lost in their own thoughts. Dmitri stared at the bird he'd carved, perched in the dirt.

"I know I've become a disappointment to you these past weeks," he said at last. "Since your arrival, really. I hope you understand now." Rotating toward her, Dmitri's face fell in defeat. "There can be no hint of favoritism. I cannot overturn jurisdiction for Boreal, however much I wish to. You have to know that I would tear apart this entire city to avenge those children. But I *must* support the Accords—they alone hold the realm together after tragedy, when tensions rise. The Accords must endure after I'm gone. For the sake of my child—Thoarne's child—they must."

"Then, *se'lah Aurynth*." Luscia released a breath of apprehension, her decision made. "I am at your complete service. I'm with you, Dmitri Thoarne. Until Aurynth."

"No." The tired prince scooped her fingers off the stone and into his own. He brought the inside of her palm to his lips for the gentlest of touches, then pressed it against the uneven beat of his heart. "The fate of Orynthia, my very life, rests in your hands. Luscia, it is I who am with you.

TWENTY-THREE

Zaethan

It had been ages since Zaethan studied anything. He hated parchment. The smell of it. The feel of it. Yet here he sat, in an office he never used, scrutinizing every map of the Proper he owned for the third consecutive hour.

He chewed on a stalk of camilla root, what was left of it, as he examined the intersecting web of streets. There was no pattern to the cross-caste murders, apart from the youth and lineage of each victim, each having been robbed of their Ascension. Zaethan grimaced, charting a path between the various marks he'd scribbled onto the parchment. From one bloodred dot to another, he surveyed the crimson lines between. With most alleyways unrepresented on palace maps, it was impossible to determine how the killer moved about unobserved.

A triplet of beats knocked at the door. Zaethan considered ordering the sentry away, as he hadn't made much progress, but neither was he about to anytime soon.

"*Uni*!"

The door cracked open and a head of sable ringlets popped through. Long fingers brushed the shelf of hair away from a boyish face to reveal a bright, crooked grin.

"*Owàamo*, Alpha Zà," the warrior tested. "You call, I come report, yeah?"

"*Uni*, Jabari. I called for your report," Zaethan reiterated, pinching the bridge of his nose.

He'd admitted Jabari Muthwali into his personal pryde six months ago, but still found it difficult to communicate with their new addition. Bred in the mountains and raised in Yowekao, Jabari's Andwele was fragmented, his Unitarian worse. Any attempt to combine the two resulted in *kakk* soup.

A crash and roar of masculine laughter came from behind Jabari, where the offices connected to a common area in the guard house. The screech of moving furniture and more voices joined the ruckus.

"Jabari, what the Depths is that noise?"

"Eh…." The trim Darakaian turned to investigate. "That be the *Jwona rapiki*, Alpha Zà."

Zaethan bit down on the camilla root until it snapped.

"Are we all calling him that now?" he growled. At Jabari's look of confusion, Zaethan rolled up the maps and motioned briskly. "Just get in here."

The youngest member of his pryde bobbed on his heels in the doorway before slipping inside. "*Uni*, Alpha Zà."

If the freshly Ascended warrior wasn't such a natural talent, Zaethan didn't know how his patience with Jabari would have fared. His thumb tapped a stout glass of water, wishing it were full of something brash and bitter instead.

"You may begin, Jabari, and do make it brief for once." Zaethan pointed to the space in front of his desk.

"Eh, *uni*. No trouble come two-night pass for prince, *ano*. Easy like breeze, but for dark and light al'Haidren come a call. Dark al'Haidren prince send away, say 'not feel well, tell her go.'" Jabari's cheerful grin returned, having also developed a dislike for Sayuri Naborū-Zuo during his stint in Bastiion. "Then, prince send small gangle boy to fetch y'siti al'Haidren. She come like moth after midnight, in sleep dress. He spend all night with y'siti in the garden, yeah—"

"Wait. *Doru*, stop." Zaethan's hand cut off Jabari's jumbled explanation. "What do you mean, 'in sleep dress'?"

Jabari danced in place as his hands mimed around his chest and middle.

"Erm...tie-dress. For night-night walkabout."

"Jabari, are you telling me the al'Haidren to Boreal—the y'siti—was brought to the prince in the middle of the night wearing nothing but *her dressing gown*?"

The warrior clapped his hands together enthusiastically. "*Uni*, yeah!"

Zaethan spit the pulverized root out the side of his mouth and shot out of the chair. "And how did our prince seem when she left?"

"Eh." Jabari wiggled a brow, chuckling to himself. "Little happy, not big happy, *ano*."

Another bang emitted through a wall shared with the common

area. Zaethan's hand clutched the back of his neck and clenched when a second followed.

"Jabari, how often does the prince send for the y'siti?"

Before he could answer, the office door creaked open again to allow a boulder of muscle through.

"*Ahoté*," Kumo interrupted. "You want to step out here."

The beta locked eyes with Zaethan and latched the door in retreat.

"We aren't done," Zaethan told the younger warrior. "You will tell me how many times this occurred and how often it happens in future. Do you understand me, Jabari? *Yeye qondai?*"

"*Uni zà*, Alpha Zà, *meme qondai.*" He bumped a fist against his chest and stepped back, allowing Zaethan to lead the way into the main room of the guard house.

His beta waited rigidly outside the door. Zaethan's cheeks went hot as Kumo sucked his teeth and jutted a bristled jaw toward a crowd of sentries in the center of the guard house. A ragtag collection of chairs had been dragged around a table, and over the heads of the sentries, dice flew in the air, eliciting a raucous cheer at their return to the wood.

Half the men should have been at their posts. Zaethan recognized more than enough faces to confirm it.

"*Owàamo.*"

A cluster of sentries parted at Zaethan's greeting, though he spoke primarily for the Darakaian audience. Across the division sat the author of the commotion. Glass of *bwoloa* in hand, Wekesa had a cross-caste laundress perched in his lap and a single muddied boot propped on the table, soaking a soiled ring into the wood surface. Zaethan knew the other alpha hadn't chosen *his* guard house for a random game of dice.

Ano. He'd come to piss in it.

"Zaeth, won't you join us?" the bastard shouted in mock camaraderie as he lowered the shallow glass of liquor. Wekesa rolled the pair of dice between bruised knuckles and let his free hand roam the woman's bare shoulder. "So much sweeter, a mix, *uni*? But our commander's son already knows this—don't you, Alpha Zà?"

Wekesa twisted his neck as if to admire the woman's teak skin, but slid his coal-black eyes toward Zaethan and smirked. The angle invited sunlight to bathe the ragged scar along the side of his skull. Zaethan anchored onto the rapidly fading reminder of his rival's defeat.

"Get out of my guard house," Zaethan barked at the laundress, hunkering down over the tabletop when she hesitated. "I said, *get out*!"

"A bit hypocritical, yeah?"

Murmurs and smothered snickers rumbled through the grouping at Wekesa's insinuation.

"Your pryde is on duty, Wekesa," Zaethan said coldly. "Yet they are here, in my guard house."

"They've earned a break." His tongue probed the side of his fat mouth before he turned to spit on the floor. "After all, it's a very involved investigation, *yeye qondai*? My pryde could be here for months doing what yours could not."

Kumo came up behind Zaethan, popping his knuckles—a series of bursts Zaethan knew too well. He bit back a volatile swell of curses at Wekesa's brazen disrespect and instead straightened his spine, plastering a grin on his face.

"You're a fairly gifted man, Wekesa."

"High praise from our Alpha Zà. *Zullee,* accepted with honor," he sneered, translating for the Unitarian sentries.

"Which is why I just can't understand," Zaethan folded his arms and paced through the gathering as the sentries shifted out of his way, "how a gifted man like Wekesa keeps overlooking one fundamental principle."

"*Uni,* go ahead. Share with us, Zaeth." Wekesa freed the dice and laced his fingers in his lap, lowering his voice when Zaethan halted near his shoulder. "Speak, while they still listen."

"The *Jwona rapiki* is free to waste his own time in Bastiion, like a weak, sniveling yancy." Zaethan bent until his chin hovered inches above Wekesa's scar. "But he keeps forgetting he's not free to waste *my* time. Each member of his pryde is *mine.* Their time is *mine.* So, since the Fate writer is free to do as he pleases, his warriors will not rest until he assumes each of their posts and personally relieves them. And for every instance of the *Jwona rapiki*'s disobedience, I will transfer one of his men to join our forces at the border of Hagarh."

Undertones of humor evaporated from the lake of faces. For the mingling of Darakaians and Unitarians, both sentry and pryde, this moment was critical. Zaethan was Alpha Zà, and he needed to hold his ground in the only manner he had left—targeting those under his own influence to punish the one currently outside it.

"*Ho'waladim.*" Zaethan reached over Wekesa for the other alpha's nearly empty glass and downed the remaining fluid. Slowly, he replaced it in front of him. "As is due you."

Turning, Zaethan nodded to Kumo as he exited the building, aiming straight for his apartments.

"I would have punched him for that," Kumo said, hurrying after him. "But you know, *kàchà kocho.* Whatever works for you, *Ahoté.*"

"Instruct Zahra to follow Wekesa. Unseen. And put Jabari back on Dmitri's guard tonight, he's on assignment for me," Zaethan rattled off as they neared the gate. "Meet me after dark. Bring Takoda."

"What do you have in mind?"

"I'm tired of these games. My father's guest is wearing out his welcome." Zaethan squinted in the growing heat and levelled with his beta. "We need to use his own tactics against him."

Four nights, Àla*maia* watched them stalk the streets of Marketown. Four nights enveloped in cloud, she refused to light their way and bled her tears for their misfortune.

On the fifth, the moon turned radiantly optimistic, casting her brilliance over the assembly of trading stalls. Unabashed, Àla*maia* shone her confidence in Zaethan's pursuit.

"*Owàa's* lover is with us tonight, Alpha Zà! Finally, she blesses our quest!" Takoda hailed over a shoulder, shifting his head of braids to the side to avoid a low-hanging clothesline.

"*Uni*, that she is," Zaethan concurred, surveying the rising silhouette of buildings on either side of the bustling alley. A few blocks back, a hag had insisted she saw movement up there the night prior, though she'd been peddling pipe marrow at the time—and of ill quality, by the look of her current stock. If the Pilarese trader two tents down hadn't confirmed the sightings of a cloaked figure sweeping the rooftops throughout the ghetto, Zaethan might have given up on his hunch that the killer wasn't traveling at street-level. Marketown and the Drifting Bazaar were the most heavily trafficked areas the killer had charted, according to Zaethan's markers across his maps.

Wekesa's valley pryde was the highest ranked in Bastiion, second only to Zaethan's own, and he didn't believe that the lack of progress in their investigation was a coincidence. The more he considered it, the more Wekesa's delay seemed intentional. After all, once the killer was named, the valley pryde would be forced to end their investigation and, consequently, forfeit their permission to remain in the Proper.

Meaning, if Zaethan wanted to remove Wekesa from his city, all he needed to do was hunt down the reason the other alpha had been sent for in the first place. It was a strategy that directly defied his father's orders, but Zaethan decided it was best to sort out the finer details on the backend.

Besides, if he allowed the *Jwona rapiki* to extend his stay in Bastiion, it might not be long before Zaethan could no longer claim the city at all. Or the pryde inside it.

"You don't believe in the Fates, *Ahoté*. Or their imprisoned." Kumo's great shoulders shook as he laughed steps ahead. "*Ano*, we do this by might. *Kwihila rapiki mu Jwona!*"

"Victory can write over fate, cousin, but I'll take all the help *Àla'maia* wants to give," Zaethan retorted, dodging the clothesline. "Keep your eyes high. If what the hag says is true, that's where victory will show itself."

"*Uni*," Kumo agreed, then jogged up the tight street to relay the same to Takoda.

Watching Kumo squeeze his breadth between the stalls, packed with hagglers and even stingier merchants, reminded Zaethan of years past. When they were cubs, his cousin used to visit Bastiion on occasion. The first time they'd explored these very streets, Kumo returned to the palace with two black eyes for the price of one. By Marketown's standards, that was a bargain.

They followed Takoda down another, narrower alley, though no less crowded. Even nearing midnight, women dragged their children from one merchant to the next, bartering with fervor. The divergence of classes here in Marketown never ceased to amaze him. As Zaethan passed a booth of baubles, an off-duty kitchen maid screamed at a noble's wife, who had just ripped a shiny object from a night-caller's grasp. One dressed in soiled linen, the second in silk, and the third a combination of the two. It was remarkable how quickly the classes forgot their stations in a vendor's tent, and how much more quickly they recalled them upon leaving.

Beyond Kumo, Zaethan saw Takoda duck when a broken bottle whizzed overhead. From a cloud of smoke, a ragged-looking man stumbled out of a dirty tent, bowling into several passersby. Another hunk of glass followed his departure, shattering across his yellowed, pipe marrow-stained tunic. Cloying vapors pooled in the street when a larger man, red in the face, erupted from the tent and hurled a bucket next.

Kumo's forearm covered his mouth as they neared the bumbling fools. "Depths, that's rancid!"

"Eh, break it up!" Zaethan pushed past his beta and through a group of gawking bystanders. "*Uni*, you!" He pointed to the second man. By the severe jaundice of his eyes, Zaethan didn't know if he'd even comprehended the order.

"Ow! *Shtàka!*" Takoda flinched when something hit him. "He said break it up, you stoned scumbucket! This yancy's puffed higher than dandi pollen. Depths!"

Blood trickled from Takoda's temple. Zaethan grabbed the lowlife and twisted his arm, inspiring him to spew the contents of his stomach onto the cobblestones. Kumo doubled over once he saw the man's vomit. Were she to ever challenge him again, Zahra should just eat a spoiled breakfast, and his beta would fold at the sight of it.

"A night in the guardhouse should sober him up," Zaethen said grimly. "Come on."

Zaethan reared back when the man's head suddenly bobbed to the side with a *crack*, knocking him out. Releasing the unconscious bum, Zaethan knelt and picked up the clay tile that had landed near his boot.

"Kumo, Takoda!" he barked. "The roof—we've got movement!"

Without hesitation, Zaethan sprinted down the alley in the direction of tumbling tiles. He spotted a launder's ladder and scaled the rungs to a second-story balcony, nearly tripping over a lady's underskirt in the process. Climbing onto an awning, he hauled himself atop the clay roofing and scanned the patchwork of Marketown's skyline. There, to the east—a dark smudge leapt from one building to the adjacent. Squinting, he realized it was not one smudge, but two.

They were moving too fast to catch up from behind, but he wouldn't need to. These streets wove an intimate network Zaethan learned long ago. Tracking their trajectory, he ran north, skidding along old tiles as they buckled beneath him. He briefly lost his balance on a section of unstable framing, slashing his shin on a makeshift gutter. Panting, Zaethan pushed forward with the last ounce of his endurance as the dark smudges became cloaked figures and continued their race over the rooftops.

Jumping off a higher platform, Zaethan caught his arms around the second body. In an awkward barrel hug, he gripped the figure's torso as they rolled down a slope of loose slats and rickety tilework. When their combined weight hit a particularly weak spot, he and the masked figure fell together through the planks and onto the floor of an abandoned upper room.

Zaethan groaned, cursing as a pang shot through his elbow. Blinking, he readjusted his hold. He'd landed on the perpetrator.

"Get off me, you clumsy buffoon!" a husky feminine voice wheezed under the weight of his body.

Immediately Zaethan sat up and ripped the hood off a head of ashy hair, the moonlight overhead revealing the y'siti's delicate features.

"You really are a cockroach!" he snarled, drawing a blade and whipping it up under her chin. "Everywhere I look, I find you scurrying about. And to think, your act the other night with Salma almost had me fooled."

"You just let him get away! I've been tracking him for weeks, and tonight I nearly had him!" the witch shrieked, disregarding the knife he held to her throat. "Weeks of progress, for nothing! Are you really so delusional? I was chasing him, you fool!"

"Why should I believe—"

"*Ahoté.*" Kumo called in search from the roof.

"Ah, Alpha Zà!" Takoda's head manifested through the hole in the ceiling. "You catch a—uh…Alpha Zà?"

"*Uni*, I've caught an al'Haidren." Zaethan's confirmation echoed through the vacant space.

"Huh. Bit problematic, yeah? What're you going to do with her?"

"*Get off me!*" The y'siti bucked under his hold. "Every minute you waste, we invite another slaying. Do you want that on your conscience, Kasim?"

"Right…" Panting, Kumo joined Takoda above. "…right behind you, *Ahoté.*"

"She insists she's innocent. Same search as we," Zaethan yelled back without taking an eye off the wriggling witch. Even with his knees pinning her limbs to the floorboards, her efforts boosted him inches off the ground. She wasn't fatigued in the least.

"*Na huwàa tàkom lai na huwàa.* Same with y'siti, yeah?" Kumo called through the busted slats.

Zaethan glared down at the y'siti and considered his cousin's counsel. Wekesa's threat to both his position and his pryde in Bastiion was imminent, and trusting her again could be his undoing—or perhaps his salvation.

Her lustrous eye flicked to Kumo overhead. "What did he just say to you?"

"He said, 'It takes a hound to hunt a hound.'"

She swallowed. "What does that mean?"

His blade inched off her ghostly flesh. Rolling back on his heels, Zaethan eased to his feet.

"It means you are either with us or against us." He clutched the knife in his hand. "So, which will it be...Hound?"

TWENTY-FOUR

Luscia

Considering the coveted view from Luscia's private terrace, a stroll through Bastiion's illustrious Drifting Bazaar was long overdue. Merchant rafts draped in bright hues and mixed textiles littered the murky waters. The scent of foreign spices hovered in the air, the source of each sharp aroma tucked under tarp and canvas as their peddlers slumbered in the bowels of each buoyant stall. Though the bay was sleepy and the hour dark, the industrious grid of floating booths looked much how she'd imagined.

Present company excluded.

Fortunately, the three Darakaians kept their distance, and while Luscia hardly appreciated playing the hound, it *was* the better alternative. Kasim had been crushing her lungs when posing the two options—neither preferable—and the lack of air hadn't assisted her decision-making skills. Climbing over a snug swing bridge to the meager gangway of another stall, Luscia hoped she'd chosen wisely.

"We already passed this booth," one of his men grumbled—the one with shoulder-length braids. His beads chattered as they crossed the crude bridge behind her. "*Shtàka*, is she just taking us in circles?"

"*Wewe huwàa…na ýsiti tàkom lai na ýsiti,* yeah?" The huge one, Kasim's second, answered the other warrior.

Luscia understood little Andwele, but the bits she pieced together were not flattering. She couldn't decide if being called a dog as opposed to a member of the undead was an upgrade or a demotion with the Darakaians.

Kasim shifted restlessly in her periphery when Luscia paused and assessed a stack of crates. She needed a higher vantage point. Encumbered by their ordinary limitations, she'd tried to chart a path the Darakaians could follow, but it was like hauling a sack of opinionated potatoes through the maze of makeshift waterways.

"You're trying my patience," Kasim warned in her ear. "I can still revise the terms of our agreement. You already failed to fulfill your end of one bargain—don't make this the second."

The hilt of his *kopar* pressed into her lower back, just above the crest of the trousers she'd procured for tonight's outing. Apparently, Kasim was still cross from their dispute that morning, when he'd again howled to use the wraiths. Instead, she'd handed him a curved staff and tied rocks to his ankles.

He'd floundered miserably.

Kasim really had a hard time letting things go.

"I failed at nothing, Lord Darakai." Luscia heaved a sigh and reached around to ease the cool metal back toward his middle. "I cannot speed your own rate of learning. That—" She peered higher, toward a potential landing. "—is your own affliction. You requested I lead this party, yet are proving to be a terrible follower."

"*I* lead, witch. You are just my means to an end." Kasim pivoted in front of her, puffing his chest out at her chin. A pleasing, smoky tang of camilla and cedar doused her nose.

"This continued infatuation with semantics is exhausting." Luscia retreated and inhaled the briny odor of the bay. "If you wish to succeed tonight, silence your sounding alarm and do shut up."

She twisted away, putting her back to Kasim. Cocking her head, she listened to the sounds of the night. The tide lapped the docks, bins and boxes creaking in the routine sway. Beneath the rudimentary layers of sound, emerging snores carried a rumbling baritone through the darkness.

With an impatient huff, the other al'Haidren murmured something under his breath.

"I asked for quiet," Luscia repeated sternly.

"*Shtàka*. No one said a word!" he barked, folding his arms. "Some y'siti ears you've got."

Luscia stretched her neck and tried once more, but the rapid whispering increased. She spun in place. The big one, Kasim's beta, shrugged to the slender Darakaian in front of the gangway. Neither man's lips were moving.

Low voices swarmed her ears when the relentless buzz engulfed her mind.

"*Niit. Niit, heh'ta!*" She shook her head violently. Luscia scrambled for a vial inside her cloak, but it slipped from her fingers with a tremor, shattering across the planks underfoot. "*Heh'ta!* Make it stop!"

Clutching her temples furiously, she tripped into the leather folds of Kasim's jacket. This couldn't happen, not here. Not with witnesses. Panting, Luscia gripped the buttery, weathered arms of his coat as the buzzing grew to a roar.

"*Ahoté!*"

"Alpha Zá!"

Through the whirring symphony, she recognized the measured, high-pitch whine as Kasim released the *kopar* from his hip. She felt his shoulder rise under her fingertips. Luscia lifted her face and met his gaze, tense under each puckered brow. Her lips parted, to ask for aid, when a loud *pop* jolted her limbs. Her head snapped toward her spine. Ringing flooded her ears.

Kasim's eyes widened as he stumbled away from her on the narrow platform. "*Depths...*"

Suddenly, her vision erupted in threads of light.

Energy from the *Other* shimmered throughout the Drifting Bazaar, dancing faintly on a gentle breeze. A single source of brightness in the shadows captured Luscia's focus. The thread, brilliant against its brothers, shivered around her torso and into the distance. Hesitantly, fearfully, she turned to watch it slither past the two Darakaians at the edge of the swing bridge.

Sensing her attention, it twitched erratically. An eerie light that she alone could see flickered over the waters.

Instinctively, her limbs rebelled and leapt to the call. Luscia dove past Kasim, toward the stack of crates, and vaulted overhead after the pulsing guide. The ball of her foot grazed the beta's shoulder for balance when she crossed the bridge in midair. Landing, Luscia rolled into an explosive sprint. She hardly heard the Darakaians yelling in her wake.

As she bounded across the rickety planks to another stall, the ringing eased and opened to pages of sound. Abruptly the shining thread convulsed and switched to the east, pulling Luscia through an open window of a vacant booth. Frantically, she skidded overtop a cluttered counter and through a swath of stale, moldering curtains, tumbling into the open.

A scream fractured the haze in her mind.

Luscia jumped to her heels. With a spark, the lumin shuddered fitfully toward a floating ghetto across a vast waterway. A system of rigging connected posts on either side of the channel. In a rush, she ran up the nearest post, freed Ferocity, and cut loose a cable. Cording it around her forearm, she swung and, with eager footwork, treaded the side of a freighter until she met the roofing.

Atop the unstable structure, the threads flashed in and out of focus. Between eroding, clustered stalls, the lumin pulsed around a circlet of darkness, even under the abundance of a full moon. The darkness shifted aside in the form of a cloaked figure to reveal a whimpering child. The pale hue of the young boy's hair shone as he struggled to escape his captor's grasp.

A sound of fury broke through her lips. Luscia abandoned the freighter and carved her Najjani blade through the air. Despite her speed, the cloaked figure whirled responsively, tossing the boy aside and catching the tip of Ferocity at their shoulder instead of the throat. Luscia's knee cracked as it made impact on the platform before she clumsily rolled to a crouch.

Tightening her grasp around the hilt of her blade, Luscia sprung after the figure. A gloved hand released their bleeding shoulder and they ran west. Lurching in the figure's direction, Luscia stopped at the cross-caste's wail of pain. Looking back, she saw a pool of dark blood soaking the planks beneath his little body where it escaped a deep gash along his arm.

Luscia growled in frustration as she watched his captor disappear in the distance, only the glint off a pair of fine boot buckles under the moonlight marking their departure. Hurriedly, she moved to the boy, who was no more than six or seven, judging by roundness of his scraped, tear-streaked cheeks.

"Shh." Luscia tore a strip off the hem of her undershirt and bound his arm tightly. It was so small. "Shh, *waedfrel*. We are safe now. *Wem*, yes, it's going to be all right."

Within minutes, the Darakaians tore through the alley of freighters, stopping short at the sight of them.

"Wh—" Kasim panted, bending over to catch his breath. "Which way did he go? Depths, why didn't you follow him?" His tied locs swished erratically as he gestured to the emptiness.

"Because he's losing blood—a lot of it." Luscia scooped up the boy, caressing the back of his shivering head. "I made a call. Deal with it."

Kasim all but snarled at her, though she knew his malice was misdirected. He wanted to catch the cross-caste killer almost as much as she did, if for different reasons—reasons she suspected had more to do with the scarred man in Salma's tavern than the lives of Boreali innocents.

"Give me the boy." He reached out, but Luscia tightened her grip. Kasim motioned angrily to her distinctive eyes. "You create complications by being here! How will you hide *those* from your own cross-caste?"

Luscia chewed her lip. He was right. In their political climate, the Boreali al'Haidren could not be seen stalking the Bazaar in the middle of the night with a bleeding child in her care. And unlike her visit to The Veiled Lady, there was no amount of cocao powder that could mask the truth from one of Boreal's own descendants.

Slowly, Luscia relinquished the boy into Kasim's stiff arms. They wrapped around his little body possessively—protecting him from Luscia. As if she would ever even dream of hurting this child, or any other.

"Where are your parents, little one?" she asked, but he only whimpered into Kasim's chest. "Your mother?" Luscia stroked his hair. "*Yeh Mamu? Mamu ou Fappa?*"

"*Fappa!*" The boy sobbed and pointed toward the eastern slums.

Luscia nodded and looked warily to Kasim. "When you find their vessel, instruct his father to stitch the wound and make a paste of pure kaleo flower and gilead leaf. He's likely a Boreali trader if the boy calls him that. He will understand."

The Darakaian al'Haidren held her gaze for a moment, his bright eyes narrowing at her instructions. Turning, Kasim rocked the boy from side to side as he issued orders to his men.

"Takoda, you're with me. Kumo—" He angled his head at Luscia. "—escort the y'siti back to the palace grounds. Unnoticed. We don't need any questions about our...association."

Luscia bristled, but started walking.

The beta, Kumo, kept pace with her as they navigated between the more forgotten buildings of Marketown. After nearly half an hour of quiet, he began to speak.

"So, eh," he tried cautiously, as if their interaction would rouse her ire, "how'd you know where to go? You smell him out, yeah? After all that, uh..." His dark, oversized hands swarmed about his skull. "*Kakka shtàka...?*"

She snorted, though there was little to laugh about.

"*Kakka shtàka* sounds accurate," she grumbled. Despite logic—for

Luscia had been right to ensure the boy's safety—it still felt as if she'd permitted a killer to run free.

"You get a look, *uni*?" The beta inched closer as they walked, but kept a hand on his *kopar*. "You saw him, I mean?"

"Man or woman, they wore a cloak, which did its job." Lusica picked a few splinters of wood from the seam of her surcoat. "He's not from any slum, though. The fresh polish of his boots gave that much away."

"Huh." Kumo's hand eased off his *kopar*. Suddenly, a pearly grin sparked on his face. "You no y'siti hound, *ano*! You like *Maji'maia*!"

Unsmiling, Luscia eyed him, suspicious of her new branding. "In other words?"

Sheepishly, his thick forefinger rose to point at Aurynth's watchman. The full moon, alarmingly bright, illuminated their steps as they turned a corner.

"When Àla'maia still has her magic." His finger shook toward the sky. "The Witchy Moon."

Slowly, with great care and exhausting control, Luscia lowered the heel of her foot to the stone of her private terrace. Even slower did she allow the rest of her body to follow.

With the gentlest *click* and turn, she nudged open the stained-glass door to her bedroom chamber. On any night, Luscia welcomed her luxuriously extravagant bed, but tonight her mind proved as weary as her extremities. Head pounding, she slipped off her hood and cowl, then bent to untie her upturned boots.

The hiss of a match kissed her ears just before the light of its flame sizzled into existence. Luscia's stomach dropped. Najjan were called Boreal's shadowmen for good reason; she was the last being who should have forgotten.

On a humble stool in the middle of her quarters, Marek slumped over the candle, elbows propped on his knees. His oceanic eyes were grim, shaded by his furrowed brow, when he eventually looked up.

"Marek, I—" Luscia started.

"You do not answer to them."

Luscia felt the warmth drain from her cheeks when Alora's outline moved through the doorway. As her own candle crossed the room, the light illuminated the whole of her guard. Declan, positioned nearest their Haidren, stood stoically, with an expression equally stern. The twins bookended her dressing table. Böwen rubbed his face with his palms, clearly uncomfortable. Collectively, their eyes remained downcast, but it was Noxolo in the corner who physically turned his elegant features toward the wall, away from his charge.

None of them uttered a word when Alora stopped behind Marek's stool. Her posture spoke volumes.

"These men have given their lives to protect the al'Haidren to Boreal," she said, her tone icy. "Yet through your petulant actions, your infantile ignorance, you've turned their sacrifice into a petty game of hide and seek. A *game*—" Alora leveled her glance around the tense space. "—that they appear to be losing. If one loses the petty games of a child playacting as an adult, how then could one possibly be victorious against a real threat?"

Many shoulders slumped at her communal admonishment.

"*Ana'Mere*, they are faultless in this. *Meh fyreon*, but the Darakaians have made a mockery of the cross-caste massacres." Luscia implored the humanity in her aunt. "I just...I needed to do something, anything in my power to—"

"*Niit*, Luscia. What you have done is jeopardize the already fractured balance of the Ethnicam." Alora's unbound veil of platinum tresses followed her like an ethereal cape as she stepped in front of the captaen. "If your selfish whimsy and childish justifications were ever discovered, the Accords would be tested beyond your limited imagination."

"The Darakaians are dragging their feet, *Ana'Mere*! Are we to stand by and watch?"

"*Wem*, as I instructed, weeks ago." In her periphery, Luscia's guards shifted uneasily. "Once the Darakaians conclude their investigation, the Najjan will be permitted to intervene. Not before."

"That investigation is a joke. You haven't seen because you weren't here!" Luscia's face warmed again with the flurry of passion rising from her gut. "You weren't here, so I made a choice. I too am Najjan—"

"*Niit*, Luscia." The etchings of age creased when her aunt's lips pressed into a harsh line. "You are al'Haidren to Boreal. *That* is your duty—to be a servant to your House. *Meh'dajjeni Dönumn, weh'dajjeni Lux.* 'My strength in the Gift, our strength for the Light.' We lay down everything, Luscia—*everything* for our people." Luscia's mother's eyes stared out from her aunt's face. "Your pride—this need for *your* version of justice—has made you blind. And your blindness," she emphasized in a detached voice, backing away, "is beyond a disappointment."

Luscia's legs threatened to buckle under her, as if she'd been kicked in the kidneys. It wasn't until Alora reached the doorway that Luscia realized she'd stopped breathing.

"*Se'lah Aurynth*, Luscia. Until the shores of Aurynth, I will endeavor to make you see."

Luscia counted her breaths in her aunt's absence, weighted by an arduous merger of anger and shame. Staring at her half-laced boots, she heard the twins leave; listened to the abrupt pause when Böwen turned to say something, but changed his mind. Noxolo whispered to Declan, too low even for her ears, and then he exited after the twins.

Luscia lifted her chin when the stool raked against the floor and Marek rose. She tried to offer an explanation, but nothing came.

"How—" Marek shook his head, huffed, and twisted the hem of his jacket between his long fingers. He must have gone out in search of her. "How could you?"

It was an accusation, not a question. Her chest compressed as he too departed.

Tears promised to spill over, but Luscia refused them. She'd already demonstrated enough weakness.

"*Ana'Sere?*" Declan held the door ajar, the last to leave. Light from his candle wavered over the braided, ginger hairs at his chin. "Just give us the night. We took a mighty tongue-lashing, the captaen more than anyone. *Boleava,* please. Give us one night to lick our wounds, *Ana'Sere,* and it will be forgotten in the morning."

"*Mey fyreon, Ana'Brödre.*" She bowed her head, pressing her eyes shut. "It seems I don't deserve you."

Before the door latched, a somber chuckle slid over his shoulder. "We've learned many things tonight, *Ana'Sere,* but that was not one of them."

Luscia collapsed onto her bed. Her fingertips sought the *solrahs* through her septum for comfort, but the luxiron's unnatural warmth did nothing to soothe her. Moments later, those same fingertips dropped to the uneven tissue of her neck, where layers of fabric hid its legacy.

No Darakaian brand, no Unitarian slur, could ever compete with something so timeless it chased her like a ghost.

Failure.

TWENTY-FIVE

Zaethan

Zaethan tapped the steel point of his quill pen against the blank parchment before him, rebelliously inclined to keep it that way. Dmitri had requested they each bring tools for note-taking, insisting there was a need. Even since their childhood education, Dmitri had loved writing down his thoughts, almost as much as he loved Uriel pie.

Zaethan hated Uriel pie.

Along with flamboyant pens.

"The gall, making us wait on her like this." A swallow of citrus and sea salt caused him to cough when Sayuri leaned over the table to pour herself a generous flute of Galina wine. "Really, who does the y'siti think she is—the ghost of queens past?"

"That's a bit rich," Ira propped his chair on its back legs and blew a kiss, "coming from you, dear."

"I'm sure she has good reason." The prince licked his forefinger and turned the page of the ledger before him, otherwise engrossed.

Fleeting and foxlike, Sayuri's eyes rolled under her lashes. Despite the al'Haidren's frequent dramatics, Zaethan found himself agreeing with her. He'd waited nearly an hour for the y'siti to show at the abandoned training room that morning. She never did. The witch had been dancing around their agreement for weeks by withholding the wraiths, but today had elected for complete absence.

There was a reason the others in the Ethnicam did not seek bargains with the Boreali: they never stuck. Zaethan stifled a groan and fidgeted in his seat. He'd been stupid to test history in the first place.

"...as if I couldn't possibly have other social engagements today. Dozens of invitations, callers, and don't get me started on the appointments—" Sayuri ceased admiring her nails when the double doors creaked and parted slightly.

A sliver of the y'siti's profile could be seen through the narrow opening. She paused in the doorway, appearing to argue with someone. A red-headed Najjan—the captaen of her guard, Zaethan recognized—stepped closer, backlit from the hall. Their lips jumped furiously, but emitted no sound. It was a characteristic of witch-tongue Zaethan had begun to notice.

When the Najjan disappeared, Sayuri tracked the witch like an archer as she seemed to float toward her seat. Her stride was fluid, strange in its unfamiliar grace, though each step was notably more reserved than her arrogance typically warranted. The bushy tail of her war-tainted crossbreed dusted the floor as he padded inches behind her, almost imitating his alpha.

"Finally decided to grace us with your undead presence?"

"Lady Pilar," Dmitri cautioned.

"Well, I for one am pleased to see you, my dove." Ira, slightly unbalanced, leapt to pull out her chair. "Life is just bl-bleak without your wintery radiance."

"Rich, indeed," Sayuri muttered flippantly.

"Per—" Ira hiccupped. "—haps, one day, I can undertake the duties of this chair." Ira attempted to wink, his eye twitching, as he sloppily slid back into his seat.

The quill snapped under Zaethan's thumb. "I'm going to find better things to do with this pen, Ira, if you don't lock it up."

"*Meh fyreon.* Forgive me, Your Highness, I—"

"Dmitri," the prince reminded her.

"—overslept," she finished, barely glancing toward the head of the table. The severe angles of her face were fully exposed today, as she'd donned no trace of kohl and contained her hair in an uncharacteristically tight braid.

Without her Najjani mask, the y'siti looked emotionless. Zaethan was startled to realize how much she resembled her aunt.

"Completely understandable, Lady Boreal." Dmitri perched forward and dropped his face to find hers, offering a smile. "You and I know more than most how difficult it is for sleep to find us."

A shrill noise escaped Sayuri's painted lips, as Ira started to snicker into his cup. Her glare seared an invisible pattern into the northern al'Haidren. Perhaps Zaethan hadn't been the only one to hear of their midnight strolls. His pryde was discreet, not prone to common gossip. Unitarian sentries, on the other hand...

To Zaethan's surprise, the y'siti turned to him. "How was your evening, Lord Darakai?"

Ironically, had she bothered to come to training, they could have discussed it. Zaethan would have relayed how he and Takoda almost lost the boy at one point from all the blood loss, or how his Unitarian mother had wailed through the night at the foot of his makeshift sling bed. And, more specifically, the distrust his Boreali father demonstrated after Zaethan mentioned the northern herbs and later pressed him for the origin of that knowledge before they'd departed the merchant's home.

Zaethan twitched irritably when he realized the others had gone quiet. Sayuri crossed her arms, while both Ira and Dmitri listened curiously. The y'siti stared blankly into her empty glass, feigning disinterest for the sake of the others.

"It—" Zaethan cleared his throat and poured a shot of water. "It turned out exactly as intended." With a cheeky smirk, he tossed the water back.

"I'm relieved to hear it." She nodded solemnly and stroked the muzzle of the highlander wolx. His forelegs were folded under her chair in order to rest his oversized head in her lap.

"Here, here!" Ira splashed his glass with sparkling fluid and nudged a shoulder into Zaethan. "As did mine, my friend, as did mine. One of Salma's finest!"

"Get your hands off me," he snapped.

"You must not have felt that way last night." Ira's hands flew up in mock defense when Zaethan raised the pen. "*Shtàka*, so temperamental! Not that there isn't a market for that sort of thing."

"By the Fates, Ira, I'm about to—"

"Right. Now that we're all settled, shall we begin?" Dmitri bookmarked the ledger and set it aside, replacing it with several pages of parchment scribbled in his own hand. "Last night, word arrived by courier notifying us that the Zôueli royals will arrive in a matter of days. Therefore, I've begun listing the arrangements we need to make. After all, their visit is more significant than a mere solstice celebration between allies." Dimtri placed the parchment down and looked around the five-sided table. "I think it's time my Quadren knew that we are courting *Bahira*'Rasha."

"Princess Rasha?" Zaethan couldn't help his surprise. After their recent arguments, he'd given Dmitri space, but he'd never imagined his friend would keep something so vital out of their conversations. "Are *you* courting her, or is the Peerage?"

"I'd prefer we use her Zôueli title. It might seem more *welcoming*," Dmitri emphasized, for Zaethan's benefit, no doubt. "*Bahira*'Rasha is a strong choice. The Peerage suggested the match, but I've...consented to their wisdom."

"Courting?" Sayuri sputtered, the smooth perfection of her brow crinkling erratically. "For what?"

"Ah, the shapely lands of Razôuel." Ira's hands met behind his mop of hair. "Think you could handle a Zôueli queen, Your Highness? They're so...bossy." He grinned.

Sayuri's gilded features fell. "Queen..."

"Thank you, Lord Bastiion. That very attitude is why I've taken the liberty of drafting some assignments, if you will. Rasha's mother, *Bahira'zol*'Jaell, will be accompanying her and her brother, *Bahir*'Tozune, to Bastiion. I'm told he is eleven or so. Ira," Dmitri rapped the wood, "write this down."

"I'm certain even *I* can remember the name of an eleven-year-old."

"Good, because he will be your charge." Dmitri's quill pen skirted over the folds in his parchment. "He enjoys riding and archery. As both activities require a sober mind, let's start drying you out."

Seizing Ira's goblet in hand, Zaethan promptly replaced it with a glass of water.

"You want me to babysit—"

"A prince. *Bahir'*Tozune, precisely. Moving on…Zaeth…" He flipped to a second page of notes. "Have you prepped the palace for the Zôueli party? I believe they are to be housed in the eastern wing, is that correct?"

"It's the most logical placement. We retain our ability to monitor their security, while they can enjoy the views. The western wing would be more secure, but I doubt their queen would tolerate the docks."

Zaethan listed other provisions, sentry counts, and accommodations for the Zôueli guard. As he finished, Ira stifled a disgruntled yawn, while the y'siti caressed her mutt absently. Sayuri reclined in wordless disbelief.

There's one benefit to this news, he thought.

"Most impressive, Lord Darakai. As always." Zaethan leaned back, pleased. It felt like ages since his friend had acknowledged his aptitude for anything. Dmitri referenced his final page. "Lastly would be *Bahira'*Rasha herself. My mother will personally host the queen, but Rasha may require a sort of…social escort during our festivities."

Smoothing her inky hair where it slipped down her shoulder, Sayuri sat up a little taller. "I suppose I could introduce the princess into my elite circles."

"Thank you, Lady Pilar. That's very gracious of you," Dmitri said, patting her jeweled fingers. "However, Rasha has evidently harbored a fascination with the lands of Boreal since girlhood." Withdrawing his hand and glancing at the y'siti, he added, "Luscia, would you be kind enough to assist me? I fear she'll quickly grow bored of my conversation, with my avid appreciation of herbaceous shrubbery and whatnot. Might you relieve her from time to time?"

Without warning, Pilar's seat skidded backward as Sayuri stood and slammed her palms onto the tabletop in front of the witch. Dmitri grabbed his cane, bewildered.

"Lady Pilar!"

Her scrutiny narrowed as she inched closer to the y'siti. Amber against snow, their noses almost touched. "I know what you are doing, you putrid northern *whore*. And you are going to regret it."

The prince shot to his feet. "*Sayuri!*"

The y'siti's strange eyes sparkled when she glanced up for the first time that morning. "Remember yourself, Lady Pilar. I won't remind you again."

Zaethan broke from Dmitri's side when her war-tainted animal's ears flattened, and his snarl revealed a set of elongated canines. Gripping Sayuri by the arm, Zaethan dragged her into the hall. Standing watch in the shadow of a column nearby, the Najjani captaen stepped into the light streaming through the wall of windows. The northman's skin, normally so pale, now rivaled the shade of his hair, and his face was twisted with rage.

Briskly, Zaethan heaved the Pilarese al'Haidren down the corridor and around the bend.

"Y'siti trash, all of them! He is utterly enthralled by her, Zaethan. *Enthralled!*" she shrieked. "Don't you see it?"

"*Depths*, Sayuri," he hissed, "of course I see it."

"Then what are we going to do about it?"

"*Shtàka.*" Zaethan tossed her into an alcove. "*We* aren't going to do anything."

Her hands planted on the slight curve of each hip. "Something has to be done about the witch before her spell infects him for an entire lifetime. We both know what I'm saying is true."

"I know, from experience, that you never tell the truth."

Sayuri prowled toward him, as if another person suddenly occupied her skin. Warm breath puffed against his chin when she leaned in, coaxing, "I told you there would come a day when you and I would need each other, Zaethan. We could make a memorable alliance in this game she's playing. *Very* memorable."

He felt her nails skim the underside of his jacket when she reached around and dragged him against her. Zaethan suppressed a smirk and let his lips brush her ear.

"Dmitri chose a 'putrid whore' over you, Sayuri. Why would I want even less?"

Shoving her aside, he straightened his sleeves and headed for the war room, her petty scream echoing at his back.

It was unclear what drove Zaethan to seek out Orynthia's notorious war room, except his longing for an empty space, his desire to breathe, or perhaps its library of maps.

He rebound his dreaded coils as he marched through the palace. There were too many moving pieces on the proverbial board. Between the cross-caste killings, Dmitri's sudden need for a wife, and Sayuri's near descent into madness, Zaethan needed to clear his head before his fists found a simpler solution. With the openness of the plains out of reach, the vacant war room would have to do.

When Zaethan arrived at the ornate entry, he reached for the byrnnzite handle, then wavered. Masculine chatter trickled through the crack between the twin doors, though to his knowledge, no military discussions were planned for that morning. Confused and intrigued, he pressed an ear against the fissure.

"...nearly ready, coming to eighty warships..."

"... impressive, Lateef. Our navy will nearly double that of Razôuel."

"*My* navy, Tetsu. Don't forget where we stand, you and I..."

"...vessels may belong to you, Nyack, but they're berthed in my waters."

Pulling back marginally, Zaethan scratched the newly grown scruff at his jaw. The king's contract with Pilar was for forty vessels, not eighty. He'd sat at the table, in that very same war room, when the agreement was signed.

If Zaethan's father, both Haidren and Commander of Orynthia's armies, had negotiated a secondary contract with Tetsu Naborū, it was a deal between Haidrens outside the crown's awareness. Dmitri's father was many things, but proficient in military dealings was not one of them. It was entirely possible the king would overlook additional warships stationed in Pilar, but the greater question was why the naval expansion had been ordered in the first place.

"...prydes will handle that, when the time comes."

"You speak as if you hold authority, little Alpha, whilst being no one with nothing to your name...keep your pet in line, Nyack, or put him outside."

Zaethan crammed his ear against the door again, wishing not for the first time that his hearing was cursed like the y'siti. Whatever bargain had been arranged between Tetsu Naborū, General Lateef, and his father, it affected the prydes. *Zaethan's* prydes.

Except it wasn't Zaethan at his father's side in the war room. It was Wekesa.

"...place in Bastiion secured. Get used to it."

"What about that son of yours, Nyack? He's your al'Haidren. Will that not spark trouble for..."

The tenor of a younger man snickered, dampening Naborū's inquiry and his father's reply.

"...never worry yourself with insignificant details, Tetsu."

Breathless, Zaethan stood mute in the empty hall, unable to move. Like a satchel of stones, his stomach plummeted to his feet, numbing his toes. He knew he'd become a disappointment to his father. A reminder of his mother's death; an ever-present barb in an unhealed wound. But at the very least, pain ensured his significance. Without that pain, Zaethan wasn't sure if there was anything left between them.

In a rush, he rolled his body to the side when a *click* of the handle signaled their exit. As the doors pushed open, Zaethan sucked in air to flatten himself between the decorated slab and the cold stones at his back. Watching them through a thin crevice, they concluded their discussion.

"...your men. Order them to be on watch. I don't want any interference, *yeye qondai*?" their commander instructed Wekesa as the pair followed General Lateef to the end of the corridor. Even from the back, Zaethan could tell Wekesa had begun dressing in the finest Unitarian garb the Bazaar had to offer. From the fine wax coating his braids to the virgin leather of his boots, he'd thoroughly transitioned to life in Bastiion, and the bastard was enjoying it.

"*Uni zà*, Commander." Wekesa struck his chest eagerly. "I will see it done."

"*Uni*, that you will."

Unable to look away, Zaethan's jaw slackened when his father lifted an arm, cabled in scars and muscle, and patted Wekesa on the back—a gesture Zaethan had never once experienced at his father's hand.

Together rounding the turnoff, they were gone.

After a few moments, Zaethan shoved the door off himself and struck the bronze-plated wood with force. Knuckles throbbing, the door flew back on its ancient hinges, threatening to bust from the framing.

"One so insignificant should be quiet."

Zaethan spun in place. Drowning under the silvery swell of his shoto robes, the reedy and jaundiced Haidren to Pilar waited patiently beside the archway. The tail of his pointed beard rotated like the hand of a compass when his head angled eerily, and he fixed his yellowing eyes intently on Zaethan.

"Just looking for my father. Jolly fellow." Zaethan stretched out his shoulders, resisting the inexplicable urge to itch his exposed skin all at once. "Seen him?"

Tetsu Naborū's lips quirked at the sides before his head propped upright again. Zaethan had never taken to the man, and this sort of *kakk* was a perfect example why not.

"I have seen many things and foresee many things to come, young Kasim." Naborū waltzed closer, accompanied by the reek of sour pipe marrow. "I foresee that an insignificance should be quiet. It doesn't think..." He touched his metal nail-piece to his temple. "It doesn't speak..." The tip dragged to his thin lips. "...unless his master ordains it. So, run along, young Kasim—run to your master and *heel*." He dropped his claw to his thigh and patted it, like one ordering a hound.

"Treat a man like a dog, Lord Haidren," Zaethan folded his arms stiffly and stepped back, "and eventually, he'll bite like one."

Refusing to lower his gaze until he put his back to Sauryi's uncle, Zaethan strolled to the turnoff, admittedly a bit faster than he'd intended.

"Oh, young Kasim," he heard the Pilarese Haidren call after him, "I'm counting on it."

TWENTY-SIX

Luscia

As a woman under the immense scrutiny of her personal guard, Luscia found it mildly depressing that she was to spend her only hour of freedom at the behest of an ill-tempered Darakaian. With a slight twitch of her finger, she signaled Aksel, her sole confidant in all matters treacherous, to follow her descent down a grand, plunging staircase. In an abandoned training room floors below, Kasim awaited her, no doubt brooding over things he didn't understand and never would.

She'd argued to Marek, rather tersely, that her station warranted the right to *some* privacy, be it a mere walk during waking hours in the company of her own thoughts and restless wolx. As such a walk encapsulated the miniscule hour of solitude left at her disposal, she hoped one day the entire House of Darakai would appreciate the sacrifices made to hone their meddlesome al'Haidren into a decent excuse for a warrior.

In Marek's lingering anger, the evidence of which balanced on the hard set of his shoulders, they'd quarreled at Luscia's exit, his words both detached and taciturn. The captaen of her guard still refused to look her in the eye after the profound bite of Alora's rebuke, for though the weight of their Haidren's disappointment fell on Luscia, her criticism had settled on the men as well, casting a net of shame far beyond herself.

Lost in thought, Luscia passed under a narrow arch and entered a less occupied corridor with her head hung low. She wished she could have explained the events of that evening to her aunt, but even more to her guard. Disagree as they may, Alora was right in her assessment of the Najjan and their sacrifice. They'd traded their own lives for Luscia's, in more ways than one. It was the call of the five, just as it was hers as future Haidren for their people.

That very call, in methodology rather than ideology, had splintered Luscia from her predecessor. Like Alora, she too hoped to submit herself for the sake of Boreal, but not by way of surrender to the will of the Peerage or the prydes. They had no right to speak for the maligned and forgotten, the trafficked and sold, the innocent and the unascended. There wasn't room for Alora's passivity in a city where people's lives held less value than the political entanglements of men unburdened by the death of Boreal's children.

Even still, her convictions didn't change the fact that Luscia was not Haidren to Boreal yet, and it had been wrong to elevate herself in such high esteem. In that, Alora had spoken the truth twice over. Luscia *had* become blind. Because of her pride and therefore disloyalty, Aurynth would sing of her unworthiness; a melody Luscia, like the five, could never unhear.

And yet...

Out in the world, there was a cross-caste boy, both frail and frightened, who had lived to see a new morning. Bittersweetly, the corner of Luscia's mouth curled, though the smile quickly retreated.

A muffled, mouse-like whimper tickled her ear when she stepped onto a lower landing. Frowning at Bastiion's fondness for public trysts, she looked to the lycran and remarked sarcastically, "And here I thought Unitarians couldn't function this early."

Her excuse for a smirk fell at the low growl from Aksel's underbelly. Changing course, she entered a narrow, shadowed corridor to the east of the landing, the highlander wolx several paces ahead. What at first had resembled a stifled moan rolled into a shuddered sob, and Luscia hastened after Askel, following him around the bend into an even darker hall dotted by a dozen cutouts built into the stone archways along either side. A silver tray and its fine contents laid strewn across the marble floor near the farthest alcove.

Without hesitation, Luscia sprinted down the hall in search of its owner. Inside the alcove, a lady's maid was pressed against stone wall, buried under the heaviness of a tall nobleman.

"*Niit, heh'ta!*" Luscia shouted as she slammed into his body. Gripping the folds of his velvet waistcoat, she used her weight to reel him off the maid. Halting her momentum when the Unitarian's back hit the wall, Luscia released the catch of Phalen's radials with each thumb. Furiously, she anchored her left blade against his gut and her right beneath his chin.

The dark-haired maid slumped in the corner. Torn fragments of her dress slipped off her slight shoulders as they lifted around her crumpled form, hiding herself as she wept.

"I know you…" The yancy's throat bobbed carefully against the edge of the radial as he glanced down. "We don't have to keep meeting like this. Bastiion houses better places meant for your kind."

"Lord Ambrose." Luscia spat the name when she recognized him as the same nobleman she'd seen with the Haidren to Pilar, in another dark corridor weeks before. In the softer light of the snug alcove, his complexion was wanner than expected, lacking the warm radiance attributed to Unitarian blood.

"You will never touch another lady in this palace again," she instructed, pushing the radial through the outer layers of costly material around his waist.

"That y'siti mutt is no more a lady than you are, dirty highlander witch." Ambrose sneered as Luscia realized he was referring to the young woman crying on the floor, not the snarling beast at her heels.

"Mark my Boreali witch-tongue, Ambrose. If you touch one of them again, I will gladly spill your entrails and serve you at a Mworran feast." Luscia dropped her left radial from his navel and slid it below his belt. Ambrose shuddered as a bead of sweat dripped from his walnut waves and past his protruding brow. "Or…I might just serve them another local delicacy."

Felix Ambrose stared at Luscia, locking on her Tiergan eye, and twitched in a manner she took for a nod. Backing away, she shielded the maid and ordered Aksel to let the yancy pass.

Stopping under the archway, Ambrose paused and licked his lips. "You smell delicious when you're angry, Lady al'Haidren."

Luscia stomach roiled as she took a deep breath and instantly regretted it. "And you smell like carrion. Leave us!" Aksel snapped at his ankles, yipping as he urged the noble further down the hall.

"M-my l-lady." A familiar, delicate hand touched Luscia's leg.

"Mila!" Luscia fell to the marble to aid her lady's maid. "*Meh fyreon,* I didn't even realize it was you!" Her hands went to assess the state of the girl, but slowed, remembering it was best not to touch right away. "Are you injured? Can you walk?"

Shakily, Mila guided herself upright and wrapped her arms around her chest, shaking her head. "He...you were in time, my lady."

A blossom of indigo was already spreading across Mila's jaw.

"Not soon enough," Luscia remarked angrily. "Come with me. I'm getting you out of this place."

Removing her outer sparring tunic, she wrapped the garment around her young friend and guided her to the safety of the Boreali suites.

Back in Luscia's apartments, she inspected Mila's surface wounds, knowing it would take far longer to heal what lay underneath.

"Böwen!" Luscia called while Tallulah fetched warm cloths. "Böwen, where is *Ana'Mere?* I need her. Now."

"*Ana'Mere* is meeting with the Peerage this morning, *Ana'Sere*... about a boy the night before last." Luscia felt a bittersweet sting at the mention of the little boy they'd saved. Böwen's eyes darted from his al'Haidren to the solemn girl in her care. Mila hadn't spoken since they'd entered the apartment. "From there, Emiere said they were to spend the evening in the outskirts of Wendylle. *Meh fyreon, Ana'Sere,* her guard didn't share anything more."

"*Shtàka*," she cursed. "And Marek?"

Returning, Tallulah tried to tempt Mila with a cup of water while she cleaned the shallow scrapes down her forearms.

"The captaen took the others to speak with the prince's sentries in preparation for the Zôueli's arrival. They stepped out after you left with the lycran earlier this morning."

Uncertain, Luscia bit her lip. "Mila, you said your mother works in the palace laundry, correct?" she inquired. "What of your sister? Is she in the palace as well?"

Mila's chin trembled as she nodded. "She's nine years old," was her only comment.

"*Wem*, I recall." Getting up, Luscia snatched a quill and parchment. "Your father was a trader from Roüwen—give me his name."

Luscia glanced up at the silence. Mila stared down at a bruise forming across her wrist.

"Mila." Böwen knelt at her feet and rested one of Tallulah's cloths over the bruise. "*Yeh fappa*...his name?"

"Caellaigh. Mac Caellaigh," she managed as a tear trailed down her porcelain cheek and splashed Böwen's hand. "His parents disowned him for marrying an outsider, before—before he died."

"Caellaigh," Luscia repeated as she scribbled a plea for her father's aid. Folding the parchment, she sealed it in wax and handed it to her Najjan. "Böwen, I need you to escort Mila, her mother, and her sister home to Roüwen. Bring this to my father. Our Clann Darragh will ensure the family takes them in."

Luscia sent up a prayer to the High One on their behalf. It was common knowledge the Boreali were a closed-off people, a fact that had surely defined Mila's upbringing in the Proper. They would need Clann authority to ensure the Caellaighs opened up their home voluntarily. One would think that, under the circumstances, Mila's grandparents would eagerly welcome the sight of their granddaughters on their doorstep. Regrettably, even the House of Boreal had its faults. Thank Aniell that Luscia's father had the influence to lessen their sting.

"All the way to Roüwen, *Ana'Sere?*"

"Mila is an unascended Boreali cross-caste, her sister even younger." Guilt drove Luscia to look away. "Today was the wickedness of one man, but tomorrow could hold even worse. I'm ashamed I didn't think to remove them from the present danger until now."

Picking up an untouched piece of bread from her morning tray, Luscia wrapped Mila's hands around it. "You must eat, Mila—no more of this courtier nonsense. We eat to become strong. Böwen, I want you to train her in the evenings. Her sister, too." She met his sea-green eyes, begging. "*Boleava*, Böwen. Like they were your own kin."

With that, she reached into her upturned boot and retrieved a hidden pocket blade from her youth and placed it into Mila's open palm. "So it won't happen again." Luscia squeezed the young woman's hand tightly and stood up, moving toward the door. "Leave as soon as you're able, Böwen. Get them out of Bastiion. Far, far away from this evil."

He nodded silently, likely shaken by the turn of events and his new charge. "Will you not see us depart, *Ana'Sere?*"

Luscia heard the pain behind his question. None of her Najjan would feel right about a separation, especially in such a tempestuous season.

She walked back to the sandy twin, sitting somberly without his mirrored image by his side, and cradled his boyish features between her hands. Luscia bent down and placed a gentle kiss atop his golden locks. "*Tredae'Aurynth, Ana'Brödre.* The High One watch over you day and night until we meet again, in life or in Aurynth."

She grabbed her cloak and snapped for the lycran. "We must go, I'm quite late."

Böwen raised his head. "Late?"

"*Wem, Brödre.* It's time to clean up my mess."

Storming into the training chamber, Luscia wasted not a second to rectify the dangerous situation at hand.

"Our bargain is over, Kasim." She stopped at the edge of the mat. In the center, he'd begun returning their gear to the trunk, apparently having given up on the notion she would eventually arrive. "It's reckless and a risk neither of us can afford any longer."

"Think again, witch." Kasim jerked the trunk up off the mat and rose to his feet. "Oaths might be meaningless to the y'siti, but a Darakaian keeps his word. You will keep yours, *uni*. I'll make sure of it."

"Run along to your boyhood companion. Tell him all about how you've betrayed him and his crown multiple times since I've arrived. *Wem*, yes." She fanned a hand in the direction of the southern wing. "Let's together inform the prince of all you've done behind his back."

"Isn't that from where you just came?" He leered, letting his gaze make a show of its voyage over her figure. "Did dressing make you late, or am I just keeping you from bewitching the next poor yancy?"

"You don't want to do this, Kasim. Not today," she warned. Luscia retreated to the door of the training space, intending to leave him to wallow in his next tantrum without an audience.

"You will teach me the wraiths as promised, or from the Depths, you will regret it."

"I won't come back tomorrow, Kasim, and neither should you."

A slight shift in the air preceded the curved training baton, warning Luscia to duck as it soared past her face and splintered against the door. Shocked by his unhinged behavior, she pivoted to face the al'Haidren to Darakai.

"You're weak," he instigated. "Scared, pathetic. Why is the realm so frightened of you pitiful creatures?"

"Because you *should* be," she growled, breathing slowly so as to not be bated by his foolish ignorance.

Kasim kicked another baton over to where she stood. "Prove it."

Luscia bent to seize the weapon, traditionally used by children on Viridis, and vaulted herself at Kasim, bypassing him to slide behind and knock his legs out in one swing. As he fell to the mat, she seized the curved baton from his grasp, claiming the complete set of beginner wraiths.

"But you're slower, heavier, and still unbalanced." Luscia scoffed as he grimaced but returned to his position. "Your ears are indifferent. They haven't listened to a thing I—"

A leather cord lashed her side, and she cried out at the unexpected pain. Taking advantage of her surprise, he tossed the *feidierdanns* aside and scrambled to the corner of the mat, grabbing the Boreali staff. Fearlessly, he ran toward her and, in midair, used both feet to kick her in the middle, launching Luscia across the room—a move he'd witnessed the day he spied on her and her five.

Aggravation spilled from her throat as Luscia rolled, reclaimed the batons, and made impact with the staff. He kept pace with her until she smashed a set of his fingers, though he refused to drop the weapon.

"You're holding back," he taunted. "Is the witchling too tired to play after a night under another yancy?"

"If you don't hold your tongue, I might just cut it out!" She struck his thigh with one baton and the side of his head with the other, then stepped back to calm herself.

"I was taught y'siti never grew tired." His eyes sparkled viciously as he blinked the pain aside. "Is it the heart or the lungs your mother eats after you're born?"

Her jaw clamped shut, veins filling with fire. She cracked her neck and stepped away. "These lessons are over."

When her boot met the stone, she turned her back to Kasim, eager to shake off his insults, but he only chuckled. It was a cruel sound, like that of his father when they'd met on her first night in the city.

"You're getting flushed, you know. I hear Boreali flesh isn't so corpselike when it's flushed. They say it burns quite beautifully in the heat of passion. *Uni*, like a *yaya* between some yancy's legs."

Lusica froze. The horrific scar tissue on her neck throbbed as she thought about Ambrose and his body pressed against Mila. The pulsing changed to a scald as her mind flooded with images she'd ached to forget and a sensation she'd strived to wash away.

"Ah, is *papyon* what makes your kind come alive, little y'siti?" She heard Kasim's poison over the rushing in her ears. "A pair of soft, Unitarian hands all over your b—"

Luscia screamed with a waking wrath that consumed her entire being. She spun in place, pulled her mother's consort dagger from its sheath strapped across her thigh. Nearly jolted by an outbreak of light, she threw Ferocity along the threads of lumin, aiming straight for Kasim's skull.

With a clatter, the dagger hit the wall and jangled against the floor. The threads shuddered at the sound and coiled in a makeshift fence surrounding them.

She tasted iron on her tongue when his fingers wiped blood away from a cut near his temple. To her shock and dismay, he grinned at the sight.

"There you are."

TWENTY-SEVEN

Zaethan

He recoiled from the taste of the words as they leaked off his lips. While Zaethan suspected them to be true, each turned sour when his voice evolved, emulating someone he'd always known to be much colder and crueler than himself.

As the witch neared the door, Zaethan's gaze burned a hole in her back. Suddenly his need for an advantage over Wekesa waned and submitted under the weight of Dmitri's disbelief in Zaethan's claims; the ache of his dismissal six years ago, and ever since.

The recent night on the docks had reminded his pryde of her true nature. Zaethan wasn't operating on absurdity, and in that moment, he resolved once and for all to make her prove it. Trapped in this wretched city, he seemed to have lost every personal battle since her arrival.

And Zaethan Kasim was done losing.

"Ah, is *papyon* what makes your kind come alive, little y'siti?" He heard his tone drop low and callous like his father. Halting, her steely demeanor began to unwind at its sound, and her fingers twitched. "A pair of soft, Unitarian hands all over your b—"

Zaethan felt a braided loc rip from the side of his head before he ever saw her turn. An invisible charge filled the room. The witch faced him on the other side of the mat near the door but, impossibly, it felt as if they were only feet apart. A chill coursed through his limbs at the terror before him.

The past resurrecting, the witch's eyes blazed unnaturally. Zaethan's heart skipped wildly when her lashes shuddered, increasing their glow. Her hair, ghostly and unpigmented, wafted around her small frame.

This. Zaethan's stomach tightened. *This is y'siti.*

A breeze passed over the tingling wound across his temple. He absently touched the wetness, disturbed by a static shock when he pulled away. Zaethan rubbed the blood between his fingertips.

"There you are," he said, grinning broadly. Vindication soothed the sting in his flesh.

The y'siti crouched low and roared. It was an unearthly sound, almost animalistic as it harmonized with itself. Springing from her position, she sprinted across the mat, seizing the whip he'd discarded moments prior. Like a tidal wave, she flipped forward and twisted in the space. The tail of the whip slashed violently through the air and snaked around Zaethan's neck. He had only a moment to clutch the northern staff within reach.

Gagged by the leather cable around his windpipe, Zaethan jerked the staff with him as he was pulled to the center of the mat and angled it, connecting with her jaw. He heard a satisfying *crack* at the impact. Breathless, he yanked the cord away, imagining the mark he'd left on her, but his victory was short-lived. Without hesitation, the y'siti stole the staff and used it to vault the distance to her dagger against the wall. She moved too quickly, practically in a blur, and Zaethan scolded himself for not taking his own advice to Kumo.

"Even as a cub, you were a y'siti demon," Zaethan choked out, voice hoarse. "You just," he stretched for the grip of the whip, "hide it better now."

She ran from the wall to seize a curved baton with her open hand, dropping low before flipping to strike it down upon his back just as he struggled to his feet. Zaethan's chin smashed into the mat. Turning over, he let the whip fly. A thrill of dominance rippled through his arm as he wrenched it back when it licked her ankle, causing the witch to tumble to the floor.

They both rose to circle each other defensively. She rotated the baton in her grasp, eerily mirroring the silhouette of the witchiron dagger in her opposite. A chunk of his loc still hung from the blade. Without warning, she spun. Zaethan ducked away, but not before the baton bruised his rib. In the same motion, her dagger skimmed his upper arm. Warm blood dripped on the mat.

"Some words should not make sound." She flexed her jaw, a bluish shadow creeping toward her lips. "And I am so tired of hearing that disgusting term."

Zaethan backed up and nearly tripped over the staff. "It's what you are." He stomped on the end, flinging it into the air, and caught it with his left hand. "Do you deny it now?"

Raising the staff, he thwarted her attempts to strike him. He saw her swallow.

"I am not at all what you say, and yet so much more."

She fell to her knees, slicing his calf.

Zaethan stumbled at the sear of the witchiron. He knew he'd feel its burn for days to come. She rotated to the side when he cracked the whip, barely missing her with its tail. He moved forward, but she flipped out of range.

"Maybe," Zaethan tested, inching closer as she skirted around the mat. "But like all men, even a witch has a weakness. Did you think I wouldn't notice?"

He'd picked up on her routine deflection during that last week of their morning trainings. The witch always seemed to avoid close combat, likely due to her small stature—coming body-to-body in a fight with a larger, physically stronger opponent would almost always put her at a disadvantage.

Her thick brows furrowed as she matched his footsteps backward, maintaining the distance of her baton, like always. Timing his strike with her next step, Zaethan whirled the staff brazenly at her middle, imitating her own tactics. Falling to the mat, he heard a snap as her wrist bent the wrong way and the dagger dropped. Zaethan kicked the blade aside and hovered over her.

A cry escaped her lips when he stepped on her injured wrist. He felt the disfigurement of the bone through the soles of his bare foot. Zaethan trapped her free arm with the other.

"What lacking could a Darakaian swine ever find in me?" she panted.

The witch virtually stood on her neck and shoulders as her legs hooked around his thighs and tugged. Zaethan's backside hit the mat forcefully. As she tried to free her ankle, crushed beneath his leg, he thrust the staff upward against her chest with the strength of both arms. They rolled as she again attempted to dislodge her ankle. Pinning him, they landed with her legs wrapped around his torso. The tip of the witchiron dagger cut into the first layers of skin at his throat. He didn't know when or how she'd retrieved it.

Zaethan smelled his flesh burning as it sizzled under the touch of the corrosive Boreali blade. He gulped cautiously. The brightness of her eyes flickered as they stared down at the metal. One bluer than Thoarne Bay, the other transformed into an eerie kaleidoscope, like those sold to wealthy children on the streets of Marketown.

"Weakness belongs to the Ethnicam," she struggled to say. Her hand shook as the blade pressed further into his skin. "Such weakness lives inside you all."

Zaethan stopped fighting. His fingers released the staff, letting it fall to the ground. Keeping his eyes locked on the orbs of light in her face, he brought his hands to her knees, suspecting the altered tactic would disarm her, given her usual prudishness and their sudden proximity. Slowly, languorously, he dragged his palms up the curve of her thighs over the men's breeches she wore.

Confused, possibly in horror, her eyes darkened, then shimmered with unexpected moisture. The blade subtly eased off his throat.

"What are you doing?" Her voice cracked.

His resolve faltered momentarily at that look in her eyes, but Zaethan had long since learned to press any advantage he found in battle. Hesitation could have fatal consequences, and the witch still held her dagger.

Newly determined, Zaethan's fingers found her hips and gripped them firmly, driving them into his own. "I told you I found your weakness."

Her face contorted, as if with pain, and she dropped her eyes to the shallow cut on his neck. Then to her hips. A look of terror filled her gaze, and she hurriedly crawled off his body, retreating onto the mat. The northern dagger trembled between them, clutched in her shaking hands.

"All of you," she whispered, scrambling to her feet. "*You're* the real monsters."

Zaethan stared after her in shock as she fled the training room. He lay there motionless on the floor long after the door clamored on its hinges, replaying those final moments in his mind. He'd thought her avoidance of close combat was merely tactical; he'd never imagined it might have been due to some other, unspoken trauma.

An uncomfortable sense of shame settled into his bones. Bleeding onto the dirtied floor, Zaethan suddenly itched to wash—and for the first time, not because of her.

Zaethan ignored the debased laughter from a nearby table as his retraced a line drawn across a map of the Proper. He moved another empty glass to flatten the corner of the parchment where it curled. It wasn't the most effective solution, but neither was studying his maps in the belly of The Veiled Lady.

"*Owàamo,* Alpha Zà." Beautifully sun-kissed arms encircled his chest from behind. "*Àlàmaia* shines for us tonight, *uni?*"

A knowing chuckle teased the back of his throat as he guided the sound of home to stand in front of his chair. Zaethan didn't like anyone at his back, especially a woman so adept at accessing men's coin.

"Not brightly enough, *ano.*"

"The best *papyon* happens in the dark, Alpha Zà. I should know." Her black curls bounced as she leaned forward, her parted lips brushing his ear. "Would you like to?"

Zaethan reached for her hand, nearly the exact shade of his own, and stroked the crevices of her open palm. She purred at his attention, a rehearsed sound.

"I would like—" He picked up a glass off a corner of the map and placed it in her hand. "—a refill."

Insulted, the night-caller sputtered and threw the glass on the floor. "I am not a barmaid!"

"Ah, but *yaya*, there's still time, yeah?" He patted her arm. "*Bwoloa*, and none of that yancy spittle Salma's peddling. The good stuff." Zaethan grimaced at the pain in his calf. He could certainly use it.

The southern night-caller sidestepped some broken shards of glass and stalked off, assuredly cursing him in Andwele as she disappeared into the crowd of patrons surrounding the bar. Hoping her return would be swift, Zaethan rubbed his leg, trying not to draw attention to his injury. While the liquor would help him forget the sting, he wished it could help him forget who he'd become in that training room. Though Zaethan hadn't known what haunted the Boreali al'Haidren—and still didn't, truth be told—he was ultimately responsible for having taken things too far. And that didn't sit well with him, despite his differences with the witch.

There was only one man he knew who would knowingly exploit such a thing, and unfortunately, no amount of *bwoloa* could rinse the taint of Nyack Kasim from his veins.

Returning to his maps, Zaethan again sought a pattern between the haphazard markings. Red lines drafted a distorted circle around the city, sprinkling into the provinces. He had only recently seen the need to classify the bodies found. Crimson hatch-marks clustered the inner Proper, where most of the victims had been drained. Miniature stars dotted Marketown and outward toward the docks, as well as the Drifting Bazaar. Sparingly, tiny squares distinguished where a victim's body was torn apart. Though spread out, the squares dominated the map outside the Proper and into the plains.

Same victim. Different kill.

Zaethan bent the corner of the map, accidentally tearing it. The pattern, though present, still didn't add up.

"*Ahoté*." A pair of enormous fists shook the tabletop, sloshing the little *bwoloa* left in his glass. "*Ahoté*, didn't you hear me?"

"*Ano*…when did you get here?" Zaethan looked around. "And where is that waitress?"

"I went to the stables, the offices, your apartments." Kumo scratched the base of his thick neck. "We've been trying to find you for hours, *Ahoté*. They made an arrest. It's sheer *kakk*, though. Just a thief, third offense…" The beta rambled until Zaethan cut him off.

"*Doru*, cousin. Just stop." Zaethan held up his hand. "Arrested for what? Lifting some bread?"

"*Ano zà!*" Kumo's forefinger pounded the center of the map. "For this! Total *kakk*. Wekesa's pryde wanted an arrest, and the commander bought it. Zahra said they rolled through your offices this afternoon and paraded the gutter rat in front of the sentries like some trophy."

"*Shtàka!*" Zaethan snarled and swiftly rolled up the maps. "Let's go."

"Go where, *Ahoté*?"

"To the accused," he yelled over his shoulder as he plunged through the crowd ahead of Kumo. "Depths, after running night after night through this city hunting the man, I want to look him in the eye."

"But I just told you!" Kumo hollered over the noise. "It's all *kakk*. A *kàchà kocho* pocket-swiper won't be able to tell us anything."

"Which is exactly why I want to talk to him."

Zaethan breathed through his mouth as they descended the spiraling stairs into the lower dungeon. Wekesa was really putting on a show, holding a common thief among the roughest criminals in Bastiion. If anyone suspected his false arrest, they'd have to endure these putrid catacombs beneath the city just to question the prisoner—an unlikely measure for most.

As they turned a corner, Zaethan mistakenly inhaled a whiff of human waste. Chains clanked and jangled against the bars of neighboring cells as he and Kumo marched past. A few prisoners called out perverse proposals, while some wailed in pain in the distance. Understandably, their visit was not well received.

"Depths, I hate this place." Kumo spat into the rag he'd used to cover his nose and eyed Zaethan peculiarly. "Are you limping?"

"Cramp," he grumbled.

"That's a limp, *Ahoté*…"

"How much further, Timon?" Zaethan asked the young Unitarian sentry at the lead.

"Just ahead, sir. *Shtàka*," the sentry swore under his breath. "I meant, Lord al'Haidren. Er—Alpha Zà, sir."

"They all suit," he assured the sentry, sympathetic that he probably didn't get out of the catacombs much.

They stopped before a slim opening between two boulders. Torches dimly lit a hollowed space where a man dangled in the center, his arms

HOUSE OF BASTIION

chained above his head. His spine and ribs protruded through his skin under the grisly lashes across his back.

"Really wanted to sell it, didn't he?" Kumo scoffed and tossed the rag aside.

"Timon, fetch the prisoner's personal effects," Zaethan ordered. "I'd like to examine his clothing, weaponry, the like."

The sentry shifted uncomfortably. "There aren't any, Alpha Zà."

"Then step outside, Timon."

The sentry promptly nodded and left. Zaethan was grateful his title still meant something in the dungeons, even if it carried less weight above the surface.

"My name is Zàethan Kasim, Alpha Zà of the Darakaian militia." He leveled his face with the thief's, noting the extreme swelling of his haggard cheeks. "I want to discuss your interaction with another alpha by the name of Wekesa."

A bloodshot eye tracked Zaethan as he mimed a scar over the side of his head, imitating his rival. The thief ground his teeth—the few left, anyway—and glanced aside.

"Eh, this rat's not going to talk, *Ahoté*." Kumo threw his hands up. "To him, we just chained him up to be punished worse than the crime he did commit, yeah?"

"I'm trying to help you." Zaethan again moved into the man's line of sight. "But help goes both ways. Where did Wekesa, or his men, find you earlier today?"

It was a wealth of moments before the thief answered. "Alley," he croaked.

"This was your third offense, I am told. What did you steal?"

His bloodshot eye rolled sarcastically. "Saoirse pearls."

"Saoirse pearls...see?" Kumo folded his arms.

"Whatever you stole, I assume it was to eat, by the look of you." Zaethan noted the depressions in the man's sternum. "I don't care *what* it was, so much as where it was."

"Agost merchant." The man blinked. "Marrow district."

Agost honey could buy a family food for a month, if sold to the right bidder. The merchant was foolish to set up a booth near opium tents. Although, Zaethan remembered, many a rich yancy found themselves addicted to the smoked herb—yancies who could also afford goods from Agoston. The type of yancy with whom Wekesa spent his time as of late.

"What was said when they arrested you? Any exchange between the alpha and his men?"

"Makes no difference." The man sniffed at the blood running from his nostril.

"A third offense loses you a hand." Zaethan lightly gripped the hilt of his *kopar*. "You've been accused of murder. There is very big difference. Unless, of course, you disagree. Kumo?" He gestured to the exit. "I think we've heard enough."

"Wait!" the thief exclaimed when they reached the opening of passage. "'Make him unrecognizable,'" he whimpered. "That's all... all he said."

"Timon!" When the sentry reappeared, Zaethan ordered, "Take this man to the secondary level. He will provide you his name. He is not to lose his dominant hand—so he may still work. Sear it with hot iron and ensure it's tended by a physician, then let him go."

"Alpha Zà?" Timon asked, looking uneasy.

"Do as I ask, and you'll be reassigned to a rotation upstairs." Zaethan pointed to the fresh air above. "Just do it quietly. No questions, no answers. Understood?"

"Yes! Yes, Alpha Zà, Lord al'Haidren. Thank you, sir!"

Zaethan and Kumo headed for the stair, trying not to vomit when they walked past a man defecating himself. Departing the lower dungeon, both eagerly climbed to freedom.

"Any fool could see that skinny husk couldn't do the damage we've seen," Zaethan mused, "let alone leap between rooftops."

"Depths, one look at his clothes. I told you the witch mentioned the shine off the killer's boot that night." Kumo shoved his fists in his pockets. "Must be a yancy, yeah? Or somebody dressed like one, at least."

Zaethan paused on a landing between floors, still inside the catacombs. Abruptly, he looked to his beta.

"Wekesa," Zaethan murmured. "He bought new boots…"

"What do we care about Wekesa's *kakka-shtàka* footwear—"

"Wekesa needed a reason to come to the city. A crisis valid enough for the commander to permit his entry into my territory." Zaethan's eyes widened as he shook his cousin's huge shoulders. "But why would Wekesa wait for an opportunity like that when he could *create* one?"

He let go and backed against the wall of the narrow landing. It was possible, but would Wekesa really go as far as hurting children to achieve his ambition? Could Wekesa sacrifice innocents simply to usurp his own alpha?

"Wekesa doesn't see them as children," Zaethan answered aloud. "He calls Boreali cross-castes the 'vermin of Orynthia.'"

"What are you saying?" Kumo asked carefully.

"There's only one person benefitting from these killings." Zaethan became lightheaded as a rock formed in his gut. "The same person capable of executing them."

TWENTY-EIGHT

Luscia

Luscia licked her forefinger and turned a page of the Zôueli compendium, fully immersed as she researched Bastiion's guests in preparation for her first solstice at court. Razôuel was said to have been founded by a vast wave of maritime wayfinders, in search of a home in the wake of the Forgotten Wars. It was unsurprising, then, that Razôuel maintained a fortified fleet barring their western border.

Luscia was unsure how that helped their fight against a cannibalistic enemy to the south. She made a note to ask someone later.

"Any word from my aunt, Tallulah?" she asked the maid as Tallulah entered the common room, tray in hand. Luscia wasn't particularly well-educated on Zôueli affairs and had hoped her aunt might provide some guidance before the westerners arrived.

Tallulah's lip hugged her overbite apprehensively. "*Niit*, Lady Luscia. Her lady's maid relays she's been summoned by the Peerage again, been in their chamber all morning." She placed the tray of small bites in front of the chaise and poured Luscia a fresh cup of steaming tea.

The vapor was a calming blend of eüpharsis and drösarra leaf, suggesting Tallulah's own lingering anxiety. Still shaken from her alter-cation with Kasim, Luscia had prescribed herself a version of the tea for the past few days. Aside from clan leadership, only her men knew the origin of her ghastly scar, and now, likely the al'Haidren to Darakai. Whatever had motivated him to revert to such despicableness, she'd shown her hand during their exchange. Feeling exposed, in more ways than one, Luscia drew the thin blanket higher and accepted the hot cup from the maid.

"*Rul'Aniell*...all will be well in time," Luscia weakly assured the older woman, accepting the tea. "*Tadöm*, Tallulah."

"*Rul'Aniell*." The maid curtsied, nodding to herself. "*Yeh'maelim, Ana'Sere*."

A timid knock came from the doors to the apartments. Wiping her chapped hands against her apron, Tallulah scuttled under the vast dome to greet their visitor. Before she could reach for the handles, Marek entered from a side hall and stopped her, seamlessly taking her place in the snug entry.

"*Meh fyreon*," he apologized to the maid before cracking open the door. "What is it?" Luscia overheard him inquire of someone on the other side. "Fine. Stay here."

Her captaen snatched the piece of parchment in his fist and closed the thin gap to the passageway. Wordlessly, he marched to Luscia's side and offered it without looking in her direction. They'd barely spoken since Alora's discovery of Luscia's nightly departures, and his coldness had worsened after her recent decision to send Mila to Boreal.

Creyvan had not been a supporter of her decision, either. Luscia spied him through her unbound hair, where he peeled an apple in the corner of the room. His typically jovial features had waned into a slack apathy in his twin's absence. She'd not heard his voice in days.

Breaking the prince's seal, Luscia unfolded the note, scanning it quickly.

Luscia,

The Zôueli are reported to arrive by nightfall.

Five vials would be prudent.

Yours,

Dmitri

Crinkling the parchment, she rose from the chaise and immediately sought her bedroom. Luscia caressed the pad of her forefinger, the same that moments prior had embraced Zôueli history. Heaving a sigh, she gripped the skeleton key hanging between her breasts and sought her chambers.

They walked in silence, with only the clack of Aksel's claws to break the hollow quiet.

"This is worse than a lecture," she muttered, draping her arm to skim the lycran's back. "Just say what you wish, Marek."

Passing another column, Marek let the moment hang before he complied sharply. "You sent them without any clearance. Böwen is a critical member of this unit."

"Your Najjan report to me before they report to you," she snapped back, keeping her voice below a whisper, "and are therefore at my disposal."

His stride stiffened in step with hers as he bent to her height. "Escorting a stray cross-caste through the Valley of Fahime is not what the elders had in mind when choosing the finest Najjan for your *disposal*."

"Mila is not a stray!" Luscia tried not to shout. "How dare you question my intent—"

His eyes flashed ahead to Callister as he led them to the main floor. "There are elements of that journey which you are unaware of, *Ana'Sere*." Marek maintained a lower volume to avoid the page's ears. "Things even Böwen does not know—things he *ought* to have known before traveling with a woman and two unascended children."

Luscia swallowed, her throat dry. She watched the tips of her boots advance across the stonework beneath her skirts. "I acted within my rights, Marek."

"Just because we have the right to do something doesn't always mean we should. A conversation would have been nice." Out of the corner of her eye, she saw his jaw clench bitterly. "I'm not asking to give you permission, Lusica. I'm asking to offer you counsel."

Pressure filled her sinuses, suddenly overcome with worry and embarrassment. If she'd endangered Mila in an attempt to protect her…Luscia didn't know how to begin fixing such a misstep.

Again.

"Callister," she called, slowing at the landing. "Wait for us ahead. I need a moment with the captaen."

The page blinked a couple times and continued, stopping short of their next turn, where he fidgeted in place. Luscia pulled Marek behind the nearest marble column and leveled with him.

"Should I send someone after them? Declan, perhaps?" She stared into his stern face until they locked eyes. She found sadness beneath their beryl and teal tones. "She's not safe here. It's this place, Marek—you don't understand. I just…I need her to be safe. Both of them."

Marek palmed his face. The shade of his stubble rivaled his crimson hair as it'd gone unshaven since he'd learned of her nightly departures. "They aren't clear of danger yet, but Böwen earned his place beside you." He raised his arm as if to comfort her, but let it drop and glanced away. "You can trust his instincts—just not everyone else's."

She reached out and grazed his chin with her fingertips, tempting it toward her. His stance froze, and his lips parted in surprise.

"*Meh fyreon, Ana'Brödre.*" Luscia kept her hand against the roughness of his cheek. "I am truly sorry, and…I will try to do better."

"*Tadöm.* This thing between you and I—" Marek's response trailed off as someone cleared their throat awkwardly.

Callister's head popped around the column. "Lady al'Haidren, please. The prince awaits." He shuffled aside, wary of the Najjan's distaste for intrusion.

Luscia smiled gingerly and skirted between them, rescuing the adolescent page from Marek's intimidation as he readjusted the sheath at his hip.

As the sun began to set, they entered a part of the palace foreign to Luscia. Through a series of ornate gates, walls of byrnnzite emerged to form a sort of temple, open to the elements. A dome of the same material covered a large dais, upheld by a series of statues, their figures undefined though no less imposing. At their feet, a healthy fire sparkled in individual altars encircled by plants, goods, and precious stones.

"You'll need to remain here, sir." Callister flinched slightly when the captaen leveled his glare at the page and growled under his breath.

"It's fine, Captaen." Luscia laced her fingers together and stepped beside the page. "I will meet with the prince while you and Aksel wait on the steps. You may go, Callister."

Without further delay, the prince's page scurried down the steps and back the way they'd come. With a nod to Marek, Luscia entered the odd structure. In front of the farthest statue, the prince sat on a stool in front of the largest altar. An empty stool waited beside him, his walking cane resting between the two.

"A bit humid for fires this time of year, Your Highness," she remarked as she took up residence on the unoccupied stool.

Dmitri chuckled. Firelight danced over his olive cheeks as he toyed with a carving in his grasp. "I'm told the Fates don't care much for the weather, and we must appease them regardless."

"With flame?" Luscia wasn't familiar with the fluidity of the Unitarian faith, much less the rest of the Houses.

"Actually, it's the burning, I think." Dmitri leaned over his knees, his richly embroidered vest crinkling with the movement. "The Fates prefer destruction to newness, so the burning keeps their lust at bay. That's what the priestesses claim, at least." He casually gestured to the women weaving incense around the temple, at an obvious distance from the prince. "I despise the smell of it. Why can't they ever smudge roses?"

"Do your Fates have an objection to roses?"

The prince set his chin on a fist quietly. Angling his head, he replied, "You know, I've never thought to ask. I'll burn them a bushel next time." Sitting upright, he murmured conspiringly, "But not the Hildureans. Those took quite a lot of work on my part."

Luscia grinned and pulled his vials from a pouch sewn into her skirt—Mila's handiwork.

"You're quiet this evening," he observed, pocketing the vials discreetly. "I now realize it might've been offensive to ask you to meet in this place. I hardly come myself, but when I learned the princess was nearing the city, I thought it best to, well…" Dmitri shrugged. "Just in case."

Rigidly, he lifted himself off the stool and tossed the wooden trinket into the flames. Some inner pain tightened his mouth as he returned to the modest seat.

Luscia considered the prominent idol rising from the altar. "Your Fates are fickle."

"Is your High One not?"

"*Niit*, not characteristically." She shook her head and studied his totem turning to ash. He'd etched such detail into its creation.

"Interesting," Dmitri commented, chucking a piece of lint into the fire. "Zaeth's people believe in what they call *Jwona rapiki*—Fate writers. They propose," he continued, picking another collection of fibers off his vest, "that the rarest of men can 'write over' the will of the Fates. Do you believe the same? Or are we all just subjects to destiny?"

Luscia laughed sourly. "I pray my actions are not that finite. How destructive it would be to hold power outside Aniell's will."

"So, you are a prisoner to destiny, as we are to the Fates?"

"No. *Niit*, I'm a…partner. To something greater." Luscia brushed the tip of the *solrahs* in her septum. "I merely hope to be a good one, and not a disappointment."

Dmitri pivoted on the edge of his stool, facing her. "Is that a regular concern of yours, Lady Boreal?"

She hesitated, wondering how candid she ought to be with him. Dmitri often made it second nature to forget his birthright in conversation.

"My men hardly look at me anymore. Each time I attempt heroics, I somehow make it worse." Lusica resisted the temptation to look over her shoulder at the red-headed captaen on the steps.

"I can empathize with the feeling." The prince sighed knowingly and smirked. "That's the riddle of heroism, isn't it? It is measured less by success, than it is our likeliness to fail." His hand gently cupped her shoulder, avoiding her skin. An intentional awareness, she recognized, for her behalf. "They forgive us eventually, Lusica. It's in the eyes."

"What is, Your Highness?" Luscia turned to find him smiling warmly.

"Love. A leader's greatest reprieve." He removed his hand from her shoulder and returned it to his knee. "If incredibly uncommon. You should cherish it."

At that, Lusica's chin tucked to look back at Marek, where he stood at attention and attempted to force Aksel to do the same.

"Forgive, perhaps," she added, and faced forward. "But never forget."

"No. No, they don't forget." Dmitri tossed a twig onto the altar as his totem disintegrated. "It's a blessing, though—their memory. Otherwise, what reason would we have to grow?"

Luscia exhaled and relaxed her neck, gazing up at the underside of the glittering, domed cupola. "Are you nervous, Your Highness? For her arrival?"

"Dmitri," he corrected, then mirrored her posture, admiring the ceiling. "In truth? Absolutely." They shared a communal laugh that loosened her limbs. "Razôuel is a daunting blend of Pilar's splendor and

Darakai's strength. The Zôueli treaty provides us with a valuable ally, however Razôuel boasts that women are not only equal, but superior in all matters. It will be a fascinating marriage, should she find me favorable."

"Is that what you'd want in a marriage—fascination?" Luscia imagined Dmitri pruning a faceless woman in a gardening pot.

"Sometimes fascination is all we get." Dmitri looped a loose thread around his thumb. "And that makes fascination quite dear."

Luscia's thoughts returned to Marek, her father's choice, contemplating the prince's sentiment. It was unavoidable in their positions. Like Dmitri, Luscia didn't have the luxury of her mother's circumstance. Had Eoine been the elder daughter, she might have lived untethered, as Alora had chosen. Alora had never needed to produce a successor, as her younger sibling had rapidly produced two, securing another generation in the line of Tiergan.

"I've been studying the Zôueli, as requested," she relayed, returning to the topic. "Their origins are curious. My knowledge of peoples beyond the Ilias is limited."

"I'm sure the princess will be happy to illuminate you further. I think you'll enjoy her company, from my recollection of when we were children. Rasha might bring a much-needed break from your experience here at court." Dmitri wavered, pursing his lips. "She, too, will feel like an outsider in Bastiion. You have that in common."

"Y-your Highness," Callister voiced weakly behind them. "It's time. The Zôueli are at the city gate."

Dmitri motioned for a priestess and gathered his cane to stand. Holding his breath, he leaned down and allowed the priestess to waft her incense around his dark, unkempt waves. Rising, the prince pounded his chest at the puff of smoke.

"Pray to all of our majestic overlords, Lady Boreal." He coughed and pointed to the sky. "We're going to need it."

A parade of starlight entered the southern gate to the inner Proper. Whirling flares and torchlight designs decorated the streets for the Zôueli procession. From the palace windows high above, the rolling tent housing the western royalty looked like nothing more than an oblong *lumilore* Phalen might have found shimmering at their feet by the edge of the *Dönumn*.

"It's been a decade since Korbin hosted *Bahira'zol* Jaell." Alora fixed her eyes on the carriage as she spoke of Razôuel's queen, unmoving at her niece's side. "This is a pivotal moment, Luscia. Every maneuver must be wielded shrewdly and with unyielding precision. More than you realize hinges on the coming days."

Luscia's teeth set, following her aunt's gaze.

"Your childhood must be laid to rest, Luscia. Further rebellion poses a risk to the prince now more than ever."

"He told me."

Alora spun away from the glass. The moon haloed her neat braid and betrayed the thinning of her cheeks, made more severe by the luster.

"The prince told you of his need for a wife, or his need for an heir?"

"He told me everything," Luscia touched the skeleton key beneath the fabric of her dress. "It was not a tale for children, nor the responsibility of one. You can set your worry aside."

She rubbed her eyes and clasped her hands together, regretting the curtness in her tone. Luscia felt her aunt reading the unseen threads around her. It was a new sensation, one she'd not noticed in the past.

"You are concerned for him, so I won't take offense at your tone." Alora's pitch dropped to a level no ordinary human could detect as several courtiers passed by, eager to witness the extravagant display at the gates. "As well you should be. We must assume there is less time than he is willing to admit. Your elixir is potent enough to keep it at bay—for now. His complexion has already improved."

"Why is my…" Luscia waited for a group of squealing attendants to drift on. "…my blood any different than yours? Do the elders know what we're doing?"

"*Niit.* The elders know what is pertinent and have little need to know what is inevitable."

She hated when her aunt answered straightforward questions as if they were puzzles. Their years together had taught Luscia when a boundary was established, and there was no use pressing through it.

"*Ana'Mere.*" She bit her lip as the tail of the Zôueli caravan moved out of sight. "How did you know our blood would save him?"

Alora's pale brows crinkled, then plummeted, dissatisfied somehow. "*History written, and history rings,*" she quoted the ballad. "You should already know that answer, for it lies at the start." Her aunt picked up her hand, tenderly pinching the healed spot on her fingertip. Then Alora let go and stepped back, tugging her linsilk shawl tighter. "If you can't answer the past, you've no sense questioning the present."

After a few steps from the tall window, Alora paused and turned back to her niece. "And I couldn't save him. I only drew out his death. Goodnight, Luscia."

Retreating against the glass, Luscia's chest caved in. She wrapped her arms around her middle and stared out through the window, down at the gate. In a single breath, it seemed all the hopeful light had vanished.

TWENTY-NINE

Luscia

With the concentration expected of the most studious shoto, the prince slid his marble across the Zôueli playing board. Dmitri pocketed three others, plucking them from depressions in the lacquered wood, carved like eight-pointed stars. Among the spoils was one of Luscia's own.

"Impressive, Prince Dmitri," the board's owner praised the maneuver in thickly accented Unitarian. Though they'd only met that morning, Luscia already enjoyed the way the princess's western lilt altered each syllable, bending their common language into an exotic chime.

"I did warn you, *Bahira*, I do love a good game. And—" Dmitri bit the tip of his tongue as he completed his second move, swiping two more marbles. "—I rarely lose."

His dimple emerged as he smugly boosted off his forearms, bolting upright, thoroughly pleased with himself. His boasting turned a bit sheepish when he glanced at the princess in question, sprawled over the lavish cushions surrounding their game. *Bahira'*Rasha lifted a brow under a dangling string of jewels, challenging him in return.

Across the multicolored set, Sayuri wound her long, silken hair around her fingers. Tossing the sleek jet strands over her shoulder, the Pilarese al'Haidren slunk forward, angling her lowcut bodice over the playing board.

"Neither do I, Your Highness," Sayuri simpered, plumping her ruby lips.

Luscia let her lids close, steeling herself. Pilar's al'Haidren was relentless, even in front of company.

"Thankfully for our sake, you aren't playing, Lady Pilar." Dmitri responded awkwardly and picked up a glass of water, accidentally splashing his trousers.

Sayuri shifted closer, producing a dainty handkerchief and dabbed the inside of his thigh. "I never stopped," she purred.

Gulping, Dmitri let out a shaky laugh and snatched the square of fabric from her, rising with vigor. As he meandered to the edge of the tent, which sheltered their gathering on the spacious lawn, Sayuri's eyes tapered like a cat, sliding between Luscia and their foreign guest. Sitting back, she brought the goblet to her mouth and smirked over the gilded rim.

Luscia surveyed the princess nervously. It was unclear if, in her assigned role, she ought to condone Sayuri's behavior or apologize for it. However, her concern was short-lived, for it appeared the Zôueli princess was not fazed in the least. Snapping a grape off its stem, *Bahira*Rasha brazenly held the al'Haidren's stare and popped the Wendyllean fruit in her mouth. The marigold-colored grapes had been harvested from the Hastings' private vineyard in Arune, and it was a blessing that *Bahira*'Rasha's brother preoccupied Ira on the lawn, rather than inside the tent, for he would have thoroughly relished the visual.

"A sweet solstice you have this year," the princess commented aloofly, seizing another grape. "Your summers are milder than Razôuel. More pleasant, I find."

As a bead of sweat trickled down her neck, underneath the thin lace collar, Luscia attempted her most believable smile. It was feeble at best. She'd long since decided that a freezing Orallach blizzard was more favorable than the humid, hedged lawn the Unitarians had selected for this picnic. Even if Thoarne Bay were drained until its last drop, it'd be no match for the moisture that suffocated the plains.

"It's best not to grow accustomed to it here," Sayuri commented, gently fanning herself. "It could be years before you've the chance to return."

"Tell me again, Lady al'Haidren." The princess stroked Luscia's arm lazily, the only indication she was being addressed instead of Sayuri. "Why does your prince need a Quadren if he's not yet a king? All the chatter from your Houses, it's so…meaningless, yes?"

Luscia shifted uncomfortably on the tufted pillow when the princess's fingertips skirted away and returned to her own lap. Even by royalty, she did not like being touched so candidly.

"Our prince aspires to build something new during his reign." Luscia nodded at Dmitri, who scratched his chin, apparently trying to make sense of Ira's clumsiness outside the breezy tent. "By engaging his al'Haidrens on a Quadren, albeit prematurely, he can leverage our strengths for the greater unification of the realm."

The princess's expression was skeptical beneath the emerald gems strung across her forehead. "And this…" She languidly pointed toward the lawn. "This is the strength?"

Following the angle of her forefinger, encased in stacked bands of rare metals, Luscia frowned as Ira thwacked himself in the eye while drawing his ornamental bow. Then, resituating the excessively feathered fletching against the bowstring, he somehow sliced his hand. Ditching both pieces, the al'Haidren to Bastiion clutched his bloody palm and danced in place. At the sound of his yelping when he stepped on the abandoned arrowhead, his juvenile companion, *Bahir* Tozune, ran to Ira's rescue so it wouldn't happen twice.

"Strength comes in many forms, *Bahira*," Luscia offered weakly.

Gratefully, the princess chuckled and patted Luscia's hand. "You, I like. You may call me Rasha, as friends do say. And I, to call you…?"

"Luscia."

Over the gaming table, Sayuri gawked in disbelief. For a woman whose eyes seemed eternally narrowed, it was a sight to see them so enlarged. Luscia wondered how the Pilarese beauty would look were she not so discontented all the time.

"*Loo-Shah*…" the princess repeated, pronouncing her name as if unrolling a scroll from her tongue. "Loo-Shah of the Boreali highlands. Your people, the northmen, come from the mist, yes?"

"*Wem*—yes," Luscia translated, dabbing away the perspiration pooling in the crest of her upper lip. "Though I'm finding there is a different kind of mist here in the lowlands."

Sayuri reclined on the cushions and ran a nail down her bare, copper-toned arm, kissed by her more accepted lineage. "You see how the Boreali putrefy under our sun, Rasha? It's dangerous to even invite them to court."

"*Bahira* Rasha," the princess sternly corrected.

Insulted, Sayuri pouted. Rising off the cushion, she strutted over to Dmitri, who continued to watch Ira from a shaded tent post, likely concerned for the welfare of his Unitarian al'Haidren. Drawing close, Sayuri threw her shoulders back unnaturally, like a pole were wedged into the boning of her corset. Swift and ladylike, she took his arm, holding it snugly.

Feeling a tug on her scalp, Luscia turned to discover the princess playing with a strand of her hair.

"The color is gone?" she questioned inquisitively, and passed it under her jeweled nose, sniffing. "Because the sun is so mighty, or does it grow empty of life?"

Conflicted about whether to recoil or to laugh, Luscia politely slipped her palest locks through Rasha's grasp. "My brother's is even lighter."

The princess beamed, her interest visibly piqued. It was remarkable how Luscia's kind were despised by her own realm, when the heir to another wished to know everything about them.

"Call your brother to us, yes? Enough of the prancer," she said, dismissing Ira.

"Regrettably, I cannot," Luscia said wistfully. "Phalen is not permitted in Bastiion."

"He...stays in the mist?"

Rasha's expression suggested she envisioned Phalen to be some woodland nymph among the toadstools, rather than a blade-laden luxiron apprentice. Peering through the wafting tent, Luscia considered

Bahir'Tozune as he foraged Ira's arrows, staked erratically throughout the grass.

"He stays in the mist, with my people. Yours is a natural archer." Luscia stood, offering Rasha her hand. "I'm sure your family is proud."

The princess rose as well. "Tozune will be a fine general, like our father. He is ineligible to wear my mother's crown, you know."

Together they walked arm in arm, joining Dmitri. Recently, Luscia had read how the Zôueli regency passed from mother to daughter. Orynthia had no such constraints, yet as Thoarne's descendants tended to be sons instead of daughters, the tenor of the Peerage mirrored the throne, favoring male delegates from the provinces. That same favoritism traditionally held less favorable for female Haidrens, even when they occupied a coveted seat on the Quadren beside their sovereign. Although their policy and deportment couldn't be more divided, Luscia and Sayuri were at least united in the disadvantage of their sex.

A fact the Pilarese had decided to use to their advantage, apparently, as Sayuri practically melted into Dmitri's camel day jacket when Luscia and Rasha reached the perimeter of the tent.

Aksel might as well teach her to mark the poor man, Luscia mentally retorted, *it would certainly be more effective.* She couldn't help but smirk at the thought, remembering the stench in Sayuri's vacated apartments.

"Dmitri, tell me something." The princess positioned herself between him and the tent post. "An Orynthian Quadren hosts four ambassadors, yet I've only met three. Where is the fourth?"

With a feminine confidence Luscia had never witnessed at court, Rasha exerted her supremacy by echoing his posture, not touching him in the least. Seconds later, Sayuri loosened her grip on his sleeve, doing the same.

Women were intricate, chaotic creatures, Luscia had decided long ago. Praise the High One her mother had only borne one. It was enough to dissect her own temperaments—navigating those of a sister as well would be an undertaking, indeed.

Dmitri unbuttoned his jacket apprehensively, waving the fabric to cool himself. "Forgive me his absence. My al'Haidren to Darakai, Zaethan Kasim, informed me that he was to spend today familiarizing your Zôueli guard with palace protocols and procedures. You are to meet him tomorrow, though," he assured her. "At the match. Bit of a confusing sport, *motumbha*, but he makes an excellence starter."

Luscia's stomach unclenched. At that moment, she realized how tense she'd felt all morning. Luscia relaxed on her heels, relieved she wouldn't be seeing Kasim until tomorrow afternoon. After their final meeting in the training room, she still wasn't ready to meet his knowing stare, both watchful and smug. Not after what he'd done, intentionally or not. Luscia didn't trust that Kasim wouldn't broach the subject again, or use its gravity against her. There were times when she forgot who his father was. That morning had not been one of them.

Absently, she scratched at her scar under the lace and swallowed. He said he'd found her weakness in combat, and she couldn't face him because of it. Not after he might have been right.

"Is the Darakaian as nimble as your fellow Unitarian?" Rasha posed cynically, watching Ira while he wrapped his uncalloused fingertips where they'd split and swelled.

"*Shtàka!*" he hollered, losing the roll of bandages between his boots.

Luscia wasn't sure of the alternative, but sober, Ira really was terribly unathletic. She nearly felt sorry for the yancy when he bit down to sever the mesh fabric from the roll. His feet unknowingly entangled, Ira tried to march toward their party and fell flat on his face, uprooting the sod.

As Ira brushed himself off, an imposing character strode across the lawn, directly toward their picnic assembly. As he neared, Luscia recognized the dark man, his notable height the first clue that Kasim's beta approached in search of his alpha. The unyielding sun melded his countenance, until the trampled lines of his square features defined inside the shadow of the tent. Unsettled in some way, the beta's forehead puckered as he bowed to their prince and beat his chest twice.

"Kumo," Dmitri greeted him by name. "Is everything all right?"

"Your Highness." He bent over a second time, thoroughly out of breath, and asked, "Is Alpha Zà with you?" As he spoke, the beta's huge skull swung from side to side, surveying the protected field. Comprehending Kasim's absence, the Darakaian rolled the twisted knots atop his head between his fingers anxiously.

"He was unable to join us, Kumo. Though I sense there is some urgency?" Concerned, Dmitri stepped forward, hands at his belt.

The beta leaned down to mutter in Dmitri's ear. Shifting slightly, Luscia tuned her northern ears toward the flutter of his full lips.

"...stable boy gone missing, Your Highness," he uttered in a hushed whisper. "Boreali cross-caste."

Dmitri lurched back in shock. Smoothing the lapel of his jacket, he lifted on his toes to whisper in return. "Here, on the grounds?"

As if he knew she'd overheard the report, Kumo's hickory eyes slid to Luscia. Grimacing, he dipped his chin to the prince. The southerner then offered her a look of pity, confirming his words.

Dread brought her hand to her stomach. Dropping it, Luscia straightened her posture, aware Rasha was studying the entire encounter. Despite the language barrier, the princess was more astute than she let on. Razôuel had no business decoding the peril of Orynthia's downcast, and Dmitri couldn't afford for them to find out.

A single weakness in the realm could became a weakness in a marriage contract. Their own Accords already posed enough.

"You should find Zaeth in the southern wing, around the Zôueli suites. Go, quickly now." Dmitri patted the beta's bicep, double the width of his hand, sending him off.

As Dmitri returned to their picnic, Ira came around from behind, his fine silk shirt covered in dirt stains. Holding a bowl of his Wendyl-lean grapes, he munched the remaining few, ogling the trio of women.

"Well, look at that. Quite a riveting sunset you've made, ladies." His cloth-swathed hand gestured down their row, calling attention to the gradient of their skins. "What a shame so many clouds are in the way."

Luscia ripped the bowl out of his grasp, covering her chest indignantly.

"I'm pleased to see someone tasted the fruits of my labor." Ira winked at the barren vine. "I trust you found them pleasantly plump?"

"Compensating, Ira?" Sayuri muttered dryly as Dmitri reen-tered the tent.

The prince wicked moisture off his temples where they had started to glisten. Luscia wondered when he'd need his next treatment, assuming the heat hastened his metabolism of the elixir.

Sprinting up to them, *Bahir'*Tozune presented his sister with a pile of busted arrows, likely Ira's doing. Lusica felt a pang through her ribs. He was old enough to work in the stables, like this missing boy. An image of the princess's brother hemorrhaging into a stack of hay flashed through her vision.

Wetness suddenly bordered her eyes. Luscia turned around, searching for her men around the outskirts of the field. Declan held his post at one end, disguised within the brush, while Noxolo remained in sight beside Rasha's quartet of guards. Luscia located Nox, a moonbeam among pillars of amber. Sensing her distress, his brow cinched over the bridge of his beaklike nose.

"Rasha, do you enjoy botanicals?" Dmitri asked as Luscia rotated forward, gathering herself once more. "Our garden is a bit of a wonder, and—"

He trailed off when another visitor appeared, curtsying just outside the tent. The dainty lady's maid lowered her abdomen, staying that way, even though the reprieve of the shade was inches away. Dmitri coughed and waved her in, clarifying, "You may enter," when she failed to look up.

The Pilarese girl, concerningly slight in stature, curtsied another half a dozen times before she relayed a message to Sayuri in their western tongue. Unexpectedly, Sayuri launched away from the post and tidied the top of her dress. An eager grin broke her smooth indifference as she snatched the girl's wrist and moved to depart.

"Forgive my brevity, Highness. I've an appointment I cannot miss."

"What did she mean, 'procedure'? Or was that 'pirouette,' perhaps? I'm embarrassed my Pilarese is rather shoddy," Dmitri explained to the princess. "'Potbelly'...no, that can't be right," he rattled off distractedly.

Remembering Dmitri's earlier mention of the gardens, Luscia leapt at the opportunity, eager to visit the stables, even if the Najjan wouldn't be allowed inside.

"Why don't you escort the princess to the gardens, Your Highness?" she suggested. "I'm sure she'd love to see the Byronia coming in. Very impressive."

"That is true. Byronia lily, such a remarkable little thing," he began, leading Rasha in the direction of the hedge maze.

Treading across the lawn past the archery targets, Noxolo's long stride fell in step with Luscia's. Under her breath, she relayed the beta's report.

"On palace grounds," Luscia murmured angrily, snapping more of Ira's stray arrows underfoot. "How did this happen? Our Najjan are concealed everywhere, both mine and those with *Ana'Mere*."

At his silence, she halted their advance.

"Well, *Ana'Sere*, you're the expert." Noxolo exhaled sharply. "How do you evade us?"

Unwilling to answer, Luscia eased back, allowing him to lead the way through the lake of discarded equipment. Slower than before, her upturned slipper stepped over Tozune's bow.

"Oh, Lady Boreal, I keep meaning to ask," Sayuri called, towing her attendant along. "How is that y'siti mutt of mine serving you? Mira, Melda—oh, does it really matter?"

Luscia stopped walking. Sayuri's lips curled as she passed behind one of the targets.

"Better for cross-castes to keep to their own kind...increased survival rate and all."

Forgetting restraint, Luscia dove for Tozune's bow in the grass. Nimble and true, she pivoted on her knee and released an arrow.

Sayuri screamed and grabbed her maid like a shield as the arrow splintered the wood of the target, striking the very top, right in line with her heart. Gasping, Sayuri shoved the girl aside and marched off, shouting in a Pilarese staccato.

At the smell, Luscia glanced behind the archery target. The small maid quivered as liquid seeped down her legs. The girl's eyes shone with tears as she gaped at Luscia.

Frozen in place, Luscia wondered what she saw.

"Come, *Ana'Sere*," Noxolo prompted her to rise. "You're needed elsewhere."

Forfeiting the bow, she quietly left the maid crying on the lawn, forcing Luscia to question if she was so different from the al'Haidren to Pilar after all.

THIRTY

Zaethan

Zaethan flipped the *motumbha* stick, rolling it between his palms. The ladles on either end hovered in anticipation over the freshly cut lawn.

Jabari whooped twice, running between their opponents. Sliding on his thigh, he tore through the green and thrust the ball of laced hide through the air, dirt and grass accompanying its flight. Zaethan shouldered another player, not bothering to watch him crash to the earth, and lowered the stick, dashing to the middle of the field. Spinning through a triplet of oncoming players, he spied the narrow goal basket.

Without hesitation, Zaethan launched the ball upright and spun the stick. Striking with the backside of the adjacent scoop, it soared over the heads of his competitors. He released a series of similar sounds, summoning his teammate. Zaethan spotted Jabari beyond the cluster guarding the basket, the Andwele warrior swiftly retrieving an arrow and aiming for the flying target.

The crowd voiced their disappointment as the arrow narrowly missed, followed by a steady clap after the ball fell into the mouth of basket.

"*Kàchà kocho*, Alpha Zá." Jabari shrugged and snatched the ball, wiping off a chunk of soil on his relaxed gunja pant. "Eh, *uni*! Knick a lick, yeah?" The warrior's accent thickened as he displayed a slash in the hide.

"*Zullee*." Wekesa snatched the ball from Jarabi's grasp and tossed it to another member of his team. A red cord wrapped about his forearm, distinguishing their opposition for the onlooking nobles. Zaethan's men did not need dye to know whom they were against. "When you run with men, instead of cubs, you're never in this position, Zaeth."

Rotating his wrist, the blue cord around Zaethan's muscle suddenly felt constricting. "What position, Wekesa?"

"Liability." His rival's playing stick swung and smashed Zaethan's calf where it was still healing from the y'siti's witchiron. Biting down, he refused to show the pain. "*Yeye quondai…*Alpha Zá?"

"Eh, *meme qondai…*I understand you've been playing a dangerous game." Zaethan crouched low, awaiting the signal for the pitch. "On the field, and in my city."

"Think Bastiion's still yours, Zaeth?" A wailing cry rang out as the ball glided above. Wekesa's murky eyes widened, exposing their whites. "*Kwihila rapiki mu Jwona!*"

The blunt end of his ladle socked Zaethan's middle, causing him to double over. Spitting out a mouthful of bile, he sprinted after Wekesa, both men tracking the lost ball between players. Nearing the bastard's heels, Zaethan roared. He whipped the stick around Wekesa's abdomen, pinning the man as he caught the opposite end in stride. Lifting the other alpha off the ground, Zaethan yelled at the throbbing pain in his leg as he careened them to the left and freed the stick, hurling Wekesa onto the green.

"*Ho'waladim,*" Zaethan bit out, striking the shredded earth inches from Wekesa's head. "*That's* what's due you." He ran ahead to his team of off-duty sentries on the far side of the field.

One of Wekesa's men hoisted the ball, preparing his serve, and howled for his archer. Zaethan searched the lawn for Jabari, whooping the same. Hailing an arc, Wekesa's player aimed for the furthest basket in front of the royal pavilion. Zaethan rushed under Jabari's arrow, trusting its trajectory. He might have been inexperienced in his youth, but Depths, the cub was a good shot.

The gong rang out, signifying the end of the match just as Jabari's arrow spliced their opponent's and impaled the hide victoriously into the third basket, stealing the goal. Zaethan rammed into Jabari and cupped his head of sweaty coils.

"*Shtàka! Uni zà!*" He shook the youngest member of his pryde triumphantly. "Rounds of *bwoloa*, as many as we can drink."

"*Owàa* lent me his eyes, yeah?" Jabari's fingers drew away from his face and toward the clouds. Strapping his bow to join the final arrow in the slim quiver, he trailed Zaethan to the secondary pavilion, where Dmitri watched the match with the Zôueli princess.

"Good game, Zaeth, good game!" Dmitri gripped his cane and stood, continuing his applause. "I tried explaining the rules of *motumbha* to *Bahira'*Rasha." He colored slightly and waved to the exquisite woman lounging to the right of his seat, elevated from the others. "I fear I may have confused things further."

"*Bahira* Rasha." Zaethan bent his knee, her Zôueli title feeling bulbous as it exited his mouth. Bowing to the woman, he recited Dmitri's lines as promised: "We are graced to host you for the summer solstice. The sun shines brighter in Orynthia for years to come." He doubted the last part sounded the least bit genuine, but offered a toothy grin nonetheless.

"I like this Darakaian arrowball, as you call it." The princess didn't get up, and seemed to enjoy the fact she didn't need to. Zaethan straightened as she looked him over. "It is barbarous."

Rasha elongated her figure as she reclined, in a way Sayuri never could. The Pilarese al'Haidren noticed as well and attempted to imitate Rasha's gestures from the end of the row near Ira, who fished something out of his empty glass. The princess dripped gold and precious stones, and her entire being sparkled when she tossed her head and laughed heartily.

"Bloody and riveting, are you." Her nose crinkled, jingling a chain that connected to a jeweled earpiece. She idly crossed her legs, enveloped in billowy pants beneath a type of skirt. Ironically, her feet were bare, though no less decorated than the rest of her.

Zaethan scanned the witch seated next to the princess. "I get that a lot. Lady Boreal, you're looking well," he offered lightly. Regret from their encounter lessened when he saw her ivory jaw was devoid of the lovely bruise he'd gifted it. "The sun does the Boreali good, after all," he commented, noticing how gracefully her fractured wrist moved as she plucked a grape off its stem.

"I keep reminding you how resilient I am," the witch said to the fruit.

"Ah, my new friend, Loo-Shah…" Rasha rolled her name and clutched the witch's arm, drawing her closer. "This wit of the northmen, I love."

"Won't you join us, Zaeth?" Dmitri motioned to the empty place in the line of spectators. "I've ordered your favorite," he added, gesturing toward an amber bottle on a valet's cart.

In Zaethan's periphery, players departed the field, equipment in tow. Passing the next pavilion, more prominent in scale and grandeur, Wekesa was called out of the pack. Breaking from the group, he sauntered up the steps and leaned into the shade for Zaethan's father to relay something. Their commander's fingers twitched as he went on in Wekesa's ear.

"Alas, I must see to the guard." Zaethan squinted under the sun. Dmitri grimaced, not entirely pleased, but ascertained the course of his thoughts, jerking his chin toward their parents.

"We'll see you at dinner?" Though posed as a question, Zaethan knew better.

"Dinner," he confirmed, and bowed to the princess. "*Bahira*'Rasha, *shàlàmaiamo*."

Zaethan picked up his pace as he walked in front of the king's pavilion, pretending to ignore the closeness between his father and the other alpha. Tetsu Naborū appeared to offer comment on their discreet dialogue. Zaethan wondered how entangled Wekesa was in Lateef's plan for additional ships stationed in Lempeii, or if the Haidren to Pilar had simply seized an opportunity to spew partisan poison to the closest party.

"Zaeth, my boy!" The king descended onto the lawn and slapped Zaethan across the back. "I put my auras on you. Sack of gold you just earned me!"

Dmitri's father sloshed his wine as he turned to the Queen of Razôuel, who seemed disinterested in his royal pocketbook. The Zôueli regent wrinkled her hooked nose at a plate of Uriel pie an attendant offered, clinking an opulent set of chains across her cheek. He understood her reaction when she flicked a dollop back at the attendant, unimpressed. Uriel pie was already dreadful, made worse in the heat of summer.

Zaethan risked another glimpse into their pavilion. His father's fist clenched and shook over the arm of his chair. Wekesa's fat braids swung as he inched away.

"I think I earned a good washing, Your Majesty." Zaethan mock scrubbed his middle and winked at the king. "I should take care of all this mud before charming Razôuel's Queen."

"Oh-ho!" King Korbin's belly rumbled at the jest. Pulling the front of his thick belt into position, he again reached out and gripped Zaethan's shoulder. "Just spectacular, my boy. Go, brush up and see to those *yayas*. Now, in my day…" His bushy brows leapt before his hand covered his mouth, remembering his wife beside the western queen. "Oh, on you go!"

Marching toward his office, Zaethan's fingers tightened around the playing stick he still carried. He bid farewell to his teammates, grateful Jareth and Brandor had been available to leave their posts and put on a spectacle for Dmitri's guests. They were his best Unitarian passers, not *kakk* squabblers like the rest of the sentries.

It was a good thing he still controlled their schedules.

Zaethan neared the hedge maze, intending to take a shortcut to the guard house. At its opening, Felix Ambrose sloshed his goblet and moved aside, off the path. Overly dressed, in typical yancy fashion, the noble dribbled sweat into his wine, intently staring past Zaethan.

Looking back, he saw the noble's gaze was fixed on the exotic princess as she rose from her seat and took Dmitri's arm.

"She's off limits, Lord Ambrose," Zaethan warned the man, then coughed as he was hit by a waft of pipe marrow. "Depths, Felix, take a bath."

He proceeded through the opening in the bushes and into the maze. Someone's swallow-call whistled from the field as they jogged around the bend.

"Do you hear the birdies, Zaeth?" Wekesa repeated the call and ran up the path, his arms draped lazily over the *motumbha* stick across his shoulders. "They're singing a certain prisoner is missing. He flew away." His fingertips flitted as he barged in front of Zaethan. "Flew like *Owàa* in the morning, yeah?"

"*Kàchà kocho.*" Zaethan's thumb wiped away a bead of perspiration from the match. "Birds fly. If you'd borrowed his wings, you might've won. Now, get to your post." His boot shifted off the gravel path. "That was an order."

His windpipe collapsed when Wekesa hooked his rod over Zaethan's head and propelled them behind a hedge, forcing a gulp of greenery down his throat.

"I played your game." Wekesa's spit sprinkled the back of Zaethan's spine. "Well, this is mine. You took from me, yeah? Now, I'm taking it all!"

"Using which prisoner?" Zaethan's snicker made it harder to breath. "You failed," he taunted, wedging a hand between the stick and his throat. "*Uni*, nothing to show the tribes but dead cross-castes." He used the little space to twist forward, wrap his arm around, and pound his knuckle into Wekesa's kidney. "Return to the valley," he wheezed, "take your pryde, leave the city, and I won't tell the commander what you've done."

Bent over, Wekesa laughed cruelly. "But Zaeth," his eyes rounded in mock horror, "what about all those helpless roach cubs? You tested *Jwona*. Freed their murderer."

Zaethan's fist collided with Wekesa's mouth. Blood foamed around the other alpha's teeth as he smiled wildly. Standing over his rival, Zaethan stepped away, though every fiber of his being wished to beat Wekesa to within an inch of his life.

"Do it...I attacked my alpha." Wekesa sneered, dripping pink saliva. "We both know who he'll punish."

Panting, Zaethan dipped down and picked up the *motumbha* sticks strewn in the grass. "You've taken back plenty," he huffed, electing to walk away. "Enough."

Zaethan unraveled the blue cord and chucked it to the ground. As he exited the hedge maze, that swallow song echoed through the exterior garden once again, partnered by a faraway promise.

"Do you hear the birdie, Zaeth? I'm going to take everything."

"*Ano, ano*. That's not how he's doing it."

The four Darakaians huddled in Zaethan's snug office, Kumo barely squeezed between the desk and Jabari. He fidgeted awkwardly to avoid the corner of the wood. Its orientation was a little too intimate for the beta's liking.

"Ah, see." Zahra punched his bicep and gestured to the topmost map on the desk. "I told you, *uni*, those tunnels are shut up. Packed full of rock and *shtàka*."

Zaethan leaned back on the hind legs of his chair, letting his third harass Kumo while he considered an alternative.

"He has to have help," he said finally, throwing up his hands and bringing the front legs to the floorboards. "Wekesa can't be everywhere, yeah? He was in Fahime when you found the first body."

"And what about Arune, and that yancy's estate maid?" Zahra added, hand on her hip. The muscles in her arm flexed when she reached for a map underneath the stack.

"Arune could be an outlier." Zaethan bounced his heel. "Ira said it resembled an animal attack. Maybe a coincidence."

"Coincidence hillman trap, Alpha Zà." Jabari's coils swung back and forth. "Never trap a trick, *ano*. Trick trap the hillman or *kakk* keep a calling."

Kumo glared at Jabari. "I hear *kakk* calling now."

The mountaineer cautiously pointed to the map. "Because you hillman, being trapped by the trick."

"Jabari's right," Zaethan interjected before someone received a black eye. "Even if he enlisted help, the killings multiplied once he arrived. Depths, he all but admitted it!"

"Alpha Zà." Zahra leaned against the desktop and leveled with him. "He tell you plain? We know your shared past. What if it's a distraction, yeah? Let you believe it's him, distract your while he rallies support for a challenge."

Kumo rubbed his neck, then dropped his arm. "Makes sense, *Ahoté*."

"Wekesa said that more children will die," Zaethan articulated each syllable, "because we let his thief escape. He looked me right in the eyes, and said they'd die for it."

Zahra shared a glance with Kumo. Her brow lifted, sending creases across the sheen of her smooth scalp, disrupting some of the inked Andwele markings. "All right, then. *Uni zà.*"

Pinned against the door jamb, Jabari watched the older three warriors deliberate. Zaethan sighed and ripped a different map off the floor, unrolled it, and massaged his temples.

"You've watched him for weeks, Zahra. Even if he walked straight out the gate into Marketown, he couldn't come back the same way." Zaethan waved to the web of streets in his lap. "Not after that. Not after what he does to them."

"Wekesa goes where we all go," she replied. "The guard house, his suite, the hall, kitchens, the war room—" She trailed off as the parchment crunched in his hands.

"The sentries on our payroll don't know anything, either." Kumo scowled. "Even threw in a couple extra dromas. Nothing."

Hammering at the door caused Jabari to jump. Zaethan nodded for him to permit the newcomer. Tripping into the already crowded room, Takodo nudged Jabari into the hall to fit in front of the desk.

"We have it, Alpha Zà!" He beat the surface of the desk and announced, "I found how he's sneaking past us! Eh." Takoda poked his thumb at Zahra and stood taller. "Past you, at least."

Zaethan's third whacked Takoda upside the head. "*Owàamo* to you, too, cocky cub-rub."

Takoda recovered and flipped through the papers, rotating a blueprint of the palace main. His index finger glided over the lower level and tapped the kitchens fervently.

"Here." He flopped his braids over, bending down. "It's an unlocked access to the sewer. Kitchen hardly touches it, yeah? Nasty, *kakka-shtàka* sludge canal, but the lock is rusted. Never fixed."

Zaethan chewed the inside of his cheek and peered at Takoda. "How'd you learn this?"

"Eh…" A rosy blush swept his forehead, and he grinned sheepishly. "So, there's this *yaya* in the pantry, and she was giving me a, uh…" Takoda cleared his throat. "…a tour."

He winced as Zahra smacked him even harder.

"And after the completion of your…tour?" Zaethan asked.

"She starts raving about dark spirits, moving buckets, puddling. *Kakk* talking, yeah?" Takoda flapped his hands around. "Somebody's been using it."

Zaethan rolled up the map and hit Takoda in the chest with it. "*Zullee*, my friend. Zahra," he ordered, pushing off the desk, "I want you with Dmitri tonight. The rest of us are needed out there. We need to arrest Wekesa in the act."

"We bringing *Maji'maia* with us?" Kumo swirled a finger around his eye. "*Tàkom lai na huwàa?*"

"*Ano zà.* Our brother has become a monster. It's Darakai's responsibility to put him down." Zaethan belted his *kopar*. The witch's accusation rang in his ears as if he still laid on the mat of that training room. "Damn the day we step aside and invite Boreal to do it in our place."

THIRTY-ONE

The figure ignored a pair of drunkards wrestling ineptly in the street as he scanned the rooftops. Near the edge of Marketown, the stench of the slums overpowered a more pleasing spice in the breeze, floating from the closed stalls of the Drifting Bazaar.

He used his thumb to itch a fingertip on his left hand, hanging onto a drainpipe with the other. He'd shed another fingernail, the raw bed of flaky flesh raking against the interior of his stiff glove. It creased as he stretched out his hand. He knew from experience that the nail would not grow back.

Below, one of the intoxicated men smashed a bottle over the other's head. Preparing to move along, eager for an alternative bouquet of smell and sound, the figure spun when Amaranth's cry shot through the night. Gliding across the slats of the rickety building, avoiding a break in the tiles, he ran in the direction of her call. Further down the boardwalk, where the edge of the slum turned into a river of colorful booths, the Pilarese hawk circled overhead.

He leapt over a steep drop and landed on a collection of homes wedged into the tight street, heading for her wings. The figure did not hesitate, vaulting to a crooked terrace and hoisting himself through the window of an abandoned structure. His cloak caught on a splintered sill. Ripping it with his momentum, he sprinted to another window overlooking the alleyway. Amaranth surveyed on the opposite side.

The figure lingered behind a weathered curtain, searching the shadows for her sighting. Huddled, shaded in the back corner of a buoyant stall, a hooded man dumped his burden onto a pile of sack grain. His own cloak concealed his identity, even as he turned to hop off the merchant boat. Moonlight spilled over the addition to the stack of burlap: a pale, lifeless boy.

Preparing to vault, the figure flung himself back into the vacant hovel. At the farthest mouth of the alley, another person appeared, starting to run toward the hooded killer.

"*Doru!*" a southern voice screamed in pursuit. "Kumo, Alpha Zà, tricker getting away!"

The figure stooped lower, hidden, as the Darakaian sprinted after, a sharp *kopar* in hand. From the other end of the alley, a second southerner flew around the crumbling corner of a shop and barreled straight into the killer, slinging them against a crude lamppost. The figure heard a *crack* as the Darakaian screamed in anguish, rattling the only torchlight in sight.

Attempting to thrust his sickle-sword into the hooded man, his body suddenly spasmed and the *kopar* rattled on the cobblestones. Gargling blood, the Darakaian tried to mouth something to his assailant. The figure leaned forward to read his lips, but the cape covered the warrior's face when it whirled. The hooded man bolted into the shadows, leaving the Darakaian slumped against the post in a growing puddle of crimson.

His kinsman arrived at his side, in not nearly enough time as the struggle had happened so quickly—even the figure shook himself to recall his original quest. Without concern for the panicked Darakaians, howling for help, the figure gripped the top of the window frame and swung onto the gable. Under Amaranth's lead, he dodged a broken chimney and trailed her deeper into Marketown's busy district.

There—between a trader's cart and the rear of a loud tavern, he spotted the hooded man weaving through a crowd of hagglers. The figure stalked his path from atop the adjacent building. Speeding up, he lost his footing over a cable. Cursing the misstep, rare as they were anymore, he watched in helpless horror as a slew of tiles scattered over the edge and plummeted into the street. The hooded figure pivoted, still disguised by the swath of rich fabric, and took off into the seedy network of trading trolleys and smoking tents.

In the scarce torchlight, as Marketown's customers preferred the anonymity of darkness, the figure leapt to the ground. He pulled his cloak close, head low, and plunged into the swarm of bustling patrons. Passing a pipe marrow tent, he breathed shallowly, refusing to allow the substance access to his shriveled lungs. Bobbing in and out of the throng, the figure soon lost track of the man, though Amaranth still hovered above. He ducked around a hanging rug when a woman bumped into him, reaching for a bushel of milled spices, and began to barter with the owner. Through the strips of the plaited fabric, he studied each passerby patiently, trusting the hawk's guidance.

Vigilant, the figure watched the movement in the street from the trader's booth for half an hour. Amaranth screeched over the racket, pulling his attention to a smoking tent across the way. The hooded man exited through the slim split at the front and reentered the crowd. Easing away from the stand of goods, the figure slinked along the narrow lane between the street sellers and a row of rowdy establishments.

Maintaining pace at the rear, the figure followed him down a vacant alley. Out of sight, the figure sprung off his heels and dove onto the killer's back, awakening the monster within.

The cowl of the figure's cloak flew off as his blistered arms snaked around his prey's neck and squeezed the throat mercilessly, crushing his knees into the ribcage. Animalistically, the glands behind his canines flooded with the expectation of the kill. Stickiness drooled from his mouth, down his chin.

The figure was driven into the wall and slammed against the old brick repeatedly as his prey tried to break free. His state of mind fractured, the figure thrashed his head and constricted his limbs tighter. Sputtering erratically, his prey's veins pounded in his ears. Snarling through his nostrils, the figure sank his teeth through the velvet of the killer's cloak. Sour warmth bathed his parched and abrasive tongue. He heard a grunt of pain, the accompanying scent of fear pleasing and sweet.

Spinning them away from the brick, his prey flailed through the alley. Savagely, the figure's jaws stayed anchored in his prey as they both tumbled into the open.

The figure heard shrieks in the distance, and his humanity tried to reclaim dominance over his curse. Something smashed into his back, hurling him off his prey and into a casket of spirits. Rolling into a crouch, he growled at the forming circle of frightened faces.

"Look at the skin—the boils! War-taint!" A plump woman gasped and hailed to the sky. "He's war-tainted!"

A chorus of screams jolted the figure back to himself. Barrels overturned, rolling down the street. People scattered as others sought makeshift weapons, looking to extinguish the sickness in their midst.

Nearby, a clothesline descended at an angle from the heights. The figure sprinted for it as a burly trader grabbed a butcher's knife and swung after him, barely missing his leg. The figure shimmied up the cabling to its anchor stories higher. In the haven of the skyline, he clutched his beating heart before heading for the western docks.

As he prowled, the figure repeated his own name, again and again.

Under the unforgiving moon, he climbed aboard a vacant ship moored in the yard. Suspended on the topmast, the figure stared over the murky waters of Thoarne Bay. He spit the killer's blood into his glove, nauseated. It tasted of waste and bile, much like his own.

He closed his eyelids, scorched from their blistering, and wished it were war-taint that ravaged his body instead of the truth. For damnation was so much worse.

THIRTY-TWO

Luscia

Luscia removed the stopper of the vial and swirled the murky fluid inside. Legs of the liquid slid down the glass, thicker than Alora's previous concoctions. Resigning herself to its bitterness, she swallowed the tonic and trudged to the edge of her lush bed, wearing little more than her linsilk shift.

As she slid under the blankets, Aksel yipped at her heel. His impatience swelled into a throaty growl when she refused to move.

"Your manners are absolute trash these days," she grumbled into her pillow. "*Niit*, you brute."

Luscia hoisted herself up on an elbow when he started to scratch at the door, growling louder at the illuminated seam between it and the floor. With a groan, she rolled off the mattress, grabbed her dressing gown, and listened from the interior, radials at the ready. There were men talking just outside, their cadence clipped and argumentative.

"*Heh'ta*, Aksel," she ordered her companion, wrapping the dressing gown tighter.

Easing into the common room, Luscia nearly tripped on the hem of her robe in surprise. In the threshold to her apartments, Kasim's beta cradled another Darakaian in his arms, limp, grey, and soaked in blood. Kasim was attempting to push through Marek and Declan, who blocked the Darakaians' entry to the foyer. From his chest up to the side of his face, both skin and leather were smothered in gore. The veins of his neck strained under the wetness, warping his expression into something unbridled and bare.

"I said, call for her! She can save him." Kasim's throat pressed into the edge of Declan's blade. His overly bright eyes searched beyond their barricade, latching onto hers. "You *will* save him!"

Marek held his stance unwaveringly as he murmured for instruction, "*Ana'Sere?*"

"Ock, Aurynth's watchman, on high!" Tallulah scurried to Luscia's side, adjusting her own floppy nightcap. Sputtering, she heaved a blanket around her curled shoulders. "Well, I'll not give them a free show!"

Luscia felt her heartbeat inside her ear canal. She weighed the ramifications of Boreali involvement, should he not survive the night. The hour aside, such a request was unprecedented—a Darakaian choosing to bypass court physicians to beseech the House of Boreal for healing.

"You will save him." Kasim's voice cracked. Worded as a demand, spoken as a plea.

Blood dripped in the entry near the beta's feet as he readjusted the weight of their friend. Kasim's man didn't have much time, if any at all.

"*Wem.*" Luscia nodded and motioned for her men to admit the Darakaians. "*Wem*, to my bedroom, quickly now. *Bolaeva*," she begged, directing the gruesome group to her quarters, "please be careful. Try not to move his abdomen."

The hulking beta tenderly laid the man on her mattress and lumbered out of the way. The injury continued to bleed, quickly soaking the fabric in an unpromising stain. A mane of shoulder-length braids spread over the crest of her pillow. She recognized him as the third member of their night raid through the Bazaar. Luscia tore a piece of linen with her mouth and thrust it into Creyvan's grasp as he entered the room, door swinging behind him.

"Hold this. Tallulah!" she shouted for the lady's maid. "Hot water, needle, thread, and all the rags you can find. Marek, cut his shirt open. *Niit*, lift it, don't touch the skin."

Peeling the filthy sparring tunic away from the flesh, red flooded to the surface, no longer contained. Yelling for Declan to apply pressure, Luscia tossed the drenched tunic into a bucket Tallulah lobbed near the bed. At Luscia's direction, Creyvan replaced Declan as she ran to the viridi box and unlocked her apothecary.

Her back to the scene, she rushed to grind gilead with kaléo, hiding the subtle twinkle of the chartreuse leaves and white stamen within the basin of the mortar. "Mila!" Luscia called, sprinkling iridescent yarrow buds into the paste. "Where is that girl? Mila, the water!"

"She's gone."

The brisk, off-putting tone caused Luscia to turn. Creyvan's jaw was set as he pinned a wad of cloth against the southerner's middle.

She moved to take his place and caught his eye. "*Wem*, that was thoughtless of me." Luscia had not realized his feelings for her attendant were so serious. His resentment likely made worse, she suspected, by the fact that Mila traveled to Roüwen with his brother. "More water. *Bolaeva, Brödre.*"

Crevyan stomped out of the room to do as asked, without retort. Using a warm rag, Luscia carefully wiped gravel out of the wound and gasped.

"Should we send for *Ana'Mere?*" Declan asked, examining the wounds with concern.

"*Niit,* not unless we have to." Luscia sent a look at Marek. He tilted his head suspiciously. "Kasim, these injuries…how did this happen?"

Kasim paced at the foot of the bed, rubbing his forehead anxiously. His gaze narrowed at the two Najjan in the room before returning to Luscia. "We regrouped. Went back out there. Found him at the edge of Marketown, depositing another body. Takoda…" He gripped the headboard forcefully. "Takoda got to him first."

Luscia avoided the looks from her men and peered closer.

"This had to have been some kind an animal, you see? What kind of blade would make such markings?" Luscia indicated the parallel slashes over Takoda's belly. Torn and savaged, he resembled the victim of a bear attack. She mimed a set of claws over the wound for Kasim and the beta. "I will do what I can for your friend, but you should prepare yourself, in the event our aid proves futile."

"*Ano zà!*" Kasim grabbed a vase and smashed it against the wall, pointing at her. "You do for him whatever you did to heal those bruises I gave you. He will *not* die!"

"This is not a bruise."

"*Ahoté…*" His beta cringed when Kasim kicked a chair over.

As Kasim reached for Dmitri's *Noculoma-Anastasis* on her nightstand, Luscia stood abruptly, needle in hand.

"Lord Darakai! That is not yours, and you will put it down immediately. Take him out of here." Luscia poked her chin toward the common room. "Declan, get them out of this room right now."

She rolled up her sleeve and wiped a bit of blood off Takoda's wound using her forearm as the brawniest of her guards corralled the other two Darakaians into the communal living space.

Dust puffed off the trim when Kasim punched the wall outside. "If Takoda dies in there, by *Owàa*...by *Owàa*, Kumo, I'm going to find him and kill him. Tonight," she heard him vow.

In her bedroom, alone with Marek and the unconscious Darakaian, she went to work. Threading the gashes into tight, meticulous seams, Luscia packed each laceration with the healing paste, praying to Aniell the kaléo fulfilled its purpose and accelerated sterilization. Unconscious and unresponsive, Takoda needed the lumin-laced remedy to do what Bastiion's physicians could not.

She moved to her apothecary chest. Luscia plucked some dehydrated bits of ennus and viridi bark, dumping them into a cup. The brew for her morning tea could suppress pain in high enough dosages.

"Are you angry with me?" she asked, her back to the silent captaen.

Marek must have deduced the partnership Luscia had forged with Kasim within the first minutes of their knocking, and the nature of her nightly activities was made even more obvious by Kasim's explanation of Takoda's attack. There were nights she was not alone when she evaded her guard and left them behind, a fact she could no longer hide from him and Declan.

"*Darakai*, Luscia? Of all the Houses, you trusted Darakai?" The tenor of his voice lifted in disbelief.

She winced when the door handle latched sharply, marking his departure. Luscia stirred the vapors steaming off the surface of the tea, thinking of all the times she could have told Marek the truth. She spun and stared into the grain of the wooden door, wishing she had chosen differently.

Nearing daybreak, as the beginnings of dawn teased through the vast windows, Luscia brought a heap of soiled linen into Tallulah's washroom inside the apartment. Scrubbing, she tried to salvage a few items, working as she let the maid sleep. They would need someone to watch their patient during the day, as she and Kasim were expected to cater to Dmitri's guests. Luscia didn't anticipate Marek allowing a member of Kasim's pryde into her quarters to do so.

She swirled her fingertips through the rosy water, its hue deceptively innocent, and considered her role in what had happened to Kasim's warrior. She'd betrayed her own men to play the hound, to guide the band of Darakaians through Bastiion's underbelly and into the den of a killer, only to ultimately abandon them in their quest. Left to their own mortal devices, Luscia couldn't help but feel a responsibility for the young man beating back death in her bed, unsure if he'd see his tomorrow. Her lashes beat back moisture as she held onto the prince's recent sentiments about the forgiveness of others, hoping he was right.

"You should also rest, *Ana'Sere.*"

Luscia stretched out her neck, blinking multiple times before acknowledging him. At the entrance to the washroom, Marek leaned against the doorframe, his hands clasped together loosely. His shoulders rounded with exhaustion under the fitted, sable jacket that normally hugged a more attentive posture.

She rung out a rag, proceeding to the next as he watched her. "*Allöh*, Captaen."

"Let me finish this, *Ana'Sere*. Even you need sleep."

Luscia propped herself against the rim of the washtub. "Every step I take is the wrong one. By Aurynth, Marek, I make a choice, believe it in my soul to be true, and then I falter. *Meh fyreon*." Her head shook as she apologized. "From the bottom of my heart, Marek, I was just trying to save them."

The floor creaked as he stepped into the snug space, maintaining a foot of decorum. "You saved the man in that room."

Luscia's throat tightened and she asked in a whisper, "And if my actions somehow put him there?"

Uncertain why she was confiding in him, Luscia lifted her gaze and stilled for Marek's shrewd rebuke. She'd certainly earned it. Except that where she'd expected to find judgment in his cerulean eyes, there was none. Instead, like the light of a *lumilore*, the crystalline ring about his irises shone in the dim washroom, untarnished by spite or resentment.

"Only the High One sees everything under Aurynth." Marek's shoulders rose and fell. "We may never know."

"You left Roüwen. You traded your independence to follow the al'Haidren to Boreal, descendant of Tiergan, daughter of the Clann Darragh, our Mighty Oak." Luscia squeezed the damp fabric, dispersing a deeper shade of scarlet throughout the basin of water. "But I only offer you a life sentence of more grief and more death in return."

Marek came to her side and took the rag from her, setting it on the bench. Hesitantly, he scooped up her chin, angling it toward him. Her breath caught at the intimacy of his gesture, unsure if she should correct it, though the heat of his touch petitioned her not to look away. "Is that why you think I'm here, in Bastiion? For accolade?"

"*Wem*, what else could possibly warrant it?"

"I'm not upset because they're Darakaian, Luscia." The lines of his mouth tensed. "Or because you care deeply for our cross-castes, or that you wanted to try to save them. I'm upset that, even still, you don't trust me enough to take me with you."

She inched back in surprise. "But you are bound to her orders above mine. *Ana'Mere*—"

"—is not *you*."

His hand slid softly to her neck, avoiding the lengthy terrain of her scar, and tipped her head back with his thumb. Marek never initiated physicality between them. Not even when they'd first met on the Isle of Viridis in her youth, before she Ascended to her station and he called to his own. But she had merely been a frail young girl at the time. Bruised, in more ways than one. Now, Marek no longer stood before a girl, but a woman, resilient and whole. The realization caused Luscia to stiffen, though only momentarily. Something sleeping inside her awoke, soothing the disquiet of her thoughts. Calming and warm, it reminded her of home.

His throat leapt as he swallowed. "Under Aurynth, I willingly give my independence to serve a woman I believe in. To protect her. To attend her." Closing the gap, Marek's hair swung out of its binding, like a flame licking his skin. "To be near her."

A wisp of it skirted her cheek as he bent down and brought his lips to hers. While his mouth was polite in pursuit, his fingers curled behind her nape, indicating he did not wish to let go. Luscia wasn't certain if she wanted him to either. It seemed like another life since she'd allowed herself to be touched in that way. A tendril of desire unfurled in her middle when Marek's foot shifted and his belt pressed into the front of her robe, as if begging to open it up to the unknown.

"*Ana'Sere*. Captaen," Declan knocked on the doorframe. Luscia broke the kiss, renewing the space between herself and the leader of her five. Blooming a flush, she retightened the robe, its closure suddenly untrustworthy. Declan palmed the strand of metal beads in his carroty beard and averted his eyes. "The Darakaian stirs."

Luscia sidestepped Marek to follow Declan down the hall with haste, preventing any potential query from the eldest of her Najjan. Instructing him to wait with the others, she caught the uncharacteristic, upturn of Marek's mouth when she backed into the bedroom and gently closed the door.

What do to about said mouth posed a veritable quandary, indeed. One she did not have the time or emotional store to properly ponder.

Twisting, she saw Kasim drooped over the arm of a chair he must have dragged to the bedside. His black locs hung freely over his shoulders, untied. She'd never noticed the detailed threadwork around a handful of them. Asleep, his head was held upright on the edge of his fist, his *kopar* unbelted and propped against one of the chair legs. Curled up beside his boot, Aksel fixated on Kasim, watching the al'Haidren doze from his spot on the floor.

Moving to the opposite side of the bed, she dabbed at the perspiration along Takoda's dark hairline as he moaned in his sleep. Minor tremors played with his slender features as he fought off delirium. Luscia pulled the skeleton key from between her breasts and pivoted to the apothecary, once again releasing the woodsy scent of the highlands.

"Kumo swore you'd refuse us," Kasim slurred in exhaustion.

Luscia jumped, then resumed scraping more ennus thorn into a clean vial. "Regardless of where we stand, I wouldn't just turn you away. Not when you brought a wounded man to my door."

"I wouldn't have blamed you if you had."

Her knife slowed. "That is a lie," she noted, setting it down. Lusica poured a few drops of nixberry into the cocktail, trying her best to remember Alora's combination for fevers.

"It went too far, what happened in that room," she heard him continue, alluding to the last time they met in the abandoned training chamber. "I crossed a line I didn't know was there. Last night, you could have punished me for it."

Luscia took a deep breath and returned to Takoda's side, noticing a pile of broken glass gathered neatly in the corner of the room. Kasim must have cleaned up the shattered vase at some point. Holding the vial, she eased the rim between Takoda's lips. The fragility of their existence struck her unexpectedly as she peered down, his shallow breaths a powerful reminder of how human they both were. Even for a child of Boreal, life was never guaranteed.

"I want to hear what you think you've discovered about me," she said abruptly in an low voice. When he didn't reply, she glanced across the bed. Fleetingly, a look of pity pinched Kasim's countenance and he looked aside. "*Say it*, Kasim."

Pulling the vial back, she waited for an answer. Gazing outside, his fist neared his mouth. "You excel only at the range of your weapon. In close combat, you become preoccupied with your defense. Distracted, even." Kasim turned back from the window and toward his friend. A tendon twitched in his jaw. "You're scared to be touched. That's your weakness."

Luscia absorbed Kasim's observation as she eased her hand behind Takoda's neck. His judgement was sound, she bitterly admitted. Thinking back on their sparring sessions, none of her men ever proposed hand-combat, always favoring a blade when she was their partner. An odd embarrassment threatened Luscia's impression of herself. Such glaring negligence in her training, and not once did the Najjan attempt to correct it.

"A weakness that might have cost me my life one day," Luscia said evenly, "had you not revealed it."

"Even still, a line was crossed. It won't happen again." His leather pants creased as he sat forward. "You have my word."

Twisting, Luscia stared at Kasim. Unblinkingly, he stared back.

"Is that the Darakaian equivalent to an apology?"

"Darakaians don't apologize."

"I see." She lifted Takoda's head to slowly tip the treatment down his throat. "*Tadöm*, for it is accepted nonetheless."

Kasim stretched out in the chair. The sun rising over the bay sent fresh light spilling into the room. Absently, Luscia started to apply another batch of paste, forming a poultice on Takoda's wounds. As she did, the rapid fluctuations of his chest smoothed to a more reassuring rhythm.

"Will he live?" Kasim asked, clearing his throat.

"Perhaps."

Luscia carried the mortar over to Kasim. Scooping two fingers into the paste, she lifted the substance toward his right temple. Edging back, his nose wrinkled at the strong, mossy odor. Luscia pitched a hand on her hip, knowing the longer it went untended, the more irritated the cut would become. Wordlessly, he swept a section of locs back to reveal the place her mother's dagger had grazed him. Evidence of the day she'd lost control.

The outline of the cut was crusted over in certain areas, indicating its slowness to scab, thanks to the corrosivity of luxiron. The fading slit under his chin fared slightly better.

"I should not have thrown that at your head," Luscia confessed, smoothing the paste over the partially healed skin.

"*Kàcha kocho,* I might've deserved it." Kasim grimaced as she layered it on. "Good thing you missed, or you really would be in the dungeon."

"I didn't miss. *Yeh'maelim*—you're welcome for that, too." She reached into the bowl and smeared what was left onto his throat. "Why didn't you take Takoda to a court physician, or one of the yancy doctors? Surely you've garnered enough coin, or favor, to demand treatment."

"You know why."

He watched her through tired eyes as she finished. The two had never been so close without injury, normally to his person. Luscia tugged at the plush collar of her robe, realizing then that she still had yet to actually dress, and began busily collecting the supplies dispersed throughout the room. Once everything was tucked away, Luscia stood against the dresser and faced Kasim, crossing her arms, more comfortable at a distance.

"The cross-caste boy taken from the stables," she had to ask, "was that who he found?"

Reluctant to reply, Kasim peered into his lap. "Nothing's been confirmed."

"Then tell me this. Your friend was on his deathbed, bleeding out into the street. When you came to my door, were you resolved to bring him to a witch, or to someone else?"

Reclining in the chair, Kasim crossed his arms as well. "I'm not sure."

She gazed straight into his hard, chartreuse eyes. "Then I propose we release ourselves from further threats at this point, don't you? We've too many enemies in this city, coming after yours and mine alike."

"I don't know what you are," Kasim reiterated, a knuckle grazing the fullness of his mouth. "Until I do, we cannot be allies."

"*Waedfrel*, then we are in agreement." Luscia tossed him the dirty rag, intending to find Tallulah so she could prepare for the event-filled day ahead. "But for the foreseeable future, we will cease trying to destroy each other."

"*Uni zà*," Kasim confirmed in his native tongue, "for the foreseeable future."

Getting up, he stooped for his *kopar*, strapped it on, and bent over Takoda to whisper something in Andwele. Kasim reached around her torso to grip the handle and reenter the common room. Stilling, he took one last glance at his kinsman and then to her viridi box on the dresser.

Just before he walked out the door, he threw the rag back into her hands. "I'm no laundress, and neither are you." He squinted at the apothecary again. "*Majïmaia*."

Granting a wide berth to Tallulah, who'd been awoken by the dawn and was clearly startled by his noisy departure, Kasim thumped his slumbering beta's leg, hanging off the edge of the chaise.

"*Owàamo*, cousin," he announced, heading into the foyer. "We're leaving."

Together, the two Darakaians marched out of her apartments and into the morning bustle. But before entering the main corridor, Kasim's beta rotated and bowed his head toward Luscia.

"*Shàlàmaiamo, Majïmaia*." The tall warrior looked up at her, smiled, and hit his chest.

Bewildered, Talluah closed the double door behind them. "Well, what in Aksel's Keep is that supposed to mean?"

Utterly exhausted, Luscia rubbed her eyelids. "It means the House of Darakai is the least of our problems, Tallulah."

THIRTY-THREE

Luscia

Under a sea of colorful lamps and suspended lanterns, Luscia took a breath and smoothed the front of her gown, appreciating how the luster glinted off its detailed beading. Out of habit, she went to straighten her collar before wading deeper into Thoarne Hall, only to remember there wasn't one on this dress. Careful not to disturb the intricate designs painted over her exposed neck, she lowered her hand, feeling a sudden flush beneath the iridescent artistry.

Unlike the temperate climate of the highlands, summer in the lowlands made it challenging to conceal the scar stretching toward her ear. Its ugliness had been camouflaged by Noxolo's handiwork, and

Luscia lifted her chin proudly, pleased to wear their Boreali custom in the Unitarian court.

"They will not notice," Declan assured her, as if attuned to her self-consciousness. By the time she glanced in the direction of his voice, he'd disappeared to his post in the shadows like the others.

Luscia bypassed a huddle of courtier women near the towering windows, who relished the sunset view over the city below, and sought the prince in the throng of clinking glass and swirling skirts. She'd left the lycran behind tonight, as the event was not in her honor, but the Zôueli. Eyeing the roasted boar on a platter, surrounded by choice fruits, she concluded it was likely for the best.

From behind, a bronze arm snaked around her own, ensnaring it. "There you are, Loo-Shah," the princess rolled her northern name, still unable to pronounce it. "Come with me, my friend. Missed, you have been."

"I appreciate the sentiment, *Bahira*'Rasha," Luscia said with a wry smile. "*Alloh'jom'yeh*."

"What does this mean?"

"May peace convene with you," she translated.

Rasha repeated the Boreali greeting as she led Luscia deeper into the swarm of guests with and air of authority. As they passed a tower of bubbling effervescence and flutes of Galina wine, the princess plucked two glasses from the top.

"For you." She extended the second to Luscia, taking a generous gulp of her own. "Now, teach me more of Boreal. Tell me of your trees, they are so tall?"

Her russet eyes lit up as she tucked in her chin, like they were two old crones discussing something scandalous instead of foliage.

"*Wem,* indeed, massive enough to host our village-fortress within the heights." Luscia gestured overhead. "All Roüwen hangs off the earth. In my home, it is said that in Roüwen, man stands closer to Aurynth, for the distance is already a foot and a flight shorter."

The train of the princess's hybrid gown trailed their path through the solstice celebration, her billowy pantlegs swishing as she walked, seeming genuinely entranced by the account of Luscia's homeland.

"The city among stars. It is..." Rasha's tongue curled over her teeth, finding the right words. "...my dream to see such a settlement. In Razôuel, my cities are dressed in jewels. Jol'Nune would fall to the ground!"

Luscia laughed, imagining it. Rasha touched the flute to her lips, but the wine sloshed onto a nearby yancy when she abruptly changed course, dragging Luscia in tow. Meandering through the Hall, the princess brought them to Ira's side. Buttoned into a pressed, velvet waistcoat, the al'Haidren almost looked sober, barring the bit of residual rouge across his cheek from his latest encounter with some nobleman's daughter.

"*Bahira* Rasha." Ira lingered over her fingers, kissing them. "And my wintery rose!" He swiveled to Luscia next, scanning the pearly patterns on her neck as he raised her hand to his lips. "I bid you both a very sweet solstice."

Lusica yanked her hand from his grasp. It was sticky, and she tried to convince herself it was only sweat.

"Lord al'Haidren—Ira, may I?" Rasha tested. "You've known each other now many years...or is it only a few?"

"You can call me whatever you please, whenever you please," Ira simpered toward the princess, deepening his voice. "My acquaintance with Boreal is just as inadequate as your own, despite tremendous diplomatic attempts to bridge our…" Tilting his head, Ira admired Luscia's fitted bodice. "…topographical differences."

The princess eyed Luscia curiously, who vehemently shook her head at the prospect. "Our differences span wider than the Ileas, Ira."

"Oh, I'm a fine swimmer." He winked and thrust his palm in the air, looking past them as he called, "Sayuri, be a pet and fetch that attendant there. No, darling, the chubby one."

Ira flipped his glass upside down, shaking it. Sayuri melded into their group, wedging herself into a gap between Luscia and the princess.

"We're not here to grab things for you, Ira," she said. "You insufferable snob."

"But you've proven such an affinity for it, dear."

Scoffing, she spun her back on Luscia to converse with the Zôueli princess, her features so similar to the other westerner. Sayuri's coastal beauty was on full display for the solstice, her curves enveloped in gilded tiers of feathery lace. Her movements seemed labored, drowning under strings of Pilar's famed pearls. Offset by the dark, glossy curtain of hair descending her back, Sayuri's splendor was a clear show of rivalry with the princess. Luscia skimmed the room to find Dmitri in animated discussion with a trio of nobles, evidently indifferent to her efforts.

"Loo-Shah was speaking of things," Rasha's head whipped around, "elsewhere things. Shall we, friend?" She extended her reach around Sayuri's tiny waist and grabbed Luscia's wrist, yanking her away from the other two al'Haidrens.

Fleetingly, Luscia worried the House of Pilar might publicly threaten Dmitri's prospective wife, but Sayuri's brows merely furrowed into sharp lines as she watched them disappear into the crowd.

"I hear Pilar speak enough in Jol'Nune. They are my neighbors, you know," Rasha stated under her breath, "and they never quiet."

"*Maji'maia.*"

Someone tugged Luscia's sleeve where it fell off her decorated shoulders. She was surprised to see that it was Kasim easing through the wall of nobles. At his appearance, the princess slowed her advance, seemingly intrigued. He kept pace with them as they headed toward another tray of Unitarian treats.

Dmitri must have ordered Kasim a tailor and a decent grooming, for it was the finest suit he'd sported since her arrival at court. Worn over trim leather pants, his satin jacket appeared to be custom-made. The crest of the short collar shone under the lively lanternlight, the depth of indigo rich and radiant. Luscia gave additional credit to the valet responsible for taming his locs into the ample topknot at his crown, save for the few locs that hung tucked behind an ear, encased in copper thread.

Kasim leaned in. "Kumo reported Takoda's transfer from your quarters. It's done."

Up close, Luscia noticed the cut had already begun to heal, enough for a barber to have shaved a tight margin around the base of his scalp, fading upward, where it'd been neatly gathered.

With the slightest angling of her chin, she acknowledged his update, and he backed away, without a word to the princess.

"So pretty, yes?" Rasha bit off a piece of sweet wafer, staring after Kasim as he crossed the hall to Dmitri's right side.

"Unfortunately," Luscia grumbled.

"Oh, Lord Zaethan!"

A bushel of taffeta bounced after the Darakaian al'Haidren, who unsurprisingly ignored her shrill cajoling. Flapping a piece of napery in the air, Flourette hastened after him, like someone signaling for help. A few courtiers stepped out of her path as she latched onto Kasim's jacket.

The princess looked amused. "Who is that, Loo-Shah?"

"That is the Haidren to Bastiion's daughter, Flourette Hastings. Ira's...very enthusiastic sister," Luscia replied, cringing for the girl when Kasim grabbed her lanky fingers, halting their progression toward the cluster atop his head.

"She has an emptiness, yes?" Rasha gesticulated around her forehead as they headed for the platform at the end of the hall, toward the towering byrnnzite antlers affixed to the throne.

"*Wem*, yes." Luscia grinned. "I suspect much the same."

Guests littering the cavernous space leisurely found their way to the long, pristine tables situated around the perimeter. The tabletops, spread with the finest place settings, sparkled under the lanterns as the sun dove into the waters of the horizon. Luscia escorted the princess to Dmitri's table, positioned lower than the king's, where Rasha's mother would dine.

An additional setting had been placed between Dmitri's seat at the middle and Boreal's to his left. Two attendants rushed to scoot both Luscia and the princess into their chairs. Serving royalty first, wine was poured for Rasha before the attendant switched to Luscia, failing to meet her eyes. Missing her glass as his hand shook, the man apologized and scuttled away.

"Orynthia is a land full of people puzzles," the princess mused, squeezing Luscia's forearm tightly. "But now, let us speak of your prince. Will he do for me, Loo-Shah, or must I pursue another? Tell me of his nature—I must know."

Luscia regarded the Orynthian prince in question near the base of the platform. He'd propped a polished boot on the first step, still engaged in some lively debate. Luscia considered the question carefully, aware the Zôueli princess would judiciously weigh her response, despite Rasha's casual and light-hearted demeanor.

"I can testify his patience is unparalleled, that is certain," she began, thinking on their most recent conversation in the temple. "He holds a great capacity for feeling, more than most rulers."

"And you believe this is good for your kingdom?" Rasha turned in her chair, resting her chin on the back of her wrist with ease.

"Do you not?" Luscia paused, studying their foreign ally.

"Men should not carry a crown." She shrugged and tapped her heart. "Too many emotions, they hold. Women are the backbone of a people. They break their body, mar their beauty, for the life. Each swallow great pain, and call it joy. Men, not the same. Great pain makes a great man crumble. This I know, Loo-Shah."

Luscia thumbed a shining copper spoon on the edge of her setting. Dmitri started up the steps with enthusiasm. His eyes gleamed, seeing they were already seated, and stopped at the other end of the table while Sayuri took her place. Laughing at something she said, his dimple came forward. A warmth filled Luscia's chest, pleased that her blood, in the mystery of those vials, granted him renewed liveliness for an evening.

"*Bahira*." Luscia faced the golden princess. "What you say holds merit. But we are not the owners of suffering, simply allies through it. I promise you, Dmitri Korbin Thoarne is no different. If you deem sorrow a prerequisite for kingship, you will not find the Crown Prince of Orynthia wanting in that regard."

"Much to consider, my friend," Rasha muttered as Dmitri's hand slid over the backs of the chairs, pulling his own out from the center, Kasim following close behind. Attendants swooped in to assist their prince, as well as the Darakaian al'Haidren, but Dmitri waved them off.

"I see you two are getting on nicely," he commented, beaming. "I do hope you've not plotted my demise in my absence, for I'm certain you'd be very effective at it."

Chuckling, Rasha slid her thick braid over her shoulder to cascade down her back. Over her head, Dmitri stretched to peek at Luscia, miming his thanks.

The great gong sounded, and Ira skidded into his seat just as the first course was served. Reminiscent of Luscia' own reception, a parade of entertainers ascended the dais, accompanying the progression of the meal, though with significantly more grandeur and costly extravagance.

"Pow prawn?" Ira raised a shining plate as he leaned closer, rubbing her arm. "They are meant to be shared—a lover's delicacy."

"You ought to learn some delicacy, Lord Bastiion," Luscia answered sharply, staring ahead.

"In time, my snow dove," he declared, slurping it down.

After unnecessary rounds of perfectly baked crumpets and a procession of soups, a wave of attendants brought the main course to the table. Like a collapsing tide, a company of shotos—likely early in their years of study, by the ashy hue of their voluminous robes—replaced the traffic of the palace staff and surrounded the dais. A series of ropes tumbled from the ceiling into their grasp, adjoined to a floating contraption mingling among the lanterns overhead.

"Oh, I do love this one." Ira perched over his plate in anticipation, clutching a hunk of braised meat. "Much better than their standard depressing recitation!"

Sayuri's uncle, the Haidren to Pilar, joined the Pilarese students. His robes were white and crisp, signifying his status as Prime over their Shoto Collective. Around the hall, most of the torches were extinguished, save for a few to cast enough illumination for their dining. Tetsu Naborū leaned over a metal dome and lit a match. As he stepped away into the dark, light exploded from the device, mirroring its beam into the ceiling. Reflecting off the box among the lanterns, the students swayed to adjust the roping like a single organism. In a flash, the head of a stag appeared on the dais, printed in shadow.

The room erupted with applause, impressed by the sight. Modifying their steps, the students twirled the ropes around their abdomens. The antlers of Thoarne's stag melted into the wings of an owl, flying in place while they continued their dance. Guests cooed in wonder, the Zôueli princess joining their praise. She clapped with delight, pointing at the scene while she brushed back a wisp of Dmitri's hair to speak in his ear.

After navigating the crowd through a series of images, Naborū moved to the opposite flank and lit an identical dome. The galloping horse on the dais broke apart and materialized into a pack of wolves running through a forest. A shadowy hawk soared above a forest of pines.

Luscia felt an odd stirring in her stomach as he struck another match for a third dome. Settled into the shade outside the circle of performance, the Haidren leveled his gaze at her. Eerily and unblinkingly, Naborū tilted his waxen, yellowing face, just as he'd done after their encounter in the passageway.

A sting panged through her temples. Panic constricted her throat, which had gone raw. She'd taken her last dose just yesterday—it was impossible that she could be having an episode so soon. The pain worsening, Luscia pushed back her chair, grateful that the guests of the hall were too mesmerized to notice her stand.

"Lusica, are you alright?" Dmitri started to rise.

"*Niit, niit*...I am fine, just feeling unwell." Luscia stepped away, reassuring him. "Stay, enjoy the show, Your Highness."

Spinning in place, she found her aunt at the king's table. Confusion tugged Alora's delicate brow. Humming consumed Luscia's hearing, drowning out the words Alora mouthed. Exiting off the corner of the hall, she plunged through an archway, collapsing to her knees on a vacant balcony. Clutching the stone balusters, she pulled herself up, rocked by the tremors controlling her limbs, contorting them unnaturally. Her head sank back, and Luscia felt her lashes flutter as the hum was overtaken by whispers. Some faint, some louder, they blended into an unwanted chorus.

Drawn into the Sight, Luscia's view of the city over the banister evolved into a shimmering network. Threads of lumin drifted hazily through the streets of Marketown, forming a luminescent map of Bastiion. The whispering waned when she recognized a unique thread, brighter than the rest, twitching in the distance. Its light sputtered as it wound through the alleys, convulsing in agitation.

Gentle pressure touched her back.

"*Ana'Sere?*" a voice asked through the distortion, its tone far and hollow. "*Ana'Mere* sent me to find you. Luscia, are you alright?"

Sound rebalanced itself, the cloud dispersing. Twisting, she discovered Marek standing nearby. She'd not even felt him clenching her hand.

"Do you trust me, Captaen?"

The skin beneath his eyes tightened as he searched her gaze. There was a newfound intimacy behind them. "I trust you, *Ana'Sere*."

She laced her fingers through his and guided him under the archway. A tingle spread down her spine. Hesitating, she glimpsed over her shoulder into the night.

"What is happening?" he asked.

The light of the *Other* disappeared, concealed behind the veil. The ominous disorder of Marketown returned, flickering in front of it.

"I'm fulfilling my promise to you, Captaen, and taking you with me."

Beside Marek, Luscia balanced over the shelf of the aqueduct, surveying a hunting ground of opulence and depravity.

"So *this* is how you've been getting around us," she heard Marek mutter.

For the first time since the clearing in the wood, Luscia voluntarily sought communion with the threads and summoned the Sight. This time in the presence of Najjan, rather than lycran.

"*Bolaeva,*" she prayed, her lids falling.

Reopening them, she saw strings of lumin entangling the buildings, connecting and dispersing in an alternate map of the *Other*. With stillness and resolution, Luscia searched for the restless thread among its brethren. Whispers replaced the vibration in her skull, louder than ever before. Searing tendrils shot up her nape and outward, like twin captors squeezing her mind.

There—among the pipe marrow tents at the edge of the docks, the harbinger thread embarked on a quivering path into the pit of Marketown.

"I see you."

At her acknowledgment, the murmurs started to scream, becoming an indistinguishable anthem. Luscia sank into a squat, clutching her head. With a pop, their song vanished.

"*Luscia...*"

She slowly turned to Marek, praying it was him at the end of the call, and not the unseen. He flinched away when her hood fell back, lips parting. Droplets fell, chiming against their weaponry, as the sky opened. Rain rolled off Marek's hair, and in the reflection of his pupils, her irises were aglow.

"Luscia..."

Marek reached out to touch her, but stopped, seeming afraid. "Luscia, your nose."

Her hand lifted to wipe away a wetness trickling from her nostril. Blood smeared her fingertips.

"Release your wraiths, *Brödre*." She rubbed her hand on the tail of her coat. "We're losing time."

Fastening the shroud across her cheeks, she restored the hood and vaulted off the waterway. Luscia struck the ground and sailed into the night after the thread, trusting the captaen to do the same.

THIRTY-FOUR

Zaethan

S he was easy to spot—a pastel specter in a lake of the living.

Arm in arm, the al'Haidren to Boreal walked with Dmitri's would-be bride. Zaethan was about as interested in forging a more intimate alliance with the Zôueli as he was with his tailor, both of whom Dmitri insisted were essential to the future of the court. But unlike the fingers of a nosy tailor, Zaethan doubted Razôuel would be satisfied with mere proximity to the real prize. Eventually, when the splendor of the union dissipated and the dust of the Ethnicam settled, Razôuel would come for it—the throne of Orynthia.

Zaethan's eyes rolled as he squeezed between a nobleman and his wife, both too in their cups to care. The Unitarian Peerage would never agree to a bride from one of the outer Houses, but a foreign princess, as rich in trade as she was in gold, rang a different story in their greedy ears. A princess who had much more to gain, and even less to lose, than his optimistic friend, Dmitri Thoarne.

Wedging his hand past a pair of yancies, Zaethan caught hold of the delicate sleeve of the al'Haidren's gown. The material fluttered off her bared shoulders, twinkling in the lanternlight, unlike anything she'd worn in the past.

"*Maji'maia*," he said under his breath, adopting Kumo's moniker for the witchling.

Striding to a nearby table alongside her and the princess, he bent to her level and whispered into her untamed hair, "Kumo reported Takoda's transfer from your quarters. It's done."

Irregularly woven gemstones tickled his nose as he pulled away and departed, not caring to hear her response. He'd committed to having Takoda moved, and it had been done. No need for commentary, especially in the presence of foreigners.

Dmitri hadn't exaggerated *Bahira*Rasha's odd obsession with the House of Boreal. The princess had practically lacquered herself to the al'Haidren since her arrival, constantly entwined, like those candied rods of twisted treacle in the market. Zaethan shrugged at the enigma of it all and tried to locate Dmitri in the crowd. Better Razôuel form friendships with the secluded highlanders than their more affluent and powerful neighbor, Pilar.

Sighting the bronze tail of Dmitri's cane, Zaethan angled for the base of the platform beneath the throne. Then he winced, hearing the ear-splitting yelps of Gregor's daughter. Under siege, Zaethan clenched his jaw, thoroughly defeated. As with all her attacks, the impact hit him from behind, bathing his coat in nauseatingly floral perfume.

"I've been looking everywhere for you, Lord Zaethan!" Flourrette wagged her handkerchief, hanging onto his bicep like a thirsty sucker-bug in Hagarh.

"Making it impossible to get away," he remarked, and swiftly snatched her hand before it could ensnare one of his locs, clustered and secured. "Let's not, Flourette. Wouldn't want to ruin the prince's handiwork, would we?"

"The prince styles your hair?" Her brown eyes widened, lashes flapping incessantly.

"Oh, *uni zà*...exactly." Zaethan seized the opportunity. It was less than Dmitri deserved for sending the squadron of barbers to his door. "It's his newest passion. Can't get enough of it."

By then, they'd reached the huddle of councilmen surrounding the prince. From the sound of it, the Duke of Uriel was making an uncompelling case for higher tariffs on the provincial exports of his competitor, Hildur. Impartial to the rebuttal, Zaethan set his palm against the back of Flourette's corseted waist and nudged her forward enthusiastically.

"Well go on, then." He waved over her shoulder. "The prince has been waiting all evening for someone to notice!"

"Pardon me, gentlemen. Yes, you, sir!" Gregor's daughter bumped the noblemen apart, carving a place for herself. "Prince Dmitri! It's masterful, really, what you've done with Lord Zaethan's glorious mane. Truly, you should be delighted with your craft!"

Flourette pocketed the handkerchief to applaud the prince, expecting the councilmen to do the same. They would, of course, as the Minister of their Peerage was her father. Zaethan stepped aside and suppressed a chuckle at the sight of Flourette conducting the circlet of yancies in a round of awkward applause.

"Should I, Lady Flourette?" Dmitri's brows jumped into his hairline, and he shot a look to Zaethan, clamping his lips into a taut smile.

"Oh, Councilmen, by the Fates, he really is the best there is." Zaethan backed away, pinched his fingertips, and kissed them. "Day or night, gentlemen!"

Picking up speed, he cut a path toward the eldest of Gregor's progeny, philandering by the windows. Ira's arms snaked around a shapely attendant, who tried to balance a tray of morsels. Her giggling ceased when Zaethan grabbed the tray, whipped Ira around by the lapel, and handed it back to the young woman.

"Your timing offends." Ira straightened the cockeyed scarf tied around his collar. "It's like you specifically target my happiness just to snuff it out. I'll have you know," he leaned in, pointing between them, "I could have negotiated something for you out of that. But it seems you've withered that, too."

Zaethan shoved him against the windows, though not forcefully enough to attract attention from other guests. "Your sister is an absolute plague, Ira. Get her in line before she makes an even greater mockery of Wendylle than you already have."

Ira dodged a glance beyond Zaethan's cluster of locs, fanning them away, and blew out a breath. "You expect me to cure that pestilence? Better to accept it early on, Zaethan." He rebuttoned his jacket, yanking the cuffs down. "Like warts on a whore, it could always be worse. Aren't you relieved it's me on the Quadren instead?"

Ira slapped him on the shoulders and tipped a flute of wine back when a fresh batch passed by.

"*Ano. Zà.*" Zeathan snatched a second glass out of Ira's grasp, handing it off to an attendant. "Absolutely not."

"Your loss, another's gain."

Drifting off, Ira meandered toward a flock of courtiers, preening themselves as they fawned over the sunset settling into the Drystan. Sauntering onto the platform, Zaethan cracked his neck, stretching it out. Even *Owàa* grew tired of the solstice, his longest flight of the year, abandoning Zaethan to endure the festivities alone.

As the dinner gong was struck, Dmitri slid into place at the middle of the table, beside the princess, and launched into spirited discussion.

"First the y'siti harlot, now this Zôueli shrew. Depths!" Sayuri pouted as she toyed with a string of pearls in her seat next to Zaethan at the end of the table. "When is she going back to her bloody beaches? That's probably why they get along so well. The y'siti are drained of blood, and the Zôueli possess a coast of it."

Zaethan ground his teeth. He wasn't sure what irritated Sayuri more—the fact that Razôuel held the burgundy beaches or that they were famous for them, neither an asset Pilar could claim.

"I'm not in the mood to listen to your soured *kakk* piss, Sayuri." Zaethan took a platter from the attendant approaching the table and thrust it under her chin. "Just shut up and eat something. You're starting to look poor."

He shouldn't have been surprised when Sayuri instantly nicked a spiced teacake and ate it, the threat of appearing impoverished worse by court standard than actual malnourishment. As the sun vanished and ceded to his lover's plight, Zaethan thanked *Àla'maia* that Zahra, his third, maintained a healthy appetite, equal to any man in the prydes.

He elbowed Dmitri in the ribs, grimacing as he scratched at his jacket. "Your royal tailor is a fraud. This thing itches like the Depths."

"Maybe if you'd held still," his friend said through his teeth, grinning for the rest of the room, "then it would fit correctly."

Twisting, Dmitri resumed his conversation with the princess and her Boreali pet. Zaethan spooned at his bowl of thissle bisque, keenly aware it shared the color of vomit, as an ensemble of woodwinds descended the dais. A line of shoto'shi, each an acolyte to their Shoto Prime, replaced the musicians just as the soup course was swapped with something more substantial.

"I hate this one," he grumbled, eyeing a box affixed to the ceiling.

"That is because," Sayuri interjected, using her butter knife to check her reflection, "you Darakaians don't appreciate the complexity of the shadow box."

"Darakaians don't like liars," he corrected. Zaethan narrowed his gaze at her uncle, about to light the first dome. "This *shtàka*—this is why the Ethnicam doesn't trust the Pilarese. What you say, what you show, is never what you mean."

"I've never deceived you, Zaethan." Her lips puckered, excessively rouged. "The fact that you are so adamant about this says more about you than it does me."

The head of a stag blossomed over the dais, the tendrils of its antlers seeping onto the main floor. Sayuri's uncle lurked outside the student formation as the shadowy antlers melted into the wings of an owl. The shoto'shi swayed, making it fly, as he prowled toward the second fixture.

"A Haidren to Pilar is always a better liar than that, Sayuri." Zaethan sat back and folded his arms, his appetite diminishing. "You ought to seek lessons from your own. I'm sure it runs in the family."

Sayuri simpered and brought a plump berry to her mouth, biting it off the stem slowly. "You should hope so…behind your father, there's so much to live up to, isn't there?"

Zaethan's head snapped up. She licked the dark juice from her lip and resumed watching the performance. His fists clenched beneath the table. Down the row, Dmitri started to rise as another chair screeched.

Told not to worry, both royals eased into their seats as the Boreali al'Haidren excused herself from dinner, leaving in the direction of the balcony. Seeing her captain follow, Zaethan ignored any budding curiosity as to what caused her to seek the evening air.

When the match of the fourth and final dome was struck, the scene dispersed across the dais and reformed into Bastiion's silhouette, the bulbous cupolas of the palace readily familiar to the audience. Movement caught his attention beyond the brightness at the center of the hall. Zaethan squinted. Kumo stood just inside the entrance, away from his assigned post on the opposite end of the eastern wing.

Locking eyes with Zaethan, his beta signaled him over, then ducked behind the gigantic doors, returning to the main corridor.

"I must check on the guard—I'll be right back," he muttered to Dmitri before abandoning the meal, an uneasiness spreading in his chest.

Outside the Hall, Zaethan found Kumo tucked behind a column, posture rigid and expression tense. As he drew near, Kumo scratched the backs of his knuckles.

"Spit it out, cousin," Zaethan ordered.

Kumo tensed, crossing his arms. "Wekesa is missing."

"What do you mean, *missing*?"

"He should have been in there tonight with you, *ano*?" His mouth tightened, tilting it toward the Hall. "Zahra said Wekesa's not gone to his apartments all evening, claims he never came back. Jabari checked the guard house, yeah. Playing no cards, nothing. But the sentries…" Kumo paused, watching Zaethan's reaction.

"The sentries…?"

"Some of the sentries say he head to the kitchen earlier—"

"*Shtàka!*" Zaethan squeezed the hilt of his *kopar* in one hand and punched the column with the other. "This night, of all nights! *Uni*, of course Wekesa planned his next attack tonight—he knew I'd be stuck in there for that yancy charade." Rubbing his busted knuckle, Zaethan shook his head passionately. "We move one step, he's already two ahead. Every time."

"*Meme qondai*, I get it." Kumo edged closer, away from any possible listeners. "Send Zahra and I back out there. Stay in the Hall, avoid questions, yeah?"

"*Ano zà*. Not again," Zaethan spat forcefully, Takoda's bloodstained sheets fresh in his mind. "I want Zahra on Wekesa's pryde, watching his men. They'll give something away eventually, if they drink too much. I'll find Jabari, assign him elsewhere. Let's keep the cub out of this."

"Then I come with you, *Ahoté.*"

"*Ano*, Cousin. I want you here in my place, with Dmitri." Zaethan checked behind them, knowing the Pilarese exhibition would conclude at any moment and that they'd soon be joined by the shoto'shi in transition. "When they exit, slip inside, yeah? Keep to the exterior, you'll be less noticeable. Don't take your eyes off the prince."

Kumo hesitated, but struck his fist to his chest. "*Uni zà*, Alpha Zà. I won't leave his side until you return."

"Takoda—I need to ask him to do something first. You said he was awake?"

"Eh, he started to come to earlier," Kumo confirmed, peering around the column as the door creaked. "Nothing coherent, *ano*."

"*Shàlàmaimo.*" Zaethan's fist left his own chest and bumped his beta's heart twice. "Don't leave the prince," he reiterated in parting, pointing at the Hall.

As the robed students departed the celebration, Zaethan launched into a sprint and sped around the bend, running up the nearest stair.

He dodged a valet, causing the man to whip his wheeled drink cart over in the process. Shards of crystal bathed the floor, spilling wasted spirits across the vast corridor as Zaethan threw up his arms and smacked into a lady's maid. Jumping over her basket of table linens, he charged up the steps toward the apartments.

As he climbed the heights, Zaethan ripped the blasted satin jacket off his upper body and flung it aside, ditching it on a landing. With a swell of relief, he spread out his shoulders, rolling them as he plunged down the passage to the suites of the northern wing. As he'd not done in ages, Zaethan pleaded with the Fates, begging for the witchling's sorcery to have brought Takoda to consciousness.

He was the only person who could provide testimony to the identity of the cross-caste killer. Should something similar befall Zaethan, leaving his pryde in the hands of a butcher, he needed to ensure Takoda's account was recorded, before it was too late.

He dashed under an archway, skidding into the doors of the Boreali suite. Standing before their height, Zaethan released a howl of frustration, remembering Takoda had already been moved earlier that evening. He slammed his palms against the wood, rattling the giant slabs within their framing. Pushing off, he started for the opposite end of the corridor, where the passage rejoined the common route to the residential apartments.

Zaethan halted when something crashed against the double door from inside the Boreali suite. A second crash rumbled the hinges, followed by warbled shouts in foreign syllables.

Zaethan rushed back and pounded on the surface. "What's going on in there?" He jostled the handle. Locked. "Open up! This is Kasim, al'Haidren and Alpha Zà, head of the prydes and local sentry."

At his command, a weight blasted into the other side, thumping him backward. The yelling increased, and the door cracked open. A frazzled and pale, doughy woman with exceptionally large teeth stood behind the gap.

"Not the best time, milord." A blonde tuft from her braid smushed into view as she looked back and shrieked, "Shores of Aurynth! *Heh'ta*, you mangy, war-tainted mongrel! I'm warning yeh, stop this insanity at once!"

The maid yelped, her teeth consuming her bottom lip, as the door wrenched from her grasp and bashed into the stone. The hybrid wolx reeled into Zaethan, hurling him to the floor. The animal's voluminous tail swished buoyantly as the enormous crossbreed dashed down the passage. Its claws, too long and dangerous to be trapped in a stone cage, clacked against the tiles as he skidded around the corner. Scrambling to his feet, Zaethan took off through the halls of the palace after the rampant wolx.

Panting, both from fatigue and genuine panic, he chased the animal as it launched down a stairs, destroying a few banisters, and escaped into the lower levels. A group of *yayas* chucked their piled platters aside, screaming when the creature bolted through the entry to the kitchens. Puffed pastries flew through the air, pelting Zaethan in the face. The wolx weaved between the servants and scurried to a stop in front of an old hatchway, surrounded by soiled meat buckets and discarded produce.

Cautiously, Zaethan unsheathed his *kopar*, angling for its throat. At the whistle of the iron, it snarled, barring its serrated teeth. Spittle leaked off its lengthy canines. But instead of attacking Zaethan, the animal's snout lowered toward the rusty padlock. The Orallach wolx thrashed its head and yipped, jaw snapping savagely.

"Your mistress—she already went after him, didn't she?" Zaethan asked it.

At his mention of the Boreali al'Haidren, the amber fur along its spine lifted, hackles rising. The wolx yowled and pawed at the hatch. With the tip of his *kopar*, Zaethan lifted the broken lock. Flinging the door open, he gazed into the darkness below.

"Show me the way."

THIRTY-FIVE

Luscia

The unrelenting rain beat down upon their backs. With her hood pulled taut, shrouding her face from Aurynth's watchman, Luscia stared through the curtain of droplets spilling over the edge, blinking it out of her line of sight.

Her spine pressed into the broad support of Marek's back as he watched the streets from the edge of Marketown. Conversely, Luscia searched the threads patiently, awaiting another disturbance.

"Anything, *Ana'Sere?*"

"*Niit, Brödre,*" she muttered, her lips barely moving.

Most of the alleys had already cleared, slickened from the downpour. The clouds rumbled and shifted overhead, casting eerie shadows over the uneven pavers reflecting the moon, mirroring Naborū's display in the Hall. Robbed of a noble audience, the clouds thundered their applause as they showered the city, the clamor for an encore pouring into the drains.

Like threads in a loom, the lumin carved patterns through the city, more radiant than she'd ever been led to believe was possible so far from the *Dönumn*. It enveloped the buildings and cradled everything in between, snaking around to the back street, to climb the heights of the busted masonry. Light twinkled and reached for its brethren across the rooftops above, as if it held Bastiion together from behind the veil. Crowding cracks in the brickwork, it balanced the brokenness, offering recompense from the *Other*.

At the thought, Luscia felt an odd sensation tickle her temples. Poised and controlled, her eyes slid, peering to the side. Beside the wet fabric covering her head, a tendril of light drifted by her cheekbone. She stared at it, allowing the rain to drown her vision. The tendril seemed to stare back, hovering inches away.

"*Luscia....*"

The tingling intensified, a severe pain forcing her mouth open in a silent wail. Luscia gasped as the tendril writhed in place, its light contorting. The rush of whispers returned, roaring and wailing.

"*Ana'Sere!*" Spinning toward her, Marek's hands clutched her shoulders.

Luscia looked up through the opening of the alley and into the empty street. Suddenly, every thread trembled, the light of the *Other* sputtering angrily. Beset by a second storm invisible to Marek's eyes, the city flashed with ethereal lightning. She felt its wrath turn her stomach over, knotting it mercilessly. Nausea clambered her throat, burning under her awful scar. Flashing as if in warning, the threads snapped into place, fortifying their glow.

"*Luscia….*"

The whispers layered in unison, harmonizing her name. Luscia spun in her crouch toward the opposite end of the alley. Brilliant and volatile, the harbinger thread appeared in the distance. The beam quivered erratically, beckoning her to follow.

Springing from her position, Luscia darted after it, plunging deeper into the glittering web in a capricious race through the *Other*. In her periphery, details in the darkness blurred, her Sight anchored onto the thread's bright, fractured light. Luscia skidded around a corner and, seizing a rusted pole, catapulted through a second-story frame. The harbinger thread shuddered, encircling it. Grasping the splintered wood, she swung her body into the dirtied apartment. The moment her upturned boot landed on the creaky floorboards, the stench of rot and waste assaulted her nostrils.

Creeping forward on the balls of her feet, she followed the crackling thread. Abruptly, a child's scream sliced her ears, chilling and horrible. Her grip on the Sight broke, jerking Luscia to the front of the veil. She shook her head, feeling suddenly bereft, but continued toward the cracked door at the end of the crooked hall.

The slightest scuffle signaled Marek's arrival at her back. Luscia raised two fingers, communicating absolute silence. Najjani silence. With another step, she touched the door, pausing to tilt her head and observe the scene within. Through the slim opening, a cloak swayed, dusting the wood floor. A tall man angled over a quaint bed. Even without the aid of the moon, her Tiergan eyes read the outline of a simple dagger as the man lifted it over the frightened child.

"*Niit*!" Luscia shouted, ramming the door open and diving for his middle.

Tumbling across the floor, the man's revolting odor filled her nostrils, making her gag. Luscia heard the cross-caste child crying from the corner of the straw bed. The man shirked her hold on his torso when she glanced to the little girl, distressed by the amount of blood on the sheets. In her distraction, his cloak fanned out, lashing her across the face. He leapt for the window, shattering the glass, his hands protected in fine leather gloves, and plummeted into the street.

"Marek, the girl!"

She pointed to the bed before unsheathing her wraiths and jumping out the small window. Vaulting over the shards, Luscia slammed into a puddle, slapping the surface of the water as she hunkered into a low squat with the impact. Luscia squeezed her eyes shut, trying to reengage the Sight for aid. Reopening them, the corner of a cloak caught her attention, sweeping past a flooding merchant cart. Down a row of patchwork tents, the man ran on foot, faster than expected.

Sprinting, she trailed him between the pipe huts, the foul smoke competing with the rain as it filled the lane with putrid steam. A few partakers, oblivious to the storm, staggered from the flaps, firmly entrenched in marrow stupor and mumbling nonsense. Thrusting them out of the way, she dodged the wasted patrons in chase of something far worse than any addict.

Gaining speed, Luscia ran up a terrace, leapt, and flipped over the final tent. Spinning through the air, she hooked her boot around the neck of the man's hood and drove them both into the street, bathing them in soiled water. With her left wraith, Luscia secured his cloak to the cobbles and ripped the covering away from his face.

Aghast and confused, her lashes beat off the torrential rain. The wraith in her right hand chimed as she raised it, wavering.

"Ambrose?"

The rainclouds parted, permitting the moon to wash over his face, or what remained of it. While his features resembled the noble from Agoston, with the same sharp nose and protruding brow, his coloring was far from the man she'd threatened and pulled off Mila just days before.

Ambrose's lips split apart as he grinned coldly, the flesh blackened in decay where it should have pinked. Curdled inkiness gushed from his mouth when he hacked a laugh. The substance congealed and seeped down his chin.

"You shouldn't have come here, y'siti spawn."

With a strength too formidable for any human, Ambrose lurched forward and sank his teeth into her upper arm. Luscia yelped in pain, the power of his jaw more animal than man. When her grip gave out and the wraith clattered to the stone, his fetid fangs opened to angle for her throat. Terrified, Luscia repelled his advance, pushing her forearms into his neck as he snarled. His rotting tongue, covered in fissures and pustules, flailed after her skin.

A savage growl, harrowing and unhinged, came from the right. A terrible force struck Ambrose, wrenching him off Luscia. Wheezing, she knelt on the ground and pivoted to see a massive Orrallach hybrid wrestle the diseased noble down the way. Hackles raised, lifted to Aurynth, her lycran dragged Ambrose by the ankle. Thrashing him from side to side, Aksel brutally attacked, his feral nature freed at her defense.

"Is that him?" Luscia jumped as Kasim ran up from the rear. Panting, he hunched over to grip his knees. "Did you find the killer?"

"How—"

"Followed the beastie." He cocked his head down toward the tussle.

Her focus drew away from Kasim's strange presence when the lycran yelped and stumbled back, slumping into a pile of garbage.

"Aksel!" Luscia wailed, running for her friend.

As Ambrose took off with renewed velocity, his ankle bent unnaturally, yet it did not slow his pace, even as she heard the *pop* of a bone snapping.

Dropping to her lycran's side, she scanned his injuries—mostly superficial, save an ugly gash on his hind leg. It would heal, though not without significant pain. Kasim skated toward her, drenched in the drizzle. Holding the partnering wraith she'd staked into the cobblestone, he huffed as she examined the whimpering wolx, combing through his bloody fur.

"*Now* you bring these out?" he criticized, flexing his hold around the central hilt. "At least tell me you caught Wekesa in the act—that's all I need for the arrest."

"Wekesa?" Lucia sputtered incredulously, tearing a strip off her belted tunic to bind Aksel's leg. "*Nitt*! It's Ambrose, Kasim. He's war-tainted, infected or something. I'm not certain, but we have to go after him now, before it spreads."

"Wait, *doru*...you said Ambrose? *Felix* Ambrose?"

"Or that's who he used to be, anyway. *Bolaeva*, please." She extended her open palm to retrieve the crescent wraith, to complete her set. Begrudgingly, he handed it over and reached instead for his *kopar*. "*Heh'ta*, Aksel," she said, ordering the lycran to stay when he whined, attempting to follow.

Luscia rattled her head agitatedly as she and Kasim rushed to follow Ambrose's escape. She petitioned the Sight, but it again denied her access behind the veil, into the *Other*. Leaping on top of an overturned barrel, Luscia listened for the whispers, but none came. She was alone.

"*Ano*, higher!" Kasim yelled, jumping for a hanging ladder.

The lowest rungs snapped beneath Kasim's feet. Luscia sprung off her heels with vigor and clutched the slippery fourth rung, but her fingers failed to reposition around the dampness. Kasim's hand swung out from the rooftop just before she lost her grip. Entwining their arms, he hoisted her up and around.

Luscia winced as she landed on the slats beside him. Numbness had entered her fingertips from the blood loss. Unbuckling her belt, she bit the leather to strap it under the wound in her bicep, fastening it tightly.

"This," she remarked, nodding to the other wraith and shaking out her arm to wake it, "is why there are two."

Atop a beam, they scanned the dodgy grid of Marketown while thunder boomed overhead. She felt Kasim nudge her ribs and followed the end of his *kopar* where it pointed toward The Veiled Lady, a few streets beyond.

"There," he confirmed. Luscia saw the dark smudge at the tip of his sword, trailing Ambrose's fitful movements under the distant torchlight of a resilient streetlamp, still blinking in the rain.

Hopping off the beam, Luscia stalked the perimeter of the roof, surveying the stories below. Moored to a tilted post, a layer of canvas was stretched over the entrance of a dingy shop, operating as both a clothesline and a canopy. Cupping her hands, Luscia folded the wraiths in front of her chest and marched off the ledge, tucking in her knees to sail down the material. Descending in a graceful arc, she waited to ensure Kasim could do the same. Sheathing his *kopar*, the other al'Haidren plunged into the buoyant fabric, landing unceremoniously.

The moment he was upright, Luscia bolted through the rising

puddles toward the popular tavern. Weaving between deserted vendor stalls, running as fast as her legs could carry her, she ducked to glide beneath a barrier of draped mats, soaking Kasim. As they rolled to their feet, Luscia shared a glance with the Darakaian, his dress shirt coated in muck. She looked around, lost. In the absence of her Sight, she recognized the streets of Marketown belonged to him and deferred to his lead. By the way Kasim grunted, swiping the rain off his face and stepping around her, he knew it, too.

Luscia tailed him as he hurried past the conventional path to The Veiled Lady and opted for another route, careering down a winding back street, vacant of lamplight from even the lodgings in the heights above. Smashing through the entry of a shabby emporium, Kasim trampled over mounds of trinkets to an archway on the other side, spitting them out into an adjoining alley behind the tavern.

The same place, she realized as they cleared a stack of crates, where she'd found Wren—drained, limp, and wrong.

"*Ano*!" Kasim released a howl and sped ahead.

Surging for another load of crates, he vaulted off and barreled into a deformed figure scaling the bricks. A patch of brittle hair shed from Ambrose's skull as Kasim tumbled with him against the building. Luscia let out a growl of her own. Fury over Wren and the others sent fire through her limbs. With a righteous roar from deep within her gut, Luscia ran, slung an empty crate over the pooling water, and skated through the alley toward their fight. Whirling the crescent wraiths in a harmonious whirlwind, she whipped herself off the crate and sliced Ambrose's thigh apart.

In a somersault, she flipped into a defensive stance and bent her knees at the ready, utterly stunned. Ambrose snarled and rose despite his injured leg, even as inky blood oozed down his shredded skin. Kasim's *kopar* lashed out, ripping the muscle out from his calf. His back curling in a sinister stoop, Ambrose hunched and tore off an embellished glove. The moonlight glinted off a set of blackened talons, no longer mortal fingers. Ambrose slashed at Kasim, carving his wrists up and flinging him into the old masonry.

Kasim's body split the bricks. Neck slack, the al'Haidren slumped into the rubble, unconscious.

"Luscia, to your left!"

She spun at Marek's unexpected voice, twirling with the wraith as Ambrose rushed for her throat, his claws outstretched. Luscia kicked off the tower of crates and rotated the arcs like a saw, severing what used to be his hand. Ambrose shrieked, guttural and primitive, like a creature from the bowels of the earth. She smelled the toxin coating the luxiron sizzling into his deadened flesh where it spurted dark, curdled gore. Lunging, Luscia severed the tendons at his ankle. Ambrose's leg crumpled under him as she rotated, but the corners of his mouth tore and opened wide in his fall, spewing oily mire into her eyes.

Blinded, Luscia cried out, dropping the wraiths to wipe the stickiness out of her lashes,. The substance, foul and acidic, stung as she desperately tried to rinse it off. In a rush of wind, she felt Marek fly across her back as she doubled over, their contact brief before his luxiron met Ambrose. Unable to see, Luscia scrambled for her weapon within the pools of water. After a succession of crashes, she heard Marek bark in either agony or frustration when something heavy collapsed onto the cobblestones.

"Quarter spin and roll!" Marek shouted, instructing Luscia through her blindness. "I'm pinned under a beam. *Waedfrel*, now dip low!"

She ducked, listening to the air shift over her head as Ambrose's remaining claw narrowly missed. A shuffling came from Marek's direction as materials shifted about. Luscia stayed down, frantically seeking the encased hilt of one of the wraiths in the water. Out of the chaos, like the resounding gong in Thoarne Hall, Marek's wraith struck a drainpipe, sending waves of reverberation through the stone and creating a field of resonance for her. Luscia inhaled and focused her other senses. Striking the pipe a second time, Marek continued to beat it, like a crude *bomaerod*.

Luscia reeled aside as she sensed Ambrose pounce, wheeling her body like a spinning top. He dove, sending a ripple through the surrounding air, emphasized by the droplets from the sky. As she twirled, his claw snatched at her boot. One of his talons pierced her toe, and he hauled her over the cobbles through the river of filth.

Pinned against the crates, Luscia struggled to fend off Ambrose's gnashing teeth, clutching his throat with one hand, hot under her palm. Fumbling beneath the fabric of her hooded tunic, made heavy by the moisture, Luscia probed the folds for her mother's blade. Stroking the warmth of the hilt, she sobbed in relief and released Ferocity, stabbing the consort dagger into Ambrose's chest. The luxiron hissed as it sank into his tainted flesh.

"We are what we become," she heard him croak. Rancid saliva hit her cheek. "Release me."

His hold loosening, Luscia drove the dagger straight into his heart until the brim of the hilt busted through the bone, meeting soft tissue. Pushing him off her, Luscia flipped him over onto the ground and withdrew the blade, encountering little resistance. Under her touch, Ambrose was slowly changing, his monstrous form dissolving.

"They will come for you, too," he rasped.

Sinew and bone turned to ash in her hands. Dim shapes came into view, her vision clearing at last. Luscia dry-heaved as she madly brushed the remnants of Ambrose off her skin.

At the sound of his voice, she crawled toward Marek. Her hands trembled as she grasped the beam trapping him, adding her strength to heave it off his middle. Nearby, Kasim let out a distressed moan.

"*Ana'Sere*, can you stand?" Marek asked.

"*Wem*, I think so," she said. "Can you?"

"Nearly," he replied, hoisting her upright.

"*Tadöm*. But first help Kasim," Luscia instructed, exhaustion over-taking her. "His shoulder might be out of place."

Marek's boots splashed through the puddles as he bent to boost the Darakaian out of the wreckage. One of the men murmured at the other, but her hearing was to fuzzy to make out their words. An ache coursed through her mind as she started to drift backward.

"Find my Aksel..." she whispered, her voice echoing far away.

Eyes rolling back, Luscia's head hit the ground, and the sound was no more.

Every part of her body hurt.

Hazily, Luscia heard someone breathing close by—in, then out. Felt a depression on the bed, opposite Aksel's familiar weight by her thigh. Suppressing a groan of anguish, Luscia thumbed the latch of Phalen's radial and sat up, releasing the hidden blade and tucking it under the intruder's chin.

Opening her sore eyelids, Zaethan Kasim stared back at her. He didn't move, didn't speak. His vivid green eyes dropped to the thin weapons riding her knuckles, and he arced a dense brow, impressed. Luscia noticed that a leather sling strapped his elbow to his side.

His gaze idled when the blanket fell from her chest, revealing the delicate shift she wore. Under his gaze, Luscia's arm itched beneath the crust of a poultice. She had no recollection of how or when it got there.

In a rush, Luscia's memories battered her mind. The girl, war-taint in the city, Ambrose. Her tongue scratched the interior of her mouth, dried from the horror of it all.

I killed a man.

As her hand started to shake, a noise pulled her attention to her bedroom door. Backlit, Marek stood inside the threshold. His hand was clenched around the hilt of his sword while he scrutinized Kasim, as if waiting for something. Still groggy, Luscia hastily assessed his injuries, but stopped, settling on his grave features. Why would the captaen of her guard permit the al'Haidren to Darakai into her chamber?

Dread told her to lower the radial. Something was terribly wrong.

The swell of Kasim's throat shuddered as he swallowed and took a steadying breath, his eyes flitting back up to meet hers.

"The king is dead. We've been summoned."

THIRTY-SIX

Zaethan

In a surreal sweep, Zaethan tugged the handle and stiffly latched the door to the Zôueli suite, locking the western royals safely inside. He scrubbed the stubble on his face with his free hand and backed into the corridor.

Zahra and Kumo flanked the exterior of the sweeping entry. Neither his beta or his third said anything as they rigidly held their posts. Discreetly, both watched him from the corners of their eyes as Zaethan awkwardly readjusted the leather sling.

Neighboring sentries continued along either side of the corridor, forming a tunnel of security. Every man stood silent, the air hung with an unprecedented heaviness as he spoke for his pryde's ears alone.

"No one comes in or out," he murmured gruffly, glancing between them. "No one. *Yeye qondaï?*"

"*Uni zà*, Alpha Za," Zahra and Kumo murmured in unison.

Kumo angled his head to level with Zaethan in a wordless exchange. Confusion and anger buckled the wide bridge of his nose. The last hour had been utter chaos, since the moment an elderly attendant discovered the king's body, drooped over the arm of his reading chair, foaming from the mouth. His utterly unexpected demise had awoken them all to a new reality—a reality where kings were slain in the silence of their studies rather than amid the glory of a battlefield.

He clenched his fist and bounced it against Kumo's chest. Pushing a knuckle into the muscle above his beta's heart, Zaethan squinted at the row of sentries, adding, "Don't trust them, cousin."

Easing past Zahra, he took hold of her elbow and nodded to the guest suite. More perceptive than her counterpart, Zahra would note any unusual traffic in the vicinity. Her ebony lids closed, accepting the assignment. For it appeared that, under the guise of the solstice, Razôuel had traveled to Orynthian soil for a single purpose. After all, with Korbin removed, a union through *Bahira'*Rasha brought them one step closer to the crown. Zaethan recalled the trunks of Zôueli gifts and goods delivered to the king's chamber upon their arrival. Any of them could have housed the means for his assassination.

Zaethan strode the passages toward Thoarne Hall with a palm tensed over his *kopar*. His locs swung like a pendulum as he hastened down the grand staircase, already delayed by his prior stop to rouse a sleeping Boreali. From shared reports between their men, he'd learned the other al'Haidren had slept through most of the day, since her Captaen Bailefore snuck them back into the palace the night before.

A troubling realization struck Zaethan as he rounded the main corridor. If her Najjan could bypass the guards, so could anyone. Even now.

Zaethan wavered before slipping into the Hall. He rebound his locs nervously, pausing before everything changed. Shaking off his reluctance, he slipped inside, knowing it already had.

On the opposite side of the immense doors, the two generations of the Quadren formed a disorganized semi-circle, surrounding the base of the throne. Dmitri sat in his father's place, his mother occupying her usual spot to the right. Zaethan's stomach knotted, assessing his friend and charge. Dmitri's left hand absently rubbed his forehead, while the other held onto his mother's trembling fingers. Deep violet pits cradled his bloodshot eyes, emphasizing the sallow wash of his already poor coloring.

Coming to stand next to his father, Zaethan struck his chest and muttered a clipped, "Commander."

Entrenched in hushed discussion with Gregor Hastings, Nyack Kasim ignored his son, folding his powerful arms and bending toward the other man as they spoke. Beyond them, the Haidren to Boreal maintained a straight posture, hands clasped neatly behind her back. Her niece, embodying the same stoicism, ignored some muted commentary from Ira.

Adjacent to them, nearest the foot of the platform, Sayuri's face tilted as her uncle whispered rapidly into her ear. His steel nailpiece tapped her arm as he hooked her closer. She dipped her chin in agreement, painted lashes dusting her sharp cheekbones at his words. Zaethan sucked his teeth, observing them, knowing this wasn't a promising sign from the Pilarese.

Zaethan nudged his father. "What's happening? What are we waiting for?"

Fleetingly, the commander glanced backward. "Keep that quivering mouth of yours shut," he hissed, "and you'll soon find out."

Barren of feeling, his eyes narrowed and scanned Zaethan, assessing him from head to toe. Finding his son wanting, the commander spun and resumed his conversation with Gregor.

Zaethan's gaze flickered to the throne. The byrnnzite antlers reached for the domed heights of the Hall, as if spindly wings sprouted from Dmitri's lean shoulders. He did not acknowledge the intimate audience in any way. A tear trailed the prince's gaunt cheek as he readjusted his grasp on Queen Lourissa, who muffled her sobs in an ornate hand-kerchief. For what seemed an eternity, Zaethan watched as his oldest friend plucked at the hairs of his brow, staring into nothingness.

In his periphery, Zaethan saw the Boreali suddenly spin toward the servant's entry off the edge of the Hall. The elder mouthed in witch-tongue to her niece. Seconds later, the modest door burst open, and half a dozen sentries entered the room, fanning out. Metal clinking echoed from the passageway, reverberating through the room, and General Lateef emerged at the tail of the procession. Trudging toward the front of the platform, he dragged a heavy chain, scraping it against the floor.

"We have the assassin in our custody, Your Highness," the general announced.

Somber and still, Dmitri shifted. At his slow nod, General Lateef yanked the chain mercilessly, wrenching a shapely woman into the Hall by a hefty collar around her neck. An excited glint filled the general's eyes when he jerked the remnants of the chain more forcefully, bringing the prisoner to her knees underneath torn, velvet skirts.

A coldness shot through Zaethan's legs when the prisoner's mess of curls hitched aside as she clutched the collar, coughing into the floor.

Wiping moisture from the corner of her mouth, Salma Nabhu's ageless eyes scanned Orynthia's elite.

"*Ano zà, Jaha*, it wasn't me," she petitioned him, stumbling to rise. "By *Owàa* and the Fates, I swear it!"

The general lashed the chain, lurching her forward. Salma slammed into the first steps as Lateef proclaimed, "Salma Nabhu, the notorious madam of The Veiled Lady, was caught smuggling Mworran pammu through the Andweles. In her black-market dealings, this cross-caste has circumvented the established cargo channels, directing dozens of shipments to this palace—many delivered straight to the king's private collection."

Bewildered, Zaethan gaped at his father. A small quiver pulsed through his pitted jawline; his only reaction as he listened to the general's report. Retaining his unsympathetic scowl and composed stance, Zaethan's father gave no indication of his foreknowledge, let alone the part he'd played in her systems of trade.

General Lateef leered at the woman, tightening her metal leash. "A young sentry came across one of her opened bottles in your father's study this evening and had a taste. He died shortly afterward."

Zaethan flipped his palms over and examined the lines in his skin, wondering if he'd been the one who'd carried death to the king's door. Raising his head in disbelief, he saw the al'Haidren to Boreal watching him, likely pondering the same. Her hauntingly irregular irises narrowed suspiciously before she turned to face the throne. Guardedly, Zaethan followed suit.

Dmitri's expression darkened as he reached for his walking cane, gripping it tightly. He released the queen. Steadying the cane between his legs, he sat taller.

"Orynthia hereby charges this debauched cross-caste as an enemy of the realm," Zaethan's father said, producing a packet of papers tucked into the back of his belt. "For her high crimes of civil lawlessness, organized treason, and the assassination of a sitting regent."

"No! No, *ano zà*! I did not do these things," Salma cried, and crawled to General Lateef across the marble, seizing his muddy boot. "I taste all my product, sample every batch myself. There was no poison—"

"The prisoner admits guilt in her black-market trade, Your Highness." Zaethan's father whipped his hand at the hysterical madam crumpled on the floor. "A cross-caste who has cultivated contacts from every corner of the realm, sowing her treasonous venom while they lie in the clutches of her whores!"

"*Ano*! I would never betray Kor—"

The general kicked her in the ribs. The queen gasped and reached out for Dmitri when Lateef repeated the assault. Whimpering, Salma wrapped her already battered arms around her knees.

Dmitri thumped the cane between his feet. "That is more than sufficient, General."

"We've received several reports from the sentry regarding this woman's open disdain for the crown. My own son," Zaethan's father clapped his back paternally, "can corroborate these accounts of her insurrectionary rhetoric. He is known to frequent her establishment quite often."

"Zaeth." Dmitri's eyes widened. "Is this true?"

His father's hand engulfed Zaethan's shoulder, considerably bruised beneath the sling and his loose, collarless shirt.

"I don't...she..." Zaethan stammered, skeptical that Salma's idle comments could ever support such drastic crimes.

His father's thumb dug harshly into the sore tissue over his shoulder blade, and Zaethan suppressed a wince.

"Nabhu has previously mentioned her…distrust in the Ethnicam," he added, absorbing the unrelenting bite of his father's grip. "But beyond that, I cannot bear testimony to anything more."

"You see?" His father sneered, squeezing mercilessly before letting go and moving closer to the platform beside the general. "The traitor voiced her treacherous views in the presence of your own Quadren, without any fear of consequence. What would stop a corrupt cross-caste like this, without the proper governance of a House, from resorting to murder to achieve her ambitions?"

Zaethan's forehead crumpled, confused as to why his father advocated Salma's guilt with so little evidence. At that, the Haidren to Pilar inched forward as well, the fabric of his pristine shoto robes wafting around his feet like a cloud. In his shadow, Sayuri appeared ill. Sweat beaded along her hairline and upper lip, as if she were about to double over any moment. Her uncle combed his sharp beard with his ugly nailpiece, addressing Dmitri and his mother.

"Perhaps our perspective is too shortsighted in this matter, Your Highnesses." Tetsu Naborū paced toward Salma, huddled on the floor, favoring her ribs. "Perhaps another, much closer to us, plotted this violent scheme by simply adopting this woman's channels of operation? Our allies may not be as faithful as they seem. Razôuel betrayed us before…turned against Aquilla during the Shield Wars. What would prevent history's repetition, with a daughter of the burgundy sands just one contract away from where your mother sits now?"

Zaethan's mouth parted, utterly shocked to hear Pilar voice his own theory. The Zôueli could've easily identified Salma's pammu runners out of Calluc, or those through the Andwele Mountains. The king's fondness for illegal imports wasn't exactly secret. Instigators could have sent word to the Zôueli, informing them of his personal breach of their treaty against Mworra. The formidable Queen of Razôuel was not one to overlook the duplicity of a king.

Dmitri sunk into the cushions of the throne and held his temples in one hand. He remained silent while Zaethan's father glowered at Sayuri's uncle. Then a peculiar exchange passed between the two men. Tetsu Naborū laced his hands together and pointed his fingers to the floor, staring intently at Zaethan's father. His fingers altered, shaping his hands into another formation, and the corners of his thin lips smirked at the commander of the Orynthian armies.

His father's nostrils flared. Snatching the chain from General Lateef, he cruelly heaved Salma forward by the neck.

"Regardless of any *implausible* partnerships," he scoffed, hauling her up the first step, "Salma Nabhu has been found guilty of forging contracts with our enemies, managing the distribution of contraband throughout the territories, and—by the delivery of poison to royal chambers—is therefore responsible for the assassination of a reigning descendent of Thoarne!" Then the commander's voice softened bizarrely. "Your father, the Fates escort his soul, would counsel you to avenge his untimely death. What will your people think, Your Highness, if you show leniency to his murderess? Is treason something the crown will tolerate during your reign?"

Instantly, Dmitri's eyes flashed open, darting toward the accused. His mouth creased into a flat line as his chest rose and fell with quick, harsh breaths.

"Salma Nabhu." Dmitri spoke lowly, the sound hoarse and depleted. "You are hereby sentenced to death for the assassination of my father, Korbin Aquilla Thoarne, a ruling son of Thoarne, the Shield King of Orynthia, and mighty sovereign of her four Houses."

"*Ano*! Please!" Salma shrieked, scrambling to climb the steps. Zaethan's father slung her backward and slapped her to the ground.

"Your death will be slow and arduous," Dmitri continued, as if no one else was in the room. "Without a House to contest these charges, tomorrow you will be banished to the Wastes. You are to spend your final days alone, thirsting for forgiveness for your crimes. May the Fates show you mercy where I cannot."

Her sentencing resonated through Thoarne Hall. The Haidren to Boreal's hand flew up to cover her mouth, the other wrapped around her niece. Stunned, Zaethan watched Dmitri heavily wave for Salma to be taken away. Zaethan's father offered Naborū a triumphant grin before he towed Salma through the servant's entry. The chains rattled down the dark passage as he disappeared.

As she crossed the threshold, Salma held onto the doorframe, refusing to leave.

"*Jaha*, please! Who else will protect my family?" Her curls stuck to her cheeks from tears and sweat as she wailed for Zaethan to save her, and those in her employ. "You know this truth, *Jaha*, you know—"

Her hazel eyes bulged when the collar bit into her flesh, suffocating her cries. Salma's fingers went limp, and her resistance faltered. The sentries escorted General Lateef toward the passage, following their commander. The last one closed the door gently, as if the leaders of the realm were merely sharing a midnight cup of tea.

Moisture and warmth flooded Zaethan's nose. Reaching back to clasp his neck, he felt the room start to spin. He could still hear Salma's screams.

The queen turned and buried her face in the handkerchief, weeping uncontrollably. Dmitri once again closed his eyes, wincing at the tempo of her sobs.

"We must speak with the Haidren to Bastiion on a matter of the utmost urgency," he stated hollowly. "I request you all leave us and make for your beds. The royal guard will accompany you to your apartments now."

Zaethan hesitated, wanting to console his friend, but made for the double doors. Sayuri clutched her middle as her uncle led her into the main corridor, clearly unsettled by the ordeal. Following her aunt, the witch was ushered into a semi-circle of Najjan waiting directly outside the Hall, each shadowman visibly more on edge than the next. Behind them all, Ira clumsily shoved his hands in his pockets and mutely departed with Zaethan, seemingly in a daze.

"Ira, I asked you to stay," Dmitri called.

Zaethan and Ira shared a confused expression, spinning toward the prince. Dmitri perched forward on the throne, gripping his cane.

Gregor looked at his son and spread his hands. "Your Highness, Ira isn't needed for these talks. Perhaps in time, he can attend these discussions—"

Shakily, Dmitri came to his feet, leaning on the byrnnzite handle of his cane for support. "I ordered an audience with the Haidren to Bastiion, not the sil'Haidren." When Gregor sputtered, the prince cautioned sternly, "You are relieved from your duties on the Quadren, Lord Hastings. Orynthia thanks you for your years of sacrifice and service to the crown. Now, leave us." His cane pointed to the corridor, then tapped his boot. "And please, Ira, don't dawdle. We've much to discuss."

Gregor reeled in place, dumbfounded. Outrage flushed up his neck, reddening the skin beneath his beard. Stalking past his son, Gregor grunted at Ira and slammed the door open.

Zaethan glanced back as he exited the room. The Prince of Orynthia produced a dry handkerchief and leaned down to wipe his mother's tears. Except, Zaethan realized, he was no longer looking at a prince.

Within the span of a few terrible hours, Dmitri Korbin Thoarne had become a king.

THIRTY-SEVEN

Zaethan

Zaethan patted Jabari solemnly on the chest as he passed into the royal gardens. Dawn teased the tips of the surrounding foliage, its golden hue challenging the bleakness of the night. *Owàa* was overstepping, too eager to spread his wings. Though Zaethan always knew this day would come, he was not yet ready to face it.

Considering the defeated bow in Dmitri's posture as he peered into the dark, neither was his friend.

Zaethan knocked his knuckles against a nearby column. Wordlessly, Dmitri tugged his suit jacket tighter, drawing the excess fabric aside to expose more room on the stone bench. Heeding the invitation, Zaethan hitched a leg over the bench, then the other. Resting his elbows on his knees, mirroring his friend, they sat together in silence. As *Owàa* gradually took flight, birds started to chirp, their morning song unwanted and out of place.

Dmitri twisted a vine in his grasp, threading it between his thin fingers. Gently, he brushed a buttery petal of one of the blooms.

"Byronia lily. Repels the bugs," he commented, sluggishly swatting the air.

"Supposedly," Zaethan added, and studied the odd little plant, doubting its effects.

Dmitri's wavy hair dangled over his forehead, shielding his eyes. Propped against the bench, his cane pointed to his feet, which Zaethen noticed lacked shoes. Bare and dirtied, his toes were coated in rich soil. His trousers, however, were delicately rolled at the ankles, free of grime. As light filled the garden, Zaethan spotted a thin trail of dirt extending out from the bushes.

When they were still cubs, the queen had become pregnant a second time, but sadly lost the child in the womb. News of the child's passing swept the palace. Dmitri, no older than eight, had then gone missing for an entire day. It was Zaethan, only a year younger, who'd crawled into the gardens and found the prince covered in soil, huddled in the greenery, hiding from his tutors.

Six years ago, Dmitri had stowed away again on the eve of his Ascension. And just like when they were children, Zaethan found him pacing through the damp earth within the shrubs, overwhelmed and undone.

"What is that phrase you're constantly spouting off?" Dmitri mused, twirling the lily. "'Every gain has a loss,' is it?" He plucked the petal, crumpling it in his fingers. "I've listened to that phrase so many times, but only now feel as though I've finally heard you."

He crossed his ankles, wriggling debris between his toes. Then he set the vine aside and knit his hands together.

"Over and over, you've repeated that to me." Dmitri lifted his head and let out a sigh. "But not once, in all these years, did you mention how significant the loss would be."

Zaethan's insides clenched, remembering the weight of that smuggled crate in his arms. Guilt coated his windpipe. Clearing his throat, Zaethan responded the only way he could.

"I will spend the rest of my life retracing tonight," he vowed hoarsely. "I'll scour my memories, searching for the way I might've prevented this from happening to you."

"I know." Dmitri suddenly straightened. Reaching for Zaethan's forearm, he angled to face him, squeezing it. "I know, because that is who you are. If there was anything you could have done, it would have been so. You may spend your life reliving this tragedy, but I will spend mine wishing you free of its heaviness."

Releasing him, Dmitri looked away. The shadows under his eyes grew more pronounced with the sunrise. "I know he became a father to you, much in the same way he was to me. Don't allow duty to prevent your mourning, Zaeth. It's just that…" Dmitri's voice hitched. "It's just that I don't think I can bear it alone this time."

Zaethan's gaze anchored onto the track of dirt leading into the pristine garden, thinking of years past. After several minutes of silence, he bent to unbuckle the backs of his boots. Slipping off his wool socks, the soles of his feet nestled into the gravel beside Dmitri's.

"You were never alone."

Dmitri's eyes glistened as he released a shaky breath. "We sometimes forget to expect the light, when all we see is the dark." Breaking into a weak grin, he pointed to the brightening sky. "And yet, despite our disbelief, it never fails us. My first act as king will be to reassign the cross-caste investigation to your oversight—the one your father transferred to the command of that visiting alpha. That was wrong of him. Today, we will make it right."

A chill rolled up Zaethan's shoulders. In all the commotion surrounding Korbin's assassination, he'd barely begun to process what he'd witnessed in the backstreets of Marketown. Alleys free of Wekesa, instead tormented by a different kind of monster. The better part of the summer had been squandered chasing the wrong man, when all along, he wasn't chasing a man at all, but a beast.

Zaethan shifted on the bench uncomfortably as the memory of Ambrose's rotting features flashed before him. The sunken cartilage in his face; the flesh darkened from disease; decay rimming every orifice. He'd only heard stories of war-taint, as it had been flushed from the bloodlines through the course of generations. No story could have prepared Zaethan for the creature Ambrose became—a creature without limit to his endurance. To his pain.

A shiver crept up Zaethan's neck, remembering the way Ambrose moved despite the carnage, driven by something else, something *other*, even as his bones jutted from his body.

No one could move like that. Not even the witch.

"It's no longer a concern." Zaethan tugged on the lacing near his throat, loosening it. "After I left the solstice celebration, there were some developments in town. Another victim, or would-be victim. We apprehended the perpetrator, but in the struggle, he was killed."

Dmitri let out a puff of air, "I bet the commander loved that, apprehending a murderer against his orders."

"I'll be sure to tell you when he finds out." Zaethan cleared his throat, choosing his next words carefully. "Dmitri, the man was war-tainted," he shared warily. "Absolute *kakka-shtàka* frenzied. No longer human. We also received a few reports of men fighting last week near butcher's row, one of them covered in boils and the like. I've not heard of it spreading, but you need to know that war-taint was here, in the city."

"War-taint...in Bastiion?" Baffled, Dmitri crooked his chin, scratching it. Briefly, life sparked behind his earthy irises, a temporary distraction from his pain. "But why target the children, and northern cross-castes specifically? Historically, victims of war-taint ravaged everything they encountered." Fatigue relaxed the tension in his brow when he inquired, "What of the body? We can't risk contamination."

Zaethan folded his arms, remembering the tale the Boreali captaen had spun. "The body was...cremated. Nothing left."

Dmitri nodded, content with the half-truth. In the aftermath of a royal assassination, neither the House of Darakai nor Dmitri's premature reign needed the additional complication of a dead nobleman, slain by the hand of the militia prydes. Or, worse, by the hand of two rogue al'Haidrens. Admitting Ambrose's death to the Ethnicam would only result in political nightmare, for him and Dmitri alike.

"Please relay all the findings of the investigation to Luscia, at least. Those poor children," Dmitri muttered. "As you can imagine, their murders have burdened both her and her aunt for some time."

"I will ensure Boreal is notified."

"That is a small gift—to know such heartbreak has finally come to an end."

Zaethan hesitated. He tucked his chin to his chest, inhaling deeply. Taking a step into the unknown, Zaethan could not predict his friend's reaction to his next statement, though he had to try.

"You could prevent another such heartbreak."

Dmitri frowned, confused. "How do you mean, Zaeth?"

Zaethan tightened his crossed arms, pinning them against his middle. "I don't think she did it, Dmitri. By *Owàa*, by the Fates, by the moon herself. I think we should wait, conduct a formal trial in front of the Peerage. It's the least we offer common criminals."

Dmitri flinched backward, creating space between them on the bench. "Salma Nabhu is not just another criminal! That woman brought that venom into my home, into his hands! He's *gone*," Dmitri croaked, a sob escaping before his mouth tightened. "He's gone, and you're really sitting here, defending what that woman did to take him away?"

"*Ano zà!* No, Dmitri. I'm not defending anything." Zaethan slipped out of his native tongue, collecting himself. "I'm asking you if we want to be the generation who continues to withhold the right of trial from cross-castes, or the generation who offers it? Maybe she *is* guilty, but what if she's not, Dmitri? The cross-caste have no representation in the Ethnicam, no one to speak for them—"

"And so *you* will?" Dmitri cut Zaethan off, fervor enlarging his hazel eyes. "Do you realize what you're asking of me, Zaeth?"

"Salma Nabhu could not have orchestrated an act of this magnitude alone, Dmitri. Razôuel could be a real threat—"

"I know she didn't do it alone!" Dmitri snatched up his cane, panting heavily. "I'm beginning a rule steeped in betrayal—the backdrop of my legacy will forever drip my father's blood! And no, it wasn't Razôuel. The proposed marriage contract limits Rasha and all of Orynthia to my governance, to extending the line of Thoarne."

"But who else could possibly gain from this?"

"The Peerage." Flexing his fingers around the cane, Dmitri glowered down at the gravel. "You don't understand the fragility of this season we're entering, Zaeth. But the Peerage, whether a single member or many, *have* realized it. In recent years, some councilmen have voiced their doubts about my succession. The province of Agoston, for instance, has had misgivings since my Ascension. One of their nobles—Lord Ambrose, I'm told—elected to not even attend the feast the other night. No one has been able to account for him since."

"Felix," Zaethan repeated. "Felix Ambrose."

"It's simply a theory, but that's the point, isn't it?" Dmitri squinted at *Owàa*'s brightness, well-seated in the sky. "Hushed theories, whispering all around us. I see your point, Zaeth. I do. But the Peerage will mistake mercy, however intended, for weakness. And if they perceive my weakness, those responsible for my father's death will just seek another Nabhu and do this again."

Dmitri's eyes slid to Zaethan's, locking onto them. His friend looked like the very ghosts he spoke of, haunting his reign. Lavender bloomed around his lids. Burdened by grief and weariness, he desperately needed sleep.

"I won't let that happen, Dmitri. I will defend you until my last breath." Rising, Zaethan collected his boots. "Now, the crown needs his beauty rest. Let me walk you."

"I would like to stay just a little longer."

The phrase was a familiar one, a subtle request for privacy. Zaethan hitched a bare foot over the bench and stood behind Dmitri, preparing to leave him in peace.

"I know what I ask of you," Dmitri stated as Zaethan took a step toward the gate. "But I am not asking it as..." His back shuddered as he swallowed, "as your sovereign. I am asking it of you as my friend."

Boots dangled from his fingertips, tucked beneath the sling. Zaethan's free hand came down and held onto his friend's lean shoulder. He did not let go.

"I will see it's taken care of."

"You have my gratitude," Dmitri whispered. His head dipped slightly. "I need you, my brother."

Dmitri's right hand stretched over and fell atop Zaethan's on his shoulder, revealing an old, faded band of crimson encircling his narrow wrist. Zaethan tightened his hold on his friend, staring at the fraying thread Dmitri had tied so long ago, simply to make a point. A point he'd never retracted.

Brothers by choice, stronger than blood.

"I am with you, brother," Zaethan assured him. "Always."

Splashes of coral and cerise blushed the horizon. Bittersweetly, the colors of *Àlàmaia's* approach painted the skies as her lover, *Owàa*, descended into the sorrow of night. Zaethan felt the sun's misery like his own.

In a stalwart sway, the waters of the Yachel Channel lapped against the hull of the *Esafit Ramali*. True to her naming, the ship navigated the vast river like a sandstorm, intrepid and commanding. Abandoning the shores of the Wastes, she embodied the precision expected of an executioner. It was the voyage she knew best, after all.

On the main deck, Zaethan turned starboard to watch the barren, cracked sands pass by. He could taste the salt in the air as the breeze licked the dust from the coast. It numbed his tongue, flooding his mouth with the hopelessness of the land, rather than the sea. Desolate and deadly, nothing could survive these endless miles of nothingness. Not even his friend Salma Nabhu, if she lived to see the morning.

"*Shàlàmaiamo*, my favorite *yaya*," he said softly to the wind.

Zaethan gripped the ratlines and watched the weeping woman

disappear in the distance, forcing himself to accept what he had done. And, because of his action, what could not be undone.

"Eh, full speed ahead, *yeye qondai?*" he heard Dhalili yell from the crow's nest, high above the decking. With a triplet of yips, his small scout swung from the basket, landing in a skip across the planks. Clutching onto the railing, Dhalili smiled beside him, grinning into the breeze. Shorter than the rest of the minimal crew—as the ship was manned by the essential members and no more—Dhalili set her hands on her boyish hips. Her billowing gunja pants caught the wind like a mast, almost sweeping her away.

"I'll keep this yancy crew in order, Alpha Zà," she declared, crossing her petite but muscular arms. "Move like sludge-runners, yeah? Even the mudmen have more grit than this *kakka-shtàka* band of Unitarian slummies, *ano?*"

Dhalili looped one of the tiny twists dotting her head, wrapping it tightly around one finger. Her youthful eyes rolled when she grimaced at a crewman gathering the line, apparently too slow for her liking.

"Ah, *ano, ano.* I show him, Alpha Zà."

As she climbed to the quarter deck, Zaethan leaned over the taffrail and peered into the wake forming over the darkening waters. Soon the *Esafit Ramali* would meet the Drystan, sealing Salma's fate under *Àlàmaia's* eye.

A heavy hand clapped the back of his jacket. Kumo bent down next to Zaethan, resting against the railing. His sleeves creaked as his massive arms crooked forward and he gazed out across the waves.

"You are restless."

"Which is why you call me *Ahoté*," Zaethan cited his cousin drily.

"*Ano.* I call you *Ahoté* because when you killed that rabid cat, you took on his spirit." Kumo palmed the buttons down the front of his jacket. "Just a young, fearless cub, you set into the wilderness and came back with its head, proving your father wrong. But ever since, you roam like the restless bobcat. Always unsettled. Always pacing, rabid for more."

"How can I be settled in this? Depths." Zaethan chucked Salma's empty shackles over the edge of the ship. "How do I know this night doesn't prove him right?"

"We are doing what you believe to be just, *Ahoté*."

"*Uni zà*," Zaethan agreed, but he shifted his face away. "I stand behind my decision."

Kumo nudged him with an elbow, pivoting on his side. "Then why torture yourself, *Ahoté*? You gave the command, and I arranged it, yeah? It is done."

Zaethan rubbed his wrist in the sling, envisioning the red thread encompassing Dmitri's. "When we act on what is right, a line is drawn. But that line..." He scowled at *Àlàmaia*'s emerging glow, capping the waters. "That line has consequences, cousin. *Kwihila rapiki mu Jwona*. No victory will be able to unwrite this night."

"*Meme qondai*." His beta nodded grimly. "But there is no regret in victory."

"I'm not regretting my decision, or the order." Zaethan's eyes narrowed intently. "I'm preparing for the day that choice will be staring me in the face."

"Then on that day, *Ahoté*," Kumo reached out and grabbed the base of Zeathan's neck, "we face it together."

Overhead, the moon took to her throne in the skies. Her glory bathed the sea as she held court in the clouds. Zaethan made for the stern of the ship, toward the magnificent ripples trailing their exodus.

The *Esafit Ramali* surged forward, full mast, fleeing the shadow of the Wastes and leaving her sins behind.

Clasping the helm, Zaethan focused on the journey ahead, wishing his own could be so easily forgotten.

THIRTY-EIGHT

Luscia

Weary and spent, Luscia waited outside her aunt's door.

Moments ticked by, unbearably slow. Her healing arm itched as irritably as her mind, swirling with conflicting thoughts and unrecognizable emotions. They'd eliminated a killer, only to uncover another.

The door creaked, admitting the captaen of Alora's guard, Emiere, into her aunt's great room. During the past months, the middle-aged Najjan had operated at a distance, likely at Alora's bidding. Made famous by his valor during the late Shield Wars, Luscia noted the versatile manner in which her aunt entrusted the elder captaen. It would be wise, she considered, to task Marek to do the same in the trying days ahead.

The Najjan slipped past Luscia without a sound. His joints, though decades older than her own Najjan, gave no hint of his movements as he glided into the domed space. Emiere offered Luscia a somber nod. The silver stubble blanketing his grimace was the only indication of his unrest—she could not recall the last time Emiere had gone unshaven. A spindle of dread spun as she traded places with the impassive Najjan and entered her aunt's chambers.

The late afternoon sun blanketed Alora's bedroom, warming the cold bareness within. Seated on a modest bench near the windowsill, Luscia was greeted by her aunt's back as Amaranth chirped her welcome. The lavender hawk preened herself, perched on a hook beside her mistress while she worked. Alora's unbound hair rustled as she ground a fragrant assembly of herbs under her pestle.

"*Ana'Mere*," Luscia tested, taking the corner of Alora's bed.

"I'd invite you to sit with me," her aunt muttered, engrossed in the mortar, "but it seems you don't want my instruction anymore."

Luscia felt heat rush into her cheeks. "*Meh fyreon, Ana'Mere*, I never intended to give that impression." She awaited a response, but was only met with silence. "I am trying my best, for Aniell and for Boreal. I need you to know that."

The air hung stalely between them. Alora rose slightly from the workbench to kiss Amaranth tenderly, stroking her feathers. Lusica bit down a familiar bitterness. It was silly to envy a bird, especially now.

"Your best is subject to your own judgment, Luscia," Alora posed evenly. "After all you've accomplished in Bastiion, have you found it to be true?"

The question fell heavily, inferring Luscia's judgment was not wise at all. She smoothed the front of her bodice, grateful her aunt's eyes were otherwise directed, although experience guaranteed her ears were tuned to Luscia's body language, listening for anomaly.

"I've found my judgment to be...commanding."

"Not as commanding as your Haidren, I've surmised," Alora added, reaching for a dropper of glistening liquid. Traces of lumin shimmered within the glass channel. "I trust your rebellion through the streets was fruitful, at least?"

"*Wem*. Boreali cross-castes will no longer be hunted like wild game, if that's to what you're referring." Luscia stiffened defensively before promptly deflating, out of habit. "The killer was war-tainted. Some yancy from the Province of Agoston, I've been told." Her words slowed as she pushed away the memory of his rotting skin, how the stench swam through her nose, suffocating and awful.

"I gathered as much from the bite on your arm," her aunt commented, plucking fresh leaves of gilead from a pot. "What your wounds didn't express, I compelled from Captaen Bailefore. He is fine, by the way, in case you were concerned that your escapade might have caused him injury."

Luscia flinched, surprised by the suggestion that she didn't care for Marek's well-being. Or the well-being of her entire guard, for that matter.

"I see," Luscia replied squarely.

"*Tadöm* to Aniell that bite was your only keepsake from an altercation with the infected." Her aunt lit a match to a dried drössara leaf, tossing it into the mortar. "And praise the High One for kissing our veins, rendering war-taint ineffective."

Suddenly, Luscia realized her rightness in sending Mila to Boreal. They'd assumed Ambrose merely wanted what all men want, when he must have craved so much more. Luscia sat taller and let out a breath. Her judgement had proven true in that respect after all.

"He was ravenous, nearly unstoppable," Luscia whispered. "I remember the old stories of war-taint, from our childhood. Phalen loved when *Fappa* would tell the tales to terrify us before bed. I just never imagined such...depravity." Luscia caressed the radials over her knuckles, missing her brother. "There are a few things I can't make sense of, though. The nobleman's rate of decay for instance."

Voicing her query, she then understood that Ambrose did seem to have made an effort to conceal the initial signs of his illness. The gloves, perhaps his overuse of pipe-marrow to ease his pain. There was no telling now long he'd been sickened. Did the ancient disease consume one's body steadily, or expedite deterioration at a certain stage?

"Little was recorded about the behavior of war-taint, Luscia. Our ancestors were much more focused on trying to be rid of it at the time," Alora chirped in response.

Luscia supposed that to be true, given the threat war-taint posed to humanity's survival in the early ages. "Well, then secondly, if someone war-tainted harbors no restraint, how could he have executed all those precise incisions used to drain the bodies?"

The pestle in Alora's grasp slowed to a calculated swirl. "Perhaps the infection took time to mature, delaying his madness."

Nodding, Luscia's brows tightened as she countered, "Then what of the outliers—the few who were found torn apart? They bore the wounds expected of a war-taint attack. Could the sickness exist else-where in Orynthia?"

"That nobleman lost his humanity to an ancient plague, Luscia." Alora wiped her tools with a scrap of linen. "You cannot seek rational rhythm in the clamor of chaos. Perhaps his urges came in waves. Perhaps he tried to hide the affliction with his neatness, only to surrender to a more visceral nature once it overthrew his mind. We cannot know, and it is a distraction to even try, when at this very hour the state of the realm hinges on the precarious allegiance of men."

Her aunt gathered her linsilk skirt and stood. She walked to the center of the room, commanding it despite her slender frame. Her hands gathered behind her back as she looked out the vaulted windows. A glare glinted off her *solrahs,* identical to the luxiron piece in Luscia's septum.

"You must put away these thoughts. Your future lies at a pentagonal table, beside your king, not in the streets like some breakaway vigilante. The honor bestowed to you, Luscia Darragh Tiergan, is greater than the others at that table." Alora's thumb grazed the veins at her wrist. Faint indigo feathered under her nearly translucent skin. "History written, as history rings."

"*Ana'Mere?*"

"Think, Lusica." Alora released her wrist and gathered her hands behind her back once more. "*Think.* How has the line of Thoarne survived centuries of war, endless bloodshed, countless deaths? You sing your history in Thoarne's own Hall, yet you refuse to believe it."

Her aunt's words stung. Luscia wished for once Alora would speak plainly, instead of seeking another opportunity to critique her. This wasn't the time for correction, but rather for answers. Answers Luscia felt she more than deserved to hear.

"But that's simply poetry," she rebutted. "You don't actually mean—"

"The blood of Tiergan will always rescue the blood of Thoarne." Alora's chin lifted. "On the battlefield or in a garden. This is for what the High One anointed us, Luscia. *This* is our charge. Your blood is sacred, precious. It cannot be spilled and wasted, like a member of your guard or one of the Najjan. You are not fodder. *Niit*, my niece, you are the remedy."

"You said he couldn't be cured," Luscia challenged, hope teasing her chest.

"Dmitri's cure is the continuation of his lineage," she answered quietly. Alora untied the stained apron around her waist, folding it as she rotated toward her apothecary. "You may not be *this* king's remedy, but in offering him time, you are Orynthia's remedy. As his coronation nears, it is imperative you practice your Sight daily. The threads...the threads will tell us how to proceed."

"Have you ever heard them, *Ana'Mere*?"

The question escaped Luscia's lips before she could stop it.

Alora froze, her back to Luscia. Gradually, her face turned over her shoulder, though her eyes did not follow. "No one has ever communicated with the threads, except in the days of Tiergan himself. This I have already told you."

Biting her lip, Luscia tread carefully. "Do you think my mother heard the lumin? The voices she talked about..."

Luscia trailed off as the side of Alora's mouth pressed into a firm line. Stiffly, she set her folded apron atop the viridi chest housing her apothic elements, much larger than the box in Lusica's quarters.

"Eoine thought she heard many things, but all of them were a delusion in the end." Abruptly, Alora spun and tilted her head. "Have you experienced something similar?"

"*Niit*," Luscia blurted.

At her outburst, Alora's gaze narrowed and darted through the air around Luscia. Undoubtedly, her aunt was reading the threads in her own way, discerning fact from fiction. Luscia's stomach clenched, hoping the luminescent energy would not betray her haunting secret, either in claiming the voice she'd heard, or worse, confirming she'd not heard it at all.

If the former, then the consciousness of the *Other*, full of mystery and power, tormented Luscia unlike any of her ancestors. If the latter, then she was cursed regardless. If she never heard the threads, if it was not the lumin who whispered, then she was heir to her mother's fate. A fate which promised a lifetime of whispers, until she could someday bear no more. And, like her mother, she would be forced to make it cease.

"I assume this is why your men relay that you've neglected your daily meditation. I'm told you've not practiced since your arrival in Bastiion." Pouring her newest concoction into three vials, Alora gathered them up and came beside the bed. "Are you still concerned your episodes are connected to what became of her?"

"You truly believe they're unrelated?" Luscia searched her aunt's eyes, seeing those of her mother.

"*Niit*. Just as I assured in your youth, I assure you again now. It is your choice to listen," she urged, placing the vials in Luscia's open palms. "We will keep improving upon your tonic. This season will be laden with instigation, likely full of triggers. It is time you put away this foolishness and trust my wisdom on the matter."

Luscia's fingers wrapped around the vials, their marshy contents darker than the previous batch. She prayed her aunt was right, but feared the alternative nearly as much. If her connection to the *Other* was wrong, unnatural and strange, it could hinder her succession. Alora, being a woman of principle and obligation, might disown her, abandoning their mentorship. Or, Luscia hoped, she might increase her oversight, were she willing to explore Luscia's torment together.

Uncertainty stifled her bravery. She couldn't lose a second mother.

"*Meh fyreon, Ana'Mere,*" Luscia submitted, "for my wayward thinking."

"I will say this only once, my niece." Alora's shoulders set. "If your disobedience was revealed prior to these unthinkable events, then this would be a discussion of severe consequence. However, supremacy changes with the crown, and you no longer answer to me." She paced around the bed calmly, head elevated with authority. "There will be consequences for your and Captaen Bailefore's actions, just not from the rule of your own House. It will follow you onto the Quadren and, once seated, may one day entrap you."

Alora's eyes met Luscia's at last. "Soon, it is you whom they will call the Great Mother of Boreal. My legacy will fade into the stars behind the others, adding to Aurynth's tapestry of old." Her graceful fingers fluttered as she turned to the door. "But mark my words. You are playing a perilous game on a much larger board than you realize, as if you see all the parts when you do not. After your succession, I will continue to offer you counsel, as your grandfather guided me."

Alora grasping the handle, pulling the door open. Mutely, Luscia rose, acknowledging their meeting had ended. As she neared the threshold, her aunt gathered Luscia's hands in hers and, with an abnormal fervor, gripped them tightly. Discomfort pulsed through her fingers as Alora pinned her inside the doorframe.

"And when I counsel you, Luscia," she cautioned, "I pray you heed it. For the sake of us all."

Gulping, Luscia nearly stopped breathing. Alora's colorless Tiergan eye sparked furiously, glowing like it never had before.

———❀❀❀———

Wrapped in cloud cover, Aurynth's watchman permitted Luscia the solace of complete darkness as she prowled through the streets of Marketown. Dulled laughter and muffled music drifted toward her from the bosom of The Veiled Lady, where the wealthy alongside the poor eagerly took advantage of the moonless night, their comings and goings concealed.

A lamppost flickered in the distance, the dim torchlight splashing the flanks of the narrow backstreet. Luscia pocketed her *lumilore*, no longer needing its light. Her vision adjusted to the intermittent flame, focusing on the evidence of the destruction they'd wrought outside the bustling tavern.

With a feather-light step, her upturned boots carefully maneuvered through a pile of crumbled brick. Over the hunks of masonry, she found the hollow depression where Kasim's body had been thrown into the adjacent building. Luscia looked up into the murky heavens, grateful she only had to answer for the death of one man, instead of two.

Further on, Luscia stopped beside the busted crates. She stooped low, crouching near the place of the killer's demise—the place where at her hand, Lord Felix Ambrose departed this world to enter the next. The pools of rainwater had long dried up, leaving only squalid remnants from the night of the solstice. Splintered wood encircled an emptiness on the ground, coated in rancid soot. Guardedly, Luscia untied the veil shading her face. Gritting her teeth, she released a shaky breath and beckoned the Sight.

Hazy threads beamed into existence, wafting in the soft breeze. Luscia tensed, anticipating the pain in her skull, but it didn't come. Neither did the whispers. In gratitude, she closed her eyes to thank the High One for her aunt's skill.

"*Tadöm, Aniell.*"

Alone in the *Other*, Luscia opened her eyes and studied the glittering patterns. She cocked her head curiously. While most of the threads meandered through the openness with ease, a few shuddered away from the sooty spot by her feet, where Ambrose had withered to ash. In their flux, the light sputtered as the threads created a void of nothingness in the middle of the air.

Intrigued, Luscia peered into the abyss. The feel of winter blew against her cheeks, like an icy wind from the highlands. She brought her fingers to her flesh. It was cold to the touch.

"Shores of Aurynth," she whispered. The steam of her breath turned to frost.

Her head whipped to the side when a canister rolled through the mouth of the alley. Fluidly, Luscia reeled behind the crates, melting into their silhouette. A man trailed the canister as its roll came to a halt. She timed her exhales with the breeze, soundless and measured. Her Sight intact, she stared between the slats in the crates. The threads bobbed around the man's long locs as they swayed. Kasim knelt next to the pile of rubble and cradled his face in his hand. Then, in a sudden huff, Kasim hurled one of the bricks at the broken wall, shattering it to pieces.

Massaging his shoulder in the sling, he turned away and glanced toward the lamplight outside the mouth of the alley. Then down the backstreet, to the back door of the tavern. Palming his mouth, Kasim's shoulders sagged as he headed deeper into the alley.

Luscia's eyes widened. Playing at his heels, partnering threads of lumin illuminated his steps as he climbed the stairs to the back door. Lifting onto the balls of her feet, she soundlessly followed. Blinking out of the Sight, she refastened the inky veil, hiding the brightness of her skin. She tucked her hair into the folds of her hood and entered the rear of the establishment.

Luscia didn't know what compelled her to nestle into the back corner of the boisterous tavern. Hidden in the shadows, she charted Kasim's journey to the bar, where he slumped onto a stool and lifted his hand for a drink. She saw his features fall after the barkeep slid his order down the bar. Kasim stared blankly into the untouched glass. Luscia filtered the noise to listen as one of Nabhu's night-callers slunk to his side.

"What is wrong, Alpha Zá?"

Leisurely, the woman draped an arm over Kasim's leg. When he didn't flinch, she crooked his chin tenderly. Candlelight glistened on her southern skin, similar to his own.

"Do you know how to make it better, *Jaha*?" she asked.

Slowly, Kasim shook his head, his expression unreadable.

"I do." She retrieved his glass and summoned him off the stool. Through the parting of heavy, velvet curtains, she led Kasim down a darkened hall and into the belly of The Veiled Lady. With a swish, the fabric closed, sealing him inside.

Noiselessly, Luscia tightened the cowl around her face and crept through the shadows, retreating the way she'd come. Reentering the night, Aurynth's watchman came into view once more. Under his eye, she disappeared into the secretive web of Marketown, just another player in Bastiion's grid of decay.

For in the heart of Bastiion, no one was who they seemed.

Not even the Haidren to Boreal.

EPILOGUE

On the rooftop, Alora's lips compressed as they watched her niece follow Kasim's heir into the tavern. It was obvious she was not pleased.

She was *angry*—and blaming herself more than anyone else, he knew, for sending him away the night of the solstice. He'd been assigned to investigate a petty brawl in the Bazaar, involving one of her Boreali merchants. All the while, her niece had charged into the torrent to face an unknown evil, alone and unprotected.

Upon the figure's return to the Proper, she'd tasked him to root out where the monster was laid to rest, so she might inspect the remains. He reported there was nothing left to examine but ash and mire, but nevertheless, his mistress insisted she be escorted into the busiest district of Marketown. Disguised in the heights, they waited for the filthy alleyway to clear.

Apparently, her niece had shared the same intent that evening.

Amaranth's claws anchored onto his shoulder. He felt the hawk shift her weight as she settled onto her favored perch, situated between her two masters. On the opposite side, Alora's spine straightened as the door, stories below, closed behind her niece.

"He's beginning to look like his father," she remarked tersely.

The figure considered the young man's lineage, but disagreed. "I still see Cyra in their son, Mistress. Others see her, too."

Pensive, Alora angled her smooth neck. The darkness disguised the pearlescent hue of her skin, unique to her and her kinsmen. His blistered tongue swelled with need. Squeezing his eyes shut, he ignored the faithful beat of her veins. After his recent encounter on butcher's row—after he'd given way to the hunger—it would take months to unhear the rhythm of her blood, calling out a promise it would never fulfill.

"Let us pray that is who their son sees in himself." Alora tucked her chin determinedly. "Orynthia cannot afford to have Cyra's son aspiring after his father's control of the realm. The effects would be catastrophic."

The figure adjusted his leather gloves, grating his scored flesh. Surveying her through the corner of his bloodshot eye, his lungs stilled. Freezing in place, he admired the way she tucked a wisp of fair hair behind an ear. It was the single blessing to his curse—the ability to see her beauty even when the light let it go. After their decades together, encompassing a host of secrets, his affection remained their most devasting secret of all.

He looked away with difficulty. "It was her captaen who assured you, Mistress." The figure fixed his attention on the alley below. "The nobleman's corpse indeed turned to dust."

When she said nothing, he peered past the rim of his hood. Almost imperceptibly, her jaw quivered, and she spun her face aside. He thought he heard her sniffle, an uncharacteristic release of emotion.

"You are not permitted to turn to dust."

The figure dropped his gaze. Stepping back from the busted ledge of the abandoned terrace, he lowered his head in retreat, adding to their separation.

"You know this was not the product of war-taint," he whispered, embracing the agony of his sores. "This happened because of the offenses I committed in another life. Dust," the figure rasped gravely, "would be a mercy."

Alora stilled several paces away. Stubbornness tensed her limbs as she entwined her arms, something she'd done in their youth when he came close to winning an argument. Sighing, she breathed his name into the night.

"I will say it again, and again, and again, until I can speak no more," she declared to the emptiness. "There *is* still hope for redemption."

He recoiled beneath the fabric of his cloak, away from the emerging sheen of the moon. As she refused his shame, the figure could not bear for her to behold his ugliness instead.

"I'll never know redemption if history repeats my mistakes," he murmured, hiding within the hood. "Coveting what was not meant to be mine. Taking what should never be stolen."

Her hand glided into a concealed pocket in her skirts. Retrieving a pouch, she cradled it carefully as she replied, "You couldn't have been the first to stumble upon your revelations about my kind, and I doubt you will be the last, as evidenced by the cross-caste slayings." Her face tilted to the side, though he no longer stood there. "Why target the children? Why the unascended, instead of the full-blooded parent?"

Her inquiry rescued him from recounting his transgressions; from recalling the moment he'd become new and unnatural, more beast than man. The figure paused, pushing past the stain on his soul. In answering, he leveraged his disgraceful studies from so long ago against his firsthand experience of the hunger.

"I'm unsure, Mistress," he offered plainly. "Possibly a mutation in the young, or some prematurity, even..."

The veining across the backs of her hands became more pronounced as she gripped the pouch tightly. "Who else would know to seek such an irregularity?"

The figure's serrated teeth raked the interior of his mouth as he ground them together, cataloging his list of contacts from his previous life. Outdated and subject to the limitations of his former station, there was no way to be certain.

"Very few parties," the figure admitted. "Least of all a rich yancy from Agoston."

Without comment, she rested the pouch on the ledge. Vials chimed inside the knotted sack when it hit the rock. Begrudgingly, the figure came forward to take them. The glasses jangled as he slipped the pouch under his cloak.

"The rules are changing, Mistress," he reminded her, redirecting her thoughts toward the future. "With Korbin's death, Boreal could be at even greater risk within the Ethnicam. Things will be different now that you are operating as the succeeded sil'Haidren."

"The rules haven't changed—the board has." Alora laced her elegant fingers. "Overnight, the political landscape has evolved in ways we could never have foreseen. Where Luscia walks as Haidren, I cannot go before her."

"Has she become aware of her condition?"

"*Niit.*" Alora shook her head firmly. The strands escaping her braid swept past her cheek. "Nor will she. The fate of the realm rests on Luscia's shoulders. She can never learn how fragile they really are."

He noted the minor tremors in her expression as she rubbed at her wrist. The years had done little to suppress his instinct to reach out and comfort her. Denying the impulse, the figure instead lifted his gloved hand and stroked the slick feathers down Amaranth's back.

"I will not lead you away from your conscience this time," he assured Alora. "Not again."

Alora twisted toward the figure. Her eyes, alight with desperation, sought the man he used to be. "One day the High One will forgive us both." She smiled weakly. "But until that day, we are still here, given the chance to redeem our mistakes. So that is what we will do." Alora stepped closer and joined him, caressing the hawk. "That is what we will do, my dearest."

Though she said it to Amaranth, Alora called her the same words once reserved for him. And for a fleeting second, she glanced past the bird.

"*Se'lah Aurynth.*"

Within the expanse of a stolen moment, the figure forgot his name, for his name had only ever held meaning when it passed her lips. Finishing her proverb, he felt a spark beneath his tongue.

"*Rul'Aniell.*"

Glossary of Terms

Visit **www.TheHaidrenLegacy.com/Glossary** to access digital
references on your mobile device.

ORYNTHIA
⨠ UNIVERSAL ⨞

al'Haidren: /al-Hay-dren/ The next representative in line to sit on the royal heir's Quadren, typically the closest blood relative from the generation behind the current Haidren

Breakaway: Term for a member of the Outer Houses who chooses to live in Unitarian lands, typically in Bastiion Proper

Cross-caste: Split lineage; an individual of two separate Houses

Ethnicam: The term used when referring to the assembly or association of all four Orynthian Houses

Forgotten Wars: Name given to the unknown events that led to the Old-World's destruction

Hagarh: /HAY-gar/ Wetlands opposite the Miraji Forest inhabited by nomadic peoples

Haidren: /HAY-dren/ A legal, judicial, and social representative of his or her corresponding House, seated on the current ruler's Quadren

House: The collection of a people and their preserved, self-governed territory within Orynthian borders, though still beholden to the throne

Interim Haidren: The next familial relation to the Haidren, though sometimes elected by the House; put in place when the rightful Haidren is deceased or incapacitated

Orynthia: /OR-in-thee-Uh/ Central kingdom comprised of four Houses and governed by the royal line of Thoarne and the Ethnicam

Outer Houses: Self-governed Houses on the outskirts of the Unitarian lands

Quadren: The committee of advisors encircling each Orynthian ruler, consisting of one Haidren from each House

The Wastes: A barren, uninhabitable wasteland on the eastern side of the Yachel Channel

War-taint: Residual, toxic poisoning as a result of the Forgotten Wars

War-tainted: An individual, animal, or land harboring the symptoms of war-taint

Witchiron: Najjani weaponry; slang

HOUSE OF BASTIION
⋙LOWLANDS & PLAINS⋘

Auras: /AUHR-rahs/ Gold coin of Bastiion origin; adopted by all Houses

Bastiion: /BAHS-tee-ON/ Crown city of Orynthia

Byrnnzite: /BERN-zite/ An organic composite of petrified ash, wood, and Old-World metallics

Crupas: /CROO-pahs/ Copper coin of Bastiion origin; adopted by all Houses

Drifting Bazaar: Merchant market of floating stalls along the bank of the Thoarne Bay

Dromas: /DROH-mahs/ Silver coin of Bastiion origin; adopted by all Houses

Inner Proper: Walled and fortified inner city of Bastiion encompassing the palace, Marketown, upper- and lower-class districts

Marketown: Mass market within the streets of Bastiion's inner Proper

Outer Proper: Royal land encircled by the Noble Provinces; the outskirts of the city of Bastiion

Pipe Marrow: A highly pungent opiate often smoked in the tents of Marketown

Province: Land bestowed to the heads of the nobility and their heirs

Vàssa Ship: /Vaah-sa/ Leisure vessel

The Veiled Lady: Popular tavern in Marketown owned by Salma Nabhu

Yancy: /Yan-see/ Universal slang for any wealthy Unitarians; the nobility

Unitarian: Primary language spoken in the House of Bastiion and the Unitarian lands; general mixture of ancient languages, refined over time

Unitarians: Orynthian bloodline comprised from a blended ancestry from centuries past

UNITARIAN

Shtàka: /ShTAH-kuh/ Shit (slang)

Y'siti: /Yuh-ZEE-tee/ Filthy Ice-Witch (derogatory)

HOUSE OF BOREAL
⋙ HIGHLAND PENINSULA ⋘

Aniell: /AHn-ee-eL/ High One; sole deity of Boreal

Bomaerod: /BOH-may-rahD/ Vented staff utilized by the Najjan; typically made of bone and/or wood, used to created audible reference points in a space while training

Boreali: /Boar-eell-ee/ Primary language spoken in the House of Boreal; term for the people of Boreal

Clann: Ruling leader of the clans inhabiting the Boreal peninsula

Clann Darragh: /Klan Dahw-rah/ Formal title of the ruling leader meaning *Mighty Oak*

Clan Elder: Elected leader of a Boreali clan

Consort Daggers: A set of short, curved luxiron daggers, ornate in design

Crescent Wraiths: A set of long, arced luxiron blades used in unison; gripped at the center; serrated or scooped at the ends

Feidierdanns: /Fee-DYER-dons/ A braided whip used to increase the agility of footwork in Najjani training

Isle of Viridis: /eyeL of Ver-EE-dees/ A remote island off the coast of Boreal; fortress where Najjan train

Klödjen: /klode-Gen/ A wooden globe surrounded by a horizontal ring wide enough to hold a man; used in elementary training by the Najjan

Kuerre: /Koo-AIR/ Luxiron sword; shorter than standard and curved at the tip

Kurtfierï: /Kert –FYE-ree/ Courtship token; an article of the father's clothing or dress, typically worn by the suited

Linsilk: Boreali fabric made of silk harvested from spiders around the banks of the Dönumn

Lumin: /Loo-men/ Sacred light energy native to the Boreali highlands

Lumilore: /Loo-meh-Lore/ Lux-stone; lumin-infused stone gathered near the banks of the Dönumn

Luxiron: Specialized Najjani iron, forged in undiluted lumin; warm to the touch, translucent in color, corrosive in nature, and lightweight; trade restricted

Luxsmith: A Najjani smithy, dedicated to the creation of Luxiron (i.e., luxcrafting)

Lycran: /LIE-kran/ Orallach fox-wolf (wolx) hybrid; genes enhanced by war-taint

Najjan: /Nah-zhahn/ Boreali warrior

Orallach Mountains: /Orr-uh-laK/ Range of frigid mountains; uninhabited

Radials: Hidden luxiron blades worn atop the knuckles like a multi-fingered ring

Roüwen: /Roe-OO-wen/ The village-fortress capital of Boreal

Solrahs: /SOL-rahs/ Half moon-shaped septum piece made of luxiron; worn by the Haidrens to Boreal

Tiergan: /TARE-ghan/ Sacred Bloodline of the Haidrens to Boreal; direct descendants of Tiergan

BOREALI

Allöh: /AH-loe/ May peace convene with you (informal greeting)

Allöh'jomn'yeh: /AH-loe zhoM-yay/ May peace convene with you (formal greeting)

Ana'Brödre: /Ahna-Broe-DRuh/ Great Brother or Brethren

Ana'Innöx: /Ahna-ee-NOCKS/ Great Harvest

Ana'Mere: /Ahna-Mare/ Great Mother

Ana'Sere: /Ahna-Sare/ Great Sister(s)

Aurynth: /Aur-rinth/ Eternal resting place; heaven

Bolaeva: /Bo-LAY-vah/ Please

Dönumn Lux: /Doe-nuM Lux/ Gift of Light

Fappa: /Fah-puh/ Daddy

Heh'ta: /HEH-tuh/ Stay; halt

lu'Lycran: /Loo LIE-cran/ Little lycran (nickname)

Mamu: /Mah-Moo/ Mommy; mama

Meh fyreon: /Meh Feer-ee-on/ I'm sorry; I apologize

Meh'dajjeni Dönumn, weh'dajjeni Lux: /Meh Dah-zhen-ee Doe-nuM, weh Dah-zhen-ee Lux/ My strength in the Gift, our strength for the Light

Niit: /Neet/ No

rul'Aniell: /Rool AHn-ee-eL/ In and to Aniell

Se'lah Aurynth: /se-Lah Aur-rinth/ Until the shores of Aurynth

Tadöm: /tah-Dome/ Thank you

Tredae'Aurynth: /Tred-AYE Aur-rinth/ Walk in Aurynth (farewell)

Waedfrel: /Wade-frell/ Good; great; exemplary

Wem: Yes

Yeh'maelim: /Yeh-may-lim/ Welcome to you

Ykah lö: /Eye-kuh Loe/ What; huh; come again

HOUSE OF DARAKAI
⫸SOUTHERN MOUNTAINS AND LOWLANDS⫷

Alpha: Leader of a regional pryde of militia

Alpha Zá: Leader of the militia prydes

Andwele: /An-DWEE-lee/ Native language of Darakai

Andwele Mountains: Mountain range forming the western border between Darakai, Razôuel, and Mworra

Beta: Second to the pryde alpha

Beta Warlord: Second to the Chief Warlord

Bwoloa: /Beh-WOE-lo-ah/ Golden liqueur imported from Darakai;

made of fermented grain and orange blossoms

Chief Warlord: Darakaian leader of all native tribes and minor chiefs

Commander of the Orynthian Armies: Appointed by the king

Cub: Child (slang)

Faraji: /Fah-rah-zhee/ Capital of Darakai; fortified mountain city; location of War Council and tribal leaders

Gunja pants: /Goon-Juh/ Loose-fitting pants wrapped at the waist and ankles; worn for drills and combat

Halona: /Hah-LOE-nuh/ Foothills of the Andwele Mountains

Kopar: /Koh-PAR/ Sickle-sword carried by the Darakaian military

Motumbha: /Moh-TUM-buh/ Arrowball; a Darakaian field game consisting of three baskets, two archers, and ladle-like sticks

Pammu: /PAH-moo/ Fermented pam sap brewed with beetles in the base of the bottle

Pryde: Localized group of Darakaian militia

Yowekao: /Yow-uh-KAY-oh/ Remote mountain tribe within the Andwele Mountains

ANDWELE

Ahoté: /Ah-HO-tay/ Restless Bobcat (nickname)

Àla'maia: /Ah-lah MY-ah/ The Moon (name)

Ano: /Ah-Noe/ No

Ano zà: /Ah-Noe Zah/ No (final)

Doru: /DOH-roo/ Stop; wait; pause

Ho'waladim: /Hoe-wall-a-dim/ As is due to you (in place of "You're welcome")

Jaha: /Jah-Hah/ Pretty thing

Jwona rapiki: /Jeh-wahn-uh rah-pee-kee/ Fate writer

Kàchà kocho: /Kah-chah Koe-cho/ This or that; so-so; either

Kakk: /Kak/ Babble; ramblings; nonsense

Kakka-shtàka: /Kak-uh ShTAH-kuh/ Dumb; shitty thing; useless (slang)

Kwihila rapiki mu Jwona: /Kwih-hee-luh rah-pee-kee moo Jeh-wahn-uh/ Victory writes over Fate

Maji'maia: /Mah-zhee MY-ah/ Witchy-Moon (nickname)

Na huwàa tàkom lai na huwàa: /Nah hoo-ah tah-KOM lie nah hoo-ah/ It takes a hound to hunt a hound

Ni yeye ràtomdai na wewe: /Nee yay-yay rah-tohm-dye nah way-way/ Do you claim rights to him/her/them/it

Owàa: /Oh-WAH/ The Sun (name)

Owàamo: /Oh-WAH-moe/ The Sun greets you (greeting)

Papyon: /Pap-ee-on/ Love; sex (slang)

Qondai: /Kon-Die/ To understand or comprehend

Shàla'maiamo: /Sha-lah my-AH-moe/ The Moon watch you (farewell)

Shamàli: /Sha-mah-lee/ If you see fit (in place of "Please")

Uni: /Oo-nee/ Yes

Uni zà: /Oo-nee Zah/ Yes (final)

Yaya: /Yah-Yah/ Honey; an attractive woman (slang)

Zullee: /Zool-lee/ Accepted with honor (in place of "Thank you")

HOUSE OF PILAR
⫸ EASTERN COAST ⫷

Chancellor: Head of the Pilarese Shoto Collective

Gakoshū: /Gah-koh-shoo/ City of Learning

Lempeii: /Lem-PAY/ Port city; station of the Orynthian navy

Shoto: /ShOH-toe/ Citizen of Pilar; philosopher; dedicated to the pursuit of learning

Shoto'shi: /ShOH-toe-shee/ A shoto acolyte; training in the ways of the Collective

Shoto Collective: Pilarese congress of scholars and politicians

Shoto Prime: Leader within the Shoto Collective

Acknowledgments

When I first embarked on the most ridiculous and unpromising venture of writing *House of Bastiion*, I knowingly exited the path expected of me and traded it in for something heartbreakingly foolish. An endeavor that would haunt me had I ignored its call, and ironically, haunts me regardless to this day.

I once read while researching what I'd committed to, that the completion of a manuscript is essentially a marathon of the mind. Having endured the many years dedicated to accomplishing *House of Bastiion*, while juggling my day job and the constant threat of becoming a hermit, I've decided this process is more akin to an unexplainable splintering of self. Never fully here, in the present, but rather somewhere else known only to the voices in my mind, bickering amongst themselves. That's what happens, you know, when you develop characters... they never shut up.

There's one person who deserves every ounce of recognition for having dealt with my splintered-self throughout this journey. Never doubting, ever praising, my husband, Aaron, has transcended into a form of sainthood while enduring my own transformation. I've evolved, as we all do, into a new entity; one that is obsessed with something he cannot see, but he must always trust is there, worthy of my obsession. Beyond his verbal support, which is reliably regular, Aaron has invested in my foolishness in countless ways, because he never found my writing to be foolish at all. He is the epitome of a partner in crime, especially when my crime is stealing his wife on occasion, so she can play with her imaginary friends. What love, to be able to watch someone leave, the focus fading from their eyes as they slip into another realm, trusting they will return to you once more. To my Aaron, my constant, the kite reminding me to look up and trust in the ability to soar – you are my home. Thank you for helping me fly away, and for reminding me why I ever needed to in the first place.

Few are aware that *House of Bastiion*, and the entire THL universe, would have never been born into existence if not for one person: Amanda Williams. This woman is the sole reason I discovered a story to tell. Were it not for her advice, I'd never have written a prologue about people I'd never met, in a world that didn't exist, on a red-eye home to Tennessee. As the wonder of lumin, an unseen light-thread of hope, glittered across my mind, my husband slept soundlessly at the edge of my tray table, none the wiser. Thank you, Amanda, for turning around in your seat as we drove to the coast of the Pacific, just to look me in the eye and suggest the ludicrous. Thank you for challenging why I'd chosen to write something I would never read, and with a twinkle in your eye, encourage me to trash it; to look beyond my need to impress, to perform, and seek something more wonderous than my own nobility. Somehow, you knew there was more. Without you, I would have never found it.

After five years of puttering around with my first draft, *House of Bastiion* would not have a home with readers if Rory Gilson hadn't adopted the cause. She picked up a banner not her own and waved it over me, encouraging me to finish, fangirling when necessary, and through her efforts fell in love with my world. Rory was the first member of Team Haidren, my rag-tag team of creatives. Without her knack for all things social, I'd still be an un-pictured recluse, buried under a clowder of cats, content to never quite finish. Completing something is terrifying… there's a finality to it. A finality I couldn't face without Rory Gilson. On my rollercoaster of self-doubt, she became my courage and many days, is still.

During the months leading up to the release of *House of Bastiion*, Team Haidren developed into, simply put, a sundry clan of randos. Most vital to this dynamic group were my Betas. The patience these people exhibit is beyond impressive, constantly receiving revision after revision from the author. Their sheer tolerance for my neuroticism is astounding. My beta readers offered *House of Bastiion* what I could not – perspective. Not only were they pivotal identifiers of underlying issues blind to my eye, they reminded me why I treasure this world so dearly. Through their developmental reading, I was gifted the opportunity to laugh with them, love with them, cry with them. No longer was I alone inside Orynthia, speaking in tongues to myself. I cherished every email and every text. These wonderfully passionate beta readers became the first fans of Luscia and Zaethan's story and now, are forever etched into its chronicle. Thank you, my friends, a million times over. Thank you for undertaking this adventure by my side.

Prior to my amazing editor, Lauren Smulski, *House of Bastiion* was a radiant labyrinth of over-used words, missed opportunities, and tedious worldbuilding. The truth of that statement is proven by this very segment, which she did not touch. While this book is my brainchild, Lauren is her cool aunt, courtside at every paragraph. She took my world, too big for my hands alone, and polished it in ways I never thought to implement. *House of Bastiion* only shines because Lauren brought the elbow grease to the table. When I was tired and spent, she breathed new life into the manuscript. Her talent, taste, and moxie were exactly what this book needed. Thank you, Lauren, for accepting me as a client. For choosing to say "yes" to that overly excited and fairly awkward debut author. Thank you for welcoming her excessive emails and digesting each one with care. I knew from the moment we connected you were the only person I wanted touching *House of Bastiion*, and the reasons are evident on every page. So buckle up, Buttercup – we're playing the long game now.

Launching a book entails much more than simply writing it. In a way, that's the easy part. Because once the manuscript leaves my desk, a pipeline of creatives contribute to the trying voyage toward publication, escorting the book out of my hands and across the ether, into your own. Thank you to Fiona Jayde, my astonishingly talented cover artist, who crafted jaw-droppingly beautiful concept art. Fiona took my ramblings and compressed them into a gem. A book is judged by its cover, and I certainly hope I did this cover justice. Thank you to Joseph Jacobson, who, inspired by that artwork, brought it to life on the screen. Joseph interpreted my vision and animated it, making it both fuller and brighter than my own imaginings. Imaginings that centered around a single melody. A huge thanks to Fleurie and Tommee Profitt for permitting us to use the same song I'd listened to while writing *House of Bastiion*, making it the very anthem of her release.

Thank you to Mary Toth, our ingenious illustrator, who gave character to each apothic element, accessible for online reference. It is only with Mary's skill that I was able to offer readers a mobile world outside these pages. Through her artistry and re-illustration of the Orynthian map, she provided me an arsenal to build a digital playground. Thank you to Brent Spears, who compiled my words and formatted them into the edition you read now. With his help to package the manuscript, this book was made ready for the masses, freeing Luscia and Zaethan from their PDF prison. And to the woman who captured my socially presentable side, big thanks to Megan Sanchez, for ensuring I never looked like a dork in any of her images.

Lastly, to everyone cheering from the sidelines, you've no clue how crucial you are to this process. My spousal-unit has the dreadful habit of announcing to anyone and everyone that I've written a novel. To those of you who never grew tired of his enthusiasm, thank you. For the individuals who took it one step further, encouraging him, by asking questions about said novel, thank you. Those who then pretended to be interested in made-up languages and regional politics, thank you. To the person who after all that nonsense, is genuinely interested in reading my novel… well, you're walking evidence we're never alone in nerdom. Between my friends and family, on either side of the marital aisle, you've knit a net of support around me for years, and I'll never forget it.

This is how we accomplish the impossible; how we prove ourselves wrong and climb a mountain of our own making—by leaning on one another. All of you, in various forms, have allowed me to lean on you and in doing so, you've held up a dream.

And guess what?

It's time to wake up and see what we've accomplished. Together.

THE HAIDREN LEGACY

Receive the **THL Newsletter** to stay up to date on books released in the series, giveaways and events, as well as insight into Luscia and Zaethan's enticing journey through Orynthia!

Visit **www.TheHaidrenLegacy.com/contact** today!

CPSIA information can be obtained
at www.ICGtesting.com
Printed in the USA
LVHW110531121120
671331LV00002B/12